Praise for *Going Dark*

"[In] Hall's outstanding thirteenth thriller . . . the action races toward a literally explosive climax at the nuclear plant. The result is both thoughtful and white-knuckle tense." —*Publishers Weekly*

"Hall is one of those rare thriller writers who can build character as he ratchets tension, who can do no-holds-barred action scenes with panache and, in the midst of bedlam, never lose sight of nuance. All those skills are on display here, as Hall assembles a full-bodied supporting cast whose stories hold our interest as much as Thorn's attempt to save his son without helping to bring about a South Florida version of Chernobyl. A fine thriller on every level." —*Booklist*

"As ever, Hall is in colorful command of his South Florida setting. . . . Compared to other mystery writers, he plays things refreshingly low key, but he's always in control, thriving on the setup as much as the payoff . . . with its nicely observed characters and lively dialogue—and terrific sex scenes—it keeps readers turning the pages." —*Kirkus Reviews*

"*Going Dark* has cinematic action all the way through and a couple of fine surprises saved for the final few pages. Nicely done." —*BookPage*

Also by James W. Hall

GOING DARK

James W. Hall

St. Martin's Paperbacks

This is a work of fiction. All of the characters, organizations, and events portrayed in this novel are either products of the author's imagination or are used fictitiously.

GOING DARK

Copyright © 2013 by James W. Hall.
Excerpt from *The Big Finish* copyright © 2014 by James W. Hall.

For information address St. Martin's Press, 175 Fifth Avenue, New York, NY 10010.

Library of Congress Catalog Card Number: 2013024718

ISBN: 978-1-250-05641-2

Printed in the United States of America

St. Martin's Press hardcover edition / December 2013
St. Martin's Paperbacks edition / November 2014

St. Martin's Paperbacks are published by St. Martin's Press, 175 Fifth Avenue, New York, NY 10010.

10 9 8 7 6 5 4 3 2 1

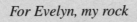

For Evelyn, my rock

By every means necessary we will bring this and every other empire down! Mutiny and sabotage in defense of Mother Earth!   —Earth First! credo

ONE

FOR AN HOUR THE MOTHER has been toiling through the tall grass searching for her newborns. The tropical night is sweltering. A lazy breeze off the Atlantic gives no relief. In a small clearing, the mother halts, surveys the landscape, changes direction. She is focused on a hump of earth overgrown with weeds.

She's forgotten where she buried them back in April. After two months of rain and erosion and the powerful ocean winds, the contours of the terrain have changed, confusing her.

But this hump seems promising. She climbs atop it, pressing her belly flat against the earth. This feels right. This, she believes, is the spot.

She gathers herself, lifts her body off the ground, fully extended as if attempting a push-up. She holds that position, then lets go, dropping all her weight against the earth. A thump echoes across the surrounding waters.

She waits a moment, then presses her jaw to the ground to listen for their cries below the surface.

A breeze flitters in the leaves of the Brazilian pepper, frogs screech, out in the darkness two owls compete with whoops and howls, and there's the endless slosh of water against the bank. But through all the night clamor she detects their voices inside the earth, their distinctive cheeps, their throaty squeaks. It's them, her offspring.

She begins to dig in the sandy soil, a few inches, a few more, clawing precisely until she exposes them to the hot night air. Two of them have already squirmed out of their shells. Ten inches long. Black and tan with gold bands. Eyes green and liquid. Immediately mosquitoes and other night bugs circle, land, and begin to track up and down their length.

All this, the unfolding drama of the American crocodile locating her hatchlings, is lit by the video camera's spotlight, which Cameron Prince operates from the bow of the airboat fifteen yards away. Onshore, crouched in the shadows only a few feet from the crocodile nest, is Leslie Levine.

Leslie shouldn't be on land so close to the nest. It's risky at a moment like this, but it happens from time to time and there's nothing to do but tough it out. A minute ago, she ducked ashore to search for drag marks, the distinctive trails crocs leave as they haul themselves across the sandy banks. Seconds after she'd climbed the slippery berm, the mother croc surfaced in the canal, swam to the bank, and trundled up the steep edge.

Cameron called a warning but Leslie raised both palms to tell him to hold steady. No worries. All she had to do was hang back, be still, watch. Sure, it was dicey, but nothing she hadn't handled dozens of times before.

Now in silence she and Cameron watch the scene unfold. The glare of the spotlight doesn't alarm the croc. With such a dominant sense of smell and keen hearing the creature relies little on sight. As long as she and Cameron are quiet, the mother will go about her business oblivious to their presence.

This is a big one, twelve feet, almost half a ton, but she digs into the mound with delicate strokes, pushing aside the mud and marl without harming the fragile shells. An amazing creature: covered in bony plates, with jaws so strong it can crush cast iron, so hardy and resilient it can survive the loss of a leg or its entire tail, yet it's capable of such deftness.

In the bright camera light, Leslie smiles. For years she's been watching scenes like this unfold, hundreds of them, but she's still as stoked as the first time. The American croc laying its eggs months before, then tracking down the right mound, doing her belly flop to see if there's anything alive inside, anything worth digging for. When she hears their cries, she begins the careful excavation, followed by the swim to a nearby freshwater source to safely deposit her offspring. A thousand times she's seen it, maybe more.

Oh, if she wanted to, she could drag out her notebooks, tally up the other nights like this, get the exact total. Everything was in her spiral notebooks. All penned in neat script just minutes after each event. Later on tonight, she'll dock the airboat at the lab and take an hour or two to transfer the data into the computer and fill out the spreadsheets. Every croc they encounter will be identified, sexed, weighed, injected with a microchip, its activities listed with signs of health or battle scars, the GPS coordinates of its active nest, number of hatchlings, and all identifying markings on the mother crocs.

The two of them watch the mother finish opening the

nest, revealing it to the camera's light. After a moment's inspection, the big female plucks two hatchlings from the nest, holding them lightly between her jagged teeth.

Next she will turn and crawl back down the bank, slide into the water to begin her swim across the canal to a freshwater pond she'd discovered earlier. That small, rain-filled pond was Leslie's creation. A month ago it didn't exist. But to be ready for hatching season, Levine requisitioned the plant's maintenance team to use their amphibious backhoe to create the pit so the crocs in this part of the canal system would have a crucial freshwater supply.

Baby crocs needed six months to adjust to salt water. In the meantime they either found a freshwater source or died. Without that pond their only hope for survival would be to skim the shallow lens of rainwater riding atop the briny canals.

In half a year's time, the young crocs can abandon their rain-filled pond and begin to roam. Nature's orderly timetable: the six-month rainy season exactly matched the half year required for their salt-tolerant glands to develop.

Even though their freshwater source is ready, other challenges lie ahead. These two baby crocs have to learn some brutal survival skills: how to hunt and keep themselves cool in the relentless Florida summer, how to conceal themselves from predators, including adult crocs, who have no qualms about eating their young. And these young crocs will have to do it without coaching or protection, because after this one gesture of maternal instinct, the mother croc will abandon her babies to fend for themselves.

Leslie certainly identifies with that.

Hanging a few yards back, she tracks the croc to the bank. She's squinting in the harsh light, trying to make out the markings on this big croc's tail, the two or three missing scutes, those knobs of gristle she herself trimmed away years ago when this croc was a youngster, a code that will tell her where she first encountered this specimen. Most likely it's one of many Leslie has microchipped, but tonight at such a moment it's way too tricky to attempt to lasso the big girl and scan her chip for an update on her travels. At this point the normally shy croc is at her most protective and volatile.

Leslie is ten feet back, staying close because she wants to eyeball the coded cuts on the tail, which will tell her if the croc is one of the hundreds from this region of neatly organized canals, or from a smaller population in northern Key Largo, or perhaps it's one of the Everglades crocs that journey to this coastal, protected habitat to lay their eggs. Charting the croc's travels is a crucial part of the research project she's completing this year.

Leslie picks her way forward with particular care because earlier that afternoon, as they headed out to the nesting sites, a squall from tropical storm Ivan blew through, leaving the canal bank a gloppy mess. Even in her cleated hiking shoes the footing is treacherous.

She's wearing her usual uniform, dark jeans, long-sleeve T-shirt sprayed with mosquito repellent, and a small backpack. She's a lean, athletic woman, thirty-two, with short auburn hair. Despite her natural agility, the steep bank is giving her trouble. Twice she slips and barely catches herself.

She motions for Cameron to keep the camera's light on the trail before her. Maybe Cameron's finger slips on the spotlight trigger, or maybe it's some electronic glitch—whatever it is, at that critical moment the camcorder's three-watt video light flickers and goes dark.

Later a Miami-Dade police detective will question him about this detail, but Cameron will be unable to say exactly what happened. He won't remember his finger slipping. And he's sure there were no previous problems with the equipment. Since Cameron's recollection of the night is so foggy, the video record is crucial in establishing the timeline.

The last clear image is Leslie's urgent wave at Cameron to keep the light focused on the path. It's possible that move throws her off-balance, or maybe the toe of her hiking shoe snags a root, or perhaps she's simply disoriented by the utter dark beyond the cone of light.

From the camera's angle, there's no way to tell what tripped her. In the murkiness, Leslie appears to throw one arm upward, then the other, as if she's grabbing for the straps on a lurching subway. That's the final image of her before the camera pitches skyward.

After this moment, the video image joggles so wildly it's impossible to determine exactly what's what. The camera swings left, then tilts up, showing the black sky, some scattered stars, a slice of moon. Cameron reported he is at this point scrambling to unhook himself from the camera straps and fumbles the equipment, sending the camera crashing onto the deck. It bounces twice, then comes to rest.

The audio recorder continues to run, capturing a splash and a grunt.

Cameron calls Leslie's name. He sounds alarmed, but not panicked. He's worked alongside Leslie for years and has absolute faith in her skills.

But everything changes fast. With the mother croc in full-protection mode, Leslie's lurch is apparently read as aggression toward the hatchlings. The croc doesn't retreat across the canal as she normally would. From the heaves and grumbles, it appears that the big croc turns on the intruder.

Leslie remains silent, no sign of alarm. This puzzles the investigators who review the footage later, but Cameron assures them her familiarity with the landscape and with crocs in general was so thorough, it's doubtful that she was even concerned.

Maybe this self-assurance made Leslie vulnerable. She dropped her guard, didn't expect the croc to turn and surge so quickly. Cameron could make out only the dim outlines of the moment of attack. Leslie's headlong tumble, the big reptile's swift move. A violent merging of the two.

The audio records violent splashes as though the animal is trying to drag Leslie underwater or tow her as far from land as possible, with Leslie fighting, thrashing. There are garbled words and heaves of breath, while the frozen video continues to show only the still and shadowy image of the grassy bank where the nest is torn open, exposing the white cluster of eggs to a milky wash of moonlight.

More than a minute of quiet is followed by splashing, and a few seconds later, a howl. A human voice that is barely human.

It could be either of them. Cameron doesn't remember yelling but supposes it's possible. He doesn't recognize the scream as his own. To Cameron those moments were a bewildering blur. Shortly after the attack began, he recalls being chest-high in the canal and smacking the water with both hands to lure the big croc away from Leslie. Not heroic, he says, just a blind reaction to the horror unfolding before him. Then he remembers backing away when he thought the croc turned on him.

All that jostling of the water rocks the airboat and somehow triggers the camera's light to flutter on again.

More silence follows, then the sound of someone slogging through the canal, and a moment later Cameron is in the camera's frame staggering toward the bank in hip-deep water.

He's massive, tall and heavily muscled, with short blond hair. He's cradling something in his arms. His face is stricken and white. He claims to remember none of this. Picking it up, carrying it to the boat.

The video shows him splashing near the bow, then lifting the object and setting it on the deck in front of the camera. This human arm was severed an inch above the elbow. Around the wrist is a rubber bracelet, a camouflage design.

Cameron is huffing as he pulls himself aboard and lifts the video camera from the deck. For a moment the lens captures hundreds of glittering lights that outline the towers and the two enormous containment buildings at Turkey Point only a few hundred yards away. With all those lights sparkling in the night, the nuclear power plant appears almost festive.

Then the video goes dark.

TWO

THORN HAD SET UP HIS fly-tying vise next to the lagoon and was almost done with his latest version of a Crazy Charlie with silver bead-chain eyes, underbody of pearl flashabou, wings of tan calf tail, and a few wispy sprigs of possum fur that he added to the rump. The possum fur was an oddball addition to the standard fly, but last week Thorn had found the creature crushed on the highway near his house, and on a whim he plucked a clump from its pelt to give the possum another shot at a useful purpose. That creature whose major survival skill was pretending to be dead was about to spend a while longer pretending to be alive.

He was making the final snips when a car rolled into his gravel drive. He watched Sugarman park in his usual spot beneath the ancient gumbo-limbo and get out of his dented Honda.

Sugar was his oldest buddy, an accomplice in more messy escapades than either of them would admit. Tall and lean, a striking mix of his pale Norwegian mother and Rastafarian dad, with a finely modeled face and a caramel skin tone a half shade lighter than Thorn's perpetual tan. Sugar and Thorn had been yinning and yanging since they met in grade school and were still doing the same crazy, out-of-kilter tango decades later.

Impulsive, hair-trigger Thorn and steady, no-nonsense Sugar. Thorn, the hard-core loner, and Sugar with a hundred friends and a sunny view of the darkest days. For years the two had undertaken risky balancing acts along precipices and canyon edges, lurching along the edges of one bottomless disaster after another, but somehow they'd always managed to steady each other and dance away just before the plunge. So far.

Thorn tied the final knot and set the bonefish fly aside and stood waiting on the gray, weathered planks of the dock.

Sugarman didn't say hello, didn't say anything as he stepped down onto the dock. He blinked and looked off as if trying to conceal the slow-motion hardening in his jaw and some unpleasant taste rising into his throat.

Sugar was dressed today in blue-and-white-striped seersucker shorts and a canary-yellow polo shirt and his best boat shoes, the jaunty look that usually meant he'd been trying to impress a prospective client.

"What happened?"

Sugar turned and glanced back down the gravel drive, shaking his head faintly, the way he did when he was fetching the right phrase. When he turned back, a grimace had stiffened his face.

Thorn backhanded the sweat from his eyes, looked out at the lagoon, where a cormorant had surfaced, a bulge in his skinny throat. He swam in ever-larger circles as he searched the water for more targets.

Sugar took a moment to scan the blue reaches of the

ocean. Processing something while he moved his lips as if doing a tricky computation in his head.

Thorn felt the rumble of storm clouds gathering in his chest. His trusty weather vane beginning to twitch.

Sugar looked at Thorn blankly, then patted him on the back. "We need to talk."

"Ah, yes. My favorite four words."

"I assume you haven't heard about Leslie Levine?"

"News about Leslie?"

"Yes."

"I've been out of the loop lately."

"Lately? You been out of the damn loop since the day you were born." Sugarman smiled wearily. Accustomed to Thorn's stubborn disinterest in the details of the modern world. "Day before yesterday, there was a crocodile attack up at Turkey Point, at the nuke plant. Happened late at night, back in those cooling canals where she's trying to rebuild the croc population. Twelve-footer versus Leslie."

"Leslie was injured by a croc?"

"She was killed, Thorn."

"Leslie?"

Sugar reached out and laid a consoling hand on Thorn's shoulder. Thorn turned his head, looked at Sugar's hand, then looked out at the lagoon. A mist burned his eyes, blurring his vision.

Around twenty years earlier Leslie Levine lived in a trailer park a half mile down the road from Thorn, and one autumn afternoon the skinny, auburn-haired teenager showed up with a fishing rod and bucket of dead shrimp she'd bummed off a clerk at the Yellow Bait House. Awkward and shy, not more than fourteen at the time, she introduced herself and asked Thorn for permission to fish off his dock. Thorn said it was okay, and the kid spent a couple of hours trying and failing to snag gray snappers from the school that lived around the pilings.

Finally Thorn drifted over and offered her a few tips on her casting technique and showed her how to grip the rod when jigging her bait, and gradually the girl got the hang of it. Later, he made sandwiches, and when Leslie wolfed hers down in three bites, he made another. The next afternoon she returned. A week, another week, a month and another month.

For most of that school year Leslie Levine apprenticed herself to Thorn, eventually applying herself to the craft of fly-tying and learning to fish the flats in Thorn's skiff. Raised by a single mom who traded sex for cocaine, Leslie was more of a lone wolf than even Thorn. But the bond between them grew until Leslie began to confide in Thorn a few details about her grim childhood.

After four or five months, she'd mastered every lesson Thorn had to teach, and her visits became sporadic. Then one day, without a formal good-bye, the visits ceased altogether, and Thorn later heard the young woman had attached herself to Mary Jo Prentiss, her high school biology teacher, a specialist in Florida reptiles and a strident environmentalist. A couple of years later, Thorn read in the local paper that Leslie had won a scholarship to the public university in Miami, where she planned to major in biology.

He'd heard nothing more about her until last year, when Leslie paid a surprise visit, appearing at Thorn's dock at sunrise one morning in a sleek flats boat. She'd matured into a striking young lady, lithe and vibrant, her chestnut hair worn boyishly short. She said she was working temporarily for some Florida state agency that had hired her to do a crocodile census in the Upper Keys. Leslie invited Thorn along for a tour of local croc habitats.

Sitting in the bow of her boat was another woman, gaunt, with flame-red hair loose down her back. Her tall frame was hidden beneath a bulky jacket and loose jeans. Her hiking shoes were battered and her skin sunburned and roughened by weather as if she'd been hiking for months through some unforgiving terrain. Leslie never introduced the young woman, just made a quick *don't ask* shrug.

The three of them spent the morning cruising the familiar back bays of the Upper Keys, Thorn marveling at Leslie's ability to spot bashful crocs from long distances, sneak up, lasso them, haul them to the boat, tag and release those toothy creatures as effortlessly as if they were backyard lizards. At sunset, before she left, Leslie stood out at the end of Thorn's dock and thanked him for sharing those hours with her as a teenage kid. The red-haired woman sat silently in the bow of the boat, staring forward as she had all day.

"You got me started on all this." Leslie gestured at the open water, the mangrove islands, the reddening sky laced with threads of purple and green.

Thorn said he was glad to have played a part in Leslie's education.

"It was more than that," she said. "You gave me a reason to go on."

Thorn smiled, opened his arms, and Leslie stepped into an embrace.

"Thank you for coming," he said, when they parted.

"Does it ever piss you off, Thorn, what's happening to it all? Losing these beautiful places."

"Hell, yes," he said. "But mostly it makes me sad."

With her fingertips she brushed the stubble on his cheek, held his eyes for several seconds, an intimacy that gave him an uneasy buzz. Then her look dissolved, she turned, climbed into her skiff, started the outboard, and was off, her passenger's hair blazing against the darkening sky.

Thorn stared out at his lagoon, at the cormorant still hunting minnows.

"How'd it happen?"

"Only witness was Leslie's assistant, a guy named Cameron Prince. Spotlight failed. Leslie tripped, a croc went for her. Prince went for help, but it was hours before any arrived. They couldn't locate the croc or Leslie. The animal dragged her off. Between the crocs, gators, and every other damn thing with teeth and claws out there, well, you know."

"Leslie Levine, Jesus Christ."

"I thought I should tell you."

"I don't believe it." Thorn settled his butt against the seawall.

"I know. Everybody's pretty shocked."

"No. I don't believe it could've gone down that way."

"Nothing suspicious about it," Sugar said. "It was dark out there, the mother croc was moving her babies, Leslie stumbled over the damn thing. Accidents happen. People get careless, even a pro like Leslie."

Thorn shook his head. "Not her."

Sugarman opened his mouth to say more, then shut it.

Thorn kept his eyes on the open water beyond the lagoon. His face was inert. Eyes focused inward. A fine mist sheened his forehead as if he had a low-grade fever. He didn't believe it. Not her, not Leslie Levine.

THREE

FROM SEVENTY FEET UP, BALANCED on the narrow railing at the top of his cistern, Thorn could only make out the man's general features. Bulky guy, pale-yellow hair parted precisely. Black cargo shorts and a camouflage T-shirt.

Ten minutes before, the man had parked in the gravel drive, gotten out, and started snooping around Thorn's property as if taking an inventory, about to make an offer on the land. It wouldn't be the first time Thorn had to chase off an overzealous Realtor.

Thorn dabbed the white plumbing grease into the fitting, smoothed it into the groves, then with his wrench tightened the two-inch pipe to the valve. Gave it one final crunching turn and wiped the excess grease away with the rag from his back pocket. He reached high and levered open the main valve, heard the squeal of water pressurizing the pipes, and watched for any leaks around the fitting. When he saw none, he wiped a fingertip around the joint to be sure it was dry. Praise the Lord, it was.

Scratch another chore off the unceasing list around his aging Key Largo home. Another finger in another leak in the ever-growing dike. Lately Thorn seemed to be running out of fingers. Barely staying ahead of the rising tide of decay.

Between the harsh subtropical weather testing every surface, the briny breezes off the Atlantic aggravating each patch of rust, the wooden house shifting restlessly on its foundation, the heart-of-pine planks shrinking and expanding with each twitch in the barometric pressure, he was spending half his waking hours staying even with maintenance. Precious time subtracted from tying his custom bonefish flies, the work that paid the bills, bought his food and an occasional luxury such as a six-pack of Red Stripe beer.

Twenty-five yards below, the man was still making himself at home, pacing the dock beside the lagoon, checking out Thorn's sixteen-foot flats boat, and bending down to peer through the windows of the *Heart Pounder,* Thorn's ancient Chris-Craft docked just forward of the skiff.

Arrogant bastard, not even going close to the house, knocking at Thorn's door or calling out hello to see if anyone was at home.

But Thorn stayed put. He wanted to see what the guy was up to, and, hell, he was in no hurry to come down from his perch. It had been years since he'd climbed the cistern tower, and he'd forgotten the dazzling views. On such a cloudless day, he could see several miles east toward the blue slit of the horizon and make out the hazy outline of the Carysfort Reef lighthouse. Just beyond it a cargo ship was steaming north along the Gulf Stream.

Closer in, the swirls of sapphire water and bottle green and turquoise interlocked like thousands of intricate jigsaw pieces, and just off Thorn's shoreline the shallow sea turned an eggshell blue where patches of white-sand flats lurked three or four inches below the surface. Just now it was low tide and a languid breeze was spreading riffles across the coastal waters, while farther out the ocean had a gentle roll.

In the other direction, west, was the Florida Bay, and beyond that the vast and spreading indigo of the Gulf of Mexico. Where else in the world but the Florida Keys could you watch the sun erupt from one sea and hours later see it melt away into another?

A hundred yards offshore, a single skiff was working the edge of the neighborhood flats, searching for late-afternoon schools of bonefish. Ollie Davis was up on the platform, poling the vessel north while his client perched on the bow and cast his fly onto the flats.

Thorn watched Ollie steer the skiff along the edge of the flat and saw the client's herky-jerky casting stroke and clumsy retrieve. The guy wobbled on the casting platform as if he might pitch overboard at the slightest rock of the boat.

Ham-fisted bunglers like him were one reason Thorn retired from his own guiding career. After all those hours in a small boat with razor-pronged hooks zinging past his face, he'd been tagged more times than he could recall.

The day finally came when he hit his limit. He had turned his back to a client to relieve himself over the stern, and on a careless backcast the angler hooked Thorn in the crotch. The Miami smart-ass holding the rod thought Thorn's plight was damn amusing. Even tried to take a snapshot of him with his shorts at his knees, grimly extracting the hook.

Thorn dropped the pliers, tore the camera from his

client's hand, and sailed it. When the asshole got huffy, Thorn shouldered him over the side as well and wouldn't let him back aboard until Thorn had removed the hook from his privates.

That was to be Thorn's last day showing strangers how to fish the flats. He never regretted the decision. Now when he went fishing, he mostly went alone, which was usually more than enough company.

Thorn took another moment to absorb the view, watching the blades of his Aermotor turn in a lazy breeze. That windmill was next on his to-do list. Time to lubricate its gearbox, grease the pump pole swivel, and tighten the connections and track down fraying and cracking in the wiring. His house lights had been flickering more than usual lately.

By the time he climbed down from the cistern, his visitor had completed his tour and was on his way back to his car. Thorn caught up, tapped the guy on the shoulder.

At ground level, he made the intruder for at least six-six. A half foot taller than Thorn, and heavier by over fifty pounds of ripped, densely veined muscles. The stranger turned slowly and, after appraising Thorn for a moment, drew in a long breath and smiled with contentment as if the air at his height had a finer bouquet than anything groundlings like Thorn could imagine.

"Can I help you?"

The man studied Thorn for several moments. "I didn't realize anyone was home. Sorry, I'll just be going."

"What do you want?"

"All right, then. How tall is your water tower, about sixty feet?"

The man was in his late twenties, with wide-set

eyes and thin lips, and the kind of well-crafted bone structure some women probably found beguiling. His camouflage shirt seemed spray-painted to his thick chest and narrow waist. Muscles so ridged and jagged he might've been chiseled from a slab of volcanic rock. The kind of freak-show he-man you'd expect to find juggling cannonballs in some traveling carnival.

Thorn had run into more than his share of bruisers and goons and had vowed to steer clear of them in the future, never again engage, to slam the door, do a one-eighty, whatever it took to preserve the tranquil cycles of his ordinary life. In the past year he'd kept that vow and gradually a familiar shell of seclusion had regrown around him. The silence, the natural phases of the weather, and the ebb and flow of the seasons were once again the shaping rhythms of his days.

After last year's bloodshed and turmoil, he'd finally managed to reclaim his old pattern—spending his days tying flies, doing sweaty labor around the property, cooling off with an afternoon swim, fishing for his dinner. At sunset taking aimless cruises with Sugarman through the sounds and coves of the backcountry, watching dolphins surf their wake, listening to Sugar gripe good-naturedly about the tedium of his work as a PI. Or on rare occasions Thorn would give a lady friend his complete attention while she discussed her troublesome kids or her ex-husbands and her fruitless search for genuine love.

But also in those months of isolation his reflexes had slowed. Otherwise he would've acted on his first impression and turned his back on this intruder's gloating smile and gone resolutely back to his chores.

"I asked you about the tower," the big man said.

"That's why you're here, to look at my cistern?"

"I've been studying them because one day I'd like to build one myself. How tall is yours?"

"Seventy feet," said Thorn. "Six inches."

"Three-thousand-gallon tank?"

"Around there."

"So that gives you a smidge over thirty pounds per square inch of pressure in the house. Minimal, not much more than a trickle."

"I never measured it, but a trickle sounds right."

"Hard to take a shower in a trickle."

"I manage."

"Can't run your dishwasher."

"Don't have one."

"Barely enough to flush your toilets."

Thorn took another dip into the shallow pools of the man's eyes. "You don't look like a building code inspector."

"And what do I look like to you?"

Thorn couldn't find a word that captured the full measure of his distaste. "Exactly what kind of bullshit are you selling?"

"Right now I'd like to know how you heat your water."

Thorn sighed. He had to give the colossus credit for sheer gall. "I've worked out a deal with the sun."

"Solar panels?"

"Exposed water pipes on the roof."

The man nodded judiciously. "Primitive, but workable. And cloudy days in winter?"

"A week or two of shivering."

"And the windmill, that's your power source?"

"When there's wind."

"So you're one of those."

"I'm not one of anything," Thorn said.

"Oh, sure you are. You're a back-to-nature true believer. Self-sufficient. In touch with the ancient ways."

"You've got it wrong."

"I don't think so. I look around and I see a guy living the pioneer life. Hard-ass maverick, don't-tread-on-me philosophical view."

"I don't have a philosophical view."

"Everybody does. Whether they admit it or not."

"The man who raised me built that cistern. In his day it was the only way to get freshwater in the Keys. There was no pipeline coming down from Miami. That's not philosophy, that's survival."

"But you're still unconnected to the public water system. You made a choice to stay true to the old ways. You're bucking the modern world."

"You have a name?"

The man considered the question for a moment, taking another leisurely look at Thorn's acreage. "I apologize for intruding on your privacy. I'll be taking my leave. Have yourself a glorious day."

Thorn's memory wasn't what it used to be, so he had to repeat aloud the string of numbers, then repeat them again as he walked back to the house to scribble down the asshole's license plate.

FOUR

"YOU'RE NOT GOING TO TELL me what this is for?"
Sugarman sat behind his desk, looking at the numbers
Thorn had scrawled on a scrap of paper.

Sugar's PI office occupied the narrow space next to
Key Largo's premier beauty salon, the Hairport. Running the length of the wall his office shared with the
salon was a shadowy one-way mirror, a legacy of the
previous owner of the beauty parlor, who'd believed it
necessary to spy on her employees.

Sugar often toyed with the idea of walling over the
mirror and disconnecting the speakers to make his office appear more professional, but he could never bring
himself to do it because the constant bustle next door
distracted him on slow afternoons, not to mention how
much he prized the tidbits of Key Largo gossip and the
invaluable insights into the riddle of the female mind.
Plus watching what happened next door could often be
a serious turn-on. The young ladies knew full well about
the mirror, and like most women, they found Sugarman
a winsome fellow, so they sometimes put on shows for
his benefit.

"I did tell you," Thorn said. "Some pushy guy shows up at my house. He refuses to identify himself."

"And now you're going to track him down and do what?"

"Can you do it or not, Sugar?"

"I usually get paid for this service."

"I'll buy you a Red Stripe. Take you on a boat ride."

"You'd do that anyway."

"Nope, not anymore. Not until you give me this guy's name."

"It's just some Realtor looking for cheap land. You're overreacting."

"This guy was no Realtor."

"You've gotten bored, now you're out trolling for trouble."

"I'm not bored, and I'm sure as hell not looking for trouble. Are you going to help me or not?"

"All right. Just to placate you. Simply to dulcify your savage breast."

Vocabulary building was one of Sugarman's hobbies, and Thorn was regularly subjected to his latest acquisitions.

Sugar tapped his keyboard. Waited. Tapped some more.

Thorn watched through the window as Molly Bright, the owner of the Hairport, ripped a long strip of adhesive tape off the inner thigh of the high school principal, Dorothy Sherman, a woman of advanced age and surprising hairiness. The speakers were turned off, so Thorn couldn't hear the exact curse Dorothy screamed, but it was sufficiently colorful to produce hoots from several of the other haircutters and their clients.

"Brazilian wax," Sugar said. "One of my favorites. Yet another reason to be grateful you're a man."

He tapped a few more keys and watched the screen. The computer made a beep and Sugarman squinted and leaned forward. "Jesus. Your instincts are sharp. This was no Realtor."

"What?"

Sugar swiveled the monitor around so Thorn could see the name blinking in a small square at the bottom of the screen.

Cameron Prince.

Thorn made it up to Miami in a little more than an hour and took Old Cutler Road through the Gables, then Ingraham Highway into the Grove, moving easily through light traffic, going against the evening flood of cars returning to the suburbs, until finally he rolled up to the address Sugarman had supplied for Cameron Prince.

A block off Tigertail Avenue, five blocks from the bay, the white wood cottage had clapboard siding and a shingle roof. Weeds and roots had pushed aside chunks of the cement walkway, and more weeds were flourishing in the gutters. The few screens remaining on the front porch were torn, and the entire house seemed to slouch several ramshackle degrees to the south as if it were slipping back into the soil from which it had risen almost a century before.

Thorn rolled past the house and parked two doors down and sat for a while considering how to proceed. Months before, he'd mourned the loss of Leslie Levine, even forced himself to go to her memorial service at the Lorelei Bar, her favorite hangout, down in Islamorada. He had a few beers too many, stood up when the tributes were given, made a few clumsy remarks about the shitty childhood Leslie had overcome, and sat back on his barstool and was silent the rest of the night. Afterward he let her loss go as he'd done with so many others in the last few years.

But for these last few weeks it nagged him. The circumstances of her death, the suddenness, the location, out in the cooling canals of the nuclear plant where she was working to restore the endangered croc population.

Most of all it bothered him that she would be killed by a crocodile at all. That last day he'd seen her, he'd witnessed her sure-handed way with those creatures, seen her roping and dragging the crocs to the boat, tagging them, weighing and sexing them, releasing them back into the wild. All done with an effortless, natural ease. That a croc had killed her and dragged away her body didn't add up.

Then for her partner in the croc-breeding program to appear at Thorn's house, nosing around, feigning interest in his water tower, then refusing to identify himself, well, damn it, that was too much to ignore.

While Thorn was still mulling over his next step, the front door of the house where Thorn was parked blew open and a white-haired man in a grubby undershirt and purple sweatpants appeared. He glared at Thorn for a moment, then stalked down his walkway, carrying what looked like a shillelagh.

The man marched up to the front of Thorn's VW Beetle and raised the gnarled club over his head and whacked the hood of the car. Then raised it and whacked again.

Thorn got out and walked to the front of the VW to survey the damage.

"I warned you assholes not to park in front of my house."

"I'm a new asshole," Thorn said. "I didn't get the warning."

The man peered at Thorn, cocking his head to the side, running his eyes over Thorn's body, as if evaluating his physique. "You're not one of them muscle boys? Them goddamn bodybuilders."

Thorn held out his arms so the man could see he was not a muscle boy.

"Well, okay." The man lowered his club. "My mistake."

"You're referring to Cameron Prince, that house?" Thorn waved at Prince's dump.

The man huffed his disgust. "Those idiots coming and going all hours, day and night, clanking them barbells and dumbbells and whatnot. Runs an illegal gym out back. Charges these turd brains good money. A dozen times I reported him to the city and the county, code enforcement, police, you name it, but does anybody give a rat's ass? Hell, no. I'm an old man, a war vet, I got asthma, I got insomnia, bad kidneys, I got herniated disks, pains on top of pains. You name it, I got it. And then him and his muscle boys. Bunch of hair balls, back there banging away. And the cars coming and going, parking right here, blocking my sidewalk, squealing their tires. It ain't right."

He raised the club again and took aim at Thorn's hood, then thought better of it and lowered it to his side. "You're not one of them, huh?"

"I was coming to see Mr. Prince on a different matter. I'll be happy to move my car."

"He ain't there." The old man bent down and ran a

finger over the fresh dents he'd put in Thorn's hood, looking mildly pleased at his work. "Ain't been there for a few weeks. But does that stop the muscle boys from using his illegal gym? No, sir, it don't. They're back there twenty-four/seven clanking away with them weights."

"Hasn't been home in weeks?"

"Fucker goes off like that. Out to his island. Stays weeks at a time. Camping on that godforsaken spit of land."

"His island?"

"Prince Key, it's out in the bay somewhere."

"Oh," Thorn said, "he's that Prince."

"You're sure you're not one of them muscle heads?"

"No, sir. Big muscles, they only get in the way."

The man squinted at Thorn. Relaxing his grip on the club. "I like that, *Only get in the way.* Yeah, that's good. What'd you say your name was, kid?"

"Sorry to bother you, sir. Good luck with the muscle boys."

Thorn got back in the VW, eased around the old man and his anger, circled back, and parked the VW behind a flashy, low-slung sports car sitting at the curb in front of Prince's house.

He walked down the driveway following the clang of metal.

In the back he found a black woman not more than five feet tall wearing a string bikini, lying flat on her back on the weight bench pressing what looked like three or four times Thorn's weight above her chest, raising it, lowering it. Puffing out huge breaths. Striated bands of muscle quivered beneath her shiny flesh. She wore earbuds and the music she was listening to was turned so loud Thorn could hear the hip-hop's lyrics from several feet away. *Thugs and bitches, knife in the heart. Killing my love.*

She pumped away, eyes open, but never cutting a look at Thorn.

The outdoor gym was simply a concrete slab with a roof of translucent plastic and walled on three sides by flimsy sheets of lattice. The backyard was overgrown and hedged with ancient coco plums and fishtail palms. Aside from the free weights scattered about, there was a single Nautilus machine with its adjustable seat and stack of weights.

Hanging on the lattice were dozens of black-and-white photos, some shots taken at bodybuilding contests, men and women holding up trophies. But mostly beefcake shots of the denizens of the backyard gym. Men in their twenties and thirties, a couple of women, a few older folks. All of them gleaming with sweat, their eyes glowing with that narcotic high that came from pushing their bodies beyond human limits for hours on end. Cameron Prince was in most of the photos, smiling, stripped down to a skimpy thong. A massive pulsing specimen. The impresario of brawn.

Thorn was about to leave when one of the photos stopped him. He turned back, stepped closer to the wall. Behind him was the thumping beat of the rap, matching the pulse of his heart.

The photo was smaller than the others, taken on a sunny day. Standing next to Cameron in almost the same spot where Thorn stood now was a man in his late twenties. He was shirtless, wearing only yellow gym shorts, and though his body was well proportioned, he wasn't in the same muscular league as the others.

His sandy hair was the color and coarse texture of

Thorn's, but unlike Thorn's it was precisely and fashionably trimmed. He had a stern set to his brow, and the solemn eyes of one plagued by grueling dreams. Standing alongside Cameron Prince's bulk, the young man seemed boyishly slender. But his stance was resolute, his head high, a shoulder-back posture.

It was Flynn Moss. Thorn's son. The young man he barely knew.

Thorn reached out and ran his finger along the edge of the photograph, his hand trembling, the ground vibrating beneath him.

From a pay phone outside a convenience store on Bird Road, Thorn called the only number he had for Flynn. After three rings his voice mail picked up and Flynn spoke in a rushed, anxious voice, saying he was going away for a while, taking a hiatus from his TV show, not sure when he'd return, telling his mom not to worry, something had come up, and he would be taking on a challenge he'd wanted to do for a long time, something important. She'd hear all about it soon. Leave a message if you want, then the beep.

Thorn broke the connection, dropped in another coin, and dialed April Moss, Flynn's mother. He let it reach ten rings before cutting off. He didn't remember her cell number, so he set the phone back, went to the VW, and drove the several miles north to her house along the Miami River.

No one home. No car, no lights.

He considered scribbling a note, but couldn't think of what to say. That their son was mixed up with Cameron Prince. That Prince had stopped by Thorn's house earlier today on some mysterious mission. That Prince had worked alongside an old friend of Thorn's, Leslie Levine, and had been present at her violent death.

The sequence unsettled Thorn, but without anything more definite than that, he decided that leaving a note for April would only scare the shit out of her for no good reason.

So he got back in the VW, joined the ruthless traffic, and worked his way across the city, back to the turnpike, and headed south to the Keys. As he drove, a loop of images rolled in his head, all of them featuring Flynn Moss. The young man's striking face, the stubborn clench of his jaw, those eyes that were both defiant and anxious as if he were always bracing himself for some fast-approaching calamity that only he could see. Thorn could even hear the kid's rich, plummy actor's voice.

Such a demanding career Flynn had chosen. Assuming the identities and mouthing the words of imagined people, giving flesh to fictions. Standing for hours before fussy directors who critiqued his slightest gestures. Required to perform his work in full view of the probing cameras, the brutal glower of lights, a man fully exposed but completely hidden. There, but not there.

Last year this talented young man, this son, had come as a staggering revelation to Thorn. He'd never imagined or wished for children, never felt unfulfilled or less complete than friends like Sugar, who had fathered two girls. But the discovery of a grown son had blindsided Thorn and left him reeling.

Flynn's mother, April Moss, was now a writer for *The Miami Herald*. But a couple of decades back when she was barely out of high school, she and Thorn had spent a few rambunctious hours in his Key Largo bedroom, then she bid him good-bye and he hadn't seen her again till last year, a quarter of a century later, when he discovered she'd borne twin boys from that single encounter. Sawyer and Flynn.

Days after Thorn met them for the first time, Sawyer attacked Thorn and April, tried to kill them both, and died in the ensuing struggle. Placing the blame for his brother's death squarely on Thorn, Flynn had rejected any future contact.

To have discovered the twins and to have lost both with such finality within days of that revelation had whipsawed Thorn so badly he'd sunk deeper into isolation than was already his habit. It had been months since he'd belly-laughed or felt a tingle of arousal for any of the women who wandered across his path. He'd been experiencing the longest period of celibacy in his adult life. A condition he'd begun to feel might last indefinitely.

And there was another thing. He knew it didn't sound like much, but in the last year, Thorn had begun to talk to himself. A new, disquieting habit. Mumbling beneath his breath, he found himself describing the rosy afternoon light or the foul reek of low tide, or whispering his complaints about the airless heat. Sitting alone at the breakfast table retelling his dreams aloud.

Sometimes he found himself quietly spelling out the step-by-step process he was using to tie a bonefish fly or the course he was navigating to some secret fishing hole. Soliloquies spoken in a murmur, his fantasies, his stray recollections. As though compelled to share his concerns and expertise, the trivia of his daily rituals, with some missing party, a ghostly presence hovering at his shoulder.

Of course he knew what he was doing and how pathetic it was. All these months he'd been pretending to share his days with Flynn, bonding with an absent son.

In the brief time he'd been around Flynn, they'd managed only a few strained conversations. He knew little of Flynn's history, almost nothing of his childhood or the source of his passion for acting. A year had passed without his seeing the kid. Yet simply encountering his image on Cameron Prince's gym wall roused Thorn like nothing else in these last twelve months.

A few miles beyond the sprawl of Miami, he pulled off at a gas station in Homestead, filled his tank, and bought a Budweiser and a bag of peanuts, and half an hour later, by the time he crossed the Jewfish Creek Bridge and entered Key Largo, he'd finished the beer and the nuts, and he'd decided what he had to do next.

FIVE

SIX IN THE MORNING, THURSDAY, the ninth of August, Claude Sellers was in a long-term parking lot near Miami International. Keeping his head down while he applied magnetic AT&T logos to both sides of the white Ford van—an image of a white globe wrapped in blue swirls.

Fuck if he knew what that image was supposed to be. The earth with Saturn rings? Did that make sense? Hell, no. But you could bet someone was getting seriously rich designing the goofy-ass crap. Rich fucks, everywhere you looked, and hardly any were doing anything useful.

He straightened the logo, got behind the wheel, backed out of the space, and headed off. Forty minutes later, out beyond the palm-tree nurseries and tomato fields, he cruised through a grubby rural neighborhood, located the street, and parked the van under a power pole a block from his target house.

He climbed back between the seats and pulled on coveralls with the same telephone-company emblem on the back and the breast. He put on a yellow hard hat, tucked the heavy, insulated gloves into his rear pocket, and jumped down from the back of the van.

He unhooked the aluminum stepladder from the roof of the van and tucked it under an arm and started down the broken sidewalk toward 11777. All the sevens in the world weren't going to save this unlucky guy.

Concrete-block houses, graffiti. Peeling paint, cracked windows. A few houses completely boarded up, several with blue tarps on their roofs, covering missing shingles blown away in the last hurricane, which for christsakes was two years ago. A few with stunted trees and some half-assed hedges.

No dogs barked, no one looked out any windows, no children playing anywhere. It was barely light, and most of the crappy cars were still parked in the driveways. He left the sidewalk and followed a dusty path to the side of the house where the electric meter was. The old-school analog model had four display dials across the top, and a wire loop held together with a yellow piece of plastic was supposed to prevent tampering. The aluminum rotor wheel wasn't revolving.

He walked down the north side of the house and found the main transmission line, which ran through the branches of a mango tree to the power pole, a single transformer serving this house and three of its neighbors. Claude looked back at the curtained window and thought he saw the shadow of someone moving behind it.

Claude opened his stepladder and climbed up to inspect the connection. And, yes, there it was, as he knew it would be. Marcus Bendell was diverting current, using an illegal hookup that was as crude as they came.

He'd shaved open a two-inch section of the service drop line and peeled back the heavy insulation. Both clamps of a twelve-foot red jumper cable were fixed to the service drop, and on the other end the two clamps were attached to the house line. Bypassing the meter.

Twenty-two thousand volts came out of Turkey Point, which the transformers upped to over two hundred thousand volts for cheaper long-distance transmission, then the substations dropped that down again, and the local step-down stations lowered it even more. The transformers on the pole behind Bendell's house cut the power back to the standard 240 volts, which, with the right amperage, was still plenty enough juice to fry someone's guts.

The red cables were hidden in the branches, but weren't well concealed. Claude had spotted them right away when he'd done his recon on this dwelling, scouting the neighborhood, deciding how to take out Bendell. Soon as he saw the hookup, bingo perfecto, he had his plan.

Claude was a burly guy. Five-nine, 180, with a cue-ball shaved head and a thick Fu Manchu cropped neat. Short of stature, yeah, but thick-wristed, heavy-boned, and possessing extra-long arms. A back-alley gorilla motherfucker.

Back in his twenties, before bucket trucks took over, Claude spent years shinnying up wooden poles like a Jamaican kid harvesting coconuts. Happiest hours of his life were on top of those power poles amid the rat's nest of step-down transformers and porcelain insulators and bundle conductors and the slender telephone lines, doing his delicate surgeries while thousands of volts buzzed around him.

Because Claude was efficient and reliable, he'd been promoted down from the sky to a ground-floor cubicle, then came another promotion and another, until now he had his own computer screen, a twenty-man staff, and a cell phone on his belt that put him on twenty-four-hour call. But his true calling was out here, working the street like today. Following his own righteous duty roster.

Claude drew out his yellow insulated gloves, pulled them on, then unclamped the battery cables from the house's drop line.

He climbed down the ladder, clamps in hand, and tucked them carefully in a clump of weeds. He took off the gloves, crammed them in his pocket. The Spectra gel came in a blue tube. He ordered it from Amazon, kept it in his medicine chest. You never knew when you might want to glop some on your heart monitor or defib paddles.

He squeezed out a handful and wiped it up and down both sides of the ladder's handrail. Probably not necessary, but Claude wanted to be extra sure this worked. He smeared a little more of the electro gel, then wiped his slimy hands on the sleeves of his jumpsuit and stepped away from the ladder.

All set, ready to go.

Reaching a hand to the window, Claude knuckle-rapped the glass, and a few seconds later the curtain swept aside and a guy's bleary face appeared. Claude gave the kid a two-finger come-here wave, and the curtains fell closed.

A half minute later the front door of the Bendell house creaked open, then slammed. Claude stood waiting by the ladder until Marcus Bendell showed—a skinny kid in his late twenties with sneaky eyes and a ponytail down his back.

On Marcus's throat was some kind of hostile tattoo. Prison art. An arrow with its sharpened tip buried in the kid's Adam's apple, five or six drops of blood trailing from the inked-on wound. Claude hadn't seen one of those before. He didn't keep up with all the hip-hop and gang bullshit, or whatever the tattoo was connected to. He didn't give a rat's ass about the complaints of turd balls like Bendell.

Bendell saw Claude standing beside the aluminum ladder and halted. A wooden club was in his right hand, like a miniature bowling pin, the kind of homemade weapon people who couldn't afford guns kept near their beds. The guy was a half foot taller than Claude, but had a spindly look, a pale cast to his skin, and teeth the dull gray of fish scales. He was wearing pajama bottoms and a T-shirt. Far as Claude was concerned, the long hair, that tattoo, the way the kid was sneering, made what he was about to do totally guilt-free.

"What the fuck, man?"

"I might ask you the same."

"Six in the morning, trespassing in my yard, you got a warrant?"

"Phone company doesn't need warrants. We own these materials. This is our right of way."

"My landline's working fine."

"Your neighbor's isn't."

"Which neighbor?"

"Tell me something, Marcus. How much that hookup cost you? Two hundred bucks? One-fifty?"

"What hookup?"

"Oh, come on, kid. You're a bright boy. You know damn well you're diverting current back here. I'm curious how much it cost you."

"What do you care?"

"Well, whatever you paid, you got screwed. There's

something you got to look at, how this thing is rigged. I'd hate to see someone get fried from this half-assed workmanship. Even an obvious asshole like yourself."

"Man, what the fuck is pushing your crazy button?" Marcus's eyes hardened and he took a better grip on the club.

"It's not my specialty, but I hear electricity thieves like you cost your fellow citizens around two billion dollars a year."

"Power company is the thief."

"Florida statutes call it larceny with relation to utility fixtures. You're found guilty in a civil action, you're liable to an amount equal to three times the cost of services unlawfully obtained. Jail time, years of probation. The state's on their side, not yours."

"They usually are."

"But a guy like you, long hair and the pissed-off tattoo, you're not stealing power to save a buck. It's politics with you, right? Overthrow the lords and masters."

Marcus stared at the ladder. "If you're from the phone company, let me see some ID."

"Look, son, bottom line, I'm not crazy about what you're doing, but I'm not legally required to report this. So this can just stay between you and me. Man-to-man."

Bendell looked out toward the street, then up into the branches. He shifted the club to his other hand.

Claude said, "Fact is, I don't give two squirts of piss if you're stealing power from the man or any of that happy-hippie horseshit. But here I am out in the field doing my job, and I'd say fuck it and walk off, except in your case, after I had a look-see, I found that you, Mr. Bendell, got yourself a serious issue with this connection. Whoever did this for you, they didn't know shit about electricity. There's some criminal negligence at work. If I were you, I wouldn't lie down in bed again till you consider the fire hazard lurking outside your bedroom."

"You want money, is that it? A bribe not to turn me in."

"You're not hearing me, pal. I got higher interests than cash. I'm a fully functioning human with morals and empathy and the whole deal. I don't like seeing my fellow man turning into charcoal from somebody's poor tradecraft. Go on, Bendell, take a peek at the mess up there in the mango branches." Claude stepped out of the way.

"I don't know what your game is."

"At this point, I'm trying to save a life." Claude swept his hand to the aluminum stepladder.

Marcus hesitated a moment, suspicious, but wavering.

"What? You think I'm going to tip the ladder over, I'm going to pull some silly prank on you?"

Marcus came over, touched the edge of the ladder with an experimental fingertip, looking back at Claude and working up some badass in his eyes, dropping the club as he started up, going two rungs, then three, his head coming close to the lower branches of the mango tree.

Marcus felt the slime on his hands and held up his right palm, puzzled.

"Up there to your left. Pull that branch to the side, you'll see what I'm talking about."

As Marcus reached for the branch, Claude pulled his yellow insulated gloves from his pocket, put them on, and stooped for the jumper cables. "See what I'm telling you?"

"I don't see anything."

"You're looking in the wrong direction."

"Where?"

"Try down here, peckerhead."

Marcus looked over his shoulder as Claude moved the clamps to the ladder, smiling up at the kid, enjoying this. Most fun he'd had in a while.

"You fucker. What're you doing?"

"I see you're packing your car, you and your girl are going to split."

"What do you care what I do?"

"Oh, I care."

"Who are you?" The kid was looking around for a clear path to jump, but the branches blocked him on every side.

"You took the feds' offer, got out of jail free, now you're sneaking off without completing your side of the bargain."

"You're with the feds?"

"Something like that."

Claude squeezed open the jaws of the clamps, moved toward the ladder.

"Wait, wait. I can give you something. We can deal. Just let me down."

"Yeah? What the hell could you give me, turd ball?"

"There's somebody else."

Claude held the jumper cables close to the ladder. He could feel the throb of voltage. "What's that mean, somebody else?"

"Out on Prince Key. Somebody you don't know about."

"Another snitch?"

"That's right. Let me down, I'll tell you everything."

"You're lying."

"He's got a cell phone, he's hidden it out there on the island. He calls some guy he knows at the FBI. Now let me go."

"You're a fucking liar."

"It's the truth. I swear."

"What's his name, this snitch? Which one is it?"

Bendell's mouth was half-open, face slack. "You'll let me down?"

"Sure, kid. Tell me the fucker's name and you're free to go."

"Put those things away. Come on, man. Don't do that."

"What's his name, this other spy? You're two seconds from going dark."

"The FBI guy he calls, his name is Sheffield. Frank, I think."

"And the spy's name?"

"I caught him talking on his phone and he admitted it. That's why I'm bailing. This whole thing is fucked. The FBI is gonna crash the party big-time."

"Who is it? Who was talking to the feds? His name, goddamn it."

"I'm coming down now."

"Not until I have a name."

Bendell lurched, tried to shove the branches aside and jump. But, fuck that, Claude was too quick. He clamped one end of the jumper cable high up on one side of the ladder, the other clamp on the opposite side.

Some people had the wrong idea about aluminum. They thought it didn't conduct electricity. But, no, aluminum was more conductive than copper compared by unit weight. True, it did tend to create an electrically resistive oxide inside certain connections, which could lead to heat cycling. Still, all in all, it was one of the most common metals used in high-voltage transmission lines, along with steel for reinforcement.

Up on the backyard pole the transformer flashed blue like a giant lightbulb exploding, and Marcus Bendell and his ponytail turned into a galvanic smoke bomb.

Not a pretty sight. His hands clutching the ladder, unable to let go, the current gripping him in place while his body bucked, and Claude guessed the kid's internal organs were already starting to melt. The kid had turned into a giant human resistor making the amps skyrocket, the voltage trying to flow, all of it mingling in a perfect brew to poach Marcus from the inside out.

The young man was completing the circuit, helping the sizzle of current find its way to the ground the way all electricity ultimately wanted. A simple wish, to return to the earth. Everyone completed that circuit sooner or later.

In another two seconds, Bendell's body broke loose from the aluminum and blew backward from the ladder in a dark, gagging cloud. The kid was dead quicker than if he'd taken a gunshot to the temple.

Claude stepped around the smoking remains and unclipped the cables from the ladder and dropped them in the grass. At this moment a light would be blinking on a control panel at the west Miami substation. In a few minutes phone calls from the neighbors would start coming in. They heard a loud pop. Their lights went off, TVs shut down, toaster won't work.

Tomorrow there'd be a news story in *The Miami Herald,* a kid tapping into the power line died while trying to save himself a few bucks. The bad economy was driving people to take terrible risks. So let this be a lesson to all those citizens contemplating current diversion.

Not that anyone read the paper anymore or took it seriously if they did.

Claude left the ladder behind, just a generic Ace Hardware brand, and was back in the van and on his way in thirty seconds.

Waiting at the first stoplight, he bent his head to the side and sniffed at the fumes clinging to his jumpsuit. Not the worst smell he'd ever inhaled.

But close.

SIX

JUST AFTER DAWN THURSDAY MORNING, Thorn started the Evinrude and let it idle while he put away the tubes of caulk and the pipe wrench he'd been using on the cistern repair yesterday.

Stowing them in the toolshed, he spotted an ancient pry bar hanging from a nail on the far wall. He took it down and weighed it in one hand, then tapped it hard against his open palm. It made a satisfying thunk.

He carried it to the dock and stepped down into the skiff and set the pry bar on the console. You never knew when you might need to force a locked door, a sticky window, or maybe whack someone across the face with a pound of rusty steel. A guy the size of Prince might require two whacks.

Back inside the house his Smith .357 was wrapped in an oily rag and stashed in a back closet. But Thorn decided against taking it. That pistol had saved his life more than once. But a handgun had a way of causing unintended consequences, upping the ante at crisis moments. He was weary of unintended consequences and even more weary of crisis moments. The pry bar would do.

Thorn was moving with controlled focus. Ignoring the shudder in his nerves. He tried to tell himself that Flynn was not in any danger. There was no conspiracy here, no sinister intrigue. Flynn had gotten mixed up with Prince for reasons having nothing to do with Leslie Levine or her suspicious death. Prince had been creeping around his property for some entirely innocent purpose. Maybe he was only checking out the cistern like he said.

But damn it, as hard as he tried to explain it away, he couldn't ignore the weird overlap, the coincidental connections that felt far from coincidental.

The Princes were old-guard Miamians. For decades the patriarch, Reginald Prince, had published the afternoon newspaper in Miami, battling righteously against political corruption and criminal enterprises of every stripe. When Reginald died, his son, Reggie, let the paper flounder. He hadn't inherited the father's warrior gene. In the fifties, Reggie married a Havana-born nightclub singer and turned Prince Key into a weekend retreat for his wife's musician friends and for writers and artists and movie stars passing through town.

Growing up, Thorn heard stories about boozy orgies and high-stakes poker, congressmen and local leaders consorting with notorious actresses and mafiosi out on that island. Eventually Reggie and his wife abandoned the island for the mainland and faded from view. Then a few years back Reggie was arrested for bribing three Miami councilmen over a real estate deal. In only two generations the family had gone from crusading newsman to low-life scum.

As a teenager, Thorn was drawn to Prince Key by its shadowy history and romance. But the day he boated there and poked around the place, he found only the charred remnants of a few wooden structures, piles of litter, and dark clouds of voracious mosquitoes, and not a whiff of romance anywhere.

Now he stepped aboard, cast off the lines, and idled into the center of the lagoon, then headed out the narrow channel. As he reached open water, he hit the throttle hard, kicking the skiff onto plane.

He kept his eyes on the silky bay before him. He was hungover from a night of fever dreams, a rising dread about Flynn. He kept circling back to that hurried message Flynn had left on his answering machine. The more Thorn replayed it, the more worrisome it seemed.

Through the long night hours, Thorn passed in and out of sleep, debating whether to get involved or stay put, tormented by a flurry of scenes of past events when he'd answered some call and things had gone badly. Flynn's face mingling with so many others, people Thorn had known, men and women, some long dead, those he'd tried to help and wound up failing, and some he'd managed to comfort or save. Snippets of fistfights and gunfire, flashes of knife blades, jerked him back to full consciousness.

Thorn's skiff sliced across the oily, flat waters, and stingrays scooted out of his path, and schools of mullet parted before him. The mirrored water reflected his white hull, his own stiff body rippling at the wheel, his hair blowing, a silvery-blue replica of himself. He kept his eyes forward. Let the wind rip away all doubts. Almost all.

He tried to push Flynn away, concentrate on his surroundings as he flew north along the eastern shore of Key Largo, a half mile off, five feet of green water. No boaters out, too early in the day for the summer tourists, no dive boats heading to the reefs to view the sad remains of the elkhorn coral, the dying, whitening twists of living rock. A mile to his east a lone shrimper was returning with his catch.

He skimmed by the state-owned lands preserved for the moment against bulldozers and chain saws, at least until some weasel-eyed politician found the temptation too irresistible, found a loophole, found enough willing officials to overturn the protections and flout the will of the people and send in the machines.

It would happen, it always happened, it was happening before Thorn was born and would be happening into the future until all of it was wiped away. The wild tangles of native scrub and gumbo-limbos and sapodillas and mangroves along the coastline, all of it densely populated with every manner of varmint, possums and egrets and endangered rodents and butterflies.

Then he came to Ocean Reef Club, the ritzy outpost for bankers, brokers, and assorted money changers who descended for a week or two in winter to luxuriate in their oceanfront mansions.

After Ocean Reef, the terrain turned wild again, and Thorn spotted his turn and cut sharply into Pumpkin Creek, then took a straight shot north, still at full throttle, faster than he needed to go, faster than was safe in such a tight channel, flying around the blind bends in the creek, gritting his teeth, unable to slow down, his wake splashing white foam high into the lower branches of the mangroves, Thorn keeping the engine wide open to match his pulse, his own racing mind. The closer he got to the south end of Prince Key, the stronger the magnetic pull.

Banking hard into Angelfish Creek, the broad river
that separated the tip of North Key Largo from the rest
of the ragged keys that trickled north for miles into Biscayne Bay, he swung the skiff into a sharp, sliding left
at Linderman Creek and cut out into open bay, circling
Prince Key to see if anything had changed since his last
pass, and, no, it was still shrouded by an impenetrable
mass of foliage and mangroves whose roots ran down to
the waterline, an island whose dock had long ago washed
away and had not been replaced, only a few rotting pilings left, and not even a spit of sand or any beachhead,
nowhere to make a landing, which left only the one
entrance Thorn remembered from long ago. If it still
existed.

He completed the circuit, then ducked back in Angelfish Creek, pushing down the waterway into a labyrinth
of smaller arteries, each one tapering narrower and narrower. He flashed past a warning sign, NO MOTORIZED
WATERCRAFT, the sign the Park Service had been post-
ing throughout the back bays of the Everglades these last
few years, putting off-limits many of Thorn's familiar
haunts, all his best fishing areas, and Thorn grudgingly
obeyed the signs, honored the state's attempts at pres-
ervation, but not this time, forging on, the branches
scratching at the hull of Thorn's boat, slapping his arms,
clawing his face, and then came more signs, hand-drawn
private warnings, NOT OPEN TO THE PUBLIC, scrawled in
red, another saying, TURN BACK, NO ENTRY, nailed to a
stake, and ARMED RESPONSE—NO WARNING SHOT, but
he didn't slow, pushing on until he entered some name-
less tributary, a waterway he thought he recognized
from years before when he was young and determined
to poke into every corner of the watery world within

the range of his gas tank, back in the days when Thorn needed to stretch his tether farther and farther from his island home, in search of some secret place, some knowledge hidden beyond the horizon, back in those years when he still believed such secret places existed.

As he slid around a sharp turn and entered a widening basin, he saw the hidden beach he remembered. An arc of white sand that glowed in the early-morning shadows like the sliver of a new moon against a dusky sky.

Thorn throttled back and rode the wash forward into the small basin enclosed by red mangroves. For a moment he was that boy again, the curious kid determined to chart every creek and canal and secret bay within his reach, the boy with big plans to someday push outward, to explore beyond the horizon, the unimaginably enormous world of bays and creeks and sounds.

To travel the earth year after year until he'd mapped every continent, hiked every mountain listed in his boyhood atlas, slayed every fire-breathing dragon along the way, pushed aside the beaded curtains of each hideaway bar from Madagascar to Borneo, and seduced the exotic ladies with his tall tales. A kid who'd grown older and traveled inward instead, abandoning those aspirations, dream by dream by dream and year by year as he was drawn into different, darker quests, defending friends, avenging wrongs, entangling himself in exploits as reckless as any of the swashbuckling silliness on the far side of the globe he'd once imagined.

Something scratched his hull. Thorn peered over the side and saw a braided net concealed a few inches below the waterline, and he yanked the throttle back, throwing the gears into reverse to keep from tangling his prop in the mesh, but he was several seconds late.

Strands of the net wrapped around the blades and shaft, almost instantly binding tight, and the Evinrude strained, belched, and the engine seized.

The cove went still.

Thorn drifted forward a few inches before the netting tugged the skiff to a halt. On two sides of the cove the mesh had been stretched to the banks, where dozens of aluminum stakes were hammered into the muck and sand to hold the main lines taut. A snare, a boat killer. Though it would have been easy enough to avoid if he'd been paying attention.

He tried to tilt the engine up, but could only raise it a few inches, the props still trapped firmly below the waterline. On his knees he bent over the transom to inspect the situation. The strands of braided nylon were thin and would be easy to slice with one of the knives he'd brought. Except the mesh had circled the shaft so many times, the metal was buried several inches deep, which meant that sawing through the tangle could take a while.

Rising, he went back to the console and slipped the gears into neutral and turned the ignition key. The engine fired up, belched, and died. He tried a second time and the engine made an even uglier belch.

So that was it. Once he managed to cut away the mesh, he'd have to tear open the engine and track down the issue. But it sounded serious, a blown piston ring or head gasket. Neither of which he was equipped to repair.

Which left nothing to do but swim to shore.

He stepped around the console and surveyed the cove.

At the edge of the sandy beach, a two-tiered wooden storage rack held a half dozen kayaks painted dull primer black.

As he was turning away, Thorn saw an odd shape slung out on the sand. He stopped, came forward, stepped up on the casting platform, and squinted to be sure.

Yes, basking in the sun on the beach was an enormous serpent, a healthy Burmese python. Its head and a couple of feet of its body were exposed, but its hindquarters were hidden in the shadows of the foliage. It was as thick as a goal post, sleek and shiny with blotches on its dark skin outlined in a shade of gold like drizzles of butterscotch. Ghastly and gorgeous.

For the last few years since pythons first appeared in the Everglades, they'd been devastating the ranks of foxes, raccoons, possums, and marsh rabbits, and multiplying so fast they'd begun to push east into the western suburbs of Miami, while others headed west into the outskirts of Naples and Fort Myers. Though these days they were being relentlessly hunted by airboat sportsmen and park rangers and herpetologists, their population was still exploding into the thousands.

Folks in the Upper Keys had thought they were safe from the invasion because the big snakes didn't tolerate salt water for sustained periods. And a lot of salt water buffered the Keys from the freshwater Everglades. But recently biologists discovered the pythons had found a clever way to cross those barriers. By moving from one brackish estuary to the next, they'd managed to hopscotch south to the Keys, where now they'd taken up residence and were snacking on local egrets, possums, and feral pigs. Even a few deer had been found under digestion in the bellies of some larger specimens.

Thorn's arrival in the cove had stirred the water, and ripples were sloshing against the sandy shoreline. That small disturbance roused the snake from its sun-dazed slumber. It lifted its head, swiveled it side to side, absorbing the situation. Then the python began a slow glide out into the sunlight, coming and coming till its length was fully revealed.

Fifteen feet, maybe longer, well over a hundred pounds. And it continued to slide forward to the shoreline, where it nosed into the water and disappeared into the basin to investigate.

SEVEN

THORN KEPT WATCH TO SEE where the big snake was headed, but lost it in the dark water. Maybe he'd spooked it, sent it off to a more secluded spot. He peered into the water for a few minutes more but saw no sign of it.

From the bow of his skiff, the shore was a good forty feet away, an easy stone's throw. A half minute's swim.

But to be sure the snake was busy elsewhere, he opened his tackle box and gathered a handful of split shot, then tucked the pry bar in the waistband of his shorts.

He stepped up onto the bow deck and edged forward until the toes of his boat shoes jutted beyond the rub rail. He looked across at the closest spit of sandy beach, chose the shortest angle.

He slung a few of the lead weights to the far corner of the basin, then waited a few seconds and plunked two more into the widening riffles of the first splashes, then sailed the last handful into the same splatter. Enough of a distraction to give him a decent head start.

Though he didn't believe he had anything to fear. Surely the snake had been dining well enough on the shorebirds and small game living on Prince Key and would have no interest in anything as large and unfriendly as Thorn.

He saw its sinuous length gliding just below the surface, heading to the ripples, which put the big snake about as far from Thorn as Thorn was from shore.

He took hold of the pry bar.

Leaning forward, he drew a quick breath and dove. He swam as smoothly as his body allowed. Slicing and pulling himself forward with his arms, but not kicking. Even though he knew this attempt at stealth was silly, for surely the python had registered his entry into the basin, knew instantly that this alien chunk of protein was out of its element.

He was well aware of the creature's method of attack. He'd encountered one earlier that summer warming its cold blood on his dock. Because it was an invading species, decimating native wildlife, Thorn had no qualms about murdering the thing. A single machete blow had decapitated the six-footer, and he'd stored its chunky head on ice until Sugar's daughters came down for their next scheduled visit.

That weekend he presented the trophy to fourteen-year-old Janey Sugarman, a devoted naturalist. And just as he'd thought, Janey was thrilled at the chance to dissect the python's head and study its structure. They'd spent the afternoon at Thorn's fish-cleaning bench, using one of his fillet knives to dismember the creature's skull and examine its strange, hingeless jaw that allowed the python to swallow prey five times the diameter of its head. Its incisor teeth were about a half inch long and curved inward, not meant for chewing, but only to lock on to the flesh of its prey, hold it in place while the supple trunk wrapped around its quarry and crushed the life from it.

Halfway across the basin, swimming smoothly, he felt a brush against his ankle. He accelerated, began to flutter-kick in earnest, and lifted his head to check his progress. He was a few seconds offshore when he crashed against the submerged branch. It thumped so hard into his ribs it felt like a short left hook from a pissed-off welterweight. A serious, breathtaking hurt.

Gasping for a breath, he halted his stroke, let his legs drop.

A mistake.

As his feet sank into the mucky sediment, he saw a shadow sneaking toward his right hip and jabbed at it with the pry bar, making glancing contact with its slippery flesh, then he staggered backward toward the bank. Twenty feet of squashy muck to cross through waist-high water.

Up to his thighs in the quicksand, he was struggling toward the soggy bank when he saw the shadow making another approach.

He waited till it was at arm's length, then waited a moment more before he slashed, missed, and slashed again. Water splattered, but he struck nothing solid. He felt the silky mass slide against his thigh, heavy and thick and undulating, its slippery flesh coiling around his hips in a loose embrace.

Gripping the pry bar two-handed, he aimed its sharp end at the golden-brown shine, searching for the head, the vulnerable eyes. But seeing only the endless tail. As far as he could tell, this monster was all tail, all heavy, dark meat, a being whose length had not yet fully arrived.

He picked a spot and hacked at the trunk looping his waist, the massive, rubbery bulk with its butterscotch markings, its slow, encircling clinch. Still not seeing the eyes, the head, the face, the mouth. Its small brain controlling the instinctive swirl of its body. This creature only knew how to do one thing. A simpleton with a single strategy. To squash the breath from what it desired. And right now it hankered for Thorn.

Before he knew it was happening, he was locked firmly. Until that moment he'd thought he was still moving freely. He'd believed he was working his way backward up the last eight or ten feet of the slushy bank, but when he looked back at the land, it had moved away. He was not just immobilized, he was being towed out to deeper water, coaxed without knowing it.

This idiot creature hadn't even bothered to bite and take hold, but just enveloped him slowly without a fight. Seducing with its slow embrace.

Then he spotted the wedged head moving past and slashed the crowbar's talon with enough force to splinter its skull and liquefy its brains. But his aim was off by an inch and all he got was another splatter of water.

His mind seemed to be clouding. He was now chest high in water and firmly in the grasp of the python, a pressuring hug that was relentless, yet so languorous that he was feeling a dreamy calm, a sense that there was nothing to worry about, a drifting away from the consequences of drifting away.

But some dim, bullheaded region of Thorn's brain was still active enough to absorb his predicament. If he didn't strike a decisive blow soon, his ribs would begin to crack one by one.

He drew a cramped breath, hacked at the meaty

weight that was hugging him. Hacked it again and once more after that. Hitting it finally, making good contact, a goddamn satisfying thunk. Getting his aim. A couple more blows bounced off its tough hide. Then a couple more.

He was breathing hard, but he also knew the snake was hurt. Saw a pale, oily liquid coiling to the surface like wisps of cigarette smoke, and bits and strands of membrane swirling up through the tannic-stained water.

Again he struck at the meat and this time nailed it good. Aiming at the section that was compressing his diaphragm, knowing that an errant blow could skid into his own flesh and might seriously wound him. But he was out of choices. He gouged at the greenish hide, gouged again, until finally the python reached its threshold.

It happened fast. In seconds the water in front of Thorn wrinkled, several small whirlpools gathered and disappeared, and the creature unleashed him and was gone.

Thorn staggered backward. He took a breath and another and the light rose around him. He hadn't realized how deeply he'd drifted into shadowland, how close to the end he'd come. He sank one foot into the muck, then sank the other foot and tore loose the back foot and moved it into the lead.

He waded ahead through the gummy sludge, peering up at the dense mangroves and viney tangle of woods but seeing no sign of any living thing, or any movement or sound. Just the glop and slop of each step, the sucking bottom that was urging him to stay put and rest.

At last he stumbled up the slope of the beach, stood for a moment surveying the basin, then turned halfway round, collapsed, and lay back panting. He stared up at the empty sky, feeling his heart sprinting for some distant finish line. He set the pry bar aside and after a moment more of rest forced himself to sit up and held that position for several minutes, his shirt dripping, his legs weak, shoes full of mire, and he looked out at the basin and tried to recall why he'd come to this forsaken place, why he'd been in such a goddamn hurry and so distracted that he'd run afoul of someone's primitive booby trap, ruined his engine in his reckless haste.

For a moment he had no clear memory of his mission. No memory of anything. Mind blank, drowsing in the shivery afterglow of adrenaline.

As he drifted through layers of fog toward the bright surface of wakefulness, struggling to breathe the summertime air, his skin sticky and fitting too tight to his bones, Thorn looked out at the cove, at this secret beach at the terminus of a labyrinth of twisty canals and creeks and backwaters that had no names and did not appear on any sane person's nautical charts.

EIGHT

"HIS NAME WAS BENDELL, MARCUS Bendell."

With one hand on the wheel of the black government-issue Taurus, Nicole McIvey cut through the traffic on Florida's Turnpike, heading south. She held out her phone and Frank Sheffield looked at the image on her screen.

A scrawny young man, midtwenties with a prison pallor and dull eyes and stringy hair, stood before a police department's height chart. Five-eleven.

"That's before." She withdrew the phone, thumbed through screens, and held it out again. "And this is after."

Frank stared for a few seconds, then looked out his window, a sphincter tensing in his bowels. For over thirty years he'd been with the FBI, the last dozen as special agent in charge of the Miami field office, so he'd seen a shitload of postmortem photos, but nothing this grisly.

"Jesus, he walk into a flamethrower?"

The naked body lay on a stainless-steel table. Chunks of the torso were missing. There was a blackened cavity in his right rib cage as if he'd been blowtorched open; the face was a charred mess, unidentifiable.

"Electrocution," Nicole said. "Happened early this

morning. Bendell's girlfriend discovered the body. Came to his house, found him out back. Metro PD sent me the JPEG a few hours ago. They knew I had an interest in him."

She set the phone in a cup holder, gripped the wheel, and sliced in front of a slow-moving landscape truck. The lady was a serious lane-warrior.

"What kind of interest?"

"Marcus Bendell was my snitch."

"Say that again?"

"A valuable asset."

"You people were running a covert operation?"

"I was running it. Me alone."

"Did I miss something? Your mission change when I wasn't looking?"

"It's not outside our parameters," Nicole said.

"You let Metro PD know but forget to inform the Bureau?"

"The terms of his parole required me to inform local law enforcement."

"It would have been collegial of you to notify us."

"My agency's mandate is to collect intelligence. Once it goes up the chain, my superiors decide who's in the loop. If the FBI wasn't included, Frank, it wasn't my decision."

"And here I thought we were all partners, trying to gel into one happy federal family."

"That's why I called you. I'm ready to gel."

Sheffield managed a smile. His bureaucratic side was irritated, but these days that was a small slice of his emotional pie.

"So here's the story. It started thirteen months ago. I heard about Bendell when he went up for a ten-year stretch at Raiford. An animal rights activist, he and six others burned down a product-testing plant outside Orlando that was using cats for experiments—mascara, eyeliner. He was caught in the act."

"Mascara," Sheffield said. "That's what we're doing now. Wasting our time on idiots like that."

"Part of my job, I follow up on these guys, find out who's visiting them in prison, monitor their correspondence, see what dots we can connect. So I get word Bendell isn't handling his incarceration well. He fits a profile we look for. With save-the-planet softies like these, it happens a lot, prison life freaks them out. A month or two they're ready to give up their mamas.

"I went to Raiford, sat down with Bendell. He seemed pliable. So I spent a couple of weeks working on him till he flipped. Homeland Security put together a package, got Justice to sign off, and Bendell took it. We put him in a house in Miami; next few months he goes to political rallies, land-use meetings, anything with an environmental edge. He holds up signs, taunts the cops, lets the local activist groups get to know him, see who tries to buddy up. Just trolling for whoever might be out there. It doesn't usually work. This time it did."

"Why didn't you just pick up the phone, let me know?"

"Didn't want to bother you. One foot in retirement, you're preoccupied phasing into civilian life."

Frank watched her weave through the heavy traffic. Behind the wheel this laid-back woman was a cutthroat. Something to factor in.

"Bendell was doing good work," she said, shooting Frank a solemn look. "He could talk the talk, had the right cred, knew people who knew people. So one day he gets a call from Cameron Prince. And, bingo, he's invited inside."

"So now Marcus is a carcass, you're in mourning."

"Jesus, Frank."

"Sorry. It sounded funnier in my head."

She was silent for a moment, trapped at the speed limit behind a plumbing truck.

"I'm not saying Bendell was an angel, but he was a decent guy. So, yeah. I'm not happy about this. We were getting close to something."

"You going to tell me what?"

"I'm working up to it."

"Okay, let me tell you what I'm hearing. You were fine sitting on this until your guy is offed, but because a federal informant is killed in suspicious circumstances, you need us. So this isn't courtesy."

"It's true, Frank. I could use your help." She cut right, swerved past the plumbing truck.

"Hey, are we in some kind of hurry? 'Cause if we are, maybe you should turn on your blue light."

"Don't have one. Why? Do women drivers scare you?"

"Nothing so global as that." Frank tugged his shoulder harness tighter.

She glanced over at him, at his shirt, and gave him that half smile. As if she was embarrassed for him and wanted to say something, but was holding fire. Fifth or sixth time she'd shown that smile, starting when she'd shown up at the Silver Sands Motel, where he lived on Key Biscayne.

Nine thirty that morning, he was waiting for her at the concrete picnic table, dressed in his best Hawaiian shirt, the yellow one with blue hula girls, and faded jeans and loafers. Showered, hair combed, ready. His brown hair going sandy and thinning in back, but his body holding up, still trim. His face showed he was nearing sixty, weathered from years in the South Florida sun, with blue, honest eyes, an easy smile, a single shiny scar on the bridge of his nose from a sucker punch thrown by a meth freak, but otherwise relatively unbattered, considering his profession.

When she'd arrived, she'd given him that teaser smile and asked if it was his day off, and Frank said, yeah, as a matter of fact. Well, she wanted him to meet someone and she was in a hurry, so there wasn't time for him to change, and he'd said fine, he hadn't been planning to.

Nicole McIvey stood there in her crisp gray slacks and silky purple top, not formfitting, but tight enough to give away her figure. Not a flashy lady, but in nearly every way he could think of, Nicole was dead center in Sheffield's hormonal sweet spot. Trim body with a hardy edge. Pale blond hair that she wore loose to her shoulders, clear blue eyes with a sharpshooter's glint. Eyebrows so light they were barely there.

She carried herself smoothly, as airy on her feet as a yoga guru. She had a take-no-prisoners sense of humor, like a woman who'd learned her first life lessons horsing around with older brothers.

First time he saw her at a Homeland Security briefing up in Lauderdale, he'd felt a twinge. She picked up on it, glancing his way more than necessary, a couple of subtle smiles. Flirting, but discreet. Second occasion, a Christmas party for some top-tier feds in South Florida, at a mansion out on the beach along the Intracoastal with a view of the downtown Miami skyline lit up in reds and greens, Biscayne Bay gleaming, soft winter breeze. Open bar. McIvey was drinking mango champagne cocktails. Sheffield was on his third Bud when she came over, started talking. Asked him if he was staring at her. He apologized, said she reminded him of somebody.

Dare I ask?

First wife, he said, but she's long gone.

An amicable divorce, I hope?

What's the opposite of amicable? he said.

She looked back at the party as if considering rejoining the crowd. Took a minute, but finally turned back to him. Never married again?

Not even close.

She hurt you that much, Frank? You'll never love again?

You're mighty quick on the draw.

You like going slow, Frank? You'd be the first man I met.

I used to think I'd never get over her. But not anymore. Twenty years, I believe I'm all healed up.

They wound up leaning against the boathouse, chatting, getting around to the weather, the cool tropical winter night, the scattering of stars, Nicole saying it looked like silver mistletoe twinkling up there, a bit of come-on poetry.

They discussed work, people they knew, the music filtering down from the big house, people laughing quietly on the other side of the lawn, then they both went silent, looking at each other, and with a tilt of her head, she offered him a kiss and he took it. He wasn't sure how drunk she was, or how drunk he was. But that kiss lasted about as long as any Frank could remember, and then came her hands, not hurried or rough, but sure, aware, the slow sensuous sound of his own zipper, her long fingers unbuckling him, you're sure about this, he managed to whisper, oh, yes, she said, then her skirt going up, panties tugged down, her sleek inner thighs, the athletic maneuvers she managed while they consummated it in the shadows of the boathouse.

After they were done, she split for the bathroom and didn't return.

Next day he tracked down her number and called her.

She didn't let him get past hello before saying it was a mistake. She never did stuff like that. What? You're a nun, a virgin? I mean the zipless thing, she said. Never? Never, she said. And it's not a good idea for either of them. Her so junior, him so senior.

Sheffield did his best to minimize all that, joking around, trying to get his silver tongue going. But when he ran out of words, she was quiet and stayed that way until he gave up and that was that, no further contact all winter, spring, and summer until this morning when she'd rung his room at the Silver Sands.

For his entire career with the Bureau, Sheffield had never once hit on a coworker, even one a step removed from the FBI. It was one of Sheffield's unbendable rules. Never dally with cops, 'cause if it came back to bite you in the ass, it would clamp hard. But as Nicole had said, Sheffield had a foot in retirement. And he could still hear that silky zipper. Still feel her sure-handed way with his belt.

On the phone at 8:00 a.m. today, Frank asked her what this was all about.

She said this had to be face-to-face. She'd fill him in on the way down to the power plant. Which power plant? You mean Turkey Point? I'll fill you in, she repeated.

"I've seen electrocutions before. Nothing like this."

"He caught fire. From the inside out, his major organs, that's what the ME told me. It's rare, but it happens."

"Jesus."

"There was a half-assed attempt to make it look accidental. But it was clear what went down. They hooked Marcus up to the electrical grid. Like a message. Power to the people. Something cute like that. That's how they think. They found out he was spying on them, they fried him."

"That's a message?"

"They're big into messaging," she said.

"Who we talking about?"

She plucked her phone from the cup holder, fiddled with it one-handed, cutting her eyes back and forth from the phone to the insane traffic heading south, everybody in a hurry to get to the Keys and relax.

She held out the phone again.

It was an image of a cartoon elf, chubby and stern-faced and wearing a green frock and a beret. His leggings were also olive drab and the toes of his boots curled up like those of the fairy-tale elves from Grimm. He was holding an oversize flintlock rifle at port arms and an ammo belt was slung over one shoulder. He was winking, but it wasn't merry. More warlock than pixie.

"Earth Liberation Front," Frank said. "Your guy infiltrated an ELF cell?"

"A month ago, there was a cyber incursion at Turkey Point. They left this image behind on all the computer screens in the power plant, and it stayed there for a couple of days until Homeland's tech guys managed to remove it."

Frank was silent, eyes on the road ahead.

"I know what you're thinking, Frank. No one advised you of this either. But how it happened, Nuclear Regulatory bounced it to me because they knew I was running an operation on ELF. I passed it up my chain. After that, like I said, it was their call who to alert."

"Your agency is under our jurisdiction, the Bureau's. I should've heard about this every step along the way."

"I'm just telling you what happened."

He considered it a moment. "Well, shit. I'm halfway out the door. I shouldn't be pissed nobody copies me on these things."

"But you're pissed anyway."

He looked at her and smiled. "Relatively pissed, yes. Six on the ten-point scale."

Frank knew all about ELF. An arm of Earth First! ELF activists were arsonists mainly. They favored primitive explosive devices to burn down ritzy housing developments built on sensitive lands, and SUV dealerships that specialized in gas hogs. They staged attacks on animal-testing labs, spiking ancient redwoods to shut down logging operations.

All loose-knit, no central command. A mishmash of beliefs. Animal liberators, anticapitalists, green anarchists, deep ecologists, ecofeminists. The entire array of next-generation revolutionaries. Everyone doing his or her thing. Save the earth, fuck the exploiters, punish the land developers, stop urban sprawl.

Business leaders upset over their economic losses had pressured the Bureau for years and finally bullied it into lumping together ELF and Earth First! and the Animal Liberation Front and a few others like them and promoting them to the top of the list, ranking their kind as the number one domestic terrorist threat.

Not the Aryan Nations or the Islamic Brothers, not the twenty-odd militias in Idaho and Michigan and Colorado, wingnuts armed to the earlobes with rocket launchers and assault weapons, targeting cops and judges and abortion doctors, just waiting their chance to bring the federal government crashing down.

No, ecowarriors were number one.

Pure silliness, as far as Sheffield was concerned. Sure, their dollar totals were up in the 40 million range, mostly from burning down those posh resorts in Aspen and trashing cosmetics-testing plants, but they'd never killed anyone and seemed to be trying their best to keep it that way. They were a bunch of idealistic merry pranksters. A ragtag assortment of dope smokers with a badass green streak. Most of the few hundred criminal acts attributed to them were so minor league, it was a stretch to call them *criminal* at all. He kept it to himself, but Frank could even work up a mild sympathy for their cause. He wasn't a big fan of urban sprawl.

"Apparently," McIvey said, "whoever hacked the plant's system wasn't trying to crash the reactors or cause a meltdown or anything catastrophic. Besides leaving this screen saver behind, looks like their mission was exploratory, testing the plant's cyber defenses. A probe of some kind, digital snooping. Possibly to identify vulnerabilities, what they call 'susceptible nodes.' Like this might be stage one, a warm-up for the main event. Or it could be just a one-shot deal. Thumbing their nose. A head fake. Pretending interest in Turkey Point, but planning to strike somewhere else."

She blew through the tollbooth's SunPass lane.

"You're running a covert operation in my backyard. Withholding information about a security breach at the largest nuclear facility in Florida. In case you didn't know, our South Florida Field Office has a cybersecurity task force, a WMD task force, we cover all those bases. Our guys are the best."

"You want the truth, my opinion, it's politics. People above me kept everyone in the dark so NIPC can score a takedown. Justify our existence."

National Infrastructure Protection Center, that was her agency. Frank had watched it all mushroom since the Twin Towers were hit, an explosion of federal programs under the aegis of Homeland Security. NIPC identified and analyzed threats and vulnerabilities in the infrastructure. Electrical grids, bridges, roads, water systems, highways, railways, navigable waterways, airports, the Internet, and phone systems. Anything that moved people or power or goods and services or information. The grid police.

Huge mandate that overlapped with about five other existing agencies, including work the FBI had been doing for most of Frank's career. All that growth was supposed to improve interagency communication, but what it did was make the turf wars even more bitter than pre-9/11. Another reason he'd decided to pull the rip cord, float back to a life of full-time Hawaiian shirts.

"So here's the deal, Frank. The computer network at Turkey Point is a closed loop. Critical areas are wired internally, but not exposed to the Internet. So a cyber attack has to be launched inside the plant using one of the on-site computers. Insert a flash drive or download malicious code. It has to come from inside the loop. But then you probably know all this."

"Refresher course is fine. I like listening to you talk."

She gave him a quick *don't go there* look and got back to driving.

Sheffield debated it. Confess now, lay his cards faceup, or keep holding out. For her part, Nicole had been concealing several major investigations, which gave Sheffield the moral high ground. If he was going to drop his own bomb, this was the moment.

But McIvey floored the Taurus and blasted by another slow mover, rocking Sheffield back in his seat, and the moment passed.

NINE

"SO, AFTER THE BREACH," MCIVEY said, "Homeland was all over it. Their techies traced the entry to a workstation in the biology lab where the croc research is based. Appears somebody spent a few hours on that computer, planting the ELF logo, poking around. This desk sits idle most of the day while the biologists are out on airboats checking on the nests or whatever the hell they do. Only two people had access to that computer. One of those was killed in a recent crocodile attack. And the other is Cameron Prince."

"I read the papers," Frank said. "Prince took over for Leslie Levine."

"The croc program, it's public relations window dressing, the power company trying to spruce up its image, look like a good environmental citizen.

"They provide the biologists an airboat and a free pass to cruise the hundred and sixty miles of cooling canals on the edge of Biscayne Bay. The berms bordering the canals, that's where the crocs nest. So Levine dies, Prince inherits the gig. In his airboat, coming and going as he pleases. Convenient access to the plant."

"And that made you suspicious of Levine's death."

"It did."

"Be awful hard to stage a croc attack."

"Well, I raised concerns with the Metro homicide detective handling the case. Marcy Killibrew. You know her?"

"Met her. Can't say I know her."

"She showed me a video of the incident. It's chaotic, hard to watch, but it seems to confirm Prince's story."

"I'm still stuck on the cyber attack."

"*Attack* isn't the right word. *Probe, snoop.*"

"Okay, *probe*. From inside the plant."

"Well, after Homeland identified the entry point, the plant's security team took over the on-site investigation with assistance from NIPC. We interviewed everyone with access to the biology lab. Did background searches, checking for any associations with ELF or other radical groups. Nothing popped."

"You polygraphed them?"

"Yeah, Prince passed. He looks legit. Has a master's in biology, virtually the same credentials as Levine. He's from old Miami money, fallen on hard times. Not overtly political, no agitator. Gives educational speeches about his croc work to schoolkids and Rotary Clubs. But he didn't feel right, so I devoted time to this guy, and one day last month, I got a hit."

Sheffield tensed as Nicole blasted by a heavyset couple astraddle a Harley.

"Turns out Prince has people in and out of his house in the Grove. He's a bodybuilder, got a home gym, charges a fee, supplementing his income. People work out, leave a few hours later, muscles all pumped. Nice glow in their cheeks. Cheaper than a gym membership and they get to rub shoulders with a second runner-up for Mr. Florida.

"So a month ago, two gentlemen turn up at his place. These guys definitely weren't weight lifters. Their photos wind up on my desk, and I recognize them immediately, the Chee brothers, Pauly and Wally. A couple of Navajos from New Mexico. Pauly was in the navy, based in California.

"These days he's a full-time ELF. His younger brother, Wally, is a high school dropout, computer programmer also with hard-core green credentials. From what we can tell, he's become a highly proficient SCADA hacker. You familiar with SCADA?"

"Something about railroads?"

"That's one thing, yeah. Stands for 'supervisory control and data acquisition.' The industrial-control computer network, adjusts railway tracks, manages oil pipelines, steers sewage into the water-treatment plants. You name it, if it has to do with infrastructure, SCADA systems run their computers."

Sheffield was silent, staring at her profile.

"Okay, so Wally and Pauly walk into Prince's Grove house and stay overnight. Next morning all three slip out, drive down to a public boat ramp in South Dade, a boat picks them up, takes them out to an island in Biscayne Bay. They've been playing patty-cake out there ever since. Prince Key, it's five miles east of the plant. Pry the branches apart, you've got a nice view of the cooling towers."

"So you were surveilling Prince. Doing all this under my nose."

"I told you it wasn't my call. Don't get huffy."

"'Huffy' isn't on my playlist. 'Ticked off,' yeah, that's a tune I know."

"We're watching Prince. We're doing it by the book. Point is, Prince is in the thick of this. Talking up the marvels of nuclear power by night, hanging with anti-nuke warriors the next. The guy's a full-fledged eco-wacko."

"Wacko?"

"Absolutely."

"Tell me something, McIvey. You a climate-change denier?"

She drew a breath and slowed for an exit off the turnpike. "What is it, Frank? Living at the beach surrounded by the great outdoors, you've turned into a tree hugger?"

"I do like trees. I admit it. Always have."

"I'm not a denier. The science is there. It's solid."

"Next question. Since it's true, polar ice melting, ocean turning acid, bigger, badder storms, you think there's anything more important on the horizon for planet Earth than total obliteration?"

"Okay, okay, we're all doomed, the end is near."

"You sit in the same meetings I do, McIvey, read the NASA updates, Department of Energy, Weather Service. The goddamn US army has contingencies for climate-change scenarios. Those guys don't waste time on fantasies. This shit is happening. The tsunami's out there, rolling our way."

"Let it out, Frank. Ventilate." Smiling at him.

"I get worked up, yeah, but this is real and we go on our merry way. SUVs getting bigger, drilling a little deeper for the same old oil."

"So you're saying what exactly? The bad guys are

right, so let them do what they want. Including blow up a power plant?"

Sheffield absorbed that for a few seconds, then said quietly, "Is that what we're talking about, that's the intel your snitch gave you?"

"Bendell didn't know the endgame. But, yeah, an attack on the reactor, that's an option. Worst case, of course. But a possibility."

Sheffield was still looking at her profile. Nice, clean Midwestern lines, sharp angles, but not brittle. Maybe a double shot of Norwegian blood. Reminding him of somebody, a Hollywood actress from way back. Big star.

"You can quit staring at me, Frank."

"It's hard."

"With you it's probably always that way." She looked over with that teasing smile.

"You got older brothers, don't you?"

"Three. How'd you know?"

"They cops?"

"One is. Indiana state trooper. The other two are lawyers. Why?"

"Growing up with all those macho men around there was a lot of roughhousing. You being the only girl, that had to be a challenge."

"I held my own."

"They didn't coddle you, protect little sis?"

"What're you trying to say, Frank?"

"Just getting to know you. See how your mind works."

"It works just fine," she said.

"Like the rest of you."

"You going to make me regret calling you?"

"Okay, okay. Sorry. That was out of line."

A car passed on the right. Some kamikaze going faster than she was.

"Okay, so you lost Bendell, your eyes and ears inside the ELF cell. What exactly do you expect the Bureau to do?"

"Raid the island, bring them all in?"

"Get serious. You got a cartoon image on the power plant computers, and there's some eco-freaks with no outstanding warrants, they're hanging out on an island grilling veggie burgers and howling at the moon. Which is one step short of having absolutely nothing."

Nicole gave him a stony look and pushed the car a little faster. "You're right. That's not much."

"Tell me this," Frank said, moving on. "Your hacker, this Wally Chee, he's smart enough to put up the ELF image and keep it up there for a few days, but he's too dumb to cover his tracks back to that biology workstation?"

"Wouldn't be the first time a smart guy does something dumb."

"Announcing themselves like that in the first place, putting that cartoon up on the plant's computers, that's just one more dumb thing? Warning everybody you're about to do something?"

"Fits their pattern. In-your-face arrogance, stop me if you can."

"Or a head fake. It's all so obvious, none of it is true."

Nicole looked over, smiled at him again. Slowing for a red light. "You're a hard-ass, Frank, but I'm glad to be working with you. I am. I'm glad we're able to do this without a lot of tension." She turned his way, smiled.

Greta Garbo. He almost said it out loud but caught

himself. She'd probably heard it a few times before. That same mysterious face, vulnerable and unapproachable at once, the pale coloring. Soft eyes that in a split second could harden and go cold.

As Nicole sped east on the surface roads, Sheffield watched the neighborhoods fly past. Then they hit the long, empty entrance corridor to the nuke plant, the first guardhouse coming up. Layer one of security. Cameras everywhere, a couple of guys in khakis, shiny holsters with automatics, milling around the heavy steel barrier.

"Rent-a-cops," Frank said.

"They get special training, nuke stuff. The NRC supervises them."

"Still rent-a-cops."

"You're going to love the head of security. Real sweetheart."

"That's who we're meeting?"

"Yup."

Sheffield glanced down at the front of his shirt. "You should've told me, McIvey. I look unprofessional."

"Would you have listened if I had?"

She stopped at the gate, lowered her window, held out her badge to the stocky guy manning the post. He stooped down, checked out Nicole, then looked across her at Frank, at his hula-girls shirt.

"He's with me," Nicole said. "FBI."

Frank flipped out his ID, leaned across to show it.

The guard grunted, spoke into his handheld, and a moment later got a scratchy answer. He stepped away from the car, reached into the guardhouse to raise the steel bar, then waved them through.

Ten minutes later, after two more guardhouses, they were inside the plant's three-story office building.

Escorted by another security guy, Nicole led the way down the gleaming hallway, Sheffield keeping his eyes forward in a businesslike manner.

Coming finally to the security office, Nicole stopped, let their escort go ahead through the door while she turned to Frank.

"His name is Claude Sellers," she said quietly. "But everyone calls him shithead."

TEN

BEFORE HE LEFT THE BEACH, Thorn buried the pry bar in the sand near the base of a gumbo-limbo. He brushed the sand over the spot and brushed it some more. He didn't want to go walking into the unknown with a chunk of badass steel in his hand, make the wrong impression.

He found a narrow break in the snarl of branches and headed up a sandy path that meandered through poisonwood trees and strangler figs and silver buttonwoods, the ground littered with chunks of limestone and jutting roots. High in the tamarind branches, a canopy of cobwebs and morning-glory vines was lit by the angled sunlight, and the dense smell of sulfurous fumes rose from the marine muds where dead plants and flecks of animal matter were decomposing.

Only five miles of calm waters separated this island from the mainland. Over there the land was jammed with the usual outlet malls, strip shopping centers, and franchise joints, and an endless maze of highways and turnpikes and avenues. Though Prince Key was so close by, this tangle of tamarind and capers and cabbage palm and this rocky pathway seemed marooned in another warp of geologic time. As harsh and brutish as the terrain was, to Thorn this was the only Florida that mattered, the landscape that kept his heart in tune, that hummed in his marrow. Lose these last few pockets of magic native land, and the game was over. Thorn might as well buy a golf cart and a chartreuse leisure suit, mix a pitcher of manhattans, and call it a day.

Branches snagged his shirtsleeves, scratched his skin, stabbed him below the belt. He ducked below a limb and glimpsed an open stretch to his left. Moving that way, he saw the glitter of metal and pushed through a last screen of acacia and stepped into a wide field, maybe three acres, grassy and treeless, open to the sun.

A solar panel the size of a picnic table was tilted up to catch the morning light. Beyond the panel was a twenty-foot wooden wall surrounded by a sandy pit, and a set of monkey bars. Nearby was a tall, wooden frame with a twenty-foot hawser hanging from the crossbeam, a heavy rope meant for climbing.

As he came closer to the primitive obstacle course, Thorn saw a dozen old automobile tires laid out in a hopscotch pattern, identical to the one for the footwork drills Thorn had run in his brief high school football career. There was a chinning bar, and a half dozen structures made of rough-hewn logs that seemed designed to torture various muscle groups.

He stood for a moment, taking it in, until he heard a groan coming from beyond the high climbing wall studded with handholds. He angled across the grassy meadow toward the noise. His clothes sopping, his shoes full of mush.

Behind the wall he found two men, shirtless, wearing only white gym shorts and flimsy tennis shoes. Each one stood atop a narrow balance beam that ran parallel to the other beam about two feet away. At the midpoint on each beam, the two were crouched, facing each other. They gripped wooden staffs slightly longer than baseball bats with boxing gloves lashed to both ends.

Jousting with the wood bats, striking and blocking and parrying thrusts, the men grunted and cursed. No protective headgear, no padding on their bodies. One of the men was clearly getting the better of the other. He was quicker and more aggressive and his strikes came in bursts of threes and fours, while the other man, slender and sandy-haired, seemed in pure defensive mode, blocking most of the thrusts, managing only an occasional counterpunch.

Stepping closer, he saw the young man's face.

Flynn Moss.

No longer skinny, the kid had added a layer of muscle in the year since Thorn had last seen him.

The other guy was cut from coarser stuff. Two puncture wounds for eyes, a heavy nose, and a thug's mouth with a belligerent jut of jaw. Rooted to the beam, whacking Thorn's son, the guy was as pitiless and composed as a journeyman boxer taking out a lifetime of frustration, blow by blow, on his latest patsy.

Thorn kept his distance, circling the men, trying not to distract the eye of Flynn Moss, who seemed with every blow he took to be about to tumble backward off the beam and fall the seven or eight feet to the sand pit below.

For a minute or two he watched them club and batter and block, sweating heavily though neither seemed winded by their combat training.

Finally Thorn's presence caught the attention of the

other man, and he lowered his staff and gave this tres-passer his full attention. When Flynn followed the other man's gaze, Thorn raised his hand in a silent salute.

The man took that opening to ram the butt of his club into Flynn's stomach, bending him double. Gag-ging, the kid somehow kept his balance and slashed his own stick in response, but the tough guy batted it away with a smile and stepped across from his beam to Flynn's, a move that must have signified an end to their workout, since Flynn relaxed his grip and lowered his own club.

"Aw, shit," Flynn said. "What the hell're you doing here?"

But the man wasn't done. With Flynn turned away, the guy lined up, cocked his bat, and nailed Flynn be-tween his shoulder blades, sending him sprawling in a long, ungainly flop into the sand.

The man jumped off the beam, landing behind Flynn, and watched the young man struggle to sit up. Edging forward to Flynn's backside, the man choked up on his club and drew it to his shoulder, aiming for the right side of Flynn's head.

Thorn covered the ten yards at full tilt and reached the sandpit as the bludgeon was starting its downward flight. He grabbed it high and wrenched it to a halt and found the man's grip was solidly fixed, so Thorn dug in his feet and pivoted, throwing out his hip to catch the guy on his backward stumble. Thorn's hip jolted against the man's thigh, a primitive judo move, a half step up from the schoolyard.

But it was enough.

Grunting, the man went down hard, slammed his shoulder in the sand, and tried to use the momentum of his fall to duck and roll back to his feet, but Thorn was waiting as he struggled to stand, the club in Thorn's hands now.

He set himself, leaned into the blow, ramming the guy in the gut exactly as the man had rammed Flynn, then thrusting into the guy's diaphragm. Knocking a long, wet cough out of him and sending him blundering backward into the sand.

He sat there trying to breathe. Staring up at Thorn while an ugly smile quivered on his lips, coming and going like a bad habit he was trying to break.

When he managed to speak, a teaspoon of sand was in his throat. "You just fucked up, sport. Nobody ambushes Wally."

Wally jimmied himself upright, groaning as he straightened.

Thorn made him for late twenties. Robust with red cheeks and a fiery gaze, but sickly around the edges. His facial skin had the oily sheen of wax paper as though he'd survived a pot of scalding coffee poured into his crib. He was about Thorn's height with wide shoulders and a barrel chest and thickened waistline and legs that were rooster thin.

"You know this guy?" he said to Flynn, edging closer to Thorn.

Thorn pitched the fighting club aside and squared off to Wally's approach. Wally cleared the sand from his throat.

"His name is Thorn."

"What the fuck is he doing here? You can't just walk in here."

Thorn was watching Wally inch forward.

"You ex-military?"

Thorn shook his head.

"SEAL, Ranger, Black Ops?"

"I'm nobody."

"Somebody schooled you on those moves."

"Nobody schooled me on anything."

"Is he lying?" Wally asked Flynn.

"I don't think so. I don't know that much about him." Flynn was brushing the sand off his bare skin. "I just met him a couple of times. He knocked up my mother when she was a teenager."

"Last time I checked, that makes him your old man."

Both of them were studying Thorn as if he were an exotic creature who'd wandered out of the mist.

"If that saying holds true," Wally said, " 'like father, like son,' then we just doubled our pussy population."

"Take a hike, Wally," Thorn said. "I want to talk to the kid."

Thorn held Wally's gaze, his body poised, ready to go the full fifteen rounds if that's how Wally wanted it.

The smile on Wally's lips fast-twitched like a loose connection. He looked at Flynn and said, "I'm getting Prince. Doesn't matter if he's your old man or not, he can't be here."

Wally gave Thorn a weapons-grade glare that was meant to make his knees knock. It didn't work.

Wally turned and walked to the chinning bar and retrieved a camouflage T-shirt that hung across it. Without a backward glance, he trudged off toward a tan barracks tent that was riffling in the sea breeze.

When Wally was out of earshot, Thorn stepped over to his son. "Are you okay?"

"Why the hell are you here?"

"Long story."

"You need to get out of here right now. I'm serious. This is a major fuckup, Thorn. Prince is going to freak."

"Why?"

"Just go, goddamn it. Leave the way you came. Do it now."

Thorn glanced across the field, watched Wally pull back the flap and step inside the tent. "Not until you tell me what's going on."

"Jesus, I don't believe this. You just walked right in."

"And I'm not walking out till I find out what's what."

Flynn brushed a rough hand against Thorn's arm as if to confirm his reality. Then cursed to himself and stepped away, his face flushed. He glanced around the open field and motioned for Thorn to follow.

He led Thorn to the shade of a mahogany that towered over the mangroves on the eastern shore of the key. There was a single rough-hewn bench long enough for three. Flynn settled on one end.

Thorn took the other and kicked off his soggy shoes and faced them toward the sun. "Look, I'm sorry you're upset. I came to see Prince. I had no idea you were here."

"You know Cameron?"

"Met him once."

"What do you want with him?"

"Another long story." Thorn was looking back across the field, past the obstacle course, beyond the solar panel, to the entrance flap of the barracks tent maybe a hundred yards away. A man stood there, holding the flap open. A big guy, thick-chested, tall with pale-yellow hair. Cameron Prince stared in their direction for several moments, then drew back inside. "Talk to me, Son."

"Don't fucking call me that." Flynn stared off at the morning sky. Then he looked at Thorn, shook his head, and looked off again. "Okay, stick with that story. You came to see Prince and had no idea I was here."

"It's not a story."

"Christ, Thorn. Are you dense? This is a dangerous situation. You've walked into something, it's way over your head."

"Over mine, but not over yours?"

"Jesus H. Christ. I can't believe this."

"What's so dangerous?"

Flynn turned his head slowly and glanced over his shoulder, checking to his left, then right. Behind him there was only the blue blaze of the Atlantic visible through the snarl of mangrove branches and roots. No one was in the field, no one anywhere around. "You came in your boat, right?"

"I did."

"Where is it?"

"In the cove." Thorn nodded toward the hidden beach.

"Good. You need to get on it right now and leave. I'm serious. Right now before they can stop you." Flynn's eyes were searching the field.

"The boat's disabled. The prop is fouled."

Flynn closed his eyes for a second, then opened them, frowning. "You ran into the net? You didn't see it?"

"I didn't see it."

"How bad?"

"Engine's damaged. It won't start."

"Shit. A guy like you, you didn't notice the net?"

"A guy like me?"

"Experienced boater."

"I should have noticed, yeah."

"Damn right you should have."

"I saw some kayaks. I could paddle home, get some tools, come back, and fix the engine."

"The kayaks are locked up. No one leaves without Prince's say-so."

"What? You're a captive?"

"Oh, I'm here by choice." But Flynn's tone wasn't as certain as the words. He stared at the sandy soil, shaking his head with an air of futility.

"Look, Flynn. I called your phone yesterday, heard the message on your machine. You said you're doing something you've been wanting to do for a long time. Is this it? Being here? With these guys, Prince and Wally?"

Lifting his eyes and gazing at the distant tent, Flynn said, "I committed myself to a cause, Thorn. You have any idea what that is? A righteous cause."

"I've heard of them."

"I gave my pledge to be part of something that truly mattered for once. Instead of the frivolous, bullshit career I've had."

"Part of what?"

Flynn hesitated, shaking his head as if to clear his thoughts.

"Part of what, Flynn?"

"Oh, it'll sound like grandiose bullshit to a guy like you."

"Try me."

"Save the planet, before it's too late."

Thorn waited through a stretch of silence, then said, "Save it how?"

Flynn gave Thorn a grim look, then chuckled. A

what-the-hell laugh that a man might make just before he leapt off some killer precipice. "We're about to knock over the first domino. After it falls, nothing's ever going to be the same again."

ELEVEN

"YOU WANT TO KNOW WHAT you walked into, okay, that's what. It's a big deal. Bigger than anything you could imagine."

Thorn wasn't going to argue.

Flynn watched a squadron of pelicans coasting low over the island, then shifted his sober gaze to Thorn and shook his head. "And here's an irony for you. You're the reason I'm here. If it wasn't for you, I wouldn't be doing any of this."

Thorn waited. A high-pitched whine was droning in his ears as if he'd dived deep into the pressuring sea.

"Last year, the day Mom brought me down to Largo, you remember?"

"I remember."

"She thought if I could see how you lived, I'd come around, start to appreciate you or some corny bullshit like that. This big bonding moment. We could all be friends. I was pissy and hateful that day. A real son of a bitch."

"I remember you scowled a lot. Didn't make much eye contact."

"I was angry about what you did. About Sawyer. I guess I still am."

"I understand."

"Do you, Thorn? I don't think so. I don't think you've ever lost a brother, have you? A twin."

Thorn said, no, no, he'd never had a brother.

"So you don't know. You can't understand. Mother doesn't either."

Thorn waited in silence.

"I know you had no choice. Sawyer went nuts, he attacked you and Mom. You defended yourself, you defended her, you probably saved her life. I know all that on a rational level. But it doesn't make any difference. Not in here." Flynn thumped his knuckles hard against his chest.

Behind him a roseate spoonbill floated above the treetops. To the east, out in Hawk Channel, a power boat cruised by. Thorn held his tongue. This didn't feel like the moment to try to set any records straight.

"The way you just came strutting into our world, this guy we'd never heard of before, all of a sudden you're standing there in our living room. It was fucked up, Thorn. How cool and collected you were."

"Is that how I seemed? Collected?"

"Like we were supposed to stand up and cheer. Look who's here. Daddy's finally showed up to the party."

"I didn't feel cool. I felt out-of-body. I still feel that way."

"Well, that's two of us." Flynn took a deep breath and released it through fluttering lips. "So, anyway. That visit had an effect. Not the one Mom intended, but it made a difference. When I got home, I couldn't shake it, how you lived. Your place, how primitive it is, but you seemed so at ease, like Tarzan in his lair."

Thorn watched Flynn struggle to find words. Though

the young man had Thorn's sandy hair, his hard cheek-bones and sturdy chin, his eyes belonged to his mother. Sensitive, shadowed with emotion, his changing moods appearing and disappearing in them when the rest of his face stayed unreadable. It was a solid face, given depth and dimension by those revealing eyes.

"Tarzan," Thorn said.

"The whole Spartan thing. So simple, basic. So free."

Thorn was silent. Not about to correct him.

"Just the opposite of me. Fucking Miami, my acting career, the fakes I have to deal with, the pompous ass-holes, the pressures. Some days I can't breathe. I liter-ally cannot draw a decent breath. Like there's a strap across my chest, it's getting tighter all the time. I know it's stress, I should just suck it up, be thankful for what I have, handle it like everybody else does, but it kept getting worse. Then I saw your place, how you managed, so isolated, so little contact with the world. Just that glimpse and something kicked in, I was inspired. It's nuts, I know. But that's the truth. Inspired."

"To do what?"

In answer, Flynn's eyes swept across the expanse of Prince Key.

"You came out here because of me."

Flynn nodded.

"Because I inspired you."

"Don't mock me, Thorn. I don't deserve that."

"I didn't mean it like that. I'm trying to absorb what you're saying. I spent the last year thinking I'd lost you."

"I was wrong to act that way. It was bitter and childish."

"Apology accepted."

"After I saw your place, it hit me how much I hated

my career, my day-to-day existence. How empty it felt, how artificial. TV acting, for godsakes. I made a promise to myself. I would simplify. Try to connect more with the natural world. The water, the outdoors."

"Nothing wrong with that."

"I bought a freaking boat, a beat-up Boston Whaler, started poking around the bay, going into the ocean, just learning my way step by step."

"And this place? It's some kind of boot camp?"

Flynn stood up, paced out into the scraggly grass, bent down and picked up a rock, and sailed it over the tops of the mangroves. The boy had a damn good arm. For an actor, for a city boy.

He came back to the bench and sat, stared toward the tent. No one there. No one in the field. But Thorn could feel the tickle of eyes watching.

"I've known Cameron for years. On the surface he's this freak of nature, the Incredible Hulk, an armor-plated aberration. But there's more to him than that. He's a sensitive guy, smart."

"So far, I've only met the armor-plated side."

"Well, I know him a little better. Four, five years ago I was doing a play at the Grove Theater and he came up to me after and we started talking about how I was handling my part. He's very tuned in to the nuances of drama. At first I thought he was trying to hit on me. I had that stupid cliché in my head, all bodybuilders are gay."

Thorn was silent. Sensitive territory.

"I'm gay," Flynn said. "You know that, right?"

"Yes, I know that."

"It bothers you, doesn't it? My sexuality."

"Hasn't yet."

Flynn tested him with a long look. And seemed to accept the answer. "So Prince and I got friendly, went out to dinner, had some laughs." He halted, looked around, swallowed a breath.

"You had some laughs, and . . ."

"And nothing. I got busy with work, lost track of him. Then last fall I was at a public hearing about Turkey Point, Florida Power and Light's expansion plans to build two new reactors on the site. The Sierra Club is protesting it because of the impact on the wetlands. FPL wants approval to drill dozens of coastal wells along Biscayne Bay for backup cooling water. It's a terrible idea.

"Pump millions of gallons a day out of the Biscayne aquifer. And the nine square miles of cooling canals that are full of heavy, hot, hypersaline water sinking into the aquifer, too, like we don't already have enough saltwater intrusion fouling our drinking supply. Thousands of pounds of radioactive waste lying around for centuries."

"You've studied up."

"It's bad. Nobody's paying attention, but it's bad. So I'd gone to a lot of meetings as part of the all new and improved Flynn Moss. Gotten to know people, made friends.

"That night Cameron and Leslie Levine were guest speakers. They talked up the croc program they run. Dodged any questions about nuclear power.

"When they finished, they came over. Long story short, Prince invited me to his house, just the three of us, and I could tell they had an agenda. They wanted to know about the Sierra Club, what I knew about their plans to protest the new reactors, how devoted I was to the antinuke thing. Feeling me out, trying to see if I might be useful somehow."

"Useful?"

"They were looking for recruits."

"For what?"

"I can't talk about it."

"Why not?"

Flynn hung his head like a beaten man.

"I'll keep your secrets, Flynn. Whatever they are."

"Why are you here, Thorn? What do you have to do with Prince?"

"He showed up at my place yesterday."

"He did? Why?"

"Don't know. He just wandered around. Didn't seem to be looking for me. We spoke a little, but he didn't tell me his name. I got his license tag, tracked him to his Grove house, saw a photo of you on the wall, thought that was weird, so I came out here to talk to him, see what the hell was going on."

"You were suspicious."

"Something smelled funny."

"Does anybody else know where you are? Does Sugarman?"

"No. Nobody. Why? What are you scared of?"

Flynn searched Thorn's face. A kid who lived among professional liars. Deceitfulness was his tradecraft, his art. "I can't tell you anything."

"Why?"

"If they found out, they'd kill us both."

That's all Thorn needed to hear. He reached out and fastened a hand on Flynn's jaw and cranked his head around so they were facing eye to eye. "Then you and I need to get the hell out of here now."

Flynn's right hand flashed up, whacked Thorn's arm away. "You can't bully me."

"Get up, we're going. I've got my push pole. We don't need the engine. I can pole us back. We're getting the hell out of here right now."

"Go ahead, leave. I'm not going anywhere."

Thorn stood up. "Come on, kid. Right now, no arguments."

"I'm not a kid. I'm not your little boy. Don't talk to me like that." Flynn rose. His face darkening, mouth tightened to a snarl.

He didn't see it coming. He couldn't have because Thorn didn't see it himself. An impulsive move. He swiveled his right hip and shoulder, loaded up, and slammed his fist into Flynn's solar plexus, knocking out the wind, squeezing shut the young man's eyes.

Flynn hacked up a yellow clot of spittle, his knees sagged, and Thorn stepped close, grabbed him, one arm around the back, fingers digging into his armpit. Holding Flynn upright while the kid gagged, he shouldered him toward the cove. Thirty yards, maybe forty, not far.

A quick plan forming. Lay him out on the beach, swim to the skiff, and slash the netting away from the lower unit. A minute or two to free it, then load Flynn aboard and pole back the way Thorn had come.

He hadn't intended to hit him so hard, just render him cooperative. It was the same gut punch he'd used in a few late-night scuffles, a first-strike, breath-stealing blow that more than once had short-circuited a slugfest and allowed Thorn to walk safely out the barroom door.

But damned if he was going to hit the kid again. The shock of what he'd done was buzzing darkly in Thorn's head. In one rash act, he'd destroyed whatever flimsy bond they had. But there didn't seem to be any other way.

Struggling to keep Flynn upright, Thorn ducked into the woods, headed down the path, staggering under Flynn's weight. The kid was deceptively heavy. A rangy, rawboned build like Thorn's.

He pushed through the last branches and stepped onto the beach. Stopped short, staring at what someone had done. His skiff had been cut loose from the netting and was beached well up on the sand. The outboard housing was gone, ignition wires slashed. His push pole lay in the sand, broken in half.

An impossible feat. Two inches thick, a composite of fiberglass and graphite. Leaning his whole weight into it, Thorn could flex it a few degrees like a vaulting pole, but the thing was indestructible. He'd never seen one shattered, never heard of its happening.

While he was registering the bewildering sight, a hand clamped on his right shoulder, a grip so powerful it deadened his flesh and sent a bolt of pain into the shoulder joint. The hand spun him around, and Thorn tripped, Flynn breaking loose from his grasp and falling away, and in that flash Thorn caught the blur of a hand as it chopped the side of his neck and saw Prince's placid face as the big man's blow turned the dazzling summer morning to darkness.

TWELVE

"WELL, AREN'T YOU THE RESOURCEFUL one, tracking me down."

Thorn was inside the barracks tent, lying on a cot in the dusky light. He looked up through an electric haze at the outline of Cameron Prince.

Dazed, his throat parched, Thorn tried to sit up, but a swirl of sickness rose in his gut, and he lay back.

"What were you doing at my house? It wasn't the cistern you were interested in."

"Let me put it this way. I was simply evaluating the location."

"For what?"

"Its strategic value. I'd heard about it, but I needed to see for myself."

"What kind of strategic value?"

"I've said enough. Now you need to answer my questions. Flynn tells me no one else knows you're here. Is that true?" Prince held his right hand up to a slab of sunlight filtering through a mesh window and snipped at a fingernail with a pair of silver clippers.

"Where is he, where's Flynn?" The words raw in Thorn's throat.

"Is that true? Yes or no. Does anyone know where you are?"

"No."

"Okay. That makes things easier. And don't worry. Flynn's fine. He's being looked after. But that wasn't very fatherly of you, assaulting your own boy. You're quite the hooligan."

"What the fuck are you people doing?"

"Why, we're living a simple life, an island life. Much like the manner in which you live, Thorn. Self-sufficient, low impact. An experiment in earth-friendly, communal existence. That's all we're doing. Why so hostile?"

"I want to see Flynn."

"Later." Cameron snipped another nail, flicked it off. "By the way, Wally is very impressed with your fighting skills. He'd like a rematch."

"If he asks nice, I might oblige."

"Apparently you fancy yourself a smart-ass."

"I don't fancy myself anything."

"It makes sense, I suppose. A man who keeps society at arm's length, it's only natural you'd maintain a buffer of sarcasm. Take nothing seriously, so nothing can touch you."

"I take some things seriously."

"Like what, Thorn? I'm curious. What do you really care about? What stirs your passions? Can you name one thing you love?"

Cameron drew another cot close and perched on its edge, then leaned forward, bringing his face inches from Thorn's, crossing the line from sociable to threatening. Thorn was forced to breathe the vinegar scent of Cameron's growth hormones or whatever cocktail he was ingesting to bulk up to such a preposterous size.

"You've got a python problem. Did you know that?"

"You encountered a python?"

"We met."

"Did the snake harass you?"

"It tried. It might need first aid."

"Oh, come on. You hurt a python?"

"I would've hurt it more but it escaped."

"You're serious."

"In the cove," Thorn said. "It wanted to dance. I didn't like the music."

"Well, Pauly won't be pleased you injured one of his pets." Cameron drew back, returning to his manicure.

"Snapper," Thorn said.

"Excuse me?"

"You asked what aroused my passions. Fresh yellowtail snapper grilled with lemon and butter. If it's an hour out of the water, my passions can get fairly aroused."

Prince gave him a pained look. "You're mocking me."

"It's so easy to do."

"Maybe I should give you another rabbit punch. Knock the rest of that pissiness out of you." Cameron worked the clipper around his thumbnail, snipping, then blowing the slivers toward Thorn.

"Did you break my push pole?"

Cameron smiled quietly. "Does that impress you? Brute force?"

Thorn peered into the man's opaque brown eyes and said nothing. There was no need to respond. A talker such as Prince could carry on both sides of any conversation. Conceit radiated like sour body odor from every pore.

"All right, let's discuss Flynn, shall we?"

Thorn waited.

"You see, you've presented us with a conundrum. You've trespassed on our island, barged in uninvited, and now we have to decide how best to proceed, given this new circumstance."

Thorn watched a cluster of mosquitoes churning in a slant of light.

"Tell me this, if you can. Do you love your son?"

Thorn stared into the big man's eyes, searching for a biting comeback.

"Oh, you needn't answer. It's clear from the look on your face. You feel strongly for Flynn, but you've got no clue how to express it because such a thing has never been required of you. Yes, yes, I'm sure you've made love to your share of women, and you have drinking buddies and the like, but you're a confirmed introvert, preoccupied with the minutiae of your day-to-day labors. It's no doubt a full-time job staring at that complicated navel of yours.

"So doing the emotional heavy lifting required of a father, it's not a task you've prepared yourself for. Am I getting warm?"

"What're you after?"

"I want to know if you love your son."

"He's my flesh and blood. Of course I do."

"But you barely know him. And he doesn't seem to have much affection for you."

"Is there a point?"

Cameron studied his nails for a moment, then used the small file to reshape an edge. When he was done, he puffed the dust toward Thorn. "To be perfectly frank, I'm looking for leverage. To see if safeguarding your son's well-being might keep you in line."

"What does that mean?"

"There's only two ways this can go, Thorn. You join our merry band or the ugly alternative." Cameron smiled again. It was hard work that seemed to strain the bands of muscles in his neck and jaw and produced something more like a grimace. "I'm told you're wild and unpredictable, and you have a sordid history of flouting the rule of law, that you live by some badass personal code, the rest of the world be damned. And you enjoy a scuffle and can hold your own against men bigger and more well trained. An eye-gouging brawler."

Cameron leaned forward into Thorn's line of vision, one eyebrow cocked. "And when you committed to a cause, you saw it to the end, no matter the risks. If you believed in something, you were dogged, ruthless, stubborn to a fault. You're passive by nature, but when the bugles sound, you can, if you choose, become a man of action. Is this accurate?"

"So this is a job interview?"

Cameron stared into Thorn's eyes for a long moment, then huffed an exasperated sigh and rose and reset the cot he'd been sitting on, aligning it in its proper place beside the others. This hulk was not to be trifled with, and Thorn had been doing just that.

"All right, get up. I've heard enough. I'm done with you."

Thorn pushed himself upright. The whirl in his gut had slowed, though his mind was foggy and his knees still soft. But the threat of Cameron Prince was reviving him fast.

"Outside," Prince said.

Thorn pushed through the tent flap and stood for a moment while his eyes corrected to the harsh midday sunlight.

Prince prodded him midback, a solid thump. Onward. Not fucking around anymore.

As they walked, Thorn cut his eyes to the sides, searching for an avenue of escape. But the dense mangroves and wild shrubs looked impenetrable. He could probably outrun Prince, but where was there to go? Get to the beach, dive in, make it a race. But that wouldn't last long. Thorn was a strong swimmer, but it was over a mile to the nearest land—no way he could outdistance a kayak.

There was the crowbar he'd buried in the sand. Close to the end of the trail. Lunge, scoop it up, swing for Prince's skull. A slim hope. Something. All he had really. Sand in the eyes, that old ploy. Take out his knees, punt him in the nuts. Run back and locate Flynn and get the hell out of here.

When they reached the edge of the beach, Thorn noted the ruffled patch of marl where the length of steel was buried and primed himself for the lunge, waiting for a moment when Prince was off balance. In his side vision he kept watch on Prince as they took the last few paces to the water's edge, past the pry bar, two long steps away.

"Turn around and face me."

Thorn did as told. Drawing a breath, staying loose-limbed, for that might be his only physical advantage with this cast-iron freak. Though he was beginning to believe his chances of surviving any hand-to-hand encounter with the giant were close to nil.

"Personally, I find you fatuous and inane. I don't like you, Thorn. But what's more important, I don't trust you. I've met your type before. You're an incorrigible maverick who'd make a highly undependable team member."

"I'm crushed."

"Okay, I know how I'm going to vote." Prince spoke past Thorn to someone in the distance. "He's all yours."

Prince turned his massive back on Thorn and strode away.

Thorn swung around and watched her step from the shadowy warren of branches and vines about twenty feet down the narrow beach. She was tall and slender and her chestnut hair was still trimmed short. She wore faded jeans and a long-sleeved fishing shirt with mesh vents and lots of pockets.

She came slowly down the sandy strip until she was within arm's length. As close as she'd been on his dock the last morning he'd seen her, that day when she'd brushed his cheek with the back of her hand and thanked him for teaching her those first simple lessons about the natural world.

"Jesus Christ."

As she came closer, the light in the cove seemed to fade.

"You're alive."

"So far," she said.

The rush of adrenaline he'd been surfing for the last half hour roared even louder in his bloodstream. "What the hell is going on, Leslie?"

She gave no sign she'd heard, just searched his eyes.

His lungs were thick, the air seemed starved of oxygen. He had a woozy impulse to reach out and touch Leslie's flesh to see if she was an apparition.

Her eyes flicked past him, scanning the quiet cove, then returned to him and settled on his. As if she'd read his mind, she raised her hand to his temple and touched it lightly, then drew away. Yes, she was real.

"Are you ready for this, Thorn?"

"Ready?"

"I'd like to give you a chance."

"To do what?"

"To save your life."

THIRTEEN

SHE TOOK A SEAT NEARBY, close to where he'd recovered from his battle with the python. Thorn lowered himself to the sand a few feet away.

"Where's Flynn? I want to see him."

"He's fine. Don't worry."

He was having trouble seeing the woman who sat beside him. The vulnerable waif who'd fished from Thorn's dock seemed to hover just below the surface of the no-nonsense woman Leslie had become.

Tethered to some mangrove roots on the north side of the cove was the streamlined flats boat Leslie had been piloting the last day he saw her. A Hell's Bay Whipray.

They were silent for several moments, then Leslie said, "It's strange, but for someone who shaped my identity, you've always remained a mysterious figure to me. May I ask you some personal questions?"

Another interview. "You can ask."

Between her outstretched legs, she was drawing circles in the sand, her eyes focused on the shapes. "You've committed crimes. Violent crimes."

"Where'd you hear that?"

"Is it true?"

"Nothing I'm proud of," he said.

"You're good with your fists."

"Average."

"Apparently Wally would beg to differ."

"Wally's a little less than average."

She lifted her head, smiled at him, then returned to the sand circles. "I also heard you've taken more than one human life." Her eyes were bourbon brown and had a weary remoteness as if she'd spent too much time staring at something a great distance away. "Have you, Thorn? Have you killed?"

"Only in self-defense. Only as a last resort."

"Good. Because that's exactly what we're doing here. That's what we're all about. The last resort. Self-defense."

"I'm not interested in joining a gang or whatever this is."

"Hear me out, please." She brushed a wisp of hair from her eyes and was silent for a moment. "I didn't think I'd ever see you again, Thorn."

He had nothing to say.

"Even though it creates a grave problem for us, I'm glad you're here. I'm glad to see you again."

"Did you arrange this? Sending Prince to my house, dropping bread crumbs. Lure me out here."

She shook her head. "Cameron had strict orders. He was to take a quick look at your property then leave. Have no contact with you. None whatsoever. I was worried something like this might happen. But he insisted on having a look."

"Why?"

She glanced off and didn't speak.

"What're you doing, Leslie? What's this about?"

"If I tell you, Thorn, then you're involved. There's no going back."

"My son is here. I'm already involved."

She stared down at the circles in the sand. "All right then." She drew a careful breath. "We're going to shut down the power plant. Turkey Point."

"And why would you do that?"

"For a lot of reasons."

"Give me one."

"To take control of our destiny."

"Your destiny?"

"That's right."

"You can do that by yourself. Alone. In a room, anywhere."

"Like you do? Disengage? That's what you mean? Retreat into solitude, keep your head down. Push the world away."

"Yes."

"Oh, I've tried that. For years you were my model, Thorn. I barricaded myself from the noise and craziness. Lived as primitively as I could. Actually I got pretty good at it. But things have changed, the earth is in deep shit, and ignoring it, being disengaged, is no longer a luxury we can afford."

"Save the planet, that's what you're about?"

"Save what's left of it."

Thorn looked out at the sky beyond the cove. The sun had bleached the ragged clouds of their early-morning pinks, and the air was already fogged with August humidity. Tucked in the dense mangrove branches across the basin, a little green heron scanned the waters. Ripples washed ashore on the small beach as if stirred by something large passing along the mucky bottom. Farther out, a school of mullet were feeding. They dimpled the mirrored surface, sending a school of glassy minnows streaking toward the edges of the cove.

"What happened to the crocodiles? You were helping the planet pretty well working with them."

"Years ago when I started, the American croc was on the verge of extinction. There were less than a hundred left in Florida. Now their status has been upgraded to 'threatened.' "

"An improvement."

"Sure. They've got a foothold, they're reproducing and spreading. They don't need me anymore. I'm finished with that." Leslie looked off at the sky above the mangroves, lapsing into silence.

First Flynn, now Leslie, their paths altered in some measure by Thorn's example. As if he'd been touting some ideal of simplicity when, the truth was, the way he lived was not a choice. It was the only way he knew.

He'd inherited the Key Largo house and land, and with only the skimpy income he made from selling his custom flies, he had to keep things basic, handle maintenance himself. It was how he made it through, patching this, refinishing that, holding it together with duct tape, nails, and sweat. When he could, he relaxed and watched the pitch and plunge of birds, tracked the migrations of fish and the cycles of the moon and tides and observed the flamboyant colors staining the sea and sky at daybreak and sunset. His days were peaceful and gratifying, but nothing he promoted to others.

Leslie came out of her brooding silence, leaning forward, peering intently at the cove as if something in the mangroves had hissed her name.

"What is it?"

After a moment she laughed and pointed at a three-foot croc swimming along the edge of the cove. "Speak of the devil. One of my flock."

They watched the young croc drag itself up onto some mangrove roots and immediately fall into a drowse. Armored with thick, bony plates, the creature might have been suited up for medieval battle. Its beauty was in the same realm as that of hammerhead sharks and feral hogs. Only a person who could see past its fierce exterior might feel affection for such a beast. Someone such as Leslie, who had been hardened by the hammer blows of a junkie mother and the mother's string of dog-shit boyfriends pawing at the young girl's bedroom door late at night; yet somehow that thick-skinned, unloved child had managed to soldier on, grow strong, and keep her vulnerable heart sufficiently intact to love the unlovable.

A gust of wind roughened the surface of the cove, blurring the wine-dark mirror and kicking up a flurry of sand from the beach. Leslie brushed her hand in front of her face as if wiping away a cobweb. The croc disappeared from its perch on the mangrove roots, off prowling.

"And how do you accomplish this? You and these people."

"We have a plan. A very good plan."

"So you break into the plant, shut off the power, you're a hero to your cause, then the next day they turn the power back on and they track down Leslie Levine and shut her away in prison. What good have you done?"

More circles, deeper in the sand, drawn faster, interlocking, concentric.

"I'm no martyr."

"You damn sure sound like one."

"I don't plan on getting caught."

"Nobody ever does."

"We're going to make as much noise as we can. There's no choice."

"Listen to yourself. You're talking like a half-baked terrorist."

She turned her head and regarded him with those rich brown eyes. Rimmed with sadness, but resolute.

"The natural world, all those things you care about, Thorn, it's being destroyed, bit by bit. And what're you doing? Tying your flies and watching sunsets and drinking a few beers at the end of a long day. Just keeping your head down, ignoring it, pretending it isn't happening. Letting somebody else fight the Huns."

It was true. Thorn was keeping his head down. His past crusades had resulted in far too many casualties. Let someone else carry the banners. Someone with a clear conscience. At this moment all he wanted was to get Flynn safely home, nothing more.

"Maybe I was wrong about you. I thought you gave a damn. You stood up for what you believed. You were my hero. You were my conscience."

He looked at her profile. And saw again the shy kid and her bucket of rotting shrimp donated by the local bait shop, her jerky casts, her sidelong looks at him, that wild, cock-eyed smile when she caught that first snapper.

She rose to her feet, motioned for him to follow, and led him down the spit of sand to the western edge of the basin. She pried apart the branches, turned sideways, and wriggled through a gap, Thorn staying close.

They ducked and wrestled for twenty yards through

the dense web of limbs until they reached the rocky shore where the blue waters of Biscayne Bay spread before them. A mile offshore a catamaran was slicing south toward the Keys, and just beyond it, along the mainland coast, was the hulking nuclear plant, its twin cooling towers, its enormous concrete dome, its dozens of outbuildings sheathed in metal girders and scaffolding, the land stripped of vegetation, a barren industrial site, ugly and forbidding.

"Right here in one of the most beautiful, fragile landscapes in the world, every minute of every day, they're sucking hundreds of thousands of gallons from the aquifer to cool the superheated steam, and inside those buildings there's enough radioactive fuel to turn South Florida into a ghost town for the next thousand years. Billions of dollars already spent to scrape the land bare and build that monstrosity, billions more to double the size of the plant in the next few years.

"Plant's forty years old, much older than it was designed to last, but the NRC just gave them a twenty-year extension. It's crumbling, pipes are leaking, cracks in the concrete. They're one accident away from catastrophe. I worked alongside those people for years. The workers know the plant's unsafe, but they're scared to complain. Last year there were dozens of anonymous tips from whistle-blowers about leaky valves and rusting seams, failed backup generators, but the regulators ignore them. Somebody has to put a stop to it."

"Who are the people on this island? Wally and the others?"

"Are you listening to me?"

"It's old, it's crumbling, about to double in size.

Yes, I heard you. Who are these people you're involved with?"

"Average citizens like me, committed to the cause."

"Who, Leslie?"

"We're activists, part of something larger."

"And how did you get involved?"

"Is that important?"

"I'm trying to understand."

"They came to me. They knew I had access to the plant. They knew I was sympathetic to the cause."

"Who came to you?"

"You're interrogating me?"

"If you want my help, I have to know what's going on."

"A woman. She wanted me to meet some people. That was a while ago. I met them, listened, and little by little, I saw the importance of what they were doing, and together we developed a plan. Nobody forced me, nobody brainwashed me if that's what you're suggesting."

"The woman in your boat that day. Red hair."

With a slow blink of her eyes she admitted he was correct.

"And shutting down Turkey Point, one plant out of hundreds. What does that accomplish?"

"You've heard of Three Mile Island, Chernobyl, Fukushima?"

Thorn nodded.

"After the meltdown at Three Mile Island, no nuke plants were built for decades. The other two reminded everyone how vulnerable they are, how dangerous. All it will take is one more disaster. Just one, and that'll be the end of it. There'll be no new plants, no more expansion. It'll wind down. One more is all it'll take. And the public won't accept nuclear power ever again."

"Disaster? You want to blow it up?"

"Shut it down."

"And how do you accomplish that?"

She gave him a disappointed look, mouth tight, not going there.

"Chernobyl and the others, those were catastrophes, radiation spread for hundreds of miles around. That's your goal?"

"No violence, no destruction." She looked at him, then her eyes slid away as if she didn't believe her own words.

"What's the group that recruited you? They have a name?"

"It's not Al Qaeda, if that's what you're thinking."

He asked her again for the name.

With a defiant flash in her eyes, she said, "Earth Liberation Front."

It was one he'd heard of, though he couldn't recall where. "They block whaling ships. Save baby seals."

"That's Greenpeace," she said.

"Oh, you're the guys that burn down Humvee dealers. Firebombers."

"Crimes against property, yes. But nonviolent."

"Bullshit."

"It's not bullshit."

"Break into Turkey Point, there's heavy security, armed men. A pacifist doesn't stand a chance. That's a suicide mission."

"We've got that covered. We're not stupid."

"And where's the money?"

"What money?"

"Who gets rich on this crack-brained scheme?"

"It's not about money."

"It's always about money."

"Not this time. This is about caring. About doing what's right."

"Wally works for free? The tents, the solar panel, this whole setup. Who pays for all this?"

"Are you really that cynical, Thorn? Money drives everybody?"

"Why get Flynn involved?"

"He shared our goals."

"A lot of people do. Why him? It was no coincidence."

"You mean because he was your son? All right, yes. I read about him in the papers, searched him out. Being your son gave him an edge. I considered asking you as well. I considered it quite often."

"Because you thought I was some kind of big-time outlaw."

"I thought you were a man of strong principles. I still do."

"Then you obviously don't know who I am."

She was silent for a moment, then said quietly, "Maybe you're the one who doesn't know who you are."

Thorn turned his back on the water and the distant plant. His ribs ached and he could still feel a lingering pressure around his chest as if the python had crushed his torso into a new shape.

"You're a man of great skills and resolve. You've been involved in some nasty business in the past, but kept your exploits off the record. I admire you, Thorn.

I always thought you'd be a perfect fit, but I knew you'd fought a lot of battles lately so I kept my distance out of respect."

"But you didn't keep your distance from Flynn."

Her face colored briefly and she looked away. "Flynn has many of your traits, Thorn. He's a warrior. Not of your caliber perhaps, but he's learning fast."

"Listen to me, Leslie. I'm putting my boat back together. If I can't fix that engine, by God I'll dog-paddle back to the mainland. But I'm going home one way or the other. When I get back, you have my word I won't call the cops or the press or anybody. You do what you have to do. Pull your prank, cripple the plant, make your big statement. Good luck with that. But I'm going back, and if Flynn wants to leave, too, he's coming with me."

Weariness was in her half smile. "I'm sorry but that's not going to happen. You're not going anywhere till this is done. We can't take that risk. And Flynn isn't going anywhere either."

"So now we're prisoners?"

"I didn't invite you here, Thorn. You found your way on your own. But now that you're here, we can't let you leave.

"In a very short while we pull the plug. Everything's going dark. It'll stay dark for as long as we can manage to keep it that way. On the day we go in, Flynn will be with us a hundred percent, as he has been from the start. I'm confident of him. And maybe you'll come on board, too. Give me a few days, I'll change your mind."

"I'm too old to be reeducated."

"If you want to resume your way of life, if you want Flynn to have a future, you'll come around. You have to. There's no choice anymore."

"You're threatening me?"

"You have to understand something, Thorn. I don't have the final say."

"And who does?"

"We're a democracy. The group will decide what to do with you."

FOURTEEN

LEAVING THE BEACH, THORN LAGGED a step behind Leslie, taking a glance at her flats boat, seeing no
keys in the ignition. Maybe with a screwdriver and ten
free minutes he could hot-wire it. More than once he'd
lost his ignition key overboard and he knew the start-up
drill on his own skiff, but wasn't sure about the more
advanced ignition system on the Whipray.

And he got a better look at the wooden rack where
the kayaks were stored. Constructed with pressure-
treated two-by-fours, the cage was bolted together and
its lid was held shut by two impressive steel hinges
mounted on each side. From each hinge dangled an
equally impressive padlock.

Even the pry bar would be no match for that steel,
but maybe he could break the hinges loose. Gouge that
pine, splinter it enough to pry one free, jimmy the lid
open a few inches to unload a couple of kayaks. Though
now that he thought about it, he'd seen no paddles anywhere.

Another problem.

Inside the barracks tent Flynn was standing stiffly
beside Cameron, Wally, and another guy, the four of

them forming a ragged line, waiting for Leslie's arrival. Behind them were six cots neatly made with sheets and pillows. Two weight benches stood nearby, along with a collection of barbells and dumbbells and stacks of heavy plates. Some backpacks lay in the corners, and by one of the bunks, oddly out of place, sat two aluminum attaché cases.

At the back of the tent a flimsy metal bookshelf was loaded with jugs of water. An ice chest with roller wheels was tucked in beside the bookshelf. A small sheet of plywood had been laid across some wooden crates to create a makeshift desk. On it sat a laptop computer attached to a mobile phone. A bright orange extension cord ran underneath the plywood desk and disappeared beneath the edge of the tent. No doubt the computer and the window fan that was agitating the air were powered by the solar assembly outside. All in all, a Spartan bivouac.

Inside the tent the air was maybe a degree or two cooler than out in the sun, but it was so saturated with sweat and body odor it was stifling.

"This is Thorn," Leslie announced to the group. "He's an old friend of mine and he's Flynn's father. He stumbled across our camp today, and he's discovered the nature of our mission, so we can't release him. I suggest we try to bring him on board. He's a resourceful man. A fighter. We could use him.

"He's not yet convinced of the worthiness of our cause, but I think we can persuade him in short order. I truly believe we can."

She introduced the one man Thorn hadn't met. Pauly Chee, Wally's brother.

Pauly was shorter than Thorn by a couple of inches,

shirtless, his exposed chest and stomach as slick and solidly molded as a slab of polished marble. His glossy black hair was pulled back into a long ponytail. He had a cinnamon complexion and a bold, hawkish nose, and his face was full of angles as if it had been whittled by the wind.

His large, dark eyes regarded Thorn with cold indifference, as though Pauly had sized him up in a split second and decided Thorn wasn't worth further consideration.

Around his neck he wore a leather cord with a beaded medallion of green and white, and on his right wrist was a silver bracelet ornamented with oval turquoise stones. Thorn didn't know much about Native American tribes, so he could only guess what this man's ancestry might be. But the flavor of his medallion and bracelet and the broad face and harsh slash of his cheekbones hinted at one of those clans who centuries ago were driven over the Bering Strait by the last ice age and had trekked down into the new continent and settled in the deserts of the Southwest.

"Some last-minute asshole," Wally said. "I don't like it. No way."

"I'm with Wally," Cameron said. "I've spoken to him at length and found him to be an arrogant man. An untrustworthy wiseass. I don't think he's capable of becoming a member of any group, much less ours. I vote no."

She drew a breath, gave Prince a disheartened look, and moved on. "All right, that's two against. But let me make this clear. If we don't accept Thorn in the group, we'll have to make a hard choice how to proceed."

"Slice his throat, dump his carcass at sea," Wally said. "That's not hard."

"I vote yes," Flynn said. Staring off at the sunlight slanting into the tent.

"And that's my vote as well," Leslie said. "So that leaves you, Pauly."

"Vote no, Pauly. The guy's a hairy-ass motherfucker." Wally danced up to Thorn, threw a couple of phantom slaps at his face. "Pauly votes no."

"Pauly? Shall we give him a chance?"

The man said something below his breath.

"What is it, Pauly?"

"Why's he here?" His voice was low and thick as though it had been days since he'd last uttered a word.

"What do you mean?"

"Why'd he come?"

"He was worried about Flynn."

"Why?"

"He thought Flynn was mixed up in something suspicious. Isn't that right, Thorn?"

Thorn nodded.

Pauly peered hard at Thorn as if inspecting a slab of meat.

"Vote no, vote no, vote no," Wally chanted.

Pauly said, "Abstain."

"Abstain!" Wally threw up his hands. "You can't fucking abstain. You got to vote no. The guy's an asshole. Look at him, he's dumber than a bag of used condoms. What're you talking about, man? Don't abstain. I'll personally do the honors, cut his smart guy's throat."

"All right, that's it," Leslie said. "Thorn stays. But it's

probationary. We have a few days before we move. Time for Thorn to prove himself one way or the other."

Thorn kept silent. Not the moment for an acceptance speech.

"I'm coming for you, douche bag," Wally said, stabbing a finger at Thorn. "Head on a fucking swivel."

Looking down at the ground, Leslie said, "Now I have some bad news."

No one spoke. Wally waved a mosquito from his face.

"Marcus Bendell was killed this morning. Electrocuted."

Flynn flinched but the others showed nothing.

Wally said, "No big loss. Bendell wasn't playing a skill position."

"Like you are?" Flynn said.

"Goddamn right."

"A hacker? Ten-year-old kids can do what you do on their cell phone."

"I'm a fucking SCADA programmer, asshole. I spent a year in a hacker dojo learning UNIX, mastering the code. I can make passenger jets crash. What the fuck do you bring to the table?"

Leslie stood silently, waiting for them to sort it out.

When Flynn didn't reply, she said, "Answer him, Flynn. What do you bring to the table?"

"I don't know. I don't know what I have to contribute."

"What's your skill, Flynn?" She spoke softly and without judgment or pressure as if she'd spent considerable time mediating between hostile men in sweaty barracks tents.

"I don't have any."

"Second that motion," Wally said.

"You're an actor, aren't you? An artist. A creative person."

Flynn said, "Sometimes I wonder."

"We all wonder," she said. "Only those cursed by hubris don't wonder about the roles they play."

"Cursed by hubris?" Wally said. "What is this, vocabulary day? We're back in tenth grade?"

"You never left, Wally," said Flynn.

Leslie let the silence grow for several moments, then said, "Marcus was an informant for the feds."

No one made a sound.

"Our contact inside Turkey Point learned that Marcus was passing information to a government agent, and our man took it upon himself to remove Marcus from the equation. He did this without consulting me or anyone else within ELF."

Flynn was staring at the bare ground at his feet.

"So much for nonviolence," Thorn said.

"This man was acting on his own. What he did was outrageous and wrong, and I've let him know we will not tolerate any more violent acts."

"So our cover's blown," Prince said. "We have to shut down. Get the hell out of here."

"No," Leslie said. "I believe we're okay."

"But the feds know we're out here, they know our goal."

"The moment Wally put the ELF logo on their system, they knew we'd targeted the plant. They don't know anything more specific than that."

"But they could raid the island, bring us all in." Prince looked at the others as if trying to marshal support, but no one responded.

"And what would they find? Kayaks, a solar panel, a

laptop computer with a sterilized hard drive, and a group camping out in the wilderness. No, they won't raid the island. We've done nothing wrong. They couldn't know our attack plan because Marcus didn't know it, and none of the rest of you do either. Even if they took us into custody, it would be useless. If one of you wanted to confess, you have nothing specific to reveal."

"When do we hear it," Pauly said, "the plan?"

Pauly's voice was deep and velvety, enunciating each syllable with the care of a DJ on a late-night jazz station.

"I can tell you this much," she said. "Wally's computer incursion has produced the desired results. They're worried about the plant's security, and they're reacting exactly as we expected."

"And how is that?" Pauly said.

"Their security team is meeting now. We'll hear the results this afternoon and we'll respond accordingly."

No one spoke. Wally shifted his weight from foot to foot as if he had to piss. Cameron stood straight, shoulders erect, hands gripped behind his back as if doing an isometric workout on the sly. They weren't exactly spellbound by Leslie, but they were listening. Something about the quiet assurance in her voice seemed to soothe this rowdy group. Thorn had never seen or imagined this side of Leslie. To him she was still the damaged kid on his dock, insecure, defenseless. But the woman who stood before this group was smart and determined, had a steady command of the situation. Nothing fragile about her.

She explained that for the next few days no one would be leaving the island except Prince, who would come and go, continuing his work with the crocodiles, business as usual.

Finally, she informed them, there was to be a change in the routine. A simple but necessary form of security. The buddy system was now in force. For the next week, they would be paired up and would never be out of sight or proximity of their buddy even for a few seconds. The pairings were as follows: Leslie and Cameron. Flynn and Wally. And Thorn and Pauly Chee.

"No fucking way," Wally said. "This peter puffer and me, you put us together, one of us will be dead by sundown, and his name won't be Wally."

"That's my decision. From this moment on you'll be in constant contact with your partner, day and night, until we've achieved our goal."

Wally started to protest again, but his brother turned to him, brought his mouth close to Wally's ear, and spoke in a harsh, guttural tongue Thorn didn't recognize. Wally flinched and sealed his lips.

With that, the meeting was adjourned.

FIFTEEN

"SO WE'RE GOOD? YOU GET a feel for the layout?" Assistant Director Emily Sheen greeted them at the door of the conference room and motioned them inside.

Nicole said yes, a good feel. Sheffield waffled his hand.

He and Nicole, guided by Claude Sellers, had completed an hour ride-around crammed in the front seat of a Ford pickup, no air-conditioning, Claude at the wheel, showing off the highlights of the three-thousand-acre complex. Afterward they'd spent another half hour covering nearly every square foot of the five-story containment building and the dual control rooms full of gleaming hardware, and, good God, ten minutes later Frank could still feel the rumble of the turbines in his sockets.

Claude had insisted on the tour. If they were going to work together, the FBI and NIPC and the plant's security team, Sellers said they needed a hands-on feel for the outdoor layout, the scale and distances, before they sat down at the table and began in earnest to refine their threat assessments.

"I've been here before," Frank said to Emily Sheen.

"Yeah, yeah," Claude said. "That's twice already you said that."

They took seats on opposite sides of a long table in the third-floor meeting room. Across from Frank was a large window that looked down on the main floor of the control room from one story above.

Men and women in blue jumpsuits and hard hats were carrying equipment, while others in surgical smocks and paper hairnets checked gauges and consulted in small clusters near the elaborate panels and banks of computers. Dozens of joysticks rose from the command consoles flanked by banks of servers and display monitors with row after row of gauges and dials of every size and arrays of color-coded LED lights. A shift supervisor manned one vast desk, with two other equipment operators stationed at another wedge-shaped desk. The room seemed as vast and intricate as a Mars mission at NASA control.

On the walls of the conference room dozens of TV screens played black-and-white videos from all the security-cam placements around the facility. The front gate, the entry to the office building, and everything in between, including views from three cameras that were set up along the coastline monitoring the waters just offshore.

Claude took a seat alongside the woman from NRC, Emily Sheen, fiftyish, with a blocky face and blunt bangs, prematurely gray, and wearing a spongy, green suit that might've fit ten pounds ago.

"Actually I was here on multiple occasions," Frank said. "First time, Freddy Manks was head of security. You were in diapers, Sellers. FBI handled the force-on-force drill, and in five minutes my team penetrated the perimeter and were having cocktails in the control room. You guys were pathetic."

"Yeah, well, those times are long gone."

Under the table Nicole nudged Frank's ankle. A professional thump. Cool it. We've got to work with these people.

Frank believed he had a solid read on Claude. The guy was a brazen bully. The way he smiled, not quite a sneer, but a snide curl in the corner of his upper lip. As if he were tolerating humankind, but only barely. His halo of testosterone stinking up the place. And his grooming, Jesus. That Fu Manchu mustache, plucked and manicured, and the way his scalp gleamed as if he buffed it with a shoe rag.

Not to mention his outfit. A tight brown shirt with epaulets, green slacks, and a white-cord bolo tie, for christsakes, with a red stone at his throat. When Frank was ten years old and didn't know better, he'd worn a tie like that once and got the snot knocked out of him after Sunday school. It was in-your-face dorky. Probably had a collection of string ties, his jerk-off trademark.

"All right, if everyone's ready," Sheen said, "let's commence."

If Frank could get a refund on the hours he'd spent sitting at conference tables like this one, listening to some federal hack hold forth on the trivia he or she was handsomely paid to spew, he'd be about twenty years younger. Maybe his back wouldn't hurt so much. And maybe he'd have a kindlier view of the wonders of government service, too.

Or if he could have spent the rest of the afternoon staring across the mahogany expanse at Nicole McIvey, revisiting their evening behind the boathouse, the time would have been well spent.

But Nicole sat to his right, which allowed him only minimal glances at her profile and a few downwind whiffs of her natural odor. The woman had lathered up during their drive-around and was now giving off a sea-salty, wholesome scent that reminded Frank of sun-dried sheets.

"As you know," Sheen said, "the NRC monitors the entire array of the nation's nuclear materials, medical, industrial, as well as anyone using or producing nuclear fuel. We police waste disposal and decommissioning of nuke plants when they're taken out of service. We supervise plant updating and reconstruction and watch over all private nuclear research and testing.

"But today's topic is security. Agent Sheffield mentioned the force-on-force drills, which is, of course, our primary method of ensuring all power plants in the U.S. are prepared to thwart attacks, and to be certain the private security forces the power companies employ are up to the task.

"The regularly scheduled drill wasn't set to take place until eighteen months from now, but in light of the recent computer incursion, the NRC believes the timetable should be altered. We've decided the drill should take place in the upcoming week."

"Your people could be ready that soon?" Frank asked.

"We're ready now," Claude said. "It's you guys I'm worried about."

"Let me get this straight," Frank said. "You're worried you've got a vulnerability and you think running a drill will find it?"

"In an abundance of caution—" Ms. Sheen began, but Frank raised his hand and cut her short.

"What you want is for the FBI to give you cover, then if something bad happens, we get the blame."

"You're misreading our intentions," she said. "A drill is simply a motivational tool. We want everyone at Turkey Point working at their highest level of efficiency, and we believe this is one way to accomplish that goal."

"Might take a little more than a drill," Frank said.

"That's a laugh," Claude said. "The feds lecturing us about efficiency."

Claude pushed his chair back, stood, and looked for a moment as if he were about to leap across the table and try to bite off some of Frank's soft tissue. Then Claude produced that slimy smile and left the room.

"He's getting the scale model," Sheen explained with a vacant smile.

While they waited, Nicole small-talked with Sheen, playing the geography game: Where've you been based, where'd you grow up?

Frank looked out the window, watching the steam swirl from the cooling towers, disappearing into an achingly blue sky. Watching birds change course around the monster vent stacks, thinking about the plant, the three thousand acres, how hard it would be to defend this place against a determined enemy.

The way force-on-force worked, an attack team was chosen by the NRC to go up against the plant's privately trained security force. Before the drill took place, both sides gathered around a tabletop mock-up of the plant or ran computer simulations. The feds proposed assault scenarios, the plant security team offered responses, the feds coming back with countermeasures to those responses, brainstorming back and forth for a day or two, war games meant to tighten security protocols.

Tabletop drills preceded the actual force-on-force exercise by a few weeks. Enough time for the plant security team to fix the flaws discovered in the mock-ups. And to tweak operational procedures, harden their perimeters, add personnel, repair any weak links in their communications network.

Thirty years back, Sheffield, a youngster, was assigned to his first force-on-force team. Gung ho going in. But by the end of the drill, he saw the whole deal was about as rigorous as a neighborhood game of capture the flag. Guys firing blanks at other guys firing blanks. Clunky, inefficient, and silly. Evaluators were posted throughout the area with binoculars and clipboards. Hard to score, hard to get a real feel for the vulnerability of the plant or the skill of the defense team.

Tedious, too. Because of the FBI's high standard for safety, before the drill even started, Frank and the rest of the team had to spend hours checking every round to be sure no live ammo inadvertently slipped into the mix.

These days it was laser tag. Light-sensitive vests worn by all participants, weapons that projected red laser dots. Easier to track and quantify after the drill was done: plug everyone's equipment into the computer, get a print-out of exactly who shot whom and where and when. But to Frank it still felt like capture the flag, the video version. A fucking joke.

The NRC ran computer simulations of various aircraft crashing into the containment structures, and they developed strategies to combat overwhelming force—sheer numbers of attackers coming from multiple directions. According to the computer models, the steel-reinforced concrete structures could withstand the crash of a passenger jet without catastrophic damage to the reactor, and there were workable ways to call in reinforcements from local law enforcement agencies in time to counter a large-scale assault. But Frank had serious doubts about those working in the real world.

Somehow, after all these years, force-on-force continued to be the gold standard for judging the security of nuke plants. To make matters even more Mickey Mouse, the NRC limited the drill to six on six. Six on the assault team going up against six plant-security guys. The drill happening in a previously agreed-upon window of three days.

Not once had Sheffield seen them game out the use of insiders. All it took was one guy behind the scenes toggling the right switch, or sabotaging a circuit board, and the best security plan was worthless.

That first time, when he'd seen how shabby the force-on-force drill was, Frank protested. Wrote memos, even took a meeting in DC, flying up on his own dime. All the congressional aides were respectful, scribbling notes, listening, asking a few questions, but nothing came of it.

And why not? Because the system was fucked. Same revolving door that operated throughout Washington. People like Emily Sheen put in a few years with the NRC, then left for cushy lobbying jobs with the power companies they used to regulate. And guys from power companies in a fit of public-spiritedness filled Emily's position for a while, policing their old pals. An endless daisy chain of collusion and back-scratching. Everybody giving everybody else a big benefit of the doubt.

Catch-22 times three. The economy was totally dependent on critical infrastructure systems. But those systems were owned and operated by private corporations. The owners of those critical systems wanted minimal government oversight, but the same owners believed it was the duty of the government to protect them against all manner of disasters and attacks.

Finally Claude and an Asian guy came back into the room carrying a plywood sheet they positioned on the conference table—a scale model of the plant, every building and tower, along with detailed renderings of the landscape, complete with the miles of straight cooling canals, the surrounding waters of Biscayne Bay, and the neighboring parks and open spaces. All of it with the molded contours of the terrain, complete with trees and boulders painted in realistic colors. Like a goddamn Lionel train set.

Claude unzipped a plastic baggie and dumped out a mix of miniature trucks, cars, and rubber soldiers. The Asian guy hung around grinning at Frank and his flowered shirt, then he shot Claude a smart-ass look and left.

"You guys don't use computers, Smart Boards, any of that?"

"I'm old-school," Claude said. "Can't hold it in my hand, it isn't real."

Claude set up six rubber soldiers inside the front gate, and six on the outside of the power plant's property.

"We're gaming it today?" Nicole said. "No prep?"

"Frank here, he's done this three times already, right, Frank? Pro like you, you don't need any prep, do you, Frank?"

"We can start," Sheffield said. "But we may need a second round."

"Suit yourself. You're the G-man."

Nicole produced a yellow legal pad from her brief-case. Fired up and eager, she clicked her ballpoint pen three or four times as if gunning a big V-8.

Then they began.

SIXTEEN

TWO HOURS LATER THEY WERE wrapping up.

Sheffield had stayed quiet, letting Nicole sketch out the scenarios. With only a half dozen players on each side, the options were limited. After she realized Frank wasn't going to contribute, she tried gamely to probe the plant's defenses. Claude shooting down each of her setups.

She tried spreading out her six attackers along two flanks. Some coming overland from the south, the others through public land from the north.

There's fences, razor wire on top, Claude told her.

Bolt cutters, Nicole said.

So you make it through the outside fence, there are security cameras every ten feet. A second fence twenty feet inside the outer perimeter. Motion sensors with alarms in the security office. Tamper with the fences, game over.

Okay, so they'd do a frontal assault with two waves. A group of four overpower the two guards at the front gate.

Do that and three more guys would be out there in half a minute. Your attackers are exposed. Security is riding around in steel-reinforced Jeeps.

Then what if two guys dressed as civilians present fake IDs. Press credentials or law enforcement. They get the green light, and once inside, the other four exit the vehicle and fan out.

Fake IDs won't cut it. All visitors have to be cleared beforehand. If he's not on the clipboard, the freaking president of the USA isn't coming in.

Went like that for two deadly hours. Given that she was winging this, Nicole was fairly inventive. Claude started out smug and got smugger by the minute. Shooting triumphant looks at the NRC lady and Frank.

"Try this," Nicole said. "Our guys are on four-wheelers, six separate all-terrain vehicles. They come in waves, take different paths toward the plant. Guys riding the perimeter would draw a crowd, right? Soon as a few of your defenders commit to chasing, the main assault breaches the front gate."

"Not a problem," Claude said.

"Sounds like a problem to me," Sheffield said.

"You're wrong. Anyone enters the front gate on an ATV or whatever the hell they're driving, they're going to be zapped."

"How's that happen?" Sheffield leaned back in his chair.

Claude glanced around the room like a kid cornered with a stolen cookie. "It'll happen."

"You need to be specific, old buddy."

"Zapped," Claude said, staring at Frank. "That isn't specific enough?"

"That's horseshit, Sellers. How do you repel multiple attackers each on their own ATV or dirt bike, or whatever?"

"My people are elite. They've seen it all."

"Nobody's seen it all."

"Every one of them is certified in police counter-ambush tactics, stealth-movement techniques, tactical covert-entry skills, forced cell extraction, countersurveillance detection, tactical roadblocks, and vehicle extractions."

"Certified by who?"

"They've had training from the best. Constantly upgrading their skills."

"That's good, that's good. Certified by who, Claude?"

"Private-sector professionals. We don't need Big Brother looking over our shoulder all the time."

"Let me guess. You took them to Peak Performance Tech, up in Aventura? Or somebody like that."

Claude was silent, glaring at Frank.

"Peak Performance," Frank said, remembering their slogan. " 'When the best isn't good enough.' "

"Damn right," Claude said. "They're top-notch."

Frank looked at Nicole, then at Sheen. Keeping his voice businesslike. No snark, no pettiness. "What Mr. Sellers is referring to is a weekend seminar. Eight hundred bucks a head gets you three days of lectures, some fieldwork playing soldier out in the Glades. They throw in a little Xbox video gaming, let you shoot at cartoon bad guys, then award spiffy diplomas at the end. The folks that teach the courses for Peak Performance, every one of them washed out of Quantico or got tossed from Miami SWAT. I know them. They're losers, all of them."

"Fuck you, Sheffield."

"As tempting as it sounds, I'll have to decline."

"There's no need for this," Emily Sheen said. "We're on the same side."

"Are we?" Frank said. "Which side is that? Team Incompetent?"

"Fuck you twice," Claude said, "coming and going."

"Mr. Sellers, please. We're all professionals here."

A professional doofus, Frank was about to say when Claude straightened his shoulders and cleared his throat.

"Okay," he said, "just so you don't go home mad, let's pretend your guys penetrate the fences. What then? Where do you go, what do you do?"

Nicole looked to Frank for help but he gestured for her to take it.

"All right," she said. "Shut down the plant's internal power source. Take the reactors off-line. Isn't that the point? ELF's dream would be to get into the control room, press the red button. Cause a few hours of panic on the streets of South Florida."

Emily Sheen was quiet, blank-faced, nodding her encouragement.

"Can't be done. There's a flicker in the plant's internal power grid, a dozen diesel backup generators kick in," Claude said. "Shut down the main electric terminal, the diesels keep the reactors glowing. The control rods are magnetically linked to the lifters, so the power goes off, the rods release, drop into the tank, automatically cool the whole reaction down. On top of the Westinghouse AP1000 there's a tank that holds around eight hundred thousand gallons of water. Enough to control reactor heat for three days. Cut the power, that tank releases its water, gravity fixes the problem. Simple as that."

"Okay, then one member of the four-man assault team peels off and incapacitates the generators, takes out the water tank."

"Soon as there's an intrusion alert, a defense team is dispatched to guard the diesels and tanks," Claude said. "You got to do better than that."

"That leaves you thin. You've got two guys occupied at the main gate. Two more at the containment-building entrances. One guy roaming, now some unspecified number at the generators."

"We'll manage."

"And you're okay with this, Ms. Sheen? No specific countermeasure offered by the plant's head of security?" Frank smiled at Sheen.

"I'm here as a neutral observer."

"Lame," Sheffield said. "Jesus Christ, I could pick up a carload of day laborers in the Home Depot parking lot and knock this place over."

Claude's cheeks were flushed, but Sheffield was relaxed now. With all the dog sniffing out of the way, his blood pressure was easing. He'd spent the last thirty years dealing with the likes of Sellers, guys with advanced degrees in assholery. Sometimes they were on the wrong side of the law, but just as often they were his own damn colleagues. Assholery was an equal-opportunity affliction.

Sheffield was focused on the cooling canals on the tabletop mock-up. Thirty canals running perfectly parallel for five miles south of the reactors; the one farthest east was only a few hundred yards off Biscayne Bay. Prince Key wasn't shown on the tabletop replica, but if the plywood were a few inches wider, it would have been sitting right there, due east of the plant.

If this truly was Cameron Prince's play, that's how his people would come. By water from Prince Key. Across that four- or five-mile stretch of shallows, then portage the kayaks to the first cooling canal and paddle straight up to the backside of the plant. Come at night when the video cameras were minimally effective.

"I have a question, Ms. Sheen."

"You're dealing with me, Sheffield, not her."

Frank kept his eyes on the woman from the NRC. "I assume when Homeland Security's whiz kids removed the ELF image from the servers, they also did a thorough housecleaning of the closed loop. Scrubbed any malware, infections, repaired any changes to the server root directory. If they didn't do that, or didn't do it thoroughly, the whole system is vulnerable to stack overflows, denial of service."

There was silence. Claude glared across the table at Sheffield, and he could feel Nicole's eyes on him, too.

Sheffield said, "Who's your head computer guy? The one that sets the Group Policies? Rules for the level of encryption and security protocols."

"We bring people in," Claude said.

"You got temps running your system monitoring?"

"Computer experts, local geeks. They do excellent work."

"That's nuts," Frank said to Sheen. "Hiring outside techies, who knows what they know or don't know? The problem is, the closed loop is your buffer, it's the one thing that keeps some teenager in his bedroom from taking over your reactor and blowing it sky-high. As it stands, the closed loop could be compromised and you wouldn't know it.

"All it would take, somebody installs a network interface card in a single computer on the loop, then that machine communicates with a wireless access point, which could be something as simple as somebody's smartphone. Bingo, the closed loop isn't closed anymore. It's wide open to the Internet."

"I'm sure Homeland Security did everything possible," Sheen said. "I have no doubt they combed the entire system. I'll be happy to pass on the Post Attack Vector Analysis. All their findings."

"Do that," Sheffield said. "I want it tomorrow first thing. And I'm sending one of our cyberjocks out here tod ouble-check."

"Of course," Sheen said. "I'm sure Mr. Sellers and his staff will have no objection."

Claude rolled his eyes. "So we're done here?"

Ignoring him, Frank went on, "What we've not considered is the fact that someone apparently spent a good deal of time probing the network. It appears that person had access to a power-plant computer for several hours, and that person is still unknown."

"Whoever it was, we got it covered," Claude said. "New protocols. You can't throw a goddamn light switch in the plant without me knowing about it."

Frank stood, stepped around Nicole, and reached a hand out to the reactor building. Twenty-five stories tall, it was about four inches high in the scale model. He touched a fingertip to the containment building. "Boiling water to keep the lights on."

"It's a hell of a lot more complicated than that," said Claude.

"Sure, there's the smashing-atoms part, but that's just to make steam to spin a turbine to keep everybody's iPods charged, right?"

"Nuclear energy is the cleanest source of fuel we have. Lowest carbon emissions per kilowatt." Ms. Sheen was smiling brightly. No doubt she'd stood before hundreds of antinuke gatherings and had all the rejoinders to all the critiques.

Sheffield glanced down at the floor of the control room. He could spend a month out there, hire a personal tutor, and he still wouldn't grasp what all that circuitry was for. He doubted anyone in ELF would have that kind of expertise either, meaning they weren't planning on being surgical, but probably meant to execute some kind of blunt-force trauma.

Frank took out his silver keychain. One of two things he'd inherited from his old man. The Silver Sands Motel and a silver keychain with a small cigarette lighter attached. Sheffield didn't smoke, but he kept the lighter operational. A corny nod to his dad. Keeping the Sheffield flame alive.

"So anyway I'm looking at this little three-story, square building. The one that's half-buried in the coral rock." Frank pointed at the grayish cube that was positioned dead center on the plywood board. "I don't think that was on our tour, Claude."

Claude gave him a sleepy look. "Couldn't show you every damn thing. We'd still be out there."

Sheffield came around the table. Claude watched him edge closer, stiffening in his chair.

"Last time I was out here," Sheffield said, "doing force-on-force, our target of choice wasn't the reactor or the diesel generators, or any red button in the control room. We weren't trying to shut the place down. We were trying to blow it the hell up. We were doing a suicide run like the jihadists and true believers would try. Our target was the seventy-five thousand metric tons of spent fuel rods you people have been accumulating for the last thirty-five years."

"So what?" Claude said.

"I'm guessing those rods haven't moved since I was here last. They're still crammed in pools of refrigerated water. Is that correct?"

With some reluctance, Sheen gave him an affirmative nod.

"I seem to remember if that water ever leaks out or stops circulating, the rods only take an hour or two to reach a thousand degrees. They get that hot, the zirconium cladding they're wrapped in catches fire; not long after that the cement walls vaporize; next thing you've got is a radioactive cloud spewing out the roof like Mount Etna shooting ash.

"Worst case, a day or two Turkey Point is in the center of a dead zone the size of Rhode Island, an area that stays toxic for centuries. Even if it's a small leak, if the wind's right, Homestead to the Broward line, five million souls are affected. If there's a quick fix, very best case, a few hundred thousand are in jeopardy. Land's contaminated for miles around, southern Biscayne Bay is off-limits the rest of our lives and our kids' lives. That's how I remember it from before. All that still true? Because I've read it's gotten worse. Even more spent fuel rods crammed in those pools."

Sheffield leaned forward a little more, clicked his lighter, got a flame, and touched it to the squarish structure north of the containment building. The plastic caught and began to crinkle and give off a chemical vapor.

"Because if this is still true, folks, this is the building we should be watching."

Everyone stared at the small replica burning, the fire spreading swiftly across the rest of the scale model. Claude came to his feet, hustled out the door, and was back with a fire extinguisher just as Frank was patting out the small fire with the palm of his callused hand. The domed containment structure was blackened but intact.

"Was that necessary, Agent Sheffield?" Sheen was on her feet, waving the smoke from her face.

"You can't hold it in your hand, it isn't real," he said. "Right, Claude?"

Claude cranked open a window. "The water can't leak out, smart guy. The walls of the tank are concrete, five feet thick, lined with stainless steel. The spent fuel tank is the size of an Olympic pool. That means pumping out thousands of gallons of water. It'd take a week. Maybe a truck full of dynamite could blast a little hole in the side, but that isn't going to happen because we got barriers on top of barriers to prevent exactly that. So your little fantasy, it ain't going to happen. Put that one back up your ass where it came from."

Voice raspy from the fumes, Sheen managed some canned closing remarks about what a productive meeting it had been. How happy she was to be working with such a highly motivated group of people. Not a trace of irony.

So it was settled.

One week from tomorrow. On the seventeenth of August, a Friday, the drills would officially begin. Starting after midnight on Thursday, the FBI team would have a seventy-two-hour window to mount their attack: Friday, Saturday, or Sunday. The attack could begin at any time during that seventy-two-hour period. Laser weapons and sensor vests would be distributed in the next few days along with reflective armbands, white for the FBI and red for Turkey Point. Sheffield was to choose six combatants, and Sellers would select six from his security team. Any of the scenarios mentioned today were fair game, or if Sheffield wanted to improvise, that was also fair.

"Good luck to all of you," Sheen said. "And the NRC will be watching with great interest."

SEVENTEEN

TEN MINUTES LATER, ON THEIR way out the exit drive, Frank said, "Anybody other than your superiors at NIPC know you were running Bendell?"

Nicole shot him a dark look. Not happy with his performance. Over the top, belligerent. Sure, Frank could've handled it better. He'd have to work on that. Learn to keep his cool. Maybe one of these days before he retired.

"No one knew about Bendell except the essential players."

"Like Claude Sellers?" Frank said.

"I don't like Sellers either. But he's the power company's security point man. We don't have a lot of choice in the matter."

"So he knew Bendell was working for you?"

"He knew I had someone in an ELF cell, but he didn't know Marcus by name. Why? You don't trust him?"

"Understatement of the month."

They drove in silence till they were back on the turnpike. Nicole going the speed limit. A deep downdraft in her mood.

"So what now, Agent Sheffield?"

"Next thing is, I'd like to watch a video."

"What video?"

"The one starring Leslie Levine and a crocodile."

"Why?"

"If Prince wanted to get Levine out of the way so he could have unhindered access to the plant, the video might give us some idea how he pulled it off. If it does, that gives us probable cause. I bring Prince in, take a look at his island while we're doing it. We get him in a room, mess with his head, maybe he'll slip, blurt something, give us a reason to take down the rest of his ELF friends. Problem solved."

"A guy's going to make a video of a murder?"

"A certain kind of guy, yeah."

"What kind is that?"

"One who thinks he's smarter than anyone in the room."

"Except for you."

"Yeah," Frank said. "Except for me."

They were quiet for the rest of the drive, and when she dropped him back at his motel on Key Biscayne, she kept the motor running.

"Buy you a beer?"

She shook her head, staring at the windshield with a stiff smile.

"Or we could raid my tequila stash. I make a nasty margarita."

"Don't think that's wise."

"Yeah, we might get tipsy, lose control, do something we'd regret."

"We already did."

Frank sighed to himself. He'd had hopes, but she sounded resolute.

"So you coming along tomorrow, take another look at the croc attack?"

"I have things on my desk," she said, distant now. All the witty banter evaporated.

"Yeah, yeah. Got to keep that desk clear. Know the feeling." He opened the door, got out, considered re-phrasing the drink offer, but saw how rigid she was sitting behind the wheel. "I'll let you know if I see anything in the movie. Then we should talk. Go over the force-on-force plan. I like a couple of your ideas."

She turned, leaned toward the open door, fixing him with a tough stare. "I'm going along, Frank. You know that, right? I'm one of the six."

"You good with a laser pistol?"

"Just so you know. I want in on this."

"Seems to me you earned it."

"Damn right I did. Damn right." She tucked a strand of hair behind her ear. "That stunt with the lighter, Frank, that was childish."

"Yeah. I got carried away."

She looked across at him, things happening in her eyes, some kind of struggle he couldn't decipher.

Then she reached out and switched off the ignition. "Okay, tell me." She released a long breath. "What's the best tequila you have?"

She had to use the john. While she was in there running water, Frank hummed a tune to himself, broke some ice out of the trays, and measured the limeade and the Patrón and the Grand Marnier. Margaritas were like a lot of things: the difference between a good one and a great one came down to money. The expensive stuff was expensive for a reason.

His room was the only efficiency in the motel. A

half-assed kitchen behind a rattan counter. A small living area that he'd furnished with secondhand art deco chairs, a couch, and tables made from some variety of blond wood and fashioned with smoothly curved edges. He'd painted the walls a pale salmon, kind of adventurous for a bachelor pad, but it seemed right because the color came from the same palette as the sunrises that woke him every day.

He'd hung some Haitian watercolors on the walls. Not the bright, garish ones the Haitians were famous for, but muted blue and white with some darker blues. Scratch paintings. Layers of different-colored paints were applied to the board, and the artist scratched them away delicately to create the outlines of fishermen and birds and a few primitive sailboats plying the smooth waters, and the mountain ranges overlooking the harbor at Port-au-Prince. He was proud of those paintings. He knew the Haitian taxidriver who'd painted them, a guy who'd finally started selling enough of his stuff to quit cabdriving and paint full-time.

When he finished making the drinks, Nicole was still in the bathroom.

"Salt or no salt?" he called out.

She opened the door a crack and peeked out at him. Through the slit he saw she'd shed her clothes and was showing a glossy sliver of her right leg.

"You like yours with salt, Frank?"

"Sure. Salt's great."

Nicole opened the door an inch, Sheffield holding his breath. Then she stepped into the room. She had a much better physique than he'd imagined, and he'd imagined it a lot. Lanky with wide shoulders and narrow hips, long legs that were muscled like a distance runner's. Her clothes disguised the taut heft of her breasts. Her nipples were strangely tiny and as dark as chocolate chips, and a fine dusting of golden down around her navel was lit by a slant of afternoon sunlight. Her flat, athletic stomach sloped down to a triangle of feathery wheat.

"If you're really into salt, Frank, maybe you could try licking the dried sweat off my arms." She held her right arm straight ahead like a sleepwalker.

Frank set the two margaritas back on the side table. "I guess I could start with your arms."

EIGHTEEN

FOUR TIMES, OR WAS IT five? Frank lost count in the blur of flesh, thrust and counterthrust, his groans and hers, his cotton sheet knotting around his ankles, even the fitted sheet breaking loose from the mattress, at one point the mattress slipping off the box spring, tipping both of them onto the floor, which didn't stop their grappling, didn't slow them, in fact helped them discover fresh angles, new and surprising pressures, both bodies slippery with sweat, her fingernails digging at his shoulders, holding on, jabbing his lower back to keep the lock tight, thigh to rump, loin to thigh, Frank noting the pain in passing, thinking he'd tally it all up in the morning, the bruises, scrapes, and long, ragged scratches, then diving back into the unthinking convulsions, the wrestling match, every hold and variation Frank knew and some he'd never thought possible, Nicole slithering away, Frank pursuing, staying inside her, and with a sudden grinding thrust she was letting go, completely letting go, she twisted, hammered her hips and thighs against his, and rolled on top, arched into the cobra pose, carnal yoga, her spine bowed forward, shoulders thrown back, yipping until the throaty cowgirl scream came again.

Four, five, six. Who could count? Why bother? He didn't. Only found himself considering it much later as she was dressing in the dark, how many times he'd come and she'd come, how many times they'd gotten close and pulled away, in the three hours—or was it four?—they'd been together, just something to consider while he watched her dress, Nicole not showering, saying she wanted to take a little bit of Frank Sheffield home, his smell, his dried fluids, his DNA, maybe scrape some off, run a lab check on him, see what came up in the National Crime Information Center, joking as she dressed, doing all the talking with silent Frank, exhausted Frank, propped up against the pillows trying not to plead, Do you have to go? Stay a little longer.

He knew how the back-and-forth would go: she had to leave, damn it; and, yes, he understood. It was late. It was tomorrow already. She had work. They both had work. Jobs to do. It was already Friday, for christsakes, practically the weekend. Hey, didn't she take off the weekend? And she'd ask him, Do you think those ELF guys are taking off the weekend?

No, he couldn't possibly blow off work for time in the sack with Nicole and her yips and her clawing nails and the lip-bruising kisses. None of that he said out loud, but he was thinking it, wanting to convince her, goddamn it, to stay there beside him, cuddle a little, milk the afterglow, but knowing that would be a mistake with a no-bullshit broad like her, Frank admitting he liked to snuggle, a tough hombre, special agent in charge, admit he was an inveterate cuddler. Spoon him just for ten minutes while they drowsed, all he wanted. But when Nicole was done, she was done and she was up and getting dressed, and who was Frank to judge?

She was over in the dark by his dresser, fumbling around, then went into the bathroom again, shut the door, switched on the light. In there for several minutes. Frank wondering, What the hell? Then she came out, the light turned off again, went back to the dresser.

"Everything okay?"

"Everything's fine," she said. "Better than fine."

On the way to the door she came over, stooped, kissed him once more, her right hand pressed hard and flat against his hairy chest, then her fingers closed, gripping, tugging on the hairs, Nicole a little more into pain than he was used to, but he accepted it, enjoyed the novelty of it, didn't question it.

"Do you have to go?" he heard himself say as she got to the door.

"You need your rest, Frank. You're not as young as you used to be. You were huffing, heart racing, I thought I might have to call the paramedics."

"Your heart wasn't racing?"

She was at the open door. The room dark, the sound of the surf. He could only see her from the bathroom light, not enough to read her face. He could've gotten up and tried to coax her back to bed, but she was right, he had nothing left. Who was he trying to kid? But it bothered him that her heart might not have been racing. Bothered him a little, but not so much he mentioned it aloud, that she'd even noticed he was out of breath, because he'd noticed nothing like that about her, noticed only the sounds she made as she climbed up the octaves to that high note she hit and hit and hit.

In the dark she said, "What exactly are you concealing?"

"What?"

"About Turkey Point, this operation. There's something you're hiding."

"I don't know what you mean."

"Oh, yes, you do."

Frank was quiet for a moment, considering, then said, "You're good."

She stayed in the doorway, a hazy moonglow behind her in the tall pines that bordered his property.

"What it is, I've got a guy. An informant. I didn't recruit him. He called me. He's gotten involved with these people, the ELF group. There was something bothering him about it all."

"What was bothering him?" She wasn't angry. Sounding neutral, patient.

Frank was relieved. "Nothing specific. He called last week. I haven't heard from him again."

"Which guy is it?"

Frank was silent, thinking. Taking too long.

"You don't trust me, Frank." Half statement, half question.

"Can we talk about this tomorrow? I'll lay it all out, everything, okay?"

"Sure. I understand. You don't want to spoil the afterglow. Don't want to mix business with pleasure. Sure."

"Now you're pissed."

"Not at all. Get some sleep. We'll talk tomorrow."

Then she backed out the door and was gone.

No one spoke to Thorn. Flynn kept his distance. At suppertime Flynn walked off and sat by the obstacle course with his Subway sandwich. Wally tagged along and planted himself a few yards away.

Thorn got the last sandwich in the ice chest, turkey

with Swiss, so soggy he could've eaten it with a spoon. He sat by himself on the rocky soil on the western side of the island. A small gap in the mangroves with a sunset view over the mainland. His minder, Pauly, stood ten yards away watching him eat.

After darkness settled, a solid wave of mosquitoes moved in, a mass so thick even Thorn was driven inside the tent. On a cot across the way, Flynn was immersed in a paperback novel. Wally was at his laptop, tapping the keys in staccato bursts. Cameron did some biceps curls with fifty pounds in each hand, while Leslie lay on her cot and stared up at the fabric of the tent. At the mesh window, Pauly stood and gazed out into the darkness.

One by one they got beneath their sheets. Cameron turned off the single lightbulb hanging from a crossbeam. There was no talk, no good-nights, no camaraderie. Just darkness, except for the blue glow of Wally's computer as he continued to click the keys in rapid bursts.

Hours later when Thorn came awake in the middle of the night, Wally's computer was shut down. The electric fan churned and men were snoring, one louder than the others with a wet catch in his throat, and damp, fluttering lips.

Thorn turned his head to the side.

Sitting on the edge of the adjacent cot was Pauly Chee. Pauly's naked chest gleamed with sweat and moonlight; his eyes were black sapphires glowing from deep within. They were fixed on Thorn.

Pauly was chewing something slowly, something thick and gummy that flexed his jaws. Watching Thorn without pause. Draped across his shoulders, a python glimmered like black jelly as it oozed between his arms and wrapped its slippery, undulating length around his torso, once, twice. Pauly uncoiled the snake and guided it onto the floor, and the python slid away into the darkness.

Thorn lay still and listened to the man's soft chewing like a dog working deliberately through his rawhide treat. On the sweetening breeze he smelled the scent of tarnished copper rising from the mangroves, and he could sense the swelling barometric pressure of an approaching storm and hear its faint cannon fire from out at sea.

He glanced over at his son sleeping peacefully two cots away, then lay back and shut his eyes, and as he drifted down a long slope back into sleep, he had a dreamy vision of Pauly's python cruising out of the tent and into the tall grasses—that giant snake heading off to track the last of the island's raccoons and mice and nesting birds, then Thorn was watching the knobby back of a monster croc sink beneath a black satin sea, sink and sink into the cold depths that were darker than any grave.

NINETEEN

AT SUNRISE FRANK ROLLED OUT of bed, pulled on his gym shorts, laced up his Brooks running shoes, stretched for a few minutes to get his blood moving, watching the morning TV news.

All the anchors were hyped about the tropical storms lined up, five of them starting off the coast of Africa and stretching into the Gulf, where Ivan was growing into a Category 4 hurricane. Juanita was next in line. Miami was in her cone, and all the storm guys were revving up their 3-D maps. Kurt was next, then two others farther out that hadn't earned names yet.

Sheffield switched off the TV. He got much better hurricane info from Matthew White's e-mail updates. Matt farmed lychee nuts down in Homestead, and as a hobby he forecast hurricanes. Though he had no formal training, Matt's tracking predictions had a much higher success rate than did those of the TV guys with all their degrees and cool devices, plus Matt did it without a bit of hype.

Sheffield walked to the beach and trotted off. Four miles on the hard-packed sand, thinking of Nicole the whole way, her line about his huffing. This was a woman worth getting in shape for.

Afterward, dripping sweat, he went over to his dresser, got his cell, flipped it open. The *Recent Calls* screen was up. A screen he rarely used. Frank stared at it, thinking of last night, Nicole's groping around on the dresser, going into the bathroom, staying for a while. He scrolled through the recent calls, incoming and outgoing, finding nothing of note. Maybe she was checking for old girlfriends. Or maybe Frank was having a paranoia flash. She was probably just gathering her own stuff off the dresser, or any number of other perfectly innocent possibilities.

Sheffield let it go. He stood in the open doorway of 106, the efficiency apartment he called home, and dialed the office. In early as always, Marta Gonzalez, his secretary for the last fifteen years, picked up on the first ring.

"Not coming in? What is it now? New drain field? Roof leak?"

For the last few years Sheffield had been remodeling the Silver Sands, the wreck of a place he'd inherited from his old man. Twenty rooms, two stories, a rectangular mom-and-pop motel from the forties with a subdued art deco style. Two hundred feet off the white-sugar sands on Key Biscayne, wedged between massive condo towers on three sides. The place hadn't been remodeled in all the years his parents owned it. It went broke, then the old man died, and suddenly it was Frank's, a run-down building sitting on primo land. In the current market the land was worth four to five million, or so the Realtors told him.

But once he picked up his hammer, hung his first sheet of drywall, started plastering, a lot of happy memories began firing off, the sweet old days when his granddad and grandmom ran the place and he'd played there every summer day while his parents were off at work, back when the key was a slow, empty island with an expansive view of the city of Miami across Biscayne Bay, back when the tallest downtown buildings were no higher than six stories.

"No, it's not the motel," Frank told Marta. "First, call Metro homicide, see who's heading up the Marcus Bendell death. Happened yesterday morning. Marcus Bendell, spelled like it sounds."

"Got it."

"I want anything they've got. Crime-scene photos, the whole deal."

"And what do I tell him it's about?"

"An FBI investigation into a possible terrorist cell."

Marta was quiet for a moment before asking if there was more, her voice more businesslike now.

"Who's our best cybersleuth?"

"Angie Stevens."

"Yeah, Angie. I want to meet her this afternoon, two, three o'clock. And I want background checks on four people."

"My pencil's poised."

He gave her the names. Pauly Chee, Wally Chee, Claude Sellers, and Cameron Prince. Told her to call the Bureau's liaison at the Department of Defense, see what kind of soldier Pauly was, service record, special training, medical history, medals, date of discharge. And the civilian side, too. High school, college, traffic tickets, all of it. Run the full background check on the others. Criminal, financial, work history.

"Later this morning I'll be at Metro PD watching a

video. Anything comes up that might endanger all mankind without my immediate intervention, I'll have my cell with me."

"Try turning it on. Much better reception."

"Another thing," Sheffield said. "We need to put together a team for a force-on-force drill. Five from SWAT." Frank gave her the names of the four he wanted, including a fifth as an alternate. "See if we can get all five together later this afternoon. I should be back by one. Anytime after that."

"Oh, Nicole McIvey called. Seemed to know you."

"Called this early?"

"Said she's an early riser."

"She told you that?"

"Oh, yeah, we had a nice chat."

Frank was quiet, not happy with where this was going. "She's with the grid police, NIPC. What kind of chat?"

"Just some girl talk."

Marta was in her early sixties. Three grown daughters, seven grandkids, thirty years on the job. More friend than subordinate.

"Girl talk?"

"You wouldn't understand. Being a man and all."

"Try five words or less."

"Is he seeing anyone?"

Frank looked out at the parking lot. A building-code inspector had arrived in his white Jeep to check the installation of the new hurricane windows. Juan Medira, a Cuban guy who appreciated Frank's stubborn refusal to sell out and as a result didn't bust his balls on the trivial stuff.

"Well, what'd you say? Am I seeing anyone?"

"Not for more than a month at a time."

"That's what you told her?"

"This is important to you, this Nicole woman?"

"I'm not sure. Maybe."

"Well, I did tell her you'd be one hell of a catch."

Juan was walking over with his clipboard, talking on his cell. He waved at Frank, and Frank gave him an almost-done wave back.

"Good answer, Marta."

"No, it's not. Moby-Dick would be one hell of a catch. Doesn't mean anybody's going to land that big old whale."

"Anything else?"

"You want my opinion of her?"

"After one phone call?"

"The lady is *muy* ambitious."

"Everyone we work with is ambitious. I'd be worried if she wasn't."

"I mean *muy*. Like, I don't know the right word. She's nice enough, polite, not pushy or anything, but there's something about her."

"Oh, come on, Marta."

"Not pushy, but intense. A lady with a plan. Eyes on a prize."

"The prize being me?"

"My guess is, you're part of it. That's for sure. But, hey, I don't want to get involved in your personal life. Too messy. Unprofessional."

"I think we're a little past that."

Over the last few years, they'd grown close. Even helped each other through bouts of cancer. Prostate for him, breast for her. Camping out in the hospital pre-op, post-op, Frank bringing Marta takeout black beans and rice from La Lechonera, her favorite Cuban joint, and badgering her nurses to quit yakking and do their damn jobs. Marta doing the same when he was laid up.

Juan took a seat at the concrete picnic table, snapped his phone shut, and gazed out at the parade of yummy mommies speed-walking on the shore.

"And before I forget," Sheffield said. "We need eyes in the sky, aerial imagery. Call our friend at NSA, see if he's willing to give us some satellite time. If he refuses, try Miami-Dade PD, see if we can rent one of their drones for a few hours."

"They've never been very cooperative."

"Ask nice."

"Can I tell them what we want a peek of?"

"Prince Key. Small island in southern Biscayne Bay, three, four miles due east of Turkey Point. I want real-time feeds, close-ups, what's going on down there. How many citizens are walking around, what they're doing, if they're armed. If county won't cooperate, hell, we'll hire a small plane, do flyovers with telescopic lens. Agent Sanford's a pilot, right? See if he's available."

"You're worked up. Haven't heard you like this lately."

Frank raised a finger to Juan—one more second.

"And we need a boat. Border Patrol, Fish and Wildlife, Park Service, somebody cruising around out there to watch for comings and goings. The kind of boat that would blend in."

"I'll call around."

"Last thing. Any updates from our guy? Phone or text?"

"Your confidential informant?"

"You heard something?"

"Not a word."

Frank was silent, staring through the palms at the white sands.

"Wouldn't he contact you directly, Frank, on your cell?"

"Yeah, probably he would. I was just double-checking."

"But it worries you, him not calling. It's been four days."

"Five," Frank said. "Going on six."

"So why not call him?"

Frank waved Juan over. "Can't take the chance. Where he is, his phone rings, it could blow the whole thing all to hell."

TWENTY

AFTER JUAN SIGNED OFF ON the hurricane windows, Sheffield showered, dressed, and drove his old Chevy Impala, his personal car, off the key, took back streets north through Brickell and Little Havana, jumped on the Palmetto Expressway, and went west out to Doral.

The Midwest District Station of the Miami-Dade Police Department was a hodgepodge of building styles, combining about five clashing architectural ideas into one sprawling complex. Part industrial park, part smoked-glass office tower, with a quirky sculpted concrete wall out front that sported whimsical cutout designs you'd expect at a modern-art museum. Like a committee slapped the place together, half of them believing law enforcement was serious business, the other half trying to attract the latest TV cop show to use the place as a trendy backdrop.

In the lobby he stopped at a kiosk, bought some heavily buttered Cuban toast and a paper thimble full of ninety-proof espresso, and by the time he was upstairs at Killibrew's office he'd finished both and was ready to put on his flying cape and soar out the third-story window and explore the heavens.

But the crocodile video calmed him down.

Killibrew sat through the first screening, answering Frank's questions, but adding nothing. Clearly put out to be wasting her time on something she'd already filed away.

She was a big woman. Fifty pounds overweight. Heavy makeup, lots of lipstick, either angry she had to explain herself to a federal agent, or else born angry. But Sheffield, still coasting on his night in the sack, didn't let her crabby impatience rile him. He had his pace, his own way of working, polite but taking his sweet time no matter whom it annoyed.

After the initial viewing, he said, "First thing I'd like to know, why are these two biologists making a video at all? Is this routine? They do it every time they go out, or is this a special occasion?"

She didn't know.

"You didn't ask Cameron Prince?"

"Didn't think it was relevant."

"You ask his supervisor?"

"I didn't think it was relevant, I still don't."

"Seems odd."

"Not to me." Arms crossed below her breasts, staring over his head. Enduring this.

"What happened to Levine's severed arm?"

Killibrew's eyes refocused on Frank.

"The arm Prince carried back to the boat. Levine's arm."

"The arm was lost in transit."

"Lost?"

It was all in the file if he cared to read it. Every last detail, so he could save them both some time if he just read the file.

"How the hell did the arm get lost?"

"On the airboat ride back to the biology lab, Prince set the arm down on the deck, and in his haste to return, it bounced overboard. The water was choppy, the airboat was traveling at a high rate of speed."

"Why'd he go back to the base? How come he didn't try to find her? He had a radio, or a phone, right? He could've called for help, stayed out there. She could've still been alive."

"He said he panicked and wasn't thinking straight."

Sheffield asked if her techs examined the deck for traces of blood from the severed arm.

"By the time we got out to Turkey Point there'd been a downpour. If there'd been blood, it was washed away."

"You double-check with the Weather Service about this rain?"

"I did not."

"So Prince tells you there's a downpour, and you don't have any other verification of that? You ask anyone else on the scene?"

"Why would he lie about rain?"

"You're a homicide detective. Why do people lie to you?"

Her frown deepened. "There was no blood."

"They luminoled it and found no trace of blood?"

"It rained."

"The question I'm asking, did you or the technicians check?"

She shut her mouth, twisted her wedding ring around and around on her finger. Sheffield pitied the man who'd picked out that ring.

"So you didn't check?"

"The ID techs saw no sign of blood. It rained. And the airboat was splashed with seawater from the ride back to the docks. Prince ran the video for us, walked us through the event. We questioned him for an hour. He was distraught, found it hard to focus, he was shivering. We returned to the scene, Prince guided us, and we searched for the body, spent all night, all morning, and into the afternoon searching that canal and the ones adjoining it, and we found nothing. There are carnivores in those canals, lots of them. It's in the report."

He and the detective watched the video a second time. When it was done, Killibrew went to powder her nose and Sheffield read the file. Minimal. Three pages long. A dashed-off, half-assed account.

Clearly she'd made up her mind early on, probably pissed she had to spend so much time on an airboat out in the sun, blowing up her hairdo, mosquitoes biting, Sheffield could only guess. But Killibrew's first impression was that the death was an accident, and she wrote it up that way, start to finish. Croc versus human. Croc won. Video verification, trustworthy first-person eyewitness report.

The half dozen photos were of the airboat and the berms alongside the canal where the incident took place. Some broken brush close to the waterline where Prince claimed the croc dragged Levine into the cooling canal. Footprints in the mud, drag marks. Case closed. Twelve hours after the croc attack occurred, Killibrew pulled up stakes and released the scene. Once you release a scene, you never get it back.

When Killibrew returned, Sheffield was halfway through the video for the third time, at the point where Prince was slogging through the water and lifted up the arm. His face was strained. Maybe he was terrified or in shock. Maybe he had acting skills.

Sheffield clicked the remote and froze it. The arm.

"I don't see any tool marks," Sheffield said.

"The image is poor quality."

"The wound is so neat it's like the arm was chopped off with a cleaver, not bit off by a crocodile. You ever seen crocodile teeth? They're all over the place, snaggly. There'd be tool marks."

"If you say so."

"What about that rubber bracelet?"

"What about it?"

"Camouflage. What does that stand for? Bracelets like that represent causes of one kind or another. Did you check out what camouflage means?"

"It's a bracelet. It's decoration."

Sheffield sighed. He massaged his forehead. Ready to strangle her. "Did you show this video to an animal expert, an outside biologist?"

She shook her head.

"Did you drag the canals for remains or articles of clothing?"

"We did an extensive search. It's in the report."

"Before you released the scene, you put your scuba team in the water?"

"No."

"You got a body missing in a canal and no one went in that water?"

"We felt it was too dangerous. We did an extensive sweep of the area and found nothing."

"The scuba guys thought it was too dangerous? That'd be a first."

"I deemed it too dangerous."

"You found no articles of clothing?"

"No."

"In the video Ms. Levine was wearing a long-sleeve shirt. But the severed arm is bare. What happened to the sleeve? Did you consider that?"

"Apparently it was lost in the struggle."

"That arm could be off a mannequin for all you can tell from the video. It could be a fake. No tool marks, no shirtsleeve, no blood."

"Agent Sheffield." Killibrew stood up. "Are you familiar with clitoridectomies?"

"Say that again."

"Mutilation of a woman's genitals. The cutting away of the clitoris. In this case with a pair of scissors."

"What the hell?"

"On the night of June the ninth, the crime scene I was working when I was dispatched to Turkey Point power plant was the seventh rape and genital mutilation in the last six months. The rapist's first two victims died at the crime scene, so as a homicide detective I was assigned the case in January of this year and have been working all the subsequent rapes and mutilations. After the first two died, the other victims have managed to survive the injuries. Though none have been helpful with descriptions. Their attacker wears a mask, and as you can imagine, the trauma is horrendous. They have great difficulty reconstructing the events."

"I've read about it. You're the lead on that?"

"Yes, I am. With all the cutbacks, that's how short-handed we are, pulling me off a case of such magnitude, to investigate a crocodile mishap."

"I see."

"So if you think about it, Agent Sheffield, you might

understand why I was not overjoyed to be removed from an active rape scene and sent to work on what was clearly an accidental death of a woman who put herself in harm's way on a regular basis. If my mind wasn't fully engaged on the effort of locating body parts, or the specific crocodile that attacked and dragged off Ms. Levine, or the whereabouts of articles of her clothing, then I beg your forgiveness. But my focus was elsewhere."

She was almost out the door when Frank said, "Can you get somebody to make me a copy of the file, and a copy of this video, too? I'd like to enhance it, take a closer look."

"Of course."

"And one last thing."

She waited at the door, staring past him at the far wall. Probably seeing those mutilated women wherever she looked. Sheffield sympathized and sure as hell didn't want to get into a pissing contest, so he kept his voice neutral.

"You happen to remember the name of the person in charge of the power company's search team? I didn't see any mention of it in the report."

"The head of Florida Power and Light's security squad."

"That would be Claude Sellers?"

"Yes, that's right. Claude Sellers. A very unpleasant man."

"Well, at least we agree on that."

TWENTY-ONE

NICOLE WASN'T PICKING UP HER cell. Her message wasn't recorded in her own voice but was a female robot telling him to leave his name and number. Saying it with that condescending edge female robots were so good at.

He refused to talk to robots, even Nicole McIvey's. So he hung up, then a few minutes later called again and hung up again, and ten minutes later did it all again, still got the robot.

By then he'd arrived in the valet parking lot of the Palace, one of Miami's more glamorous assisted-living facilities, a block down from Miracle Mile in the Gables.

Last year Johnny Greening had retired from U.S. Fish and Wildlife after thirty-five years of undercover work, busting biker outlaws for selling endangered snakes and killer pit bulls to other outlaws, and once infiltrating a primate-smuggling operation that supplied orangutans to rock stars and wealthy perverts, and for a decade he'd worked the Everglades beat, which put Johnny up against a handful of hard-core poachers who'd survived a couple of centuries too long, living far away from the rule of law, in the middle of that river of grass, and had the battered faces and the dead-eye aim to prove it.

Johnny had taken his savings and bought himself a penthouse at the Palace, where he'd become the darling of dozens of well-endowed widows who vied ruthlessly for his attention.

The valet slipped Sheffield a claim check, frowned at Frank's humble ride, then drove the Chevy off to a dark corner of the garage where it wouldn't contaminate the Maseratis and BMWs. Sheffield passed through a lobby drenched in red velvet and gold brocade, walking past the white-marble concierge's stand, across deep-pile Orientals lit by massive chandeliers that blazed as brightly as the souls of recently departed billionaires.

He stood at the bank of elevators, nodded hello to a sharp-eyed woman with a complicated stack of silver hair. She wore a skintight red tracksuit and strappy sandals and had impossible breasts.

"You in the market?" she said.

"Just visiting."

She ducked her hand in her pocket and came out with a business card. "When you're ready, give me a call. They're going fast. I can still get you a sunset view for under two million, but that won't last long."

"Nothing ever does."

Johnny Greening was waiting for him as the elevator doors opened in the foyer of his penthouse. He'd styled his white hair into a rigid flattop and had put on twenty pounds around the middle, but still looked fit enough to wrestle a ten-foot gator if called upon.

"Need your expertise, Johnny."

"Having trouble with the ladies?"

"Doing fine with the ladies. It's this." Frank held up the DVD. "You got a disc player, right?"

"Have to eject *Debbie Does Dallas*, but, sure, let's have a look."

They went into Johnny's playroom, tricked out with wet bar and blackout curtains. As if he'd been inspired by some Shanghai opium den, the room had no furniture, but the burgundy wall-to-wall carpet was covered with lush pillows of every shape and size. One wall was devoted to electronics. Flatscreen TV and six-foot speakers and a stereo system that had nearly as many dials and gauges and blinking lights as the control panel at the nuke plant.

Johnny ejected the disc from his DVD player, set it aside, and slid in the croc video. He took the remote over to a pillow the size of a kiddie pool and lounged back on it. Frank stayed on his feet, leaning against the wall.

"What is this we're watching?"

"That's what you're going to tell me," Frank said.

They viewed the video without comment, then Johnny replayed it. A big croc appears at the edge of the canal and climbs up the steep slope. Cameron Prince calls out a warning to Levine, and Leslie waves him off. It was cool, her wave said, no sweat. The big croc in the spotlight wanders a bit, then spots a hump of earth and climbs atop it, seems to listen for a few seconds, then lifts herself high on her stumpy legs and drops hard on her belly. The croc digs into the hump, discovers the eggs and freshly hatched crocs. Leslie Levine is smiling in the shadows as if she's stoked by the scene unfolding in front of her.

Plucking two hatchlings out of the nest in her mouth, the mother croc heads back the way she's come. Leslie follows five yards behind, treading uncertainly across the slippery ground.

"Good-lookingw oman."

"How unusual is this?" Frank asked.

"Good-looking women? I find they're pretty rare."

"I mean a croc digging up her newborns. These two guys stumble on this, is it a one-in-a-million shot, or is it happening all over the place out there?"

"None of the above," Greening said.

"Would you care to elaborate?"

"You feds, I love how you talk. Bunch of egghead college boys."

"Lots of syllables, I know. Part of the training."

"Well, you're asking is it common what you're seeing? Yes and no. This time of year for a few weeks, yeah, it's the season when mother crocs uncover the eggs to see if their babies hatched, probably happening in the low dozens I'd guess, and it's mainly happening in those cooling canals. The crocs are squeezed into that one tiny coastal area. Can't go inland, too many shopping malls. Can't go north, it's Miami, all concrete and random gunfire; can't go south because it's salt water and the young can't survive salt water, so this is ground zero for croc nesting. That one little stretch.

"So, yeah, sure, if you knew your way around out there in those canals, which I understand Levine did, and if she's keeping good records, a running total of what nests have eggs and when they were laid, I assume she could've made a good guess where to go on any given night. It's not foolproof, but it's neither of the things you said. It's not happening all over the place and it's not one in a million."

"You ever meet Levine?"

"Heard about her, never met her."

"What'd you hear?"

"Knew her business. Not just crocs either. She was our own Jacques Cousteau, quite the environmental campaigner. Plus she gave the power company a shitload of good PR. Did a lot of TV; whenever they needed an expert on crocs or gators, Leslie got the call. Very media-friendly face."

"Unlike yours."

"I've always been happy in the shadows." Greening froze the video with Prince holding the arm up to the camera. "Who's the steroid freak?"

"Cameron Prince, Prince Key."

"Oh, so that's the kid."

"You know him?"

"Met his granddad once. Back in the day, he was Miami upper crust."

Both were silent, looking at the frozen image of Cameron Prince.

"And that severed arm? What do you make of it?"

"It's bullshit."

"Because there's no tool marks? No blood?"

"Well, there's that. Hell, I'm no medical guy, so I can't say absolutely. To me it doesn't look real, but, hey, the picture quality is crap. Reason it's bullshit is because no croc is going after somebody like that. It just flat isn't going to happen. Even a mother with her hatchlings, she's protective, yeah, on alert. She might snarl or do a quick face-off. But even then, you could step right on the old girl and ten times out of ten, all she'll do is bolt. They're shy as shit, want to be left alone. Now if that was an alligator, hell no, then you're talking serious damage to the human body."

Frank said, "In the movies there's always giant crocs sunning along the riverbank, they see some babe out in the middle of the river paddling her canoe, and all of them go sliding into the water and head after her. So that's just Hollywood garbage?"

"Those movies, it's usually the river Nile, someplace like that, darkest Africa. That would be *Crocodylus niloticus,* now there's your man-eater, the Nile croc. But the *Crocodylus acutus,* that's the American croc, its habitat is south Biscayne Bay, that's what we're looking at here. It's laid-back. Bashful."

"What else is out there in the cooling canals? They got sharks?"

"No sharks. Water's gotten too salty for them. But there's still some big-ass barracudas and gators back there. Shit, the gators and the crocs get into it sometimes. Got some World War Three territorial battles going on."

"So a body falls into the water, maybe a gator could've scarfed it up?"

"Could happen. Be pretty unlikely. Gators aren't going to be hanging around croc nesting sites. They'd give mother crocs a wide berth."

"So, bottom line, these crocs, the Americans, they're not man-eaters."

"Until this so-called attack happened, there'd never been a reported lethal encounter between croc and human in Florida. Not one, ever. Which means there's never been a reported case in all of America, since this is the only place in the damn country these beauties exist, mostly at Turkey Point, a few dozen roaming around Key Largo. Now you go down to Belize, that's a different story, there've been a few attacks by American crocs, but all of those were being fed regularly by humans in nature preserves or zoos or whatever, and the crocs lost their fear. That's when the fuckers get dangerous. Losing your fear of humans, that can be a serious issue."

Johnny rose from his pillow, popped the disc, and handed it to Sheffield. "That what you wanted to know?"

Frank stretched his back and groaned. His night with Nicole had strained some muscles. "Never lose your fear of humans. Words to live by."

"Always glad to help. You stay safe, pal."

TWENTY-TWO

BACK AT HIS OFFICE, SHEFFIELD gave Marta a fifth person for background checks. Leslie Levine. The dead biologist. Gone but not eaten.

He looked through the notes Marta had left on his desk, found the lead detective on the Marcus Bendell homicide, and called Detective Pedro Alonzo. After the prelims, Alonzo said, "Looks accidental. Guy was trying to rig up a line to bypass his meter, save himself a buck, he bumps the jumper cables against his ladder."

"ME agrees? That's how you're calling it, accidental?"

"Would be. Except for one thing."

"Which is?"

"First tell me why the feds are interested in this punk."

"Bendell was a snitch. He was inside a group we're interested in."

"An informant?"

"Low-rent tipster."

"You're not going to tell me what this group is?"

"If it becomes relevant, but right now, no. Sorry."

"Typical. You want what I got, but I don't get a peek the other way."

"It's an ongoing federal investigation, okay? Now what's the one thing that suggests Bendell's death was other than accidental?"

Alonzo was quiet for a moment, weighing his options. Then he sighed. "You know what electro gel is?"

"Why don't you tell me, Detective."

"Let's say you were going to climb up a ladder and fuck around with the power line running through your backyard. Before you climbed up that aluminum ladder, would you smear it with an electrical conducting agent?"

"On the ladder?"

"Same stuff they coat a cardiac patient's chest with before they shock him back to life."

"No, I don't think I would," Frank said.

"Me either. But this Bendell fellow, he apparently thought it was a good idea."

They talked awhile longer, Frank getting nothing more of substance, then he asked Alonzo to keep him abreast of developments. Alonzo said sure thing and hung up.

Frank tried Nicole's cell again and got the robot and hung up on the bitch.

At two, he met with the five SWAT guys he'd picked, told them to keep their calendars clear for a week from today, seventeenth through the nineteenth. Explained where they were headed, that the operation plan hadn't yet been charted out, but as soon as it was, he'd let them know and they'd have a longer sit-down.

All of them had done force-on-force drills before, and none was thrilled at the prospect of doing another.

Even super–gung ho Billy Dean Reynolds, the shortest but toughest guy on the team, red hair, green eyes, freckles, the kind of dude if you hit him in the forehead with a sledge, he'd go down, pop back up, and you hit him again and he'd pop up again and after that. The guy you wanted along, the guy who didn't quit.

Billy Dean stood in Frank's doorway after the others had drifted back to their cubicles and said, "The power plant, that place is a joke, Frank. My mother and her bridge group could knock that place over."

"It has to be done," Sheffield said. "We're trying to keep them honest."

"They're not honest to start with. Game is rigged. We could test them from now till the corn is tall and they'd never improve. Those security guys, I met a couple of them, they couldn't handle Barney's job in Mayberry."

"It'll be fine. After it's done, we'll all go out and have a pizza and down some cold ones, wash it all away. Keep the bounce in your step, Billy Dean."

Frank, the cheerleader, not believing a word he was saying. He felt himself rising out of his own body, looking down at himself, thinking, Who the hell is that guy conning Billy Dean? Is that me? Really?

Marta was in a blue pants suit today, one from her endless collection. After Billy Dean left she came in with the files for the Chee brothers, Cameron Prince, and Claude Sellers. She set them on the desk, stepped back, and gave him her secret smile.

He should never have told her about Nicole. Now he was going to get that smile all day, every day. Marta wanted him married. Worried it would shorten his life span if he stayed single. There were statistics about that. She'd cut out newspaper articles and left them on his desk. Single guys died early. Worse than smoking. What was he thinking?

Frank picked up the four folders, weighed them one-handed, and dropped them back on the desk. "That's it?"

"The Chee boys have been playing nice. Pauly's military record is thin, which to me is suspicious. You don't spend six years in the navy and have such a flimsy file unless you were doing something covert."

"You evaluated the files?"

"I evaluate everything," Marta said. "Does that make me bad?"

"Anything else?"

"NSA rejected the satellite-surveillance request, got too many military uses in play, tracking terrorists in Yemen, same old same old. Miami-Dade said if you wanted to rent one of their drones, you needed to call and discuss."

"And the boat?"

"Park Service would also like to talk to you, find out what you have in mind and how you plan on paying for it. The number is on the Post-it there."

"Let me ask you something, Marta. You ever wanted to just vanish, start over as somebody else?"

"Are you kidding? Who doesn't?"

"How would you do it?"

"Save up till I had forty thousand, enough to last six months, get new ID, new Social, a bus ticket to California, find a job cutting hair."

"You've thought this out."

"Haven't you?"

"Not in such detail."

"So is that helpful?"

"Would you consider staging your own death?"

She grimaced.

"Does that mean you wouldn't?"

"Well, it would be kinder. So your loved ones didn't have all those unanswered questions. Your spouse wasn't out driving around all day and night looking for you. My way would be easier to pull off, less likely to fail, but staging a death, it's actually the more considerate thing."

"Yeah," he said. "More considerate."

"That's all?"

Frank's eyes strayed to his window, afternoon clouds building over the Everglades. Ivan had moved away into the Gulf. Juanita was heading their way. They were in the cone of probability. "I need that background stuff on Leslie Levine. In particular, any relatives, loved ones, friends she had. The kind of person she might be trying to spare some emotional pain."

Marta left. Frank read the files. She was right, nothing much on Wally Chee, except some medical issues. A birth defect with his legs, which some pediatrician in New Mexico blamed on contaminated drinking water on the Navajo res where his people had lived for generations.

He and his brother had been raised by a single mom. As Marta had said, Pauly's military history was too light to be real. Heavily blue-penciled. Something worth checking.

Claude Sellers, now that shithead was intriguing.

Sellers had been with the power company all his working life. Started as a lineman, worked his way up to district supervisor of field maintenance, then jumped over to security, an odd zigzag that seemed to have no basis in new training.

Divorced four times. No children. Second marriage only lasted three months with a messy finale. A restraining order from the ex. No abuse charges filed, but there had to be some kind of harassment to get the restraining order. Claude, the bully, probably didn't take rejection well. Wife three and four survived a year with Claude before they bailed. Cycling through women. Fucking up, then fucking up again.

Sellers had a concealed-weapons permit, a mail-order college degree from some no-name place in Arizona. Never been arrested, rented a starter condo out in Kendall, where the young marrieds and recently divorced lived.

The thing that must've caught Marta's eye was his credit history. His score was so low, Claude couldn't have bought a toaster on layaway. The guy filed for Chapter 7 bankruptcy seven years ago, then filed under Chapter 13 last year. Wiping his debt slate clean twice. Frank double-checked and saw from the court records there was alimony in all four divorces.

Money problems. His salary from the power company was damn good, within a few thousand of what Frank made, the prick. But all that alimony was eating him alive.

Frank got out his legal pad, started jotting down the things that jumped out. Claude's money issues, the empty military record of Pauly Chee, the gel on the ladder, an informant dead, the video of an unlikely croc attack, Prince Key.

Marta buzzed and told him Angie Stevens was

waiting to see him, their top cybersleuth. Nice young woman, blond with a perky smile. Not a single tattoo showing anywhere, zero piercings, normal shoulder-length haircut. Nothing like the movies. More debutante than hacker.

Frank sketched out the situation, gave her the cyber-attack analysis sheet that Sheen had faxed over, and asked Angie if she could find some time this weekend to drive down to Turkey Point and check over the current security status of its computer network.

"If you don't have some kind of scheduling conflict," he said.

"You mean other than the big one-day sale at Macy's?" It sat there for a few seconds, then she beamed at him, a jokester. "Happy to do it, boss."

He was about to tell her to call him Frank, but Angie Stevens had already turned and walked out of his office without a good-bye. Frank thinking, There it was, the computer-nerd thing, the klutzy lack of social skills.

He buzzed Marta, told her to call their FBI liaison at the Pentagon, see if there was any more on Pauly Chee they could shake loose.

"Bottom of my list or top?"

"Tippy top," Frank said. "Try hard, stamp your feet if you have to."

He worked through the afternoon, running his own computer searches on the principals, hours slumped at the screen but finding nothing.

He killed his computer, shut his door, called Nicole's cell, and it rang three times. Frank, expecting the goddamn robot again, was about to slap the receiver down when he heard her voice, husky, different.

"I catch you at a bad time?" Frank said.

She cleared her throat, sounding almost normal when she said, "Hey, Frank. How's it going?"

Sheffield brushed aside the weirdness and asked what she was doing later.

TWENTY-THREE

"MY CALENDAR'S CLEAR," NICOLE SAID. "What do you have in mind?"

From the foot of the bed Claude Sellers shook his head. He wanted her to stay the night, finish what they'd started. The idiot had a few more gallons of horny juice stored up.

But, no, Nicole went on and made a date with Frank, while Claude, feeling snubbed, began to massage her right foot, then her left, working her toes, digging into the meat of her arches.

Ignoring him, Nicole was saying uh-huh and no and okay, but mainly listening, as Claude finished with her feet and started working up her right leg, kneading the knots in her calf muscles, then sliding his hand up farther, above her right knee, across the slick inner thighs, going to give her a little thrill while she listened to Sheffield.

Claude only made it a few inches before Nicole kicked him in the shoulder with her right foot, knocking him away, squinching up her pissed-off face, saying to Sheffield, "Okay, that's strange. They're not man-eaters?"

Claude slid off the bed and stood in her line of sight, swinging his wiener from side to side like a caveman with his club, playing around, making a pucker with his lips, trying to get Nicole to grin, but she looked at his dick and watched it going back and forth and said to Sheffield, "Sure, the Boater's Grill at six. No, no, make it six thirty, that's better. I have a couple of things to sort out. . . . Good, yeah, see you then."

She clicked off, set the phone aside, and said to Claude, "Okay, tell me, idiot child, why the hell did you smear the goddamn ladder with gel?"

Claude stopped swinging his wiener. "Just to be sure. Probably would've worked without it, but, you know, electricity can be unpredictable, so I went the extra mile."

"Jesus Christ. Conducting gel. That's blood in the water for Sheffield. He'll have a forensic hard-on until he has the serial number of the tube it came from."

"Speaking of which, tell me about Sheffield's pecker."

She stared at him as he climbed into the broken-open sheets beside her. "Christ, I should've seen what a moron you were from the first."

"But my pheromones overwhelmed you. You couldn't help yourself."

She pulled the sheet up to her neck, staring at the ceiling, trying to think, weigh the danger. Frank had confided in her about the gel and what he'd learned about the docile nature of crocs, his doubts about the video. Which meant he was still keeping her in the loop. Unless this was his ploy. Playing her, stringing her along until he had all the evidence he needed to come after her. She wasn't sure. She'd thought she had a good read on him, that he was under her influence. Now not so sure.

"Listen, sweet stuff," Claude said. "Let me remind

you. You seem to have forgotten a few things about our personal interconnectivity.

"You came to me because I'm the guy with the keys to the locks. The secret codes. I'm Mr. Open Sesame who can make everything you want happen. I can plant the eco-freaks' flash drive, I can get everyone worked up about that screen saver. I can let that guy, Wally whatever, have remote access so he can poke around the system. It was me, me and me alone, sweetheart, who set this deal in motion because that's what you wanted.

"And sure enough, the force-on-force drill is going down. A week from today, exactly the time frame you asked for. Me, Claude Sellers, the inside guy you needed so you could score the biggest takedown of a terrorist cell in US history. So you could be a hero, strap a booster rocket on your stalled-out career. You used me and you're still using me, which, by the way, puts me at serious risk of incarceration, but am I complaining? No, because the quid pro quo, sweet cheeks, the tit for tat, is that I get to use your sweet, tight body for my gratification. Which, I got to admit, so far is worth putting my life in serious jeopardy.

"And the gel, hey, that's nothing. I used it because I wanted to be a hundred percent sure Bendell got zapped. So what if special asshole in charge Sheffield is suspicious? Big fucking whoop. We knew from the get-go that would happen.

"The logical deduction is the ELF guys found out they had a snitch in their midst, so they exterminated his ass. So what if there was gel? It's ELF gel. It's on them. Does that help explain it to you, sweetness? Does that help put your fears to rest?"

She hated to admit it, but Claude was right. Right

about everything. She felt her body relax. Still anxious, still needing to sort it through one more time, make sure she had it all set perfectly in place, but not now. Later. When she was alone, when she could think. Not with this meathead grinning at her.

"Okay, good, we got that settled," he said. "Now tell me about Sheffield's cock."

"You're fourteen years old."

"So?"

"Not even that. You're twelve."

"How big is it? Go on, tell me. I can take it."

"I warned you from the beginning, Claude. I told you I'd already been with Frank once, and if things worked out, we were going to be intimate again. You said fine. You didn't mind. So cut the jealousy shit."

"It's bigger, isn't it? That's why you don't want to talk about it."

"I didn't notice his dick."

"You were with him all night and didn't notice the thing sliding in and out of you? The thing you had in your mouth when he was busting a nut?"

"It was normal. Average, nothing unique about it."

"Fatter or skinnier or identical to me?"

"I'm not doing this."

"'Cause I'm pretty thick myself, right? Fatter is better than longer. I never met a woman thought otherwise."

"He's a pencil dick. Okay, Claude? A pencil dick."

"Number two pencil?"

"Yes, that's right, superskinny. Kind you can break in one hand. And you're thick as a German salami. Okay, you happy now?"

"Tell me you're not sweet on him."

"What matters is, he's sweet on me."

"Is he?"

"Most definitely."

"Okay, then, I'm not jealous anymore. I'm over it. I was, but now I'm okay. I'm totally secure. I know you're sacrificing your sexual dignity for the plan, to get the big advancement, office with a view. I know that. So I'm not jealous."

As he cuddled beside her, pressed his cheek against her left breast, Nicole stifled a shudder, took a long breath, forced herself to stay loose because he was right, damn it, right about her needing him, even if it meant she had to endure his bungling sex, his juvenile insecurities, his rancid Old Spice smell. She'd become a pro at swallowing her disgust.

Reminding herself, as she did so often, that this degradation would be purified later. She would absolve herself, isolate these hours with Claude, keep them compartmentalized. A skill she'd begun to develop a decade earlier, on her first job out of college.

Assistant to the senior special agent at GAO, a step above a flunky. Herbert Marshall, an investigator of white-collar crimes, waste, fraud, abuse, government corruption. Less than a year into that first job, off in Las Vegas at the yearly GAO convention, she'd joined Herbert in the hotel bar. She'd expected the whole gang, but it was just the two of them. Nicole sipped a martini. She wasn't a drinker, never had been. But after two sips the night was an ugly whirl of violent colors and music and noisy voices, and she woke in her hotel bed at ten the next morning in agony.

Remembering nothing after the second swallow, but feeling the ripping ache between her legs. She touched herself, screamed at the blood, screamed when the hotel doctor touched her, screamed again at the hospital. Herbert showed up, acting horrified, telling the female police detective that he'd helped her back to her room the night before, that she was drunk. There'd been no sex. None at all. He claimed Nicole had tried to kiss him, said she wanted to party, do the town, but he refused. A happily married man.

Her urine test was positive for roofies. Drugged and raped, the physician said, multiple times. Bruised cervix, a tear in the posterior fourchette. Injuries that would take months to heal. Others that never would.

The detective urged her to press charges against Herbert, but she didn't want to expose herself to the public shit that was sure to follow, that would dog her forever, stain her career.

She stayed on the job, applied for promotions, transfers, but was passed over and passed over again. Her workload increased. Herbert ignored her. For a year she hung on, and then 9/11 came, the Twin Towers went down. Overnight new federal agencies were born, new opportunities. She moved to NIPC, a demotion, a pay cut. But it was work.

A month on the job, her new boss hit on her. She was aloof, simmering with fury but hiding it. When he persisted, she made a decision that altered her trajectory.

She flirted back, discreetly at first, bedroom eyes, keeping a tantalizing distance. A mirage, a temptress, beguiling insinuations that were never kept. The false promise of promiscuity. She kept him in a low-grade swoon and won a small upgrade and another.

She shifted departments. Repeated the process. The alluring word, the dangled bait, the fleeting smile, beckoning but withholding. Same thing again after that. Seduction became work. Work became seduction.

Cold inside, fueled by hate and hurt, cunning, aloof, moving ahead step by bewitching step. The look that hinted more, the quick touch on hand and arm that was almost a caress, the touch that seemed certain to lead to sex. But never did.

Her power grew. GS-9, GS-10, working up the pay grades. Her own titillating revenge. Making her giddy, a little crazy, her one and only goal was to rise so high that she was invulnerable, that she could lift her foot and grind them under her heel, any of them. All of them.

When she crossed the line, let one of them into her bed, she remained two steps removed, watching from afar. Keeping her true self sober and safe. Sex was only to close the deal, to set the hook deeper, to move up and up again. She thought of her vagina as a wound that never healed.

What shame she felt she put into boxes. She assembled one for Herbert, one for each who followed. She stacked the boxes neatly, edge to edge, shelved them in the far back corner of her history where they gathered the dust of forgetfulness. Claude now had a box. When it was time, she would seal it, set it beside the others, perfectly aligned in the airless vault. The archives of her humiliations and her triumphs.

Someday soon, Sheffield would have his, too, take his place on the shelf.

She turned to Claude. "Frank's suspicious about the video, about Leslie Levine. He's consulted with some croc expert. He thinks she could still be alive, the whole croc attack was staged. This isn't good."

"Let him be suspicious. Not a problem. What's he going to do?"

"He could send SWAT out to Prince Key. Take down the operation."

"I could intervene," Claude said.

"What?"

"Distract him. I'm good at distracting."

His lips grazed her nipple, a damp nibble. Again she suppressed a cringe, looked down at his slick scalp. She touched it with her fingertips. Knowing he liked that, stroking with her palm against the bristles.

"Distract him how?"

"Put a hurt on him. Go to his place, bash him around, send him to the emergency room. Knock that probable-cause shit right out of his head."

Her hand stopped moving against his head.

"What do you say, Nicky? Can I do it? Bust him up?"

"We need Frank. You can't put him out of action. Absolutely not."

"I can modulate my behavior. I can be very nuanced."

She considered it, then went back to stroking his head.

"So come on, Nicky, give me the green light."

"I'm thinking."

They lay still for a while. Nicole listening to the white noise of traffic out on Kendall Drive. Television chatter coming from the apartment above.

She nudged Claude away, reached over to the side table, and retrieved her phone and purse. She propped herself up against a pillow. Claude drawing back, watching her.

"What're you doing?"

"Bendell told you there was another snitch on Prince Key. We need to find out who it is and remove him."

"How you going to manage that?"

She dug through her purse, found the index card where she'd scribbled the numbers, and dialed the first one.

Got an old Cuban lady, hung up.

Dialed the second. A pizza place on Key Biscayne.

The third was a department at the FBI. She disconnected quickly. That same number appeared twelve times. Frank's office.

"These are Sheffield's recent calls. One of these is his guy. Bendell said the guy called Frank from out on the island, so it wasn't long ago. I've got every number for the last week. Incoming and outgoing. Twenty-two of them."

The next five numbers were from some Miami-Dade building inspector. Scratch those. Nicole dialed the next number, got a car repair shop, hung up.

The next was next to last on her list. It rang five times, then went to voice mail. A guy sounding rushed, out of breath.

"Hi, listen, I'm going away for a while. Taking a hiatus from the show, I'm not sure when I'll be back. If this is Mom, don't worry. I'm safe. It's all cool. I'm doing something I've been wanting to do for a long time, something important. Fill you in later. Don't worry, really. So leave a message if you want. You know the drill."

She clicked off.

She called the last number, the pizza parlor again. Frank liked his pie.

"This is him." She pointed at the phone number on her list, the hiatus guy.

"Yeah?"

"Contact Leslie. Have her call this number, she's going to recognize the guy's voice. She needs to eliminate him, whoever it is. Let her know that. Eliminate him immediately."

"And Sheffield? If he's laid up, he's not sending SWAT anywhere."

Nicole set the phone aside. Put the index card back in her purse. She settled back against the pillow.

She considered it a minute more, then turned and looked at Claude, reaching out beneath the sheets and finding him. "Call Leslie, eliminate this guy," she said quietly. "I'll handle Frank."

Sheffield was still at his desk, smiling to himself, when Marta cleared her throat in his doorway. She was holding her dime-store steno notebook.

"You got two calls while you were chatting."

"Tell me you weren't listening in, Marta."

"I never press my ear to the wall. But if you want total privacy, you should consider soundproofing."

Sheffield shook his head. He and Marta were hopelessly enmeshed. "And the calls?"

"I contacted Agent Sanford about the flyover of Prince Key. He called back to say he'll do it later this afternoon if that's okay. If you want him to shoot anything specific, you should ring him. He gave me his cell."

"Call him back, Marta. I want shots of the island, surrounding waters. Boats, people, dwellings. Whatever's down there. No more than two passes, nothing that would arouse suspicion on the ground."

While she scribbled on her pad, she said, "The second call, that's the intriguing one."

"Okay."

"From NCIS, Threat Management Unit. Special Agent Zach Magnuson. Said to tell you it was urgent. Call as soon as you're off the phone. It's Pauly Chee. The calls I made about him, I guess it rang someone's alarm."

"Well, well."

"Yes," Marta said. "This is heating up. No?"

Frank picked up the phone, smiled at Marta, and waited until she was out the door before he dialed.

Twenty minutes later, he hung up, rocked back in his chair, and stared at his yellow legal pad.

While the special agent was speaking, Frank had scribbled a list:

1. Paul Chee, E-6 Petty Officer First Class, SEAL team 2
2. Munitions specialist
3. Desertion and Possible Larceny of Government Property
4. Heptanitrocubane HpNC—most powerful non-nuclear explosive compound
5. Theft of 7 pounds, Naval Weapons Station Seal Beach, CA
6. Magnuson arrives Miami Saturday sixish.
7. Bringing NCIS team, meet Saturday 8PM at 4 Seasons
8. Set up SWAT for Sunday night—Prince Key takedown

"So?" Marta was standing in the doorway.

Frank said nothing, his eyes still fixed on the list.

Marta walked over to his desk. "I guess it must be exciting news."

"Yeah?" He looked up. "How can you tell?"

"On your arms, the goose bumps."

TWENTY-FOUR

IT WAS LATE AFTERNOON, THE sun grazing the tops of the mangroves, golden arrows of sunlight firing through the dense foliage. Light wind from the east, new moon, tide coming in. Perfect fishing weather.

He'd convinced Leslie that after they finished their construction project, he should take the guys out, catch tonight's dinner. Fresh fish instead of the fast-food shit the group was surviving on. Teach them how to cast the bait net, get some pilchards, threadfin herring, or minnows, then find a coral head or patch of turtle grass, snag some snappers.

Suspicious at first, Leslie finally relented. Gave him a sharp, cautionary look, then headed off in her flats boat on an errand she didn't reveal. Cameron was gone, too. Shortly after a breakfast of cold pizza slices from the ice chest, he'd paddled away to work at the power plant's biology lab. Staying with his routine, keeping up appearances.

At the moment just the four of them were on the island, and it seemed unlikely Thorn would have a better chance to make a break.

Only steps from where they stood, the pry bar was

buried in the sand, but going for it, then taking on both Chee brothers hand to hand was too risky. Once they were out on the water, though, the balance of power would shift. The sea was Thorn's second home. And he had a plan, nothing fancy, a way to stall the Chees long enough for him and Flynn to get a decent head start.

He knew he'd get one chance and only one. If he blew it, there'd be no democratic vote this time. And he had to brace himself for the prospect that Flynn might side with the others. If that was how it went down, Thorn was prepared to leave Flynn behind, return as fast as possible with backup.

While Pauly hauled the last of the four kayaks from the storage rack, his brother stood at the shore practicing with the cast net—trying to sail it out into the cove, but fumbling yet again.

At the waterline sat the slatted box they'd spent most of the day constructing. Thorn guided them through Leslie's blueprint, making use of the handsaws she provided, the hammers and nails. It was a rectangular cage, so large it would be a tight squeeze in the bed of a pickup.

Leslie didn't say what it was for, just that it would play a role in their plan. To Thorn it resembled an over-size lobster trap.

Thorn stepped over to Wally as he was hauling in the handline, once again the entire rig snarled in a mad tangle of loops and netting, the lead weights knotted in a clump.

Six times he'd failed, but each time Wally dragged the net to shore, methodically untangled it, and hurled it again—failing, failing, failing, but on a compulsive mission to get it right.

Thorn asked Wally if he wanted to walk through it one more time.

"Fucking thing is impossible."

"Loop the handline around your left wrist, then take the line and make even coils, and hold the horn of the net in your left hand."

Wally followed the instructions with the grim focus of a child tying his shoelaces for the first time.

Thorn walked him through it again. Wally's face was flushed from the exertion, the waxy skin shining and his brutish eyes crinkled with focus. Wearing yellow Bermuda shorts and a black T-shirt and leather sandals with white socks, Wally struck Thorn as oddly childish, as if perhaps a mangled gene had scrambled his code. His focus shifted continually while he glowered and muttered below his breath as if reciting some profane nursery rhyme.

"Okay, last step. Reach down, pinch the skirt about midway, and take one of the sinkers between your teeth."

"This is where I fuck up. You need three hands."

Wally lifted the edge of the net and bit on one of the lead weights that fringed the bottom, the rest of the net balancing precariously in both hands.

"You're almost there. Now rotate to your left, pull the net back, and throw it like hitting a backhand in tennis. Release everything at once, except the handline."

Wally pivoted left and swung back around, lofting the net out into the cove. It swelled open nicely this time, a ten-foot, perfect circle parachuting into the water and sinking fast.

"Now hit the handline hard and haul it in."

"I did it," Wally yelled. "Hey, Pauly, I fucking did it." Wally dragged the net up onto the beach. A couple of finger mullet flopped on the sand at his feet and wriggled back into the dark water of the cove. "Hey, Pauly. I caught some goddamn bait. Look at this shit. I'm fucking Hemingway."

While Wally wrestled with the net, Thorn edged over to Flynn and said, his voice low, "I'm making a break. You with me?"

Flynn swallowed hard as if slugging down a dose of bitter medicine.

Thorn lay a hand on his son's shoulders and Flynn tensed at his touch. "This stunt won't work. You'll go to jail, people could get hurt."

"You've done worse."

"And I regretted it later. We need to get out of here."

"Go ahead. I'm staying."

"You're making a mistake."

"You're a goddamn bully, you know that?" Flynn gave Thorn a shove and stepped away.

Hell, the kid was right. Flynn was an adult. Years of tough decisions behind him, a mature, sensible man who'd succeeded in a competitive business. Which was a shitload more than Thorn could say.

Sure, without meaning to, Thorn had become an authority on twisted fucks like Wally and Pauly and the brutal games they played. But what kind of expertise was that? What rights did it give him to dictate to Flynn?

Maybe, in the last year, all those mumbling monologues Thorn had carried on with an absent Flynn had seduced Thorn into believing he and his son had forged a real connection. When the fact was, Flynn Moss was still a stranger. Aside from biology, Thorn wasn't the kid's father in any meaningful way. He was just a guy who'd stumbled into the young man's path.

Thorn's adoptive father, Dr. Bill Truman, had guided Thorn with little more than a nod, a rare word of support or praise, never a heavy hand. Thorn's notion of manliness, his sense of honor and loyalty, were not forged from strong-armed discipline or overbearing lectures.

Then again, could he just let this gang of zealots put Flynn's life in peril? Wasn't that the crucial job of any father, to protect his kids? Wasn't that the whole goddamn point of parenting? Take all necessary actions to spare the kid pain even if the kid was an adult, even if bullying was required?

When Pauly had all four kayaks nosed into the water, the four of them spent a few minutes stowing the rods in the tight compartments, then one by one they climbed into the cockpits and settled in. Thorn arranged the cast net in the forward hold.

They rowed out of the cove and into the narrow creek that snaked to the bay. Wally leading, Flynn following close, with Thorn tucked in behind his son. Thorn glanced back to see Pauly bringing up the rear, paddling strongly and easily.

In fifteen minutes they reached the bay, emerging on the ocean side of Prince Key. To their west the nuke plant was hidden behind the tall trees of the island. Farther to their south was the long span of Card Sound Bridge, and beyond that, out of sight, lay Key Largo, with its channels and back bays and creeks, a hundred familiar places to hide. But Key Largo was at least ten miles off. An impossible distance.

The shortest route to safety was to head a mile south, duck into the main channel at the Ocean Reef Club, and get his ass to the dock at the oceanside marina, where armed security officers patrolled day and night.

"Okay, smart guy," Pauly said. "Do your thing."

The wind was light, the water close to shore with barely a chop, while farther out in the ocean was a polished slab of cobalt spangled with silver coins of light, a flawless slick that stretched endlessly toward the horizon.

A dying wave from the wake of a distant cabin cruiser lifted the four kayaks and rolled on toward Prince Key, carrying with it a mat of seaweed and a battered styrofoam cup. Six feet down the bottom was visible, a couple of coral heads and spatters of white sand where minnows darted across the open ground, exposed for a blink before disappearing into the swaying patches of turtle grass. The hot summer air was thick with the vinegar scent of barnacles on the roots of the mangroves exposed by the not-yet-risen tide. And a sharp stink came from the trees along the shoreline where roosting pelicans had smeared the upper leaves with white streaks of guano.

Thorn scanned the adjacent waters, choosing a spot as distant from Prince Key as he thought he could sell to Pauly.

"Over there," he said, motioning south.

"Get on with it." Pauly fell in behind him.

Passing Flynn, Thorn glanced his way, but couldn't read him.

Pauly kept pace with Thorn, allowing no distance to grow between their kayaks. Stroke by stroke Thorn led them farther from Prince Key.

One cast, that's all he needed. Best cast he'd ever made.

Thorn pictured the perfect layout of the four kayaks, and how it would work, step by step, a sharp, vivid scene without a lot of fuss. Cast the bait net once, then when everyone's guard was down, he'd turn and lasso Pauly, hit the handline hard, cinch the rope, add a hard knot, and Pauly would be trussed up like a holiday turkey.

While Pauly fought the netting, deal with Wally. Whack him overboard, shove his kayak out to sea. And get the hell out of there.

Just one good cast, something he'd done a thousand times.

Thorn pointed toward a patch of ruffled water. "Bait," he said, giving Flynn a quick look. *You with me?*

And got no response.

A mass of gunpowder-gray clouds was scudding out of the west, dimming the sun and turning the blue sea to pewter as if nature were having the same grim mood swing as Thorn.

The arrangement of the boats he'd been picturing wasn't happening. The rising wind had spread the kayaks helter-skelter. Pauly was drifting farther from the group, almost out of range.

Thorn cast the net out to the open water and hauled it in. On that throw he captured a single needlefish, which squirted through the knotted cords as he drew the net close.

"This is fucked," Wally said. "We'll be out here all night."

"Fishing takes patience," Thorn said.

"Fuck patience. Patience is for assholes with nothing better to do."

Thorn gathered the net and got set. He took a second to arrange his grip and aim, then swiveled in the cockpit and launched the net.

Pauly saw it coming, jammed his paddle deep, and

tried to scoot out of range, but Thorn had guessed he'd respond that way and led him by a few feet. The net fluttered around him like a lariat over the horns of a rodeo bull.

But as Thorn was yanking the handline to tighten the noose, Flynn slid next to Pauly's kayak, dropped his paddle, took hold of the bait net, and whisked it off.

"Jesus, Thorn," Flynn said. "I thought you were good at this."

Pauly looked Thorn's way, his mouth widening a fraction. A cramped smile. "Nice try, hotshot."

"It was the wind," Flynn said.

"Sure it was," said Pauly. "The wind."

Hand over hand Thorn was dragging in the net when a flats boat idled into view from the opening of Pumpkin Creek, then with a roar, it rose up on plane and in a handful of seconds was veering alongside him, its wake rocking Thorn's kayak so hard he had to grip the sides to keep from capsizing.

Wearing a broad-brimmed sunhat, Leslie Levine stood at the wheel of her Whipray. The bow of Thorn's kayak scraped hard against its sleek white hull. She throttled back and maneuvered the boat out of range.

On her face was the kind of unruffled look you'd expect from some forgiving kindergarten teacher who dealt every hour of every working day with the shortcomings of her wayward charges.

"Any luck?" she said.

Wally opened his mouth to rat Thorn out, but Pauly cut a stony look his way and he halted.

"We're just getting started," Thorn said.

"There's plenty of bait around," said Flynn. "Looks promising."

"So there's no trouble, Pauly?"

Pauly looked at her and grunted. Nothing he couldn't handle.

"I'll get the grill ready," she said. "We'll have a cookout."

Wally was staring at each of them in turn, trying to decipher the meaning of this moment. Not sure what he was missing. Thorn was just as mystified. Pauly was giving him a pass. A simple word from him and Thorn was done.

"You need me to stick around, make sure everything goes smoothly?"

"Got it covered," Pauly said.

As Leslie moved her hand to the throttle, out in the western sky, breaking through the thickening clouds, a single-engine Cessna headed toward them, swooping low, thundering only a few hundred feet overhead, then continuing a mile or so out over the Atlantic and circling back for another pass over the island before it headed back in the direction it had come.

Leslie watched it disappear, then took another look at the four of them and kicked the skiff up on plane and roared off.

In the next twenty minutes, as the tide was coming in, Thorn nabbed a dozen glassy minnows and two stray ballyhoo. He handed out the bait and they fished until twilight.

Slow at first, until they found a rocky patch with a hungry school of gray snappers and some white grunts and a good-size spotted sea trout. Before they were done, even Wally caught a lane snapper. A dozen fish in all.

Paddling back in the gathering darkness, Thorn drew alongside Pauly.

Around them, in the thickening dusk, the bay glowed bluish silver as if the water were hoarding the last seconds of daylight within its depths.

"So this was a test," Thorn said. "See if I'd try to make a run for it."

"She wants to trust you," Pauly said. "She thinks you're hot shit."

"Why'd you give me a pass?"

"We need six people to make this work. Don't want it to fall apart."

Pauly drew his paddle out of the water, looking Thorn in the eyes as they coasted side by side.

"Plus I'm sick of those turkey subs."

They stroked in unison for a while.

"Good thing we caught fish then," Thorn said.

Not looking over, Pauly said, "Must be your lucky day."

TWENTY-FIVE

SOMETHING WAS MISSING WITH THE sex. Like that Chinese-food thing, gulping down a five-course meal, ten minutes later he was famished. His body yearning for nourishment.

Or maybe Nicole had just revved up Sheffield's appetite so high, now he was hungry all the time. He couldn't tell. And sure as hell didn't want to believe anything was wrong. Didn't want to analyze and overthink the whole thing and destroy it.

Probably it was just his own free-floating doubt, not sure what a smart, attractive lady such as her found so appealing about a man nearly twice her age, a man who had just huffed toward the finish line of yet another romp.

Lolling side by side in the mangled sheets, they stared up at the ceiling.

It was Saturday, early afternoon. The beach in full weekend roar. Fifty yards away on the wide stretch of white sand, competing music blared. Rap, rock, salsa. Laughter, the rolling crash of surf. Out his window he could see some idiot throwing bread up into a screaming cyclone of gulls.

"You need to paint something up there." Nicole pointed at the white plaster. "Clouds or stars or the moon."

"On the ceiling?"

"Or maybe a mirror."

"You find my ceiling boring?"

"I wouldn't say that. But it wouldn't hurt to jazz it up."

"I'm pretty jazzed up as it is. I think I just topped my personal best."

"You keep records on your sexual exploits?"

"Don't you?"

"Oh, great. Are we about to have the sexual-history conversation? Compare our lifetime totals?"

"You mean I'm not your first?"

"What matters, Frank, is being the last."

He liked that. Something to shoot for. The one that didn't get away.

More staring at the ceiling.

"A mirror would be nice," he said. "I could see all your angles at once."

"I like to think I've got more angles than that."

"Oh, really? Angles I haven't seen?"

"Angles nobody's seen."

"You going to show me? Or they off-limits?"

"This is why I don't like postcoital conversations."

"All our conversations are postcoital."

Droning overhead, one of those slow-moving planes hauling a banner.

"A mirror up there, I'd always be worried it'd come crashing down."

"You worry about things like that, Frank? You have anxiety issues I should know about?"

"I've made a pretty good career out of worrying."

"Maybe we should just lie here and be quiet."

"What'd you mean about the angles?"

"See, that's what I'm talking about. Frank-the-interrogator, can't shut it off, got to keep digging. We should just shut up till the rush subsides and we're normal again. Right now we're too naked. We shouldn't talk."

Can you be too naked? Frank wanted to say, but didn't.

He was silent, staring at the white ceiling. Wondering what they'd just been talking about. How it had turned testy so fast. Trying to run it back, hear it again, tease out the hidden messages. But he was too fuzzy-headed, too mellow. But still, something was off. Something he couldn't name, didn't want to name. If he could only shut down that part of his brain, the part that was always itching to go one layer deeper, peel the onion all the way to the pearl, he'd be a happier guy. A different guy, too. Dumber, but happier.

They napped for a while. Frank woke and watched her sleeping. Then lay back and went away for half an hour. A lazy Saturday.

When he woke again, she was in the tiny living room watching tennis on his TV. Wearing one of his T-shirts, an old, paint-spattered one he'd picked up in Cabo San Lucas years ago.

He stood in the doorway and watched. It was some tennis match. Two blond banshees screaming when they hammered the ball, two different shrieks. One a two-part woo-hoo and the other more like an orgasmic wail.

He went back into the bedroom, pulled on a pair of shorts and a T-shirt. The bureau drawer was still open from Nicole's helping herself. She hadn't asked where he kept his T-shirts. She must've looked through his drawers till she found the one she was wearing. Making herself right at home at the Silver Sands, room 106. Which Frank didn't mind at all.

"You a tennis fan?"

"It's the channel that was on."

"Play any sports?"

"StairMaster. Is that a sport?"

"If it makes you sweat, I think it qualifies."

"Well, if that's all it takes, then August in Miami, standing around in the shade, that's an Olympic event."

She looked back at him and gave him a smile.

"Something I wanted to show you," he said.

"Oh, good. I was afraid I'd seen everything you have."

Frank retrieved his briefcase from the bedroom, laid it on the coffee table, and dug out a manila folder.

"Couldn't get NSA to cooperate with satellite imagery, and Miami PD wanted too much for their drone. Anyway, that fricking thing is so loud they'd hear it coming a mile away. So one of my guys, Sanford, he's got his own Cessna, he did a flyover yesterday. Slid these under the door this morning while we were otherwise engaged."

Frank laid the stack of photos out on the console seat, dealt the top one.

Four black kayaks trailed a white fishing skiff, Prince Key's eastern coastline visible at the edge of the shot.

"Four guys and someone in a floppy hat driving the flats boat."

"So?"

Frank put that one on the bottom of the stack and held up the next.

The island itself from about two or three hundred feet.

"Sanford came in lower than I wanted. Not far over the trees."

"It's out of focus."

"The other ones are better."

They looked through the rest of the shots. One small tent was on the island, and a much larger one, a single solar panel, and other structures.

"Looks like an obstacle course," Frank said. "Like they're training for something. A wall, a balance beam, old tires for agility drills."

She was silent.

"And the kayaks, that's interesting."

"What about them?"

"You ever seen a black kayak?"

"Why? Is that unusual?"

"I'd say so," he said. "Normally they're bright red, yellow, orange, colors you can see from a distance, so you don't get run down by speedboats. Black is rare. It suggests to me they may have done a custom paint job, picked black so they can disappear in the dusk or at night."

"ELF is going to attack the nuke plant at night? That's what you're suggesting? Converge in kayaks."

"I'm just thinking out loud, brainstorming. What's wrong? This is your operation. You don't seem very engaged."

"It *was* my operation. Now I'm not sure."

"You think I'm running off with it."

"You had a plane do a flyover and didn't tell me. You talked to some croc expert, you interviewed Killibrew about the Levine case, and the other detective assigned to Bendell's murder. Is there anything else you haven't told me about my case?"

"These photos," Frank said. "It looks to me like they might be doing some kind of maneuver. Training exercises."

"You didn't answer my question."

Sheffield looked at the tennis players, whooping at every shot. "There's an agent from NCIS coming in tonight. We'll be meeting at the downtown Four Seasons, eight o'clock. My SWAT guys will be there, and this agent is bringing his guys. He wants to hit Prince Key tomorrow night."

"Jesus, Frank. You're just dropping this on me. This fait accompli. No discussion, nothing. What the hell is going on?"

"The ante has just gone up."

"Quit playing with me, Frank. What's this about?"

"You ever hear of a chemical compound called HpNC?"

She stared at him, her lips pressed into a flat line as if she were holding back a spew of curses.

"It's an experimental high explosive," Frank said. "Makes dynamite and TNT, C-4, Semtex, look like firecrackers."

Nicole pushed the hair from her face and stared at Frank.

"This NCIS guy is going to fill us in tonight. Now you'reu p-to-date."

She said thanks, but it didn't sound as if her heart was in it.

Six calls, no pickups. Claude was sitting at the bar at his favorite strip club, Stir Crazy, staring up at the skinny girl with angel wings tattooed on her shoulder blades, watching her hump a silver pole.

He dialed Leslie's number again, and again got nothing. Straight to voice mail. He clicked off. He'd already left three messages. He tried another text, sending the phone number Nicole had given him, the traitor working with the FBI. Then typing *Call this #. This guy's a spy. Off him.*

While he was typing, another hoochie mama came up to Claude and pressed her bare boobs against his arm.

"Nice look," she said. Reaching out, toying with the tips of his bolo tie.

"My fashion statement."

"Yeah? What's it say about you?"

"I'm not your average cowboy."

"You look lonely, hun. You want a private dance?"

Claude leaned back and checked her out. Tight body, gym rat. Not more than twenty-five. Pretty brown eyes, kinky black hair gelled smooth.

Claude pressed SEND and heard the text whoosh away.

"Three dances," Claude said. "Twenty bucks."

"Dream on, sweetie."

"Twenty-five."

"That'll get you one."

"It's a long time till payday, sweet cheeks. I'm living on PB and J as it is."

"Time's are tough all over," the stripper said.

"How 'bout two for thirty?"

The girl frowned and her eyes strayed down the bar to the next chump.

"Thirty for two, and I'll give you a tip up front," Claude said.

"Yeah? What kind of tip?"

"Floss every day, and you won't be spitting out all those stupid gold teeth when you turn thirty."

Claude slid off the stool, walked toward the exit, the stripper shouting at him that he smelled like a bucket of shit.

He stood in the parking lot next to Dixie Highway, thinking about Sheffield and Nicole. Thinking about them together last night and today. Then he bent his head to the side and sniffed the shoulder of his checked shirt.

Hell, the stripper was right. He did smell pretty ripe. Maybe it was only his imagination but he believed he detected a lingering trace of Marcus Bendell, the human smoke bomb.

Which gave him an idea.

TWENTY-SIX

AT EIGHT ON SATURDAY EVENING, Magnuson and
his men were waiting for Sheffield in the sixth-floor
conference room of the downtown Four Seasons. Pan-
eled walls, halogen lighting turned high, four long tables
squared up in the center, covered with white tablecloths,
each place setting with a bottle of Evian water, a leather-
bound notebook, and a laptop computer.

Special Agent Magnuson was about Sheffield's
height but ran twenty pounds lighter and maybe ten
years younger. As gaunt and sturdy as a Tour de France
bike racer. He had white-blond hair and his pale blue
eyes were probing and stern. Lips so thin, his mouth
resembled a knife slit.

He shook Sheffield's hand, gripping with excessive
force, then introduced his three-man team. Rogers, Har-
ris, Pipes.

He and his men were freshly barbered and decked
out in versions of the same outfit. Spit-shined shoes,
khaki trousers, and dark polos that hugged their brawny
physiques. Behind him Sheffield's SWAT team filed in
a ragtag bunch. They checked out the competition,
whispering remarks to one another. His guys looked as

if they'd been called away from a variety of Saturday activities. Backyard barbecues, movie dates, yard chores, and little Billy Dean Reynolds dressed as if he'd spent the day busting a string of wild broncos. Dusty jeans, beat-up cowboy boots, a red long-sleeve shirt with white pearl buttons.

After everyone had shaken hands and taken their seats, Nicole appeared in the doorway, standing for a moment in a black tailored suit, her hair piled up and pinned with two strands broken free and framing her face. She struck a pose that was both businesslike and suggestive, as if this very professional woman had just rolled out of bed after hours of spirited lovemaking, which Frank knew was exactly the case.

She walked over to Frank and he introduced her to Magnuson, who seemed utterly unaffected by her charms. Not so with the other eight men, who watched with various degrees of restraint as Nicole walked to one of the last open seats and took her place behind a laptop.

The meeting lasted an hour. Magnuson ran the show, laid out the plan, explained the seriousness of taking down this target.

Paul Chee was a master bombmaker who'd been trained by the best demolition experts the navy had. He'd demonstrated extraordinary skill at both disassembling and assembling munitions of every kind. He'd defused and dismantled IEDs in Iraq and Afghanistan and grenades and unexploded artillery shells on battlefields and in sensitive public locations throughout Europe. He'd also planted highly sophisticated explosive devices in a variety of black-ops maneuvers that were classified but which Magnuson hinted were highly successful in removing leaders of various terrorist organizations.

Sheffield's guys listened, no questions, no whispering. The NCIS guys had obviously already been briefed on Chee's history, but they kept their eyes fixed on Magnuson. A disciplined bunch.

"During his time as a SEAL, he acquired the reputation for slipping in and out of hot zones with such stealth that some of his buddies began to consider his abilities supernatural. Now that Chee is on the run and has affiliated himself with a terrorist group, he's still living up to that reputation.

"Four times in the last two years we've had him in our sights, and when we moved in, he's eluded capture. It is important to note that after each of those close calls, he has dropped off the radar for sustained periods."

Magnuson played a series of headshots of Paul Chee on the laptops. An exotically handsome man. The Navajo blood was clear, but his Anglo genes softened the angles in his face so he might easily pass for Greek or Italian. A strong nose, hard-edged cheekbones, dark, intelligent eyes, lips that seemed sensuous in some shots, severe in others. Chee might have impersonated an international banker, a manual laborer, or even a high-fashion model.

"He's physically strong, adept at martial arts, in excellent health. He's a formidable enemy on any field of battle. But the fact that we believe he has in his possession several pounds of HpNC puts him at the very top of our list. HpNC was first synthesized in a lab in California a few years ago. It remains the most dangerous explosive in our arsenal, the one with the greatest density of any nonnuclear device."

Magnuson called their attention to a series of videos on their laptops.

The clips featured steel-reinforced concrete walls, extrahardened and cast in place, built specifically to withstand direct assault. The kind of wall that surrounded military complexes, diplomatic stations, and the White House.

These demonstrations had taken place at a military testing range in a desert setting where six walls of this type were subjected to different explosive assaults. TNT, dynamite, C-4, Semtex, HMX, and finally HpNC. In the first four cases, after the blasts, the walls were ruptured to some degree, but no breach was made in the concrete.

In the next-to-the-last clip, the HMX opened a hole that a man might have slithered through, but the structural integrity of the wall remained firm.

"Now this is why we're concerned," Magnuson said. "HpNC is a different animal."

And, yeah, the final detonation was something else entirely. No dust and debris sprayed into an explosive cloud. There was simply a bright flash, a whoosh. After the air cleared, only the foundation of the concrete wall remained among some smoldering rubble.

"The explosive charge used in this final test consisted of a half pound of HpNC. Like most military explosives, it is detonator sensitive but bullet safe. Can't be set off during a firefight by a stray round. But unlike all other devices of this type, after an explosion all components of the bomb and its detonator are obliterated. Which of course makes identifying the fingerprints of the explosive virtually impossible. A perfect terrorist weapon.

"We believe Mr. Chee has in his possession about fourteen times the amount used in that video. And furthermore we believe he's been scouting for some time for the appropriate target. The maximum effect."

Billy Dean Reynolds came to his feet. "We were told this group, Earth Liberation Front, they're into arson. Burned down some SUV dealers and a ski development in Aspen. That's the intel we have. How's that match up with a guy like this?"

Without looking up from the screen of her laptop, Nicole said, "A new generation is taking over. They've evolved from Molotov cocktails, turned themselves into some dangerous fuckers."

Everyone, including Magnuson this time, took a long, avid look at Nicole. Head down, still focused on her screen, she seemed to Frank to be basking in their attention, then she lifted her head and looked around the room, making eye contact with each one of them until finally settling on Frank. "Wouldn't you agree, Agent Sheffield?"

The way she spoke his name, the intimate sound of it on her tongue, made his SWAT guys turn to each other with lifted eyebrows and half-hidden smiles. All was revealed. Somehow she'd managed to expose everything that had happened between them with that simple question.

Frank sat back in his chair and looked down at the table. Feeling a flush growing in his face. Had she meant to do that? Then thinking, hell, yes, Nicole was flaunting it, putting herself center stage. You better take me seriously, guys, I'm screwing the boss. Frank raised his eyes, glanced around the room, no one returning his gaze. As if maybe it hadn't been as obvious as he thought. Either that or they were trying not to make it harder on him.

In the next few minutes they decided they would rendezvous tomorrow at Black Point Marina in south

Dade County at 10:00 p.m., hit the island around midnight. The Coast Guard would supply Zodiac rafts with high-powered electric trolling motors for the landing on Prince Key. Forecast was for thunderstorms, possible tropical-storm conditions.

Frank was about to share the reconnaissance photos taken by Agent Sanford in his Cessna when Magnuson clicked his computer mouse and sent each of them detailed images of Prince Key. They were recent satellite images that could only have come from NSA. Frank sighed and pushed his folder of photographs to the side.

The big tent, the obstacle course, a solar panel, and a small lagoon that led to a narrow creek that snaked through the mangroves and joined other creeks and canals, all of them eventually feeding into one broad waterway that led out to the Atlantic. In the various shots, Magnuson counted a total of six ELF members on the island.

They chose the best landing spots for the five Zodiac teams. The attack teams would fan out and surround the island, with one team blocking the entrance channel, and on Magnuson's signal, all groups would come ashore in unison and head toward the barracks tent, which appeared to be the center of operations.

In addition to the Zodiacs, members of the Special Response Team based at Homestead Air Reserve Base would be manning two UH-60 Black Hawk choppers flying in support. If anyone on the island managed to slip through the net, the choppers would track them.

When Magnuson finished laying out the attack plan, he and Sheffield spent a few minutes hashing out the rules of engagement. Sheffield arguing for operational restraint, Magnuson making the case for a more aggressive approach. In Magnuson's view, the level of threat that Chee posed was so dangerously high that some collateral damage was acceptable.

"Not to me it isn't," Frank said. "I haven't heard any irrefutable proof that Paul Chee has this stolen HpNC in his possession. Yes, he had the opportunity, and he went AWOL around the time the explosive disappeared, so, yeah, I understand your assumption. But invading a privately owned island in the middle of the Biscayne Bay National Park with guns blazing is not warranted by any information you've presented so far."

"There'll be no guns blazing," Magnuson said, looking at his three agents. "Is that clear, men?"

They nodded one by one. Frank studying them, doubting their sincerity.

The meeting lasted another half hour, Magnuson holding forth, going over the attack plan a second time, then a third.

Frank sat quietly at his laptop and replayed the video. That steel-reinforced, indestructible wall disappearing in a whoosh. He played it again and again until the meeting ended.

TWENTY-SEVEN

"HEY, LADY," WALLY SAID. "YOUR phone's buzzing."

"Her name is Leslie," Cameron said. "Stop calling her *lady*."

In the tent, Leslie lay on the weight bench, pressing a hundred pounds again and again, down to her chest, then pumping it overhead, working up a good lather while Prince spotted for her.

Pauly lay on his cot, flat on his back, eyes open, doing nothing, but doing it with such fierce focus that Thorn couldn't stop watching him.

"You hear me, lady? Somebody's calling you."

"She hears you," Prince said.

Leslie's arms were quivering when she grunted for Prince to take the weight. He settled it into the rack and Leslie toweled her face and sat up, breathing hard.

She wore a white T-shirt and light cotton pants with a drawstring. The shirt was damp, revealing the shape of her breasts, the tightened nipples.

She glanced at Thorn, shot him a forced smile, got up, walked across to Wally, and looked over his shoulder at the scrolling code on his screen. "You still inside Turkey Point?"

"Finished it yesterday. I'm just poking around inside another system."

"What system?"

"South Florida Water Management. These idiots, their security is so out-of-date, it wouldn't protect a taco stand."

Her phone vibrated on the shelf, crawling sideways like a wingless bee.

"How long has this been ringing?"

"Hell if I know," Wally said. "I'm nobody's secretary."

"The last hour," Thorn said. "Ever since you started pumping iron."

"And nobody told me?"

"I thought you were ignoring it," said Thorn.

Fiddling with her phone, Leslie slid her finger across the screen, moving through her text messages. She stiffened. Then she drifted off to a corner of the tent and tapped in a number and pressed the phone to her ear. But she'd left the speaker on, and when the connection was made, Thorn heard Flynn speaking. His voice-mail message.

"Hi, listen, I'm going away for a while. Taking a hiatus from the show, I'm not sure when I'll be back. If this is Mom . . ."

Leslie fumbled with the phone, switched off the speaker.

Flynn was watching her, his eyes dimming with dread.

Beside the weight bench Prince was doing more curls, oblivious. Pauly stared intently up at nothing while his brother continued to type and type.

Leslie turned her back to them and brought the phone

to her ear again. In a minute when she was done, her shoulders sagged and she bowed her head, nodding several times as though counting off sufficient time to gain control of herself.

She stepped behind the dressing curtain that hung before her bed, and Thorn heard her rustling through her knapsack. When she slid the curtain aside, her smile was strained, a failed attempt to hide the distress in her eyes.

"Flynn." She motioned for him to follow. "We need a minute."

She took one of the battery lanterns from the storage shelf and headed toward the exit. As she passed by Thorn, she angled her body away from him, but Thorn spotted it anyway. Hidden beneath the tail of her shirt was a hard, angular bulge wedged into the waistband of her cotton pants. Over the years he'd seen far too many of those bulges and knew the grim results they usually signaled.

He let a moment pass before he followed them out of the tent. Staying several yards behind as Leslie led the way, holding up the LED lantern, which sent a cone of harsh light around the two of them.

Stars blazed in a cloudless patch of sky, and a breathless wind was sifting through the mangroves bringing with it the electric scent of rain from out in the Atlantic. He heard the uncertain trill of an owl and the drone of mosquitoes circling in. In the east, muted by the clouds, lightning throbbed like an erratic pulse.

When she reached the climbing wall, she stopped, turned to Flynn, lifted the lantern to his face. He raised his hand to block the glare, but Leslie stepped closer and kept him blinded.

"I heard some disturbing news. What I want to know from you, Flynn, is where you've hidden your cell phone."

Flynn opened his mouth, then shut it.

"I know it's here. Don't lie to me."

He shook his head and sighed in frustration.

Leslie swung the lantern to her left and found Thorn standing at the edge of the sand pit.

"Step over here." She had the pistol out but held it loose in her hand, pointing at the ground. A stainless-steel revolver. "That's close enough. Right there. I'd hate like hell to hurt either of you. But if I have to, I will. Make a move, there'll be no hesitation. So get it out of your mind, Thorn. All your tricks."

"Leslie, Leslie, Leslie." A lament.

"Now, where's the phone?"

Flynn stared at the ground and shook his head once more. He blew out a breath, glanced at Thorn, then lifted an arm and pointed to his left. "Buried in the sand, below the balance beam."

"Go get it, bring it back."

While he was digging, Thorn said, "If you try to hurt Flynn, you're going to have to kill me. You know that, right?"

Leslie was silent, the lantern steady. "Step forward where I can see you better. One step, that's enough."

"What's this about, Leslie? What the hell happened?"

Flynn returned with a phone and presented it to her.

Leslie waved it off. "Turn it on. Go to recent calls."

Flynn brought the device alive, and in the glow of its screen he tapped it twice and held it out.

With her gun hand, she slid her trigger finger down the screen once, then again and again, scrolling.

"Whose number is this?" She held out the phone to

Flynn, pointing at its screen. In its radiance Thorn could see Flynn's agonized face.

"He's the head of the Miami FBI, Frank Sheffield."

Thorn groaned to himself.

"You called him a week ago. While you were here on Prince Key."

"Yes."

"Why?"

"In a moment of weakness, but that weakness is gone. I'm where I want to be. Doing what I need to do."

"What did you tell this FBI agent?"

"Nothing specific. I didn't know anything specific."

"But you told him where you were. Here on the island."

"Yes, I told him I'd gotten mixed up with some political activists, and I was getting a little worried what they had in mind."

"And what did he say?"

"To stay put. Call him if anything happened he should know about. He didn't seem particularly concerned. But he's a laid-back guy. So I don't know."

"Have you called him again?"

"No."

"You're telling the truth?"

"I made a mistake," Flynn said. "I was confused."

"But you're not confused anymore."

"I'm where I need to be. Doing what I need to do."

"How do you even know this guy, this federal agent?"

"He's a friend of Thorn's."

She turned Thorn's way. "Is that true?"

Thorn nodded. "We worked together on a situation in the past. I wouldn't say we're friends. He's buddies with Sugar, from Sugarman's days as a deputy sheriff."

"Did you know about this, Thorn? Flynn being in contact with him?"

Thorn said he didn't. Leslie stared at him for a long moment, tapping the pistol's barrel against her thigh. Then she turned again to Flynn. "You understand, don't you, what you did was a betrayal. You could have put all our lives in danger."

"I understand."

"This operation is more important than any single member. We're all expendable. You understand that, too?"

Flynn nodded.

She held Flynn's gaze for several moments, and even in the bad light Thorn could read in that exchange of looks something that was more charged and personal than he could fully absorb.

"Okay," Leslie said. "I'm going to trust you. You say you were confused but you're no longer confused. I accept that."

Flynn whispered, "Thank you."

"Well, I don't. I don't accept any of it. This is total bullshit." Cameron Prince stepped into the circle of light. "You can't make a decision like that on your own, Leslie."

Thorn stepped aside. Leslie set the lantern at her feet. She tucked the pistol back beneath the tail of her shirt. Prince bristled with a dark radiance as though some dormant power source within him had been activated. Standing only a few yards away, Thorn could feel the hum of threat.

"From the very outset you've been usurping the power. That ridiculous vote on Thorn, letting this unreliable piece of shit walk right into the heart of our group.

And now this. Flynn collaborating with the feds, and good God, you're simply going to take his word for his change of heart.

"I know what's going on. I see it, Leslie. You've got a weakness for these two. You're simply too emotional to be a leader, and that puts us all in jeopardy. I won't have it. I won't fucking take it anymore. Risk my goddamn life and everything we've put into motion, for what? These two punks?"

"And what do you propose?"

"It's time we adjusted the pecking order." He turned his head and scowled at Thorn. "I'm promoting myself. From now on, I'm assuming leadership. Understood? And my first official act will be to rid ourselves of these two. Starting with this one, then his little boy."

"We need them," she said. "We need all six to make this work."

"Jesus," Thorn said. "That's your best argument?"

"See, that's exactly what I mean," said Prince. "This derisive attitude."

"Hey, meathead, forget the pecking order," Thorn said. "You want to adjust something, see if you can adjust my attitude."

From the get-go, when Thorn had confronted Prince prowling his property, there had been an instant clash. Ever since then Thorn and the pompous hulk had been headed toward this moment. Better to do it in the darkness where Thorn had at least a remote chance to catch him off-balance.

Prince came at him quicker than Thorn expected. Nothing in how he walked or moved hinted at this propulsive speed, a sprinter's surge. Head down, arms pumping, and just before contact, he spread those big arms wide, to tackle or sling or crush. His crude martial art.

His right shoulder aimed at Thorn's midsection.

Managing a quarter turn, Thorn deflected a fraction of the weight with his hip, but the impact sent him sprawling into the sand beneath the climbing rope. On his back, he was stunned, fighting for breath, as Prince gathered himself, came to his feet, and sneered at Thorn.

"That's it? That's all you've got, Mr. Back Alley eye-gouger?"

Behind Prince's bulk, Thorn caught sight of Flynn shaking loose from Leslie's grip. She grabbed his arm again and hung on, trying to spare the kid this nightmare of anabolic steroids and mindless brawn.

Thorn tried to rise, but groaned and sagged against the sand as if that single blow had ruptured something in his entrails. A possum's trick.

So cocksure of his supremacy, Prince bought the act and sent Leslie a gloating look. Just that second.

Long enough for Thorn to roll, and roll again, building up sufficient thrust to ride up hard against the front of Prince's shins, bowing the ankles back, the knees straining against themselves, whiplashing his body. Something inside the meat of his legs crackled like gristle sizzling on the fire.

Prince staggered and danced two steps, legs rubbery, howling with rage.

Thorn got to his feet, reached up, and grabbed the hawser, thick as a tugboat's towline. He retreated a yard, then swung feetfirst at Prince's bulk.

Arcing high, he timed his flight, lifted his legs, and scissored them around Prince's neck, locked his ankles, clamping the big man's neck, then wrenched sideways as if levering the cap off a beer bottle.

But Prince's neck was too braided with muscle for this to make an impression. With a spurt of fury, he growled and vise-locked his hands on Thorn's ankles, pried them apart, then took a step backward and wrenched him loose from the rope and began a slow twirl, around once, and a second time, swinging Thorn like a sack of corn.

Prince rocked unsteadily on his gimpy ankles, but managed to build up enough velocity with the next rotation to hurl Thorn against the climbing wall with such force that bottle rockets and willow trees of flaming sparks fired across the black sky of his consciousness.

He felt himself sliding down the wall and thudding into the sand.

Bleary and disoriented, he floundered on his side and tried to crawl away, escape whatever delights Prince had in mind next. Blinded by sand, his body half-numb, with a broken rib perhaps, an aching shoulder, his jaw clicking on its hinges, Thorn only made it a few feet.

Prince grabbed him by the scruff of his shirt and dragged him upright and swung him around to face Leslie and his son.

"As I was saying," Prince spoke over Thorn's shoulder. "After I snap this one's neck, I'll do the kid. We'll just have to manage with two less men."

He took Thorn's chin in one mitt and gripped the back of his head in the other. One good twist from the end.

Leslie commanded Prince to stop. She released Flynn and went for her pistol, but it was too late. Prince had already cranked Thorn's neck to its limits, pointing his chin back of his shoulder blade, his cervical verte-brae so strained that the darkness grew twice as dark.

Thorn exited the scene, became a spectator, viewing this from afar, his hands going through the motions, scrabbling and clawing at Prince's meaty arm. To no avail. But it didn't matter. Thorn was safe somewhere else, watching it unfold, watching Flynn spring across the grass to jump the goon. Protect his old man. Good kid. Brave kid.

Then for some reason Flynn halted, and from the great, comfy distance where Thorn was perched, weight-less, observing these inconsequential events, he saw Prince's hands break loose from their hold on Thorn's head, felt air seep back into his own lungs.

Thorn didn't witness the exact footwork or handhold or throwing technique that Pauly employed. All he saw were the results: Prince staggering, then pitching away to his right, going airborne, his heavy arms flailing, a shout coming from somewhere as he body-slammed face-first against the earth, an impact so violent that a yard away the lantern toppled onto its side.

From the great precipice where he'd been so pleas-antly removed, Thorn swooped back to his body on the ground. Tasting the blood in his mouth, his big joints throbbing, stretched out of alignment.

After an interval, Thorn grunted and sat upright, wiped away a smear of blood from his lips, and rubbed his hand clean on his shirt.

Pauly squatted before him. His inexplicable savior. His buddy. Pauly, whose martial arts skills came from a more exalted plane.

"You okay?"

"Never better," Thorn said.

Leslie helped Thorn to his feet, made him extend his hand to Cameron Prince and declare a truce. Thorn said something and the hulk huffed an empty apology and lumbered off to attend to his wounds with Pauly shadowing him. Maybe Leslie sent them both away. Maybe they left on their own. Thorn wasn't following the specifics too closely. He was concentrating on staying upright, keeping his legs beneath him, drawing breath.

Sometime later he found himself slouched on the wooden bench. Leslie and Flynn stood nearby, watching him as if he might tip over. She set the lantern on the grass.

Then Leslie dropped Flynn's phone on the ground in front of Thorn. Raising the heel of her hiking shoe, she crushed it, splintering the glass face. Then she lifted her foot again and stomped on the phone and stomped a final time on the broken remains.

With the tip of his tongue, Thorn was exploring his mouth, going from tooth to tooth, touching the jagged edges. Three so far, a molar loose, a rip inside his cheek.

"Can I trust you, Thorn?"

He looked at Leslie. Her face a blurry shadow. He said nothing.

Flynn said, "He can barely keep his eyes open. Can't this wait?"

"I need to know where he stands. No, it can't wait." She took a seat beside Thorn on the bench, brought her face close. "You're still not with us, are you? You haven't committed."

"What choice is there? I'm with you, damn it." A second molar loose.

"I want to trust you, Thorn. I want to believe you."

"Maybe we should close up shop," Flynn said. "Get the hell away from here. Reschedule the whole thing."

"No," Leslie said. "We're on track. We're fine. As long as you're telling me the truth about Sheffield." She kept looking at Thorn, trying to read him.

"It's the truth," Flynn said. "Sheffield's in the dark."

When Thorn was able to stand, the three of them walked back to the barracks tent. Somewhere along the way, Thorn laid a hand on Flynn's shoulder to steady himself and as a gesture of gratitude for Flynn's attempt to help. Flynn didn't shrug his hand off, which Thorn took as progress.

Around them the breeze was picking up, stirring the fronds, heaving waves against the mangrove roots and the rocky shoreline. Out in the Atlantic a bright branch of lightning lit the blackness briefly. Then a single ragged shaft struck the waters closer to Prince Key. Thorn waited for the thunder but it didn't come. No further sign of the approaching storm except for the rising wind that trembled the walls of the tent as one by one the three of them stepped inside and Leslie shut the flap.

TWENTY-EIGHT

SUNDAY NIGHT, JUST AFTER 10:00 P.M., all their gear was prepared and the assault plan had been laid out for both teams, critiqued, tweaked, and agreed upon. Both groups assembled at Black Point Marina. Sheffield's guys and the NCIS bunch. Everyone seemed more uneasy about the weather than raiding Prince Key.

After stewing for a couple of days in the overheated waters south of the Bahamas, tropical storm Juanita had become a Category 1 hurricane. Tonight one of her outer bands was whipping in from the southeast, and even the mile-long protected channel that led from the marina out to Biscayne Bay had a three-foot chop.

The bay itself was a wall of six-foot swells with whitecaps that blew away like seedpods exploding in the darkness. Small-craft warnings. Not the night for a five-mile cruise in electric-powered inflatable rafts.

Magnuson raised the possibility of a weather delay, but Frank said no. He was spooked. That video clip of the reinforced-concrete wall obliterated by the experimental explosive had become in his imagination the walls of a containment dome at Turkey Point. Frank was picturing a catastrophic rupture releasing a radioactive cloud so toxic that the city that was his lifelong home and where he planned to live out his days would be changed forever. Magnuson was focused on Chee. Frank was thinking about a few million of his neighbors.

The ten SWAT guys were huddled inside the marina's enormous storage barn, an indoor boatyard where five-story racks of powerboats towered behind them. An employee from the county had been summoned to open up the facility for their use, and he stood fifty yards away across the vast cement floor smoking a cigarette and looking up at the ceiling as if expecting it to be peeled off by the heavy winds.

"The storm's turning south," Frank said. "Half an hour it's out of here."

"Not according to the Weather Service." Magnuson, like the rest of his men, was suited in a black rain suit, his Kevlar body armor underneath.

"My info's better," Sheffield said. "She's being sheared, about to take a hard left, get torn up by the Sierra Maestra mountains in Cuba. Thirty minutes this wind'll die down, an hour at the most. If we head out now, it'll be sloppy, but by the time we reach Prince Key, wind should be down to fifteen to twenty. Rough sailing, but also damn good cover."

Magnuson looked around at his men as if taking their silent vote.

"Your choice, guys," Frank said. "Stay here, stay dry, or come with me and costar in the movie."

Frank was drenched, cold, and fighting back shivers by the time they made it to the end of the channel and faced the howling bay, thinking maybe this was a mistake. Nicole kept her head bowed against the wind, the hood of her rain gear cinched so tight only a small oval of her face showed. The pretty parts: her mouth, nose, those Garbo, high-voltage eyes.

Their night-vision equipment was useless. Between the pelting rain and the lightning, they were better off with their naked eyes.

Frank led the armada out of the choppy water of the channel, and once they entered the bay, they were plastered from every direction by swells, their rafts pitching high over crests, then wallowing for a moment before hammering into the troughs. Hard as hell to hold a heading, but Frank outwrestled the wheel and managed to keep the GPS arrow pointing due east toward the island.

Buffeted by headwinds, the two Black Hawks skimmed low overhead, then split apart, moving into position. One would hover a few miles north, and the other a few miles south, of Prince Key. Out of range of hearing, but near enough to swoop in when the five teams came ashore.

Twenty minutes into it, everyone was still fanned out on either side of Sheffield. With each lightning stroke, he caught their silhouettes. Every minute or two his radio squawked, but Frank made out only a few garbled words.

An hour into the crossing his GPS said they had a mile to go before they reached Prince Key, a mile for his forecast to come true.

As the water shallowed, they fell into the lee of the island and the wailing dropped to a moan. Spitting rain speckled the water that sloshed around the floor of the raft, and small waves jostled them as they worked to shore. By God, the storm had made its hard turn to the south. Once again his friend Matt White, the lychee-nut farmer, had nailed it.

Nicole loosened her rain hood and released her terror grip on the bench seat. She stretched her neck and reached inside her black rain suit and withdrew her handgun, a compact nine-millimeter Sig P229.

In a hushed voice, Sheffield told her she wasn't going to need that.

"Bet me," she said.

Because he was piloting the lead Zodiac, Sheffield's role was to await the radio signal from Magnuson indicating all teams were in place around the island. Meantime, hold his position just offshore, spend the time looking for an entry spot among the dense mangrove roots. Five minutes max.

The radio squawked a couple of times, more static. Sheffield kept it close to his ear, waiting for the green light, one intelligible word that everyone was set. Five minutes became ten, then fifteen, and Frank, growing anxious, was moving the mike to his lips to whisper a query when the gunfire erupted.

He dropped the mike, hit the throttle, rammed the nose of the raft into an opening between two large black mangroves. Scrambling over the bow, he dropped into muck to his knees and held his hand out for Nicole. She had other ideas. Male assistance not required. From the starboard side she jumped onto a shelf of roots and branches, slipped, then hauled herself upright, drew her weapon, and pushed off into the dense cross-hatching of flora.

Frank lashed the raft's bowline to a tree trunk and slogged up the bank as another burst of automatic fire sounded. He tried to hail Nicole but she'd already bulled ahead into the darkness. Shit, shit, shit.

Branches snatched at his shirt and stabbed his flesh

as Frank hauled ass in the direction of the shooting. It was coming from straight ahead, which put it around the larger of the two tents.

He would be approaching the tents from the rear while Magnuson's team and the other two in the NCIS group would have landed fifty yards closer, coming from each flank.

Sheffield's guys had been assigned the eastern shore, all the way on the other side of the island, which meant they'd be approaching across an open field, moving past the obstacle course, and heading toward the tent's front opening—the longest distance to travel. And the most exposed.

Frank drew his Glock.

Everyone was supposed to move on Magnuson's signal, a simultaneous landing, then proceed in unison toward the barracks tent. They'd set up a perimeter around the barracks tent, but no one was to approach the tent, no one would do any damn thing on his own until everyone was in place. Fire if you're fired upon, only then.

Frank smacked into another branch, almost put out an eye, and knew with even more certainty that things were fucked as some idiot up ahead fired his automatic weapon. Sounded like he'd held down the trigger till the clip was empty. Nothing disciplined about it. No way that could be a SWAT member. No way. It had to be an ELF guy. Goddamn, had to be.

Lights blazed to his left and he cut that way, staying in a crouch. Ahead, maybe twenty yards, flashlights were mingled with the bright blue flash of the barf beamer.

That's the name Pipes, one of the NCIS guys, had used back at the marina, showing it off to the FBI team. Sheffield had heard of it, never seen one. An incapacitator. It used light-emitting diodes to shoot superbright pulses of light at rapidly changing wavelengths. Supposed to disorient its subject, bring on nausea.

What the hell use it would serve in an operation such as this he had no idea, but he didn't want to get into the weeds with Magnuson, so he hadn't squawked. Another check mark against him.

Sheffield yanked aside the bushes, plowed through the dense brush, no longer concerned with the noise he was making, even drawing out his flashlight and switching it on. Pistol in one hand, flashlight in the other, backhanding the branches. Ten yards ahead was open ground, stray voices, someone barking commands. Loud, angry, though Frank couldn't make out the words, blocked by his own heaving breath, his rush through the scrub.

Breaking through the last of the undergrowth, Frank lurched onto a field, grassy and wide open, flashlights dancing up ahead, and the barf beamer holding steady on the side of the tent. All weapons aimed at the cone of light where the tent's fabric was shredded, pocked with dozens of bullet holes.

No way to tell if they were incoming or outgoing.

"Hold your goddamn fire!" Frank hustled toward the others.

He aimed his flashlight at his own face and slashed a hand across his throat to call them off.

Thirty feet from the tent, Magnuson stood at the rear of his three men, all kneeling in shooting position. Sheffield's crew was still arriving, out of breath, automatic weapons raking across the patches of darkness surrounding them.

Inside the tent a single lightbulb swung from a cord.

The torn fabric rippled in the wind. From inside the tent the shadow of a man rose from a squat to a standing position. One hand appeared to be raised above his head. Maybe surrendering or, hell, who could tell, maybe he was about to toss a grenade. The men on Magnuson's team tightened their aims.

"I said stand down."

Then Frank called out for the man to drop his weapon and do it now.

But the shadow stayed put, one arm raised, the man beginning to turn in what appeared to be a circle, a sluggish pirouette.

"Area's clear, Frank," his team leader, Dinkins, hissed in his ear. "We did the grid search, found no one. No boats at the beach. Nobody's here. The shitheads jumped ship."

"Except for that individual," Magnuson said.

"Are the choppers in play?" Sheffield asked Dinkins.

"They're working the quadrants, sir. Seen nothing yet."

"Who fired their weapon?"

Agent Pipes raised his hand, then reset it on his AR-15. His barf beamer was propped between two rocks two yards away from him. If the light drew fire, he was distanced.

"Why'd you shoot?"

"Because of him," the agent said, nodding at the tent.

The shadow Man made more noises. Babbling something.

"Agent Pipes, is this man armed? Did he fire on you?"

"He was holding a weapon. What looked like a weapon."

Shadow Man was speaking in a hoarse, incoherent stream.

"I believe that's one of ours, sir," Agent Dinkins said.

"One of ours?"

"Billy Dean Reynolds, sir. I think it's him in there."

Frank flashed his light around the group, searching for Reynolds.

"When we landed Billy went ahead," Dinkins said. "Running point."

Frank did a quick head count, and, yes, Billy Dean was not present.

"Agent Reynolds!" Frank shouted at the shadow man. "Is that you? You inside that tent, Billy Dean?"

The man in the tent spoke again, doing another slow circle, one arm in the air, the other clutched around his midsection as if he were dancing with himself. Then his knees buckled and he collapsed.

Frank made it through the tent flap behind Agent Hale, who fell to his knees over Billy Dean and stripped open the fallen man's rain gear. Shining his light directly on the wound.

"He's torn up bad, sir."

"Call in one of the choppers, land in the field, we need to evacuate him now. And get a medical kit in here fast."

Hale sprinted off. Sheffield tugged the bloody clothes aside and aimed his light on the shredded flesh, heavy white bones splintered, strands of meat and muscle torn to hell. Several rounds had sneaked past his Kevlar and had ravaged the shoulder joint. Frank had seen enough gunshot wounds to know this would take months to heal, require multiple operations, a long rehab, might even put

Billy behind a desk the rest of his career. Assuming he survived.

Sheffield stripped off his own rain gear, then his blue FBI T-shirt, and folded it into a square and pressed the cotton hard against the wound.

Hearing the men outside getting into it with each other, his guys yelling, Magnuson's voice in there, too, trying to quiet the mutiny.

Billy Dean opened his eyes. With a hazy grin, he looked up at Frank and said quietly, "Did we get the bomber?"

TWENTY-NINE

AFTER THE CHOPPER LEFT WITH Billy Dean, both teams did a methodical search of the island. Look, but touch nothing, Sheffield told them.

Sheffield put on his T-shirt, sticky with Billy Dean's blood. Nicole watching him, her face slack, a bruised light in her eyes. She looked faint and Frank asked her if she was all right. She nodded that she was. But then kept nodding and nodding, looking even sicker. Frank went to her, guided her to a bench, and sat her down.

Fifteen minutes later both teams had reassembled outside the barracks tent. Speaking for the group, Dinkins said the area was clear of hostiles.

"Stay here, right here," Frank said. "Nobody wanders from this position until I give the okay. Is that clear?"

"What is it, Frank?"

"Just stay put."

Sheffield walked out into the field and used his cell to call dispatch. He identified himself, gave the agent an update on their mission, and told him to alert the Evidence Response Team, the Bomb Recovery and Analysis group, in case any trace of explosives had been left behind. Sheffield told the young man to notify the commander of Underwater Search and Response. Maybe during their getaway the ELF guys had tossed incriminating materials into the nearby waters. A long shot, but at this point everything was.

It was Monday morning, a long time till dawn. Everybody would be grumpy as hell, but they'd show up within an hour or two, no questions asked, and they'd work their asses off till the jobs were complete.

When he disconnected, he said to Dinkins, "No one leaves this spot."

"I wish you'd tell me what's going on."

Frank wasn't sure what put the quiver in his gut. But there it was. A reliable sensation that had saved his life a half dozen times. He hadn't felt it for years. Thought he was past all that. Quiver-free for good. But no.

He looked at Dinkins and pointed at the ground. Stay put.

And Sheffield rejoined Nicole and Magnuson inside the tent.

Though it was clearly the group's headquarters, not much had been left behind, and there was little to indicate the nature of the group or their mission. Weights, barbells, six cots, one of them set apart from the others, hidden behind a curtain, a makeshift table, an ice chest with its lid open. Inside it were the remains of Subway sandwiches floating on a bed of melting ice.

They looked, didn't touch. Treating it as a crime scene, treading carefully. Nicole was on her feet. Pale, shaky, but coming around.

Forensics would be arriving soon and county PD. Later on Monday a whole shitstorm of Washington agents—Critical Incident Response Group, the Counterterrorism hotshots, probably CIA, everybody from

National Security Branch eager for a junket to Miami—
would be flying in. They'd be tramping around Prince
Key, taking video, photographs, clicking their ball-
points, asking questions, not liking the answers, talking
on phones to their superiors, asking more questions,
writing up forms. There'd be an inquiry. Everyone interviewed. It was quiet now, still dark, but in the next few
hours, holy Christ.

"They ran power off that solar panel," Frank said.

"For one lightbulb?"

"Must've been running other things."

"Like what?" Nicole was sounding queasy again.

"Like computers, communications, radios, hell,
maybe they had a flatscreen out here, watching Oprah
and the nature channel."

"Why's the one bed separate, and that screen?"

"The boss," Nicole said. "Wanted privacy."

"Or a shy woman," said Frank. "Like Leslie Levine."

Nicole grunted, dubious but not up to arguing. She
was probably as bleak as Frank because she was bound
to take serious heat for this mess. Even though it wasn't
her operation, still, she was third on the chain, and she
already had a dead informant on her hands, and now
this disaster. Not good.

They spent half an hour in the tent, turning up
nothing that suggested the current location of Chee or
the rest.

"Okay, we're done," Frank said. "This is a waste."

"You were expecting a forwarding address?" Magnuson said.

"A guy can dream."

"Chee's like those game fish you have down here,
gray ghosts."

"Bonefish," Sheffield said.

"Yes, like those fish, you get one shot. But if you spook them, they're gone and you won't see them again for a long damn time."

To Sheffield it looked as if the group had made an orderly exit. No sign of panic, nothing silly left behind. They'd had enough time to gather their clothes, pack their valuables, probably enough time to wipe the place down. Though there'd be DNA. Sweat, hair, flakes of skin. There was always DNA. Maybe it would tell them something they didn't know, but he doubted it.

Nicole made one last circuit of the room, stopped beside the ice chest, and reached out to shut its lid, but Frank swung around and knocked her hand away.

Nicole jerked from him, grabbing her wrist. "Jesus, Frank!"

He stepped to the side of the ice chest and squatted down, took out his flashlight, and shone it in the narrow gap between the chest and the tent. "Aw, shit. Here we go."

Magnuson and Nicole stood at his shoulder and leaned in.

"Holy mother of Christ."

"Is that what I think it is?" Sheffield said.

"The right color, yes," Magnuson said. "I'd say a quarter of a pound. Roughly the amount that took out that retaining wall in the video."

Sitting on the bare ground, a sealed plastic container was filled with what looked like lime Jell-O speckled with BBs. A rack of nine-volt batteries were attached to the lid, red and black wires running from the battery pack into the container, and a white wire was strung tight between the triggering device and the lid of the ice chest.

"The detonator," Frank said. "It's that simple?"

"It's a trip switch. Those insulated wires are attached to a high-resistance bridge wire. It acts like a match head. The pyrophoric material is almost certainly a mixture of azide, lead styphnate, and aluminum. Hit the switch, the bridge wire heats, ignites the pyrophoric material, which then sets off the explosive. One of the virtues of HpNC. Once the compounds are assembled properly, it's very easy to rig the trigger."

"Jesus," Nicole said. "How'd you know, Frank?"

"It's why they left it open," Magnuson said. "They wanted to take out as many of us as they could."

Nicole was staring at the ice chest, rubbing the spot on her wrist where Frank had smacked her.

"So much for this being a bunch of pacifists," Magnuson said.

"As long as we're writing the history of this," Nicole said, "just for the record, okay, I'm here as an observer. I had no input on the plan or the execution of the plan. Are we in agreement on that?"

Frank turned to her, held her eyes for a moment, seeing only a cold light, her mouth hard and impersonal, a woman he barely recognized. He felt a lightness in his body as if his personal share of gravity had been suspended for a half second. Then he nodded to this woman, Nicole McIvey, that, yes, she was off the hook. Completely off the hook.

"The lady is *muy* ambitious," Marta had said. *"Muy."*

Outside, Frank instructed the men to retreat from their current position. Assemble near the obstacle course and stay put. When Dinkins asked what was going on Frank told them straight out. A booby trap in the tent. Same kind as destroyed the retaining wall in the video

Stay at a safe distance while Frank and Magnuson made one more quick pass around the premises.

"Shouldn't you wait for the bomb guys?" Dinkins said.

"Yeah, probably should," said Sheffield, and headed off.

They left Nicole behind and walked to the cove, picking their way carefully, seeing nothing unusual. At the small beach, in the rising light, the sky was overcast and the water in the cove was the color of drying cement. Fallen branches littered the beach, and the wind was still rattling through the tattered leaves of the mangroves, bringing with it a whiff of ozone, the last traces of the storm.

In a wooden storage rack seven black kayaks were lined up neatly. By the water's edge, half a dozen depressions in the sand might have been footprints, but the rain had eroded them to little more than dents.

Magnuson said the obvious. The ELF group had escaped in powerboats. Sheffield confirmed that he'd seen a white fishing skiff in the flyover photos his agent had shot the day before. Maybe later on they could identify that boat—clean up the photo, see if they could read the registration ID on the hull.

Magnuson was quiet. He kept rubbing at his thin lips, grinding his palm back and forth across his mouth as if trying to wipe away a sour taste. "He's getting away. Right now."

"They knew we were coming." The quiver inside Frank was gone. Something else was missing, too, something he couldn't name. In its place a familiar hollow was taking shape.

He'd had hopes for Nicole. Even pictured a future.

Not long term, not growing old together or any of that dizzy horseshit. But a month at least, two months, three. Maybe make it to Christmas.

Magnuson rubbed his lips some more.

"They were here Friday late afternoon when my guy did the flyover," Frank said. "Could be a coincidence they abandoned ship the day we raid."

"It's no coincidence."

"Which means we have a leak. In your group or mine."

Magnuson lowered his hand and gave Sheffield a solemn look. "It appears we do."

THIRTY

"**DO YOU HAVE A HANDGUN,** Thorn? Or any other weapons?"

It was shortly before sunrise, Monday morning, the darkness easing; a reddish glow had appeared in the east as if a single bloodshot eye were peeking above the horizon. Thorn was standing on his own dock again, along with Flynn, Cameron, Leslie, and the Chee brothers. Should've felt good, being home, but he was a long way south of good.

Hours earlier, during their long journey across Card Sound, the squall line had passed by, thrashing the bay into a heavy, dangerous sea, but now there were only the ragged remains, occasional bursts of rain and heavy gusts that creaked the big limbs, ripped away leaves. Then just as abruptly as they came, the winds died and there was stillness.

Thorn's skiff was back in its berth, towed from Prince Key behind Leslie's Whipray. The big wooden box they'd constructed on Friday was crammed onto the deck of Thorn's boat, and inside one of its two compartments the monster python was coiled, the same one Thorn had battled. Two deep gashes, one near its head, the other halfway down its length.

The trip from Prince Key to Key Largo should've taken less than an hour but required most of the night. With a boat in tow through such rough seas they'd been forced to slog along just above idle speed. Then there was all the ducking into protected coves and creeks to recover from the pounding.

Pauly moved into Thorn's line of sight, reached out, and placed a hand on Thorn's shoulder. An almost-smile on his lips. "Pay attention. The lady asked you a question. Do you have weapons?"

His .357 was in a jewelry box Dr. Bill had fashioned out of native lignum vitae, stashed on a shelf at the back of the guest-room closet. This bunch might miss it if they searched, but after Thorn took a quick look at Flynn's grim set of jaw, the glaze of anxiety in his eyes as he stared at Thorn, the decision was made.

"I'll show you," Thorn said.

Pauly stepped away.

"I don't like this place," Wally said. "Where the fuck are we?"

"This is Thorn's house," Prince said. "Three acres."

"Five."

"And your closest neighbor?" Prince pointed south, then north.

"North is a nature preserve," Thorn said. "And south is the Morrison place. They go away summers. Won't be back until November."

"And he has no friends," Cameron said, eyes on Thorn.

Prince was back to his pompous self. Limping and bruised, but no longer sulking about the beating he'd taken from Pauly. Probably chalked that up to being blindsided. Mirror-lovers such as Prince were so used to being the fairest of them all, not much could shake their arrogance.

"Thorn has friends," Leslie said. "Where does Sugarman think you've been for the last few days?"

"I didn't tell him anything before I left."

"He stops in, right? On a regular basis."

"Off and on. He's a busy man."

"Everyone take note," Leslie said. "Sugarman is a tall African-American. He's a private detective, a former deputy sheriff. So if you encounter him, come to me and let me know he's here. Don't try to take him on alone."

"I can handle Sugar," Thorn said.

"No," Leslie said. "If he drops by, don't go near him. Is that clear?"

Thorn eyed her for a moment, then nodded.

"This is fucked," Wally said. "It's not safe here. Pauly, we should split. Deep-six these losers and move on. Find another project."

Pauly looked off at the water and didn't reply. Considering it.

"It'll be fine here," Cameron said. "This is better than the island. We're on the mainland now. Easier to come and go. By boat or car."

"All right, if everyone's satisfied," said Leslie. "Same rules apply. Keep your buddy in sight at all times. One change. Cameron, you're with Wally now. I'll watch out for Flynn."

Flynn swallowed, eyes darting from face to face as if expecting an objection or wiseass remark.

"Later today I'll lay out the plan," she said. "Right

now we all need some rest. We've been up all night. We need to be fresh for what's coming."

She turned to Thorn and motioned for him to lead on. "The gun, Thorn. And any other weapons."

With Prince hobbling beside him, Thorn led them through the house to the guest room, took down the wooden box, and presented Leslie with the .357. She opened the cylinder, cleared the six rounds, and dumped them in her pocket. She handed the pistol to Pauly and told him to take it out to the dock and pitch it into the lagoon.

"Knives in the kitchen, a meat cleaver, a rolling pin. Better toss them overboard while you're at it."

"We'll take our chances with the cutlery," Leslie said.

She and the Chee brothers went wandering through the house, checking the layout. Flynn stayed put, staring at the floor, lost in a dark mood.

Beside him Cameron studied a photograph on the wall. A black-and-white shot of a teenage Thorn holding up a giant tarpon and grinning for the camera. So young, so full of resolve. Sweat gleamed on his bare chest, muscles roping his arms.

"What a strapping lad," Cameron said. "That smile, I've seen Flynn with the same one, though not lately."

"Catching a tarpon that size might get it back," Thorn said.

Flynn huffed, dismissive. More important things to do than fish.

Prince said, "Be thankful, Flynn, you have someone who can teach you such things."

"Unlike your father?" Thorn said.

"Fifty years in Miami, the man didn't know a tarpon from a polar bear."

"He's the Prince who bribed politicians, got thrown in jail."

"And died there," Cameron said. "Good riddance."

"So you, you've skipped a generation."

"What?"

"Your granddad Reginald, the newspaperman, the idealist who battled corruption, he's your hero."

"Ah, Thorn the historian."

"I'm trying to get a feel for you people. Why you're doing this."

"We people, as you say, all have quite different reasons for being here, but we're unified in our desire to bring a halt to the menace of nuclear power."

"Is that it? Or is it something simpler?"

Flynn stepped closer to Thorn, eyes slitted in disdain. "You're losing it, Thorn. This is about nukes. Simple as that. The fuel rods that stay radioactive for centuries. The impact on the aquifer, the wetlands. It's about the earth, the future." Flynn shook his head and turned his back on both of them.

"Oh, sure, that's part of it. Nuclear power."

"And the other part?" said Cameron. "Please enlighten us."

"Your family," Thorn said. "The Princes were a big deal once. But your father pissed it all away."

"You should ask for a refund on that psychology degree."

"I think Flynn's heart is in this, but you, you don't strike me as a man worried about spent fuel rods. This is your come-from-behind finish, a farewell gesture to Miami. You pull this off, you're as big a deal as old Granddad. At least to a certain crowd you'll be a folk hero."

"You're dead wrong. I have no ambition to become a celebrity."

Leslie and the Chee brothers returned. The green python was slung over Pauly's shoulders like a stole, its tail trailing behind him along the floor. The snake observed Thorn briefly, flicked its tongue, then twisted its head back and forth, surveying the hallway. One long, heaving strand of muscle.

Leslie made the room assignments. Thorn and Pauly would bunk in the twin beds of the guest room. Cameron and Wally were to share the master suite where Thorn's parents, Dr. Bill and Kate, had spent their married life. Which left Leslie and Flynn in the small bedroom across the hall where Ricki, Thorn's adoptive sister, had endured her gloomy high school years.

"Everybody get some sleep. We gather at noon, I'll go over the plan."

A moment after they parted in the hall, Thorn took a backward glance and saw Leslie brush her fingertips across Flynn's lower back, a gesture so intimate and natural Thorn felt a whirl of recognition. Flynn and Leslie. A tenderness and familiarity between them Thorn hadn't noticed or accounted for.

Sure, Leslie's bond with Cameron Prince had a certain sad logic, a man who'd bulked up to bulletproof himself against a hostile world had partnered with a woman whose gift was seeing past the armored plating to the secret heart within. But Leslie and Flynn were a more natural match. Both had suffered agonizing losses, wounded in ways only one similarly damaged might fully grasp. In that simple consoling touch, Thorn glimpsed the strength of their connection.

Thorn went into the guest room. Pauly followed and

elbowed the door shut, then used both hands to guide the python onto the floor.

He left again and was back shortly with his two aluminum suitcases. He set them beside his bed, then lay back on the quilted bedspread while the big snake oozed around the edges of the room.

Pauly's black T-shirt and jeans were still wet from the boat ride, but he didn't strip them off. Just folded his hands behind his head and stared up at the ceiling. As far as Thorn could tell, Pauly hadn't slept in the last three days. The kind of stonyhearted man who didn't require the healing effects of rest.

The pry bar Thorn had tucked down the waistband of his baggy shorts had been digging into his spine for the last few hours. Earlier, as they'd exited in the darkness and rain, he'd managed to scoop it out of the sand, and now as he slid beneath the sheets, he drew it out and tucked it between the mattress and box spring. Not a .357, but it would have to suffice.

"Tell me something, Pauly." Outside the window a mourning dove was moaning in the sapodilla tree. "What's Wally's problem?"

Pauly turned his head slowly and eyed Thorn but didn't speak.

"You protect him, watch out for him. He's not quite right. His skinny legs, there's hardly any muscle. What is that, polio?"

"What do you want?"

"I'd like to know who I have sleeping under my roof."

Pauly shook his head. Not interested.

"You were in the military," Thorn said.

Pauly resumed his inspection of the ceiling.

"I'd guess the marines."

"Fuck the marines."

"Reason I ask, you don't fit with these people. You're no flower child."

A gust of wind rattled the palm fronds outside. A jet heading into Miami rumbled overhead. On the wall above the dresser the shadows of a passing flock of gulls flickered and disappeared.

"It's the uranium," Pauly said.

"What?"

"A mine on Navajo land, uranium tailings in the water, in the soil, it got into the mud bricks of the houses. My people got fucked up by it. They're still fucked up by it."

"That's what's wrong with Wally? His legs?"

"What counts is his brain. Wally's smart, a different kind. Musicians, chess players."

"Smart with computers," Thorn said. "A math whiz."

"How he's wired. Never needed school. Born like that."

"And you?"

"I'm Navajo. That's all you need to know." Pauly sank back into silence, but a grim energy was pulsing inside him. A hum in the room.

"It won't work. I don't care how good the plan is, the security's too tight at that place. It's going to fail."

"Take a nap."

"We're all going to wind up dead or in jail."

"Their security is shit. A circus clown could lead a string of elephants straight in the front gate."

"What's in the suitcases?"

"Go fuck yourself."

"Don't think I haven't tried."

Pauly drifted away into another tense silence, then after a minute, he turned his head on the pillow and stared at Thorn. "You're a lousy father."

"I know. The more I try, the worse I get."

"Then quit trying."

Thorn nodded. Sage advice. "No children yourself, or is Wally enough?"

When Pauly spoke again, weight was in his words as if he'd been harboring them for years, their energy compounding in his dark interior. "My old man," he said, then stalled.

"Yeah? And what was he like?"

"Never met the asshole. Growing up, not a word about him. Just another Navajo drunk, dumped his wife and kids."

A story on his lips. But wavering. Thorn could hear the python rustle across the hardwood floors. He kept his mouth shut, giving Pauly room.

"Five years back . . ." Pauly hesitated again. Lying there in silence until he'd collected himself. "Five years, I get an e-mail out of nowhere. Some old fuck in his nineties, a white man, he's tracked me down, claims he's my grandpa. My old man was his bastard son. Now this old white man says he has to see me before he dies. Never knew he existed till that e-mail."

"So you went."

"Fucker wanted to talk. Had something to confess." Pauly looked at Thorn, back at the ceiling. "Los Alamos. You know about that?"

"The A-bomb."

"Metallurgy, that's what he did. Physics, chemistry. How Wally got his brains. Skipped a generation, all went to him."

"What'd he want?"

Pauly chuckled without humor. He clenched his jaw. A clash inside him. Words he'd never spoken aloud, and now opening up to a stranger. A guy he didn't trust. Thorn didn't know why that happened, but he'd seen it more than once. Had done it himself, turning to some unknown on the next barstool, drunken sharing.

The python had slung itself out between the two beds. One of the guys.

"Sad old fuck. Lying there, all the tubes and monitors. Barely keeping his eyes open. Goes on about the bomb, how sad he was for what he'd done, him and the others. What it led to. All the dead. Way it changed everything, made it worse. It's eating him up, he says, all his life, eating his guts."

Thorn lay back on the bed, turning his own eyes to the ceiling, trying to picture what Pauly was seeing.

" 'Put the genie back in the bottle.' That's what he said. Wanted to know could I help. 'That's my last wish, *son*.' Calling me *son*. 'Put the genie back in the bottle.' I stood there listening to him. Didn't speak a word the whole time. Hour later he died."

Thorn let a few moments tick by. "Never met you before, he gives you a mission."

" 'Genie back in the bottle.' Like that's possible."

"But you're trying anyway. Make him happy, even though he's dead."

"Can't put genies back," Pauly said. "Can't put anything back. Once it's out, it's fucking out. Best anybody can do, slow down the genie. Trip her up."

Thorn watched the shadows of a branch sway on the wall. "And that's why you're here, under my roof. Wally's legs, the genie."

Pauly was quiet for a minute, drained. "Take a nap, smart guy. You're going to need it."

"One more thing."

"Take a fucking nap."

"Why'd you save my ass from Prince? Why not stay out of it, let him tear my head off?"

Pauly closed his eyes for a while as if maybe he'd shut down. When he spoke again, his voice was velvet and slow, back to his late-night radio sound. "I saved your ass because we're buddies. We look out for each other."

"But we're not buddies."

Pauly looked over. "We are now."

One hundred and thirty-eight mousetraps.

That's what Thorn dreamed. Not intending to nap, believing he was too wired, too on guard, just laying his head back on the pillow to relax his muscles, thinking about who these people were. What was going on. The A-bomb, Turkey Point, Prince Key, a fuck-you to Miami. Then he was into the dream, 138 mousetraps.

His eleventh-grade science teacher. Mr. Jacobs. Coral Shores High, the guy in his late sixties, gray hair, rail thin. Been teaching smart-ass punks like Thorn for thirty years and was still energized. Today in class he was wearing an Indian headdress. Hundreds of bright feathers. No shirt and Pauly's medallion around his neck. An IV hooked up to his arm, dripping chemo.

Mr. Jacobs, the Navajo from Los Alamos. Dream logic.

Thorn and his classmates gathered at the head of the class staring at a terrarium on the table. Big glass box full of mousetraps. All those traps set with yellow

Ping-Pong balls. Why 138? Thorn couldn't recall. It didn't matter. But he remembered the number.

Mr. Jacobs was chanting an Indian ritual song. The class circled the terrarium like a tribal fire. Twenty-five smart-asses making jokes. Mousetraps covered the bottom of the glass case, each wooden base flush against the other. One thirty-eight. Jacobs opened the lid.

Holding up a single red Ping-Pong ball. See this. An electron. A stray electron. He gave his headdress a shake, feathers fluttering.

Dropped the red ball into the glass box, shut the lid. The red ball sprang a trap, a yellow Ping-Pong ball exploded, set off another trap, then a few more mousetraps sprang shut, firing their balls against the glass walls, ricocheting, setting off more traps, and then whoosh, in a handful of seconds, all the traps fired. One thirty-eight. Terrarium full of exploding Ping-Pong balls, a whirlwind, a crazy yellow chain reaction.

Nuclear fission.

Like that. Whoosh.

Thorn dreaming it as vividly and real as the day it happened. Whoosh. That high school science guy wearing an Indian headdress, hospital tubes attached to his arms.

THIRTY-ONE

"EVERYBODY'S GONE." A WHISPER NEAR his ear.

"Gone?" Thorn heard himself speak the word, still groggy with dreams, a bleary residue from his midday nap.

"I sent them away, food shopping." Leslie was alongside him on the bed. Her body flush against his. "We don't have much time. Half an hour maybe. Are you awake?"

Lips next to his ear, the tickle of her breath, her head sharing his pillow.

Thorn was back from the mousetrap dream and others he couldn't recall. Turning, he found her face inches away, seeing the fine down on her cheeks brightened by the streaming sun. Light rippling on her skin.

He drew back an inch. Blinked. Her eyes were bemused. She reached out and touched the stubble on his cheek and with a finger traced his jawline as she had on his dock that day a year ago or more when she'd dropped by. Her fingernail crackling against the bristles.

"What is this?"

"This is me lying next to you."

He opened his mouth, but she touched a shushing finger to his lips. "Twenty minutes. Do this for me."

What he saw was the fourteen-year-old, the waif on his dock. The troubled eyes, her sad, bruised aura. "No, Leslie. No."

"Because of the age difference?"

"That's one thing."

She slid her hand to the top button on his shirt, undid it. Smile gone, a serious look, a determined eagerness. "Doesn't bother me you're so damn old."

He gripped her hand, halted it. "You're not serious."

"Dead serious. Since the first, your dock, the snappers, those long afternoons, the talks we had, I imagined this."

Yes, he remembered the talks. Mostly Leslie's terse retelling of nights in the trailer park, the rough, horny men who screwed her mother, leaving behind tiny bags of white powder, then sauntered down the hall to shake the knob on Leslie's door. Wanting a slice of ripe dessert. She'd managed to keep them away, blocking the door with furniture. But someday it would happen. The door wouldn't hold.

Once she'd mentioned a couple of names, guys who'd pounded and budged the door open. Those two Thorn tracked down, the first a redneck with gaudy jewelry and a cowboy hat, the second a black dude whose truck had giant wheels, loud exhausts, and fuck-you decals. Both sneered at him when he asked if what Leslie had told him was true. Both he left unconscious, broken teeth, bloody, the redneck's right arm busted up, Thorn's own knuckles shredded. Neither bothered her again.

"You think you owe me something? You're wrong."

"Not about owing. About wanting." Her fingers trickled down the front of his shirt, slid along his belt.

He caught her wrist, held it firm. His goddamn prick hardening anyway. "It won't work," he said, but no longer believed it.

She pried free of his grasp, brushed a hand against his crotch, gripped its length through the cotton fabric. An appraising smile. "Seems to be working fine. For an old man."

"Leslie, I understand what you're trying to do."

"You damn well better."

"I'm going along on the attack. You don't need to win me over."

"Then just lie there and I'll carry on without you."

"Stop."

"This is it," she said. "This is our chance."

"I don't feel that way about you."

"Doesn't matter. I feel enough for both of us."

"No, goddamn it."

"Just a kiss. Grant me that. A kiss."

Her mouth moved to his. Slowly, tempting. And he allowed that much. Believing this was an act, an attempt to finalize the deal. Bring him solidly into the fold. Confirm with their bodies that Thorn was committed.

Her lips grazed his, light and teasing, searching for a fit, elastic, Thorn resisting, his body taut, withheld. Then, goddamn it, okay, the kiss became real. Her tongue slipping in, seeking his. Her warmth, her sleek skin, the snug fit.

By fractions Thorn's restraint melted, then melted more, until he didn't care what her reasons were, didn't care if this was a test, didn't care about their age or their shared history or anything else. She was no longer that girl on his dock.

They worked in unison to make the kiss come alive, to disappear into each other. It had been so long. He'd lost count of the months of abstinence, and he was there with Leslie, rekindling old reflexes, warming up memories of other kisses as deep and exploratory, as briefly hesitant, then no longer so.

They breathed into each other, a mutual resuscitation, all reluctance gone, a blind fumbling of hands and thickening of breath, with mouths joined, the softness of her, the power just below the skin, Leslie Levine, a troubled waif, but now a woman who'd outgrown all that, gotten strong, a woman who knew her way, was making risky, bold decisions. This being one, an act committed in full daylight, the door of his childhood bedroom ajar.

She stripped off her shirt. No time for unbuttoning. She motioned for Thorn to raise his arms and she dragged his off. A rushed impatience as if something were appearing from a long way off, something coming fast toward them, a dark onrushing mass, and they must hurry before the certain collision, this woman, stronger than her slim body appeared, rolling upright and planting herself on him, his hands reaching out to cup her bare breasts, to learn their shape and weight, watching her eyes shut as she sat astride him, pants still on, Thorn fully hard, pushing into her crotch.

She groaned deep in her chest like an animal feasting, her hands gripping his hands, clenching them harder against the small, perfectly rounded flesh, nipples jutting between his fingers; she rocked her head back, ready to howl. A long time coming. Beginning in his own prehistory, and hers, a bond he'd never admitted, one more deeply rooted than he imagined. The two entangled now in something complicated and serious.

This one time together would be all. This one time.

She shuddered and peeled away his hands and bent forward and kissed him, pressed her lips so hard, so insistently, he could not return the kiss. She tore open his shorts. He arched up, lifted his butt from the bed, and let her drag the shorts away. And she dismounted, whisked her own pants off, slung them toward the door.

From the bedside she bent over him and took him into her mouth, drawing him in, all of him. Back and back against the tight fit of her throat, down the length, then holding him still, she swiveled, brought her narrow butt to him. Thorn on his back, Leslie lowering herself onto his mouth, the soft patch of hair, its tart, intricate folds, spreading open, opposite poles joined, mouths devouring, Thorn learning his way among the petals while she worked her tongue over him, sampled each ball, drawing them in, holding them, letting go, then swallowing him again, all of it, so deep, so sure, Thorn found himself close to the edge, too close, teetering, and began to withdraw from her mouth inch by inch until he was free.

She rose and came back around, straddling his chest, bent forward, brought her mouth to his, a sticky kiss. Long and fragrant.

Caught in the undertow, the flood of pent-up nights alone, an unspoken ache of voluntary isolation. Starving himself. Believing himself unfit for anyone. Now this, breaking his fast with Leslie, a woman risen from the dead, a plotter. Damn him. Damn his body, his predictable hungers, the froth that replaced his reason,

the heady, downward, unblinking plunge. Bingeing on
Leslie.

A kid who'd fallen in love with an older man and
managed to jigsaw the pieces into place so that years
and years later on, Thorn was inside her, inside the
slick, tight groove of her. Slippery skin in the overheated
room, his and hers, oily hands, oily flesh, no place to
hold, no purchase. Like the snake on the floor, the python writhing restlessly beneath the bed, its greasy,
powerful body.

He couldn't hold on. She was underneath him, then
she was atop, riding him, up there, high against the ceiling, all of it finally, finally, finally overtaking her. Leslie
shook her head from side to side, no, no, no, as if trying
to cling to a few last precious seconds, shaking her head
as if to sling away a drop of sweat tracking across her
face. Mouth wincing, an ecstatic grimace. A song rose
inside her chest, all vowels, chords so low and deep their
echoes might vibrate in the walls of this room for years.

Thorn matched hers with his own grunts and heaves.
All hesitancy gone. The coiled spring that was tightening for months, tightening until finally it was sprung,
released in one long, unclenching surge. Fission and
fusion. And everything went out of him as she collapsed
against his chest, their naked bodies slicked with sweat,
smearing themselves against each other, shadowing the
sheets, sweat burning his eyes. Both of them winded,
amazed, chuckling in the giddy, thudding after-thrall,
while beyond the window a noon sun rang like a relentless chime above the trees.

Then a car's horn.

Sugarman's twin toots. The long crunch of tires on
gravel.

Thorn slid away from her, was off the bed and out the bedroom door, jogging across the living room, through the kitchen, out the French doors, naked, still erect, panting, waving both hands at Sugarman to go away, leave, back up, get the hell gone from this place. Go, go, go.

"What is it?" Out of the car, standing, staring at his naked friend.

"Damn it, Sugar, go, now. Now, goddamn it. Get in your car and go."

"Aw, shit. What'd you do, Thorn? What the hell did you do now?"

Thorn's prick was wilting. Heart still at redline.

Sugarman's gaze shifted left, to the slow tread of footsteps on the rock. Her bare feet padding across the sharp, pulverized stone. Thorn turned and watched her come. In her hand the .38. She was naked. Body glistening.

"Hello, Sugar."

"Leslie?" His eyes slanted away from her exposed body. Shy Sugar. Polite Sugar. "You're alive. Thank God."

Thorn said, "A gun, Leslie? A goddamn gun?"

"Come inside. Both of you. We'll talk. We'll figure this out."

Before they could take a step toward the house, Thorn's VW rolled into the drive, Cameron crammed behind the wheel, Pauly riding shotgun, with Flynn and Wally in the back. Grocery bags in their laps.

Leslie walked toward the VW, waving the .38 at Cameron, directing him to pull in behind Sugar's Honda. Holding both hands up to measure the distance between bumpers until Cameron tapped Thorn's car against Sugar's, blocking him in. Tree in front, Thorn's Beetle behind.

The four of them piled out, Wally gawking at Leslie, coming closer. "Not bad. Little puny in the tit department, but all in all . . ."

Pauly told him to shut up.

Leslie went over to the driver's window of Sugar's Honda, reached in and grabbed the ignition keys, slung them toward the lagoon, where they splashed. Then she turned back to the gathering.

"This is Sugarman," Leslie announced. "The man I told you about."

Flynn was staring at Thorn, small, outraged shakes of his head.

Leslie handed the pistol to Cameron.

"Take him inside, make him comfortable while we get dressed."

"That's it?" Flynn said. "No explanation?" He waved at her nudity.

"It's what it appears to be. Why? Is that a problem?"

Thorn watched his son absorbing this. Eyes flinching as if he'd taken one blow and was waiting for the next.

"When do I get my turn?" Wally said.

"Everybody inside," Leslie said. "Put the groceries away, it's time we discussed the plan."

"And him?" Pauly nodded at Sugarman.

"He'll be staying. Our guest. Cameron will watch over him."

"And afterward, when it's done. What then?"

"We'll see," she said. "When it's done, we'll see."

Sugar shot Thorn a look. Man, oh, man. What the ever-loving shit had Thorn done now?

Thorn said, "We're shutting down Turkey Point nuke plant."

Sugarman nodded as if such a thing were completely routine.

Flynn stripped off his T-shirt and handed it to Leslie, and she slipped it over her head and tugged it to cover herself. A minidress.

She said, "We're not going to harm anyone or do any permanent damage. It's a publicity stunt to draw attention to the environmental dangers of nuclear power."

"You'll be breaking the law though," Sugarman said.

"Wrong answer," Wally said.

Leslie came forward and stood in front of Sugarman. "It's an act of civil disobedience. We've tried repeatedly to make our voices heard through all the normal means—public petitions, demonstrations, education seminars, speeches at commission meetings. We've tried to use the political process, but the entrenched power is too strong. No one listens, no one is responding. So now we're stepping outside the law. Yes, it's true. We're putting ourselves at risk for what we consider a greater good."

Sugarman nodded. Thorn knew that Sugar had stepped outside the law once or twice, put his life on the line for one greater good or another. "And you're in this, Thorn?"

"A hundred percent." His lie spoken as resolutely as he could.

"Risk all this?" Sugarman motioned at the house, Thorn's life.

"I think it'll work," Thorn said. "Our intentions are pure."

"And me?"

"We're sorry you've walked into this," Leslie said. "We only ask that you don't try to interfere or escape. Friday, we'll be done, and we'll be on our way, then you're free to go to the authorities or do whatever you feel you must."

"You try to escape," Wally said. "We'll cut your fucking throat."

"That's not true," Leslie said. "Our group is nonviolent."

"What group?" Sugarman said.

Leslie eye-checked with the others, getting no dissent. She told Sugarman. Earth Liberation Front.

"Yeah, I've read about you guys." Sounding neutral, as if he were making up his mind. Thorn thinking this was the moment they might have to make a break. Picking his path to the woods, yank Flynn by the arm, drag him along.

"You form an opinion from your reading?" Prince asked.

Sugarman drew a breath and smiled at Thorn. "You're not altogether bad. Well-intentioned."

"He's lying," Pauly said. "He's saying what we want to hear."

"I believe him," Leslie said.

"Can't allow this," Pauly said. "Another guy walking in, a lawman." He edged a step toward Sugar.

"Pauly. Relax. We'll work this out. It changes nothing."

"No. Makes it too messy."

Pauly moved so swiftly Sugar didn't have time to flinch. Pauly's roundhouse kick snapped into the side of Sugar's right knee and crumpled him where he stood.

Before Thorn could move, Sugarman was sprawled on the gravel, the right leg bent beneath him at a savage angle.

"You son of a bitch."

"Put a splint on it," Pauly said to Thorn. "If he's any kind of man, he'll be walking in a month."

Thorn squatted at Sugar's side. He was groaning, eyes shut hard against the pain. Thorn tried to ease the leg free from beneath Sugarman, but he moaned and rolled onto his side.

"Maybe two months," Pauly said.

"He needs to get to a hospital."

"We all need a lot of things," Pauly said.

Leslie hung back, her face stricken. No longer in control.

If she ever was.

THIRTY-TWO

FLYNN AND THORN HAULED SUGARMAN into the guest room and laid him on the bed still warm and rumpled. Thorn tucked one pillow under Sugar's head and used the other two to elevate his broken leg. Sugar was drifting in and out of consciousness, one minute telling Thorn he was fine, don't worry about him, the pain was manageable, then sinking away into a groaning haze.

Thorn scissored off Sugar's pant leg. The knee was bruised and swelling, turning a deep purple. He went to a hallway closet, dug out two ancient fishing rods. Skinny shafts of fiberglass he'd used as a kid, keepsakes. He broke each in half. Padding the pressure points with wads of gauze, he ran the rods along the sides of Sugar's leg, and while Flynn held them in place, Thorn added ring after ring of adhesive tape, binding the shafts as tightly as he thought Sugar could tolerate. Then he sent Flynn to the kitchen for a bag of ice and covered Sugar with a blanket from the closet. It was all the first aid he could think of.

In a while Sugar's breathing evened out, his heart rate resumed a steady tick. No sign of fever, no chills. Stabilized for now.

Flynn stood beside the bed shaking his head in disbelief. "Is he going to be all right?"

Thorn nodded. Sure. Sure.

"It's just Pauly that's dangerous. The rest of us are peaceful."

"I know," Thorn said.

"Are you with us? You committed?"

Thorn glanced at the open door. From decades in that old house, he knew every creak and crackle of floorboard. Someone was standing just beyond the doorway.

"Absolutely," Thorn said. "I'm with you to the end."

Later that afternoon, while Sugar dozed, Leslie laid out the details of the assault. She stood behind the kitchen counter in a fishing shirt, long, baggy trousers, sandals. Her hair still damp from the shower. Over by the French doors, both of them flung open to the warm breeze, Wally was tapping on the keyboard of his laptop, which was plugged into his mobile phone. Pauly lounged in a cocked-back kitchen chair, bare feet on the table, staring at the pots and pans hanging from the overhead rack.

Thorn and Flynn stood side by side at the counter where a nautical chart was rolled open, held in place with beer mugs at each corner. South Biscayne Bay and the Upper Keys. Turkey Point with its long, straight miles of cooling canals clearly delineated, running south of the nuke plant.

When Leslie finished spelling out the scheme, she asked if there were questions. Everyone was silent. No eye contact, each of them waiting for someone to go first.

To Thorn, the plan sounded insane. Insane enough it just might work. "Hauling that box loaded with critters? We can barely lift it empty."

"We'll manage," she said. "Cameron takes one end, the rest of us handle the other. Not far, thirty yards at most. That's why we've been pumping iron. Those thirty yards."

Flynn asked her about the handcuffs.

She drew a white plastic cable tie from her back pocket. "Flex-cuffs."

"I don't know," Flynn said. "These federal agents, these FBI guys, they won't be able to get free? You're sure? They're SWAT, right? All that special training. That strip of plastic is going to keep them out of action?"

She handed one of the cuffs to Flynn and he examined it.

"They work," she said. "Want me to demonstrate?"

Flynn handed it back and made a face. Thanks, but no thanks.

Leslie turned to look at Thorn, appraising his silence. He kept his face as neutral as he could manage.

"Getting free of them would require wire cutters," she said.

"Or a Zippo lighter," said Pauly.

"It'll work," she said. "The force-on-force drill uses NRC protocol. All weapons are unloaded for safety. Lasers mounted on handguns. It's a ho-hum, routine thing for them. Nobody's carrying wire cutters, Zippo lighters, any of that. We cuff them, leave them in a ditch. Take their radios, phones. Even if they somehow managed to get free, they're miles from the action, no way to stop us. They'll be out of commission at least an hour. By then we're gone."

"And after it's finished?" Thorn said.

"Enter by car, leave by water, like I said. Weren't you listening, Thorn?"

"I heard you. Take the airboat down the cooling canals. It's dark, but you know your way. Get as close to the bay as possible, exit the airboat, cover twenty yards of open ground, cross the steel barriers, get in your skiff."

"Exactly," she said.

"And where then?" Thorn said.

"Back here."

"Oh, no, you don't."

"Only long enough to sort things out, then we part ways."

"They'll track us. There'll be cops everywhere, something this big. Coast Guard cutters, choppers in the air."

"You're underestimating the chaos. Even on an average day, Miami is teetering on the edge. And timing's on our side. We'll be gone before they know what happened. An hour max, we're in and out. Miami's dark, Fort Lauderdale, all the way to Boca, maybe beyond. Happens in a blink, we're already on our way back here."

"Where does the escape skiff come from?" Flynn said.

"You'll bring it."

"Me? How?"

"You stay here until it's time to take the boat to the escape point."

"I'm not coming along? Why? You don't trust me?"

"Nobody trusts you, ass-breath," Wally said.

"It's just the four of us going to the plant," Leslie said. "Thorn, Cameron, Pauly, and me. You and Wally have other roles. This is your landing spot."

She touched the ballpoint tip to a location along the coast, the closest point to the southern-most cooling canal.

"This is bullshit," Flynn said. "I want to go to the plant."

Leslie seemed not to hear. Her gaze wandered around Thorn's kitchen and the living area beyond as though her eyes were refocusing on some distant time. Perhaps it had just hit her. The house where she'd first felt safe so many years back. This place of refuge. Something else now.

"Leslie," Flynn said. "You can't leave me out of this."

The long-ago look in her eyes faded and she returned. Her expression had softened from the journey.

"Somebody always drives the getaway car. It's as essential as any other piece of this."

"You're trying to protect me. Giving me this bullshit role."

"I'm not going to argue. The decision's made."

He heaved a disgusted sigh and stalked to a chair across the room.

"Using my house," said Thorn. "That was always the plan, wasn't it? That day Cameron came, he was checking the place out. You were already familiar with it, but Cameron had to have a look, a scouting mission. Checking out its strategic value."

"I didn't think you'd mind," she said.

"You were just going to show up here, the bunch of you, no warning, middle of the night, walk in, and you thought we'd have a big happy sleepover?"

Leslie traced a fingertip along the grout between the countertop tiles. She looked at him and gave a *so what?* shrug. "We're here. And so far it seems to be working out."

"And separating Flynn and me, that's insurance, to keep me in line."

She held his gaze. "Why should we keep you in line if you're as committed as you say?"

"Hey, ass-wipe." Wally's hands were on the keyboard, head turned toward Thorn. "What mile marker are we at?"

"Why?"

"What're you doing, Wally?" Leslie asked.

"I'm writing code, boss. Doing my job. So what mile marker is this?"

A remnant from the days of the Overseas Railroad, the small, green markers ran the length of the Keys, counting down each mile to Key West.

Thorn gave Leslie a questioning look and she shrugged. So tell him.

He gave Wally the number of the closest mile marker, and Wally turned back to the computer and resumed typing. "Okay. So where's the pipeline run around here?"

"What're you talking about?"

"The water line. Florida Keys Aqueduct Authority. Pumped from a well field near Florida City down here to the Keys."

Leslie went over to the desk where Wally had set up his laptop and looked over his shoulder. "Why're you playing around with that?"

"I finished all the jobs you gave me. Everything's set. Ready to pull the trigger. So I'm goofing on something else."

"Pipeline is about a hundred yards west of here," Thorn said. "Runs along the side of the Overseas Highway."

"Good," Wally said. "So we can see it."

"It's buried."

"I'm not talking about the pipeline, ass-face, I'm talking about the water that runs through it." Wally's fingers flew across the keyboard for several moments, then he turned around and smiled at them, lifting a single finger over the keys. "And away we go." He plunked his finger down. Stood up, walked through the open doors onto the porch. "Which way is it?"

Thorn pointed west.

Leslie came over and stood next to him, Flynn and Thorn drifting outside, everyone staring out at the hummock of slash pines and wild tamarinds and spice and mahogany.

"What've you done, Wally?"

"Hold on. It'll take a minute. You got a 130-mile transmission line, water pressure at 250 pounds a square inch, pipe begins at thirty-six inches, narrows to twenty-four, then south of here goes to eighteen. Eight-hundred-horsepower electric motors suck it out of the ground and shoot it south. When there's a power outage, they got two-thousand-horse diesels that kick in.

"Then two miles north of here you got a booster pump station, and another one down in Long Key, Marathon, Ramrod Key, they're jacking up the pressure every thirty, forty miles. Got thousands of gallons a minute flowing inside that pipeline. A few million gallons every day sucked out of the ground.

"So it's like this. Say the Key Largo booster station just up the road, it keeps pumping its ass off, but south of here at the pump station in Long Key, they got a malfunction and have to shut down. Their power just switches off. Some kind of computer glitch. Software goes haywire. Their pumps quit."

He turned around and gave them an impish grin. "Hey, something happens like that, where's all that water go? Well, they got a half-assed safety system, shut-off valves every few miles to prevent backflow. And they got a com network, it sends a message up to the Key Largo pump station, warns it to shut down.

"But say some hacker, he overrides that com network, the Largo station keeps pumping water, pumping and pumping. Then that hacker tells the Key Largo station their fucking water pressure is dropping and they need their pumps to work harder. What do you get? Anybody want to guess?"

"You idiot," Thorn said.

"Okay, no guesses. So the answer is, all that water pressure is building up in that twenty-four-inch pipe. Building, building. Then, hey, suddenly for no reason, the relief valve at this very mile marker opens wide, and badda bing. I'm tearing that relief valve a new asshole."

"Wally. Undo it right now. Put it right." Leslie was staring helplessly at the computer screen, the rolling lines of code.

"Too late."

"We don't need this," she said. "This'll bring heat. And for no reason."

"Hey, is that it?" Wally pointed off at the tree line. "Yeah, I think we got ourselves a gusher."

About a half mile away, a silver-blue geyser of water was shooting straight up, maybe a hundred feet into the blue afternoon sky. A fountain of pure aquifer water appearing in the middle of the native forest that separated Thorn's property from the Overseas Highway.

"See," Wally said. "That's the kind of shit I do, ass-breath. That's what I bring to the table." Speaking to Flynn, then glancing at Thorn. "So lay the fuck off me, or I'll blow your shit up, too. Don't think I can't."

"Shut it down, Wally."

"No can do. Has to be fixed by hand. Wrenches and shit."

A car rolled into the drive. Nobody Thorn knew. A ten-year-old SUV with dark windows. It was covered in dust and the grill was badly dented as if the car had collided head-on with a telephone pole. An out-of-state license tag was mounted on the crushed bumper.

Cameron left the porch and trotted over to the car, stood by the driver's door, and waited till it opened. Since Thorn had seen her last, her red hair had been cut pixie short. It blazed scarlet in the afternoon sunlight as she marched across the lawn, following Prince toward the house.

Same uniform as the day they'd spent together in Leslie's boat, counting the croc population. Fatigue jacket, scruffy jeans, hiking boots. She cast her gaze around the premises, surveying the layout with an almost mathematical precision. Pretty eyes, but a misshapen mouth with awkwardly protruding teeth. Still, something about her was fierce. The fiery resolve of a field commander on the eve of battle.

"You stay here," Leslie told the group. "This doesn't concern you."

She went down the steps and crossed the lawn, and the two women shared a stiff embrace, touched cheek to cheek. More ritual than personal.

Leslie spoke to Prince and he edged away, giving them privacy.

When their conversation was finished, Leslie waited

while the red-haired woman walked back to her SUV, opened the rear hatch, and hailed Prince. She handed Leslie a liquor box, and from the cargo hold Cameron dragged out a large sheet of fiberboard covered by a white sheet. With both hands he raised it above his head and carried it to the house.

The red-haired woman handed Leslie a set of keys, turned, and headed back down the drive on foot. In the distance, the geyser continued to spew. Sirens were screaming out on the highway.

Prince angled the fiberboard through the French doors and laid it on the dining-room table. The long, rectangular oak table where Thorn had eaten his first meals, learned what table manners he knew, and later on, when the house became his, shared countless dinners with friends and lovers.

Leslie set the liquor box on a counter and walked over to the fiberboard.

"What's in the box?" Wally said.

"Uniforms. FBI." Leslie took hold of the end of the white sheet and drew it away.

In all the years Thorn had passed the place offshore, he'd never paid much attention to the Turkey Point nuclear plant, so he hadn't realized how vast it was, how numerous were its domes and smokestacks, cooling towers and guardhouses and office buildings, roadways and transmission lines. An industrial city. Twenty cooling canals shot straight south for about ten miles, the crocodile breeding grounds that Leslie once patrolled.

This scale model was meticulously crafted with plastic windows in the office buildings and runty trees lining the entrance drive and half-inch hard-hatted workers scattered around the site. Each structure had a printed label attached. Cars, trucks, earthmoving equipment, even an airboat docked beside a small, rectangular building that was labeled BIOLOGY LAB.

Pauly and Cameron stood on one side of the table, Flynn and Thorn and Leslie on the other. Even Wally broke away from his laptop to take a look.

Leslie lifted the lid off one of the structures. Inside were more handcrafted details. An enormous control room full of electronic hardware with sweeping desks and podiums and a wall of computer screens.

As one who created miniature replicas for a living, Thorn marveled at the detail. The model had required months of work by a highly skilled craftsman. Every door, beam, column, truss, pipe, valve, tube, tank, storage area, skylight, stairway, elevator shaft. Ladders and machinery and earthmovers.

"You'll be studying this layout until it's as familiar as your face in the mirror. You'll learn where every visible defensive device is placed, and where all the hidden trip wires and motion detectors are planted, the entire sensing system. From this point on, there'll be no more games. This is real."

"Who's the babe?" Wally said. "I'd take a dip in that spasm chasm."

Leslie fixed him with a cold smile. "Her name is Cassandra. Don't worry, you'll be seeing her again. As soon as we're done."

Leslie's tone had hardened. Even Wally heard it and shut the hell up.

THIRTY-THREE

MONDAY MORNING ON HIS WAY to the office, knowing this would probably be the last free minute he had for a few days, Sheffield swung off I-95 at Seventy-ninth Street and headed east into Little Haiti. Operating on an hour's ragged sleep, but still so wired from the night before, the disastrous raid on Prince Key, Frank tapped out a mindless beat on the steering wheel the whole way.

He parked in the lot of Motel Blu on Biscayne Boulevard, a block down from Seventy-ninth. The sign out front said MIAMI STYLE AT AFFORDABLE RATES. Behind Motel Blu he could see a cool, shady section of Little River. Frank got out, walked over to the small bridge along the boulevard, and looked down at the sluggish green flow.

About a mile east the river emptied into the northern end of Biscayne Bay. Despite the heavy traffic on the thoroughfare behind him, standing there you got a peaceful hint of how this part of town had been once, maybe fifty years back, locals picnicking along the riverbank, fishing, napping in the shadows of the cabbage palms. Snowbirds staying at motels like this one, back in its earlier incarnation before all the seedy bars and nudie theaters, hookers and Haitian markets, and fast-food joints moved in.

As a motel owner himself, one who was trying hard to revive his own slice of Miami history, Sheffield wasn't impressed with the attempts at rebirth along this stretch of Biscayne. The gentrifiers had given the architecture a new name, MiMo, Miami Modern, and designated it historic. Space age with bold angles, lots of plate glass, and extreme, weird-angled roofs. The 1950s version of Tomorrowland. Or a bowling alley built for the Jetsons.

To Frank it told a different story. Mom and Pop got scared and sold out thirty years ago and fled when the hookers and the crack dealers and the johns moved in, and now a bunch of thirty-year-old trust-fund kids had scooped up the places supercheap, slapped on trendy colors, added tubes of neon, then rechristened their best rooms Bayview and Ocean Vista even though the bay and the ocean were miles away. But Frank was willing to bet real money that those kids hadn't gotten around to throwing out all the bloodstained mattresses or patching the bullet holes.

It had been a while since he'd cruised this stretch of Biscayne. He was here now because of Leslie Levine. Over the weekend, while Frank and Magnuson were making a mess of things on Prince Key, Marta had sacrificed Sunday, going to the office, where she'd spent the morning online, then worked the phones and tracked through Levine's records, which eventually pointed to this kitschy dive along a polluted stretch of Little River.

First, she discovered Leslie's paychecks were automatically deposited in her bank account, and that ac-

count used a post office box up in Aventura for a home
address. She used the same PO box for tax returns and
other assorted mail. Cash payments for the mail drop.
Dead end there.

Her driver's license showed an address in Kendall,
but according to the apartment manager, Leslie had
moved out a year earlier. No forwarding address. When
Marta asked the apartment manager if Leslie had any
friends, anyone who might know her current whereabouts, the lady told Marta no friends ever stopped by.
Not even men friends? Marta asked her. No men. And
as Marta was about to end the conversation, the woman
said, well, one woman used to visit pretty regular. You
wouldn't call her a friend. What would you call her?
Marta said. Her mother, the manager said.

Mother? Yeah, yeah, her name was Geraldine. She
and the manager had gotten friendly, what with Geraldine hanging around so much.

Why was she hanging around? Marta asked.

Babysitting, the manager told her. Babysitting Leslie's
daughter, Julie, cute as a speckled pup.

Geraldine Levine. Julie.

Did the apartment manager know how Marta could
locate Leslie's mother? Well, yes, she'd visited Geraldine once. Last time she saw her, Geraldine lived in an
efficiency attached to Motel Blu up near Little Haiti.
But the manager didn't feel safe in the neighborhood
and never returned.

Sheffield could understand why. It was a dodgy section, trying hard to catch the next fashionable wave, but
not there yet. Not even close. The pedestrian traffic alone,
a steady stream of greasy-haired guys pushing grocery
carts and a sauntering parade of scrawny ladies in

leopard-skin spandex, was reason enough for Kendall
apartment managers to stay away.

No one came to the door of Geraldine Levine's
apartment. Sheffield knocked again, then worked his
way around the small concrete structure, peeking
through the venetian blinds, seeing only a small room
cluttered with plastic toys and stuffed animals.

On the grassy bank next to the Little River, he found
Leslie's mom. She was sitting in an aluminum chair
reading a paperback while a baby lay awake in a shaded
bassinet beside her. The kid wasn't a year old, but she
had a wild patch of Leslie's auburn hair, and her serious
deep-blue eyes peered with interest at Sheffield as
he came up beside Geraldine's chair.

Geraldine's hair was bleached a harsh yellow, the
roots showing gray at the part. She wore a pair of white
shorts and a tight green top and no jewelry or makeup.
A woman in her early fifties with the look of someone
with a seriously misspent youth. Battered by too much
sun, too much booze, too many nights she'd rather not
remember.

"Hi, Julie," Frank said.

The kid kept looking up at Sheffield until he made a
goofy face and she grinned and gurgled something.
Geraldine dog-eared a page and shut her book and laid
it in her lap. But didn't turn around.

Sheffield drew out his ID, squatted next to her chair
and presented it.

"A croc ate her," Geraldine said, eyes on the dark
green water. "She's gone and not coming back. That
means I'll be raising this beautiful girl myself. Which is
okay, I'm not complaining. Not every mother gets a
second chance."

And for the next half hour that was all Frank Sheffield could get from her. Versions of that same statement no matter what question he posed. As if she'd rehearsed the speech, knew that Frank or someone like him was coming to ask for Leslie's whereabouts. A tough nut who would never crack.

Marta was right again. The reason someone went to the trouble to stage her own death was to be considerate. To create a cover story that could be told to a child who would one day grow up and ask the inevitable question: Where's Mommy?

So he could take Monday off, Claude Sellers pulled two ten-hour shifts on the weekend, going over various assault scenarios with his security squad. They did walk-throughs on all the attack plans Nicole had raised in their tabletop meeting with Sheen from NRC and Special Asshole in Charge Sheffield. Claude knew these predrill exercises with his team were total bullshit, but he needed to cover his ass for the inevitable inquiry that would follow the force-on-force exercise, after it went kablooey.

He knew what the real plan was, and exactly how he was going to foil it single-handedly. He also knew how he was going to keep Nicole out of the action. No heroism gold medal for her. Fuck Nicole. He was cutting the broad loose.

After how she'd been snarling at him, unappreciative, toying with his affections, Claude had decided, as of now, he was one hundred percent doing this for himself. It would be Claude Sellers walking away as the white knight who saved Miami from nuclear disaster. The kind of press he'd get after this, he could write his own ticket.

He spent those two days cramming with his guys, a handpicked team. Two days stressing the countermeasures they would take to each of Nicole's attack methods. The ATVs, the multiple attack points. Laying out each one, then asking the guys what their response would be. Even inviting the numbnut plant supervisor, Ronald Silbert, to sit in for a while, so he could duly note Claude's professionalism.

Monday morning crack of dawn, Claude parked the van with the magnetic AT&T logo in the huge lot of a condo next to the Silver Sands Motel. Pulled on his jumpsuit, his insulated boots, his hard hat, then a pair of safety goggles for the sake of the security videos that were lurking around the vicinity.

He got out, worked his way onto the property of the Silver Sands Motel, found a thick hibiscus hedge with a good view, and started surveilling room 106. At just after eight that morning, Sheffield came outside in gym shorts and a T-shirt, looking groggy, hair disheveled. He drank a mug of coffee at the concrete picnic table, stared through the palms at the water, then went back inside. Half hour after that, all showered and shaved and dressed in street clothes, he locked the front door, got in his Chevy, and drove off.

Claude came out of the bushes and swung into action. Pulled on his work gloves. Jiggered the lock, pushed the door open, and stepped into the room. Before he got to work, he took out his tube of electro gel and glopped some on the outside aluminum doorknob. Smeared it thick, then closed the door but didn't let it latch. He carried his work bag over to a rattan table in front of the TV.

He spotted the closest wall plug to the front door, took the microwave capacitor out of his bag, and wired it to the exposed leads of a heavy-duty extension cord, then screwed on the yellow junction caps. Now the 120 volts coming out of that wall socket would flow into the capacitor and exit as 4,000 volts, so hot it would approximate direct current.

He attached the heavy cable exiting the other side of the capacitor to the copper mount he'd fashioned in his workshop at the plant. It clamped tight to the knob on the inside of the door of 106. He stretched the cord out, made sure there was enough slack to reach the plug. Which there was. A foot extra.

He drew open the door. Walked over to the socket, plugged the sucker in, listened to its pleasant, deep-throated hum. Then went back to the door. Nudged it open, his glove on the wood frame. Stepped outside with his tool bag, then with one finger, he tugged the door until it was nearly closed.

Given the bleary state he was in when he left this morning, Sheffield would think he'd forgotten to close the damn thing. He'd grip the knob, and, bam, you'd have yourself a special asshole-in-charge smoke bomb.

THIRTY-FOUR

FRANK SPENT THE REST OF Monday morning sitting in the waiting room outside his own office, in a chair across from Marta's desk that was usually reserved for the next agent in line desiring to have a word with Sheffield.

He'd been ordered to do so by the official presiding over the internal investigation, a guy named Banks, sent down by the attorney general.

Inside Frank's office, along with Banks, there were a couple of guys Frank knew vaguely from DC seminars, one woman he'd had drinks with years ago. All of them taking regular smoke or pee breaks, walking out of Frank's office and coming back a few minutes later without comment or eye contact.

As he'd predicted, the full range of federal officialdom had descended overnight. Eager beavers couldn't wait, took the breakfast flight from Reagan. The forensic specialists went directly to Prince Key, while the debriefing group settled into Frank's office.

Two in matching suits and crisp white shirts from the Office of Professional Responsibility worked under Director Mansfield himself. They were the disciplinary crew who would listen to the stories of all involved, and after careful consideration they'd dole out whatever punishment was decided.

The woman, Gayle Holly, was from the Office of Integrity and Compliance. Doing the right things, the right way. That was their credo. Sheffield was pretty sure neither he nor Magnuson would be charged with doing much, if anything, right. Processes and procedures, violations of laws, regulations, and policies, misconduct, staying within the letter and spirit of all applicable rules. The barf beamer, the faulty radios, the flawed chain of command, and vague rules of engagement. Sheffield was confident that the letter and spirit of lots of applicable rules had been violated and re-violated.

And three more. Two women in their thirties who chatted noisily on their way into the office, speaking a brand of Spanish even Sheffield, who was halfway fluent, could not begin to decipher. Those two were from the Office of the Inspector General, young ladies no doubt recruited from the top of their respective law school classes, who reported to the attorney general about such matters as integrity, efficiency, and effectiveness in operational situations. OIG was looking for criminal misconduct. Not just a demotion or a turd in Sheffield's file, but real, actual jail time.

Then there was a gentleman in his late sixties wearing a bow tie and suspenders with his silver hair in a braided ponytail. Hippie inquisitor from the Security Division. A polygraph guy and cyber-expert whose job was to ferret out unreliable employees, ones dabbling in espionage or using their Web access to commit crimes, leak information, or download off child-porn sites.

One by one, Magnuson's men and Frank's SWAT

guys had been parading by Sheffield into his office, looking worried when they entered and more worried when they exited. A lot of tight faces and sweat-stained shirts. No one spoke to him or looked his way.

"They're rubbing your nose in it," Marta said quietly after Pipes, the barf beamer, had gone into the office and shut the door. "Make you sit here, outside your own office, them inside. They could use the conference room, but, no, this is for humiliation."

"I'm aware of that," Sheffield said.

"And it doesn't piss you off?"

"Is this conversation being recorded?"

Marta made one of her faces, squinching at a putrid smell.

Pipes left; Dinkins came in a few minutes later.

He stopped and said to Frank, "We're still on for Friday, right? The force-on-force?"

"Don't know if we'll have jobs on Friday, Dink."

"Oh, come on. It's not that bad."

"That what you're hearing from the others, it isn't that bad?"

"The shit's going to fall on Magnuson, that's how I'm hearing it."

The door to Frank's office opened and one of the Latinas said, "You Dinkins?"

When Dinkins was inside, Marta said, "They're Brazilians, those two. In case you were wondering. Knew each other in Rio. Both unmarried. That's Portuguese they're speaking."

"You're a font of information."

"And Zach called, wanted to talk to you face-to-face."

"I don't know a Zach."

"Agent Magnuson."

"You're first-naming with this guy?"

"I first-name with all the handsome men around here. Except you."

"Why'd he want a face-to-face?"

"Didn't say. Maybe to get your stories straight before all this started. It was early this morning. I told him to call your cell, but he'd tried and you had it turned off as usual. So I told him where you lived; he said he might just drive out to the Key and speak to you before the day got started."

"Well, he didn't make it."

Another half hour passed. Marta was typing, Sheffield on his phone, surfing the Net, shopping for outdoor light fixtures, something to illuminate the bases of the palm trees around the Silver Sands. He was giving serious consideration to some solar-powered tiki lights that flickered yellow. Very retro. Give the place a *Beach Blanket Bingo* vibe. Which got him thinking about Annette Funicello, Sandra Dee. Then he was exiting the light-fixture site and typing Nicole McIvey's name into the search box, something he hadn't done till now. Not wanting to invade her privacy, and, hell, truth be known, he didn't want to find out something that cooled his feelings toward her.

But after her performance at the Four Seasons, then last night, her self-preservation speech, distancing herself from this shitstorm, the cooling was in process.

He found her professional listings, scanned for anything he didn't know. Just the usual stuff, college degree, then her jobs. Hired at GAO, General Accounting Office, about as boring as it got. Then the jump over to NIPC, guarding the nation's infrastructure. After that, her pay grade made a steady upward push, reaching GS-10, then leveling off. Shifting to the South Florida division a couple of years back, and after that, still no promotions. Seemed odd she'd moved up so fast, then stalled out, as if she'd lost her drive. Or maybe not. Maybe it was just the economy, things slowing down, federal budget cuts, shrinkage.

"Can I speak to you, Agent Sheffield?"

Frank bobbled his phone, nearly sent it flying.

Angie Stevens, the cybergeek, had sneaked up on him and was standing so close, her skirt was brushing his shirtsleeve.

He leaned back and looked up at her face. Noticing for the first time that her blond bangs were cut at a cock-eyed angle, at least an inch higher on one side than the other. Maybe some screwy new style he wasn't aware of. Frank was no expert on makeup, but her blue eye shadow looked glopped on. More showgirl than FBI agent.

Angie was looking down at him, her eyes not meeting his, circling his face as if searching for a safe place to land. "I drove down to Turkey Point like you asked. Homeland's guys missed something. A software bomb."

"A software bomb?"

"Yeah. I defused it. It took a while. The guy that wrote it, and I could tell right away it was a guy from how it was done, well, it was pretty intricate.

"Turkey Point's operating system uses a version of RuggedCom. The systems are deployed in harsh environments, heavy-usage applications like traffic-control systems, railroad communications, military sites, electrical substations. And in power plants. Beyond networking, these devices provide serial-to-IP conversion in SCADA systems."

"And?"

"Thing is, RuggedCom is known to have an undocumented backdoor account with a factory-enabled password that's dynamically generated based on the device's address. A hacker like this guy who's good with SCADA systems has to know about this vulnerability."

"And this software bomb?"

She reached up with one hand and swished her hair awkwardly. Like a gesture she'd copied from a sultry movie star, then practiced in a mirror but hadn't worked out all the kinks. "Software bombs have a trigger and a payload. The trigger for this one was a fluctuation in the electrical power. If the lights at Turkey Point flicker, even a little variation, this thing was set to go off. Pretty clever trigger." Her eyes circled off as if she were watching an insect roaming the air.

"And what was the payload?"

"It's set to delete files. You can delete so many it will render the entire system helpless. It'll cause a general shutdown. But this code wasn't written to do that. It was just set to delete some payroll stuff, some e-mails and general announcements. More like a paintball than a bomb."

"So it was harmless?"

"Not exactly. See, I also found a signature. The guy's nom de plume. And I did a search on him. I'd never heard of this guy before, but I've read up on him now. He's been hacking for several years. Getting more sophisticated.

"Last couple of years he's specialized in infrastructure projects mainly in the western states. I sent you an e-mail with a list of all I could find. Ports, railroads, oil refineries. But he really gets off on water-treatment plants. He likes to contaminate water supplies, run trains with chemical cars off their tracks into lakes, redirect sewage lines into reservoirs. A lot of his early cyber attacks were crude, then the last year or two, they got better.

"So you see the problem."

"The guy's gotten slicker."

"That's right, and it looks like he's become so fanatical, once he gets inside a nuclear plant, and he's gained administrative access to all the plant's systems, well, to me it doesn't make sense he'd leave something as simple and harmless as a software bomb that only deletes a few random files."

"So you think there's more malicious code you didn't find?"

Angie did. She'd head back down there pronto and keep digging.

When she was gone, Frank said, "You're sure she's our best?"

"All I know," Marta said, "some big shots at the National Security Agency keep trying to recruit her. Last time they offered her four times what she makes here, but she turned it down."

Frank went back to his chair and sat, waiting his turn on the hot seat.

Five minutes, ten. Marta took a phone call. Listened, then hung up. "That was Angie. Back at her computer."

"Yeah?"

"Some pipeline just blew up in the Keys. Water spraying in the air a hundred feet."

"So?"

"She thought you'd be interested."

"What was it? A bomb?"

"Cyber attack," Marta said. "Angie's on it. She'll get back to you when she knows more. She said it had the hallmarks of our guy."

"Call her back. Tell her to forget the frigging pipeline. Get her skinny ass back to Turkey Point on the double."

"Those words?"

Before he could answer, the door beside him opened and Nicole McIvey came in, glanced down at him, held his eyes for a moment. "Wow, that hangdog look, Frank. I've seen that expression before."

"Yeah? Where's that?"

"Troublemaker waiting to see the principal, bend over, grab his ankles."

"Call her back now," he said to Marta. Then to Nicole: "I'm not scared of these guys. I've been paddled by the best."

THIRTY-FIVE

NICOLE TOOK THE SEAT BESIDE him, gave Marta a token smile, and they waited in silence for a while. Marta spoke to Angie Stevens on the phone, passed on Frank's message, then she excused herself to take a bathroom break.

"Alone at last," Nicole said.

"A software bomb. You know what that is?"

Nicole said of course she knew what a software bomb was. Frank explained the rest of it. Malicious code that seemed harmless, possibly a red herring, something to waste their time. Which raised the likelihood that still more code was hidden somewhere in the power plant's network.

While she was digesting that, he told her about the Keys water pipeline. Saying it sounded like Wally was still in the vicinity.

That got a scornful frown. "That's not how he works. The raid on Prince Key spooked them. The Chee boys are long gone."

"You're positive? You know these guys so well you can predict what they'll do next?"

A flush crept into her cheeks. With a tone he hadn't

before heard from her, as if she were indulging an addled child, she said, "The Keys pipeline thing, that could have been on a time delay, too. He could've set it long ago. Or pulled it off remotely. No reason he has to be nearby. Ask Magnuson if you don't take my word for it. He's studied Pauly's movements. The guy's gone. And his brother goes where he goes."

"Okay, *tranquilo*. I'm just raising the possibility."

"Don't *tranquilo* me, Frank."

Dinkins came out. Someone inside the office shut the door firmly behind him.

"How'd it go?"

"Who can tell? Like I said, they seem to be circling Magnuson. But, hey, with pros like these, they're asking shit so fast, one from this direction, one from that, rat-a-tat-tat, my head was coming unscrewed."

Door opened, the latter-day hippie curled his finger at Frank.

"Kick ass," Dinkins said.

"Sit up straight," Nicole said, smiling at Frank.

"The Chee brothers are still around," he said. "Believe it."

Her smile dwindled away.

Frank followed the suspenders into his own damn office.

When he entered, everyone was standing, and they stayed on their feet until Frank took a seat in a chair across from his desk. Like an all-rise moment in a courtroom. The silver-haired hipster from the Security Division sat behind Frank's desk, tapping Frank's favorite ballpoint pen against his ink blotter. The hippie was running the show. A surprise. Or maybe they'd been taking turns. Test-driving the desk of the special agent in charge of the Miami field office. See how it handled the tight turns.

The others were arrayed in a semicircle with various views of Frank's profile. He looked around his office, having never studied it from this angle before. Never tried to make his office a home away from home, but now he realized from this vantage point it looked stark, no knickknacks, nothing personal to soften it up, a little forbidding.

Though he'd done it once when they'd first met, the security guy formally introduced himself, Miles Shuster, then went around the room naming everyone, giving their titles.

"You understand, Agent Sheffield, we're here to debrief you."

"Well, it shouldn't take long. I'm not wearing underpants today."

Nobody smiled. Maybe they'd heard the line before. Or maybe they were professional sourpusses.

It took Frank five minutes to lay out the order of events, the lead-up to the raid, the raid itself, the shooting, the aftermath. Shouldering the blame like a good soldier. Whole time he was telling the story, he was picturing the Silver Sands and hearing the sea breeze ticking through the palms, a whiff of coconut suntan oil. Come on, how bad was that? Fired from the FBI, forced to live full-time at the beach. Shit. He was burned out anyway. Do your worst, bureaucrats.

The only thing tipping the scales the other way, okay, yeah, he wanted somebody to put these ELF assholes out of business before they exploded some nasty gadget and sent a plume of fallout over the city, and he wasn't sure anybody else was up to the task. And, yes, he very much wanted to speak to Flynn Moss again, make sure the kid was okay.

"Before we begin, Agent Sheffield," the aging hippie said, "I want you to take a look at something our forensics people found on Prince Key a few hours ago. It's rather mystifying."

He reached into a brown paper sack and came out with a human arm. Small, slender, with a camouflage rubber bracelet around the wrist. He held it out, offering it to Sheffield. "Prints have been lifted, forensics done. You can handle it if you like."

Frank took the arm. It was fashioned from some kind of synthetic rubberized material. Had the weight and the feel of a real arm. The fingers were lifelike, nails and all. Not a mannequin, something much more realistic.

"There's an ID stamp on the stump," the security man said. "Forensics did some calls, traced it to a local TV production company. They're shooting some crime show here in Miami. It's one of their props. Somebody reported it missing a few months ago."

The hippie asked Frank if he knew anything about he arm, but before Frank could answer, his office phone ang.

The security hippie picked it up, listened, then held t out to Frank. "A message from a Mr. Juan Medira. Jrgent."

"Building-code inspector. Probably my septic tank unneth over." Frank took the phone, smiled at the hunorless suits filling his room. "This better be good," he aid to Marta.

"Oh, no, this is bad. This is very bad."

When she finished, Frank handed the phone back to Miles Shuster. Frank's head was swimming. The room was ten degrees warmer and his face felt as if it had begun to slowly inflate.

"Is there a problem?" Shuster said.

Sheffield stood up. Jaw tight, grinding his teeth as he went from face to face. Sizing up this bunch of office dwellers who were deciding his fate and the fate of his field agents, these twerps insulated in the upper-floor offices, knowing nothing about the street, about kicking in doors, taking down an island full of bombmakers and assorted radicals in the total dark, the middle of a tropical storm.

"Yeah, a problem," Frank said. "That was Juan Medira, he's a building-code inspector for Miami-Dade. I'm doing some construction at my place so Juan's around a lot. He stopped by a few minutes ago to inspect some roof tile I installed, and he found a corpse on my front porch."

Nobody gasped, nobody did much of anything. As if corpses were someone else's department.

"I hope it wasn't somebody you know."

"I knew him, but not very well. Agent Magnuson."

That got an eyebrow lift or two, some sideways glances, and a few looks of consternation.

"Must have been suicide," the security man said.

The others murmured in agreement. Self-righteous pricks, proud of their power to intimidate and destroy.

"No," Frank said. "Magnuson was electrocuted. Looks like he walked into a booby trap intended for me."

Sheffield sat at his concrete picnic table, watching the Miami-Dade homicide detectives and ID techs working alongside his own forensics team, taking photos of Magnuson's twisted body with the burns and blisters on his right hand and arm and some kind of evil rash on his face, while other cops were still interviewing Juan Medira over by the swimming pool.

Yellow crime-scene tape was strung from palm tree to palm tree. Cops going in and out of 106, all the usual state-of-the-art science, which had produced nothing at Marcus Bendell's house and would produce nothing here. Some greasy substance had been found on the doorknob, probably electro gel from the same tube as that found on the ladder at Bendell's.

First time in Silver Sands' long and not always stellar history there'd been crime-scene tape and cops parading around the place. His Eden was tainted. He wouldn't be stretching out in his bed tonight in 106. Or anytime soon.

From the start there'd been a killer floating around the edges of this ELF operation. A straight line from Marcus Bendell to Zach Magnuson. Was it an eco-terrorist? Leslie Levine? He doubted it. More likely the guy who rigged this trap was somebody who thought Frank was getting too close to discovering something. Which was nice to hear because he didn't feel close to solving anything. The Bendell murder? Leslie Levine's disappearance? The cartoon elf on the Turkey Point computer system? The software bomb? The Chee brothers? The guy that blew up the water pipeline in the Keys?

This case had been scrambled from the minute Nicole picked him up last week, drove him down to Turkey Point.

Sheffield tried it again, running through the last few days, the step-by-step replay of everything case-related since Nicole showed up, from Marcus Bendell's electro-cution to this electrocution, looking for the thread that had to be there, wishing he had his yellow legal pad so he could draw connecting lines between events. Then going back again to Nicole, the drive down to Turkey Point, the meeting with Sheen and Sellers, the whole force-on-force thing.

Frank could feel a swell of heat in his chest. He was onto something, a glowing presence very close, like a word he'd been working to remember, fetching, fetching, until there it was, appearing from the haze but, damn it, still just beyond his grasp.

Then a few yards behind him some grievous asshole pulled a big black Lincoln over the edge of the asphalt lot, rolling right onto the patch of pristine sod next to the shuffleboard court. The sod had been laid two weeks ago. The seams between the squares were still clearly visible. Sheffield had been watering that patch an hour a day. Religious about it.

He stood up, ready to ream somebody out. But, no, it was the hippie security guy, Miles Shuster, and another guy from Professional Responsibility who got out of the Lincoln and ambled over.

"Move your car. And do it slowly so you don't dig up my new grass."

Miles looked back at the Lincoln. "Look, Frank," the security man said, laying an unwelcome hand on his shoulder. "We came out here to let you know in person that with serious reservations, the panel has decided to clear the Prince Key case. We all agree there was a considerable dereliction and reckless disregard, and we may need to revisit the situation later after the field reports come in, but given these unfortunate circumstances with Agent Magnuson we're suspending—"

"Put it in a memo," Frank said. "Just get your fucking gas hog off my new grass."

When they were gone, he checked the time, half past five, and called Marta. He knew she'd be in long past quitting time today, with an agent down.

"Look up a number for me," he said.

"You okay?"

"Everybody keeps asking that."

"Well, are you?"

"Her name is Sheen. She's NRC. I don't know where she's based. But this is her area, region two. Get her number and call me back."

"You sound frantic."

"The number, Marta."

She was back in five minutes with three numbers. Sheen's home in Palm Beach, office in Lauderdale, and her cell.

Frank tried her cell first. Got her right off. Good sign.

"Agent Sheffield, how nice to hear from you."

"I've got a question."

"About Friday's drill?"

"That's right. Friday's drill."

"Well, shoot." She chuckled. "No, no, I guess that's the wrong thing to say to a federal agent."

Sheffield pushed on. "Whose idea was it, the force-on-force? The ELF logo shows up, then you guys got involved. It's the NRC's call, isn't it, when to do a force-on-force?"

"Yes. We're charged with oversight. We make the determination when all such inspections or drills are required."

"And is that how it worked this time? Your call?"

She said, "What's the problem? You sound very stressed."

Frank closed his eyes and held the phone at arm's length. Everybody concerned about his blood pressure. It just made the pressure worse.

He brought the phone back to his ear in time to hear her say quietly, "Claude Sellers proposed the idea and Mr. Sellers set the date."

"And Agent McIvey?"

"What do you mean?"

"Was she collaborating with Mr. Sellers before you came on board?"

"Collaborating?"

"Did they double-team you? Pressure you to schedule the drill?"

She was silent for a while. When she came back, her voice was firm and precise as if these words were being recorded for some official record. "I wouldn't say *pressure*. But, yes, before I was consulted, Ms. McIvey and Mr. Sellers had discussed the situation and mutually agreed that such a drill was necessary. And they made their case to me very forcefully."

"So that was the purpose of the ELF logo, why they put it up there in the first place. To get everybody hot and bothered, to justify running the force-on-force."

"And why would anyone do that?" Sheen asked.

"Why indeed?"

THIRTY-SIX

BY SUNDOWN THAT MONDAY WORK crews from the Aqueduct Authority along with engineers from South Florida Water Management had the pipeline repaired. The geyser sprouting above the treetops sagged, then sagged some more and disappeared.

While it was still spewing, Prince had driven out to the highway and joined the crowd nosing around the rupture and gathered what information he could from cops and bystanders. He stayed for an hour watching the backhoes and the welders and the dozen guys in the shovel-wielding road crew.

When he returned, he reported that the FKAA folks believed a software glitch was responsible for the mess. Apparently Wally's high jinks would have no further repercussions. But Leslie warned Wally if he tried anything like that again, he'd be excluded from the operation.

"You can't cut me out. No way you could pull this off without me."

"You're right," Leslie said. "Which means I'll yank the plug on the whole thing and walk away. If that's what you and your brother want, then fine, just one more prank like that and it's finished."

Wally looked across at his brother, saw the cold menace in his face, took a swallow. "Whatever you say, boss. All I wanted was these assholes to see the kind of shit I can do."

"We're blown away," Thorn said. "You're a world-class adolescent."

Wally glared at him for a moment, then picked up his grouper sandwich and took a sloppy bite.

While Cameron was out, he'd run down to market 103 and gotten take-out dinners from Sundowners—sandwiches, fries, coleslaw, and slices of key lime pie. A feast that seemed to cheer everyone up, except Pauly, who didn't seem to have that emotional gear.

When the meal was done, Thorn checked on Sugar again. He was awake. Thorn set a sandwich and a bottle of Red Stripe within reach on the bedside table and went into the bathroom and brought back a bottle of aspirin. He drew back the covers and took a look at Sugar's leg. The knee was swollen double its normal size, a purple grapefruit.

Voice hoarse, Sugar said, "I thought of something."

Thorn looked back at the open doorway, hearing that same faint creak, a woman's weight on those old floorboards.

Sugar lifted a hand from the sheets and motioned for Thorn to lean close. In a whisper so quiet Thorn could barely hear, Sugar said, "Glove box."

Then formed his hand into the shape of a pistol.

That evening, Leslie did another walk-through of the plan, using the replica of the plant, pointing out the entrance road they'd take, exactly where they would park their vehicle, the spot where the ambush would go down

Ambush, handcuff, commandeer vehicle. Transfer age to the back of the feds' SUV, talk their way through he front gate. Once inside, call Flynn to head off in the kiff, then proceed to the plant's operation center. A rear oor left open. Carry the critters inside, let them loose, lear the place out, then shut down the power.

"And the backup generators?" Prince said. "They'll ick on when the plant loses juice."

"Wally's got that covered. Right, Wally?"

"I've got the diesels programmed to stay on for ex- ctly five minutes, long enough for you guys to finish our work, then it all goes black. That's all you get. ive minutes of light."

Leslie nodded and returned to the plan.

After the four of them enter the control room, Pauly eparates, sets a diversionary explosive device at a stor- ge shed a few hundred yards away. During the confu- on the group reunites at the airboat dock behind the ology lab, takes the airboat to rendezvous with Flynn.

"You stay with the skiff, Flynn. No matter what. Do ot come ashore."

Flynn said, "What about the loading docks? They're uch closer to the action. Your rendezvous point is a uple of miles away. The loading docks are like two ndred yards."

"Too risky," she said. "Lots of security at the loading cks. Can't take that chance."

Flynn nodded.

"If things go bad," Leslie said, "and we're not at the at exactly an hour after you've left Thorn's, you get e hell out of there. Half hour to get to the rendezvous int, and no more than a half hour waiting time."

"Just leave you there?"

"One hour after you depart Thorn's. If we're not a
the pickup spot by then, it's because we were captured."

"Or crushed like maggots," Wally said.

"Nobody's dying," Leslie said. "This is a peacefu
raid."

"Yeah, right," Wally said.

For once Thorn was tilting toward Wally.

"After that hour is up, you get the hell out of there
return here, and wait for Cassandra. She'll get you t
safety."

Flynn absorbed that in silence for several moments
Captured or worse. Frowning as if this wasn't anythin
Flynn had considered.

"These explosions," Thorn said. "That's the alum
num suitcases?"

No one spoke, then Leslie waved a quelling han
Back off. "We've chosen targets that won't endang
anyone. What you need to do, Thorn, is focus on you
own role. Don't worry about anyone else."

"Who leaves the door ajar?"

"Our inside guy."

"You trust him? Seems like a lot depends on th
door. What does he get out of it?"

"He hates the place as much as we do."

"Block the highway, ambush an SUV full of F
guys?" Thorn said. "That's how we're kicking off th
stunt?"

"Trust me," she said. "That will be the easy part."

Pauly bent over the replica of the plant and tapped o
of the buildings. "You sure about this?" he asked Lesl

"About what?"

"Storage pool for spent fuel rods. Sure this is label
right?"

"Absolutely. Stay away from that."

He set his finger atop a building—one story tall, nondescript—on the northern flank of the plant.

"This scale model is accurate. It was done from blueprints of the plant. Your targets are the diesel backup generators and the maintenance shed. The shed's here." She lay a finger atop a building east of the containment domes. "Get it straight, Pauly. An explosion, or fire in the storage pool, that would be catastrophic."

"Hell, yes," Flynn said. "Anybody downwind, that'd be a lethal dose of radiation. You're talking about millions of people. Not to mention us."

"You got it, Pauly?"

He glanced again at the layout, gave Leslie a bland look, then went back to his chair and sat.

It was close to midnight when everyone returned to their rooms. Sugar was awake. Thorn retrieved another handful of aspirin from the medicine cabinet, and Sugar lugged them back with a glass of water. He'd finished his sandwich and made a dent in the coleslaw, left the beer untouched.

Getting him on his feet and into the john was a wrenching series of awkward lifts and swivels, groans, grunts, and gasps. Pauly watched from his bed. Shirt off, his smoothly muscled torso glowing in the moonlight.

When Sugar was settled in bed again, Thorn lay on the floor beside him.

"It'll never work," Sugar said. "Turkey Point is too secure."

"Go to sleep," Pauly said. "Or I'll bust your other knee."

Thorn reached up and slid his hand between the

mattress and box spring. Where he'd stashed the pry
bar. He felt nothing.

Dug deeper. Still nothing.

He drew his hand out and tried a different spot,
closer to the headboard.

"Looking for this?"

Thorn sat up.

Pauly was holding up the crowbar, the steel glinting
in the golden light.

"It's for Sugarman," Thorn said. "I'm not leaving
him here unarmed, alone with your brother."

Pauly was silent. Handling the crowbar, testing its
weight. Thumping it a couple of times into the palm of
his other hand. Enjoying himself. "I'll think about it.
Now it's lights-out."

For the next hour Thorn lay awake listening to
Sugar's gentle snore, listening to the possums rattling
in the fishtail palms beyond the window. Trying to hear
any sign of Pauly sleeping. He waited longer, then longer
still. Thinking about Flynn down the hall, thinking
about Leslie, how strong her body was, the heat of her
skin, its sweaty shine, her hunger and his matching up
so intensely. He listened to the wind. Strained to hear
any sign of Pauly.

He got up, padded into the bathroom, shut the door.
He waited several minutes, eased the window open,
climbed out.

Staying close to the house, he circled to the front,
checked every direction, saw nothing. At the back corner he waited. Watched a feral cat stalking something
along the dock. Saw moonlight sifting through the
palms, printing zebra stripes of light and shadow across
the grounds.

He heard nothing beyond the familiar night sounds. The papery clatter of fronds, the tree frogs, the distant rumble of the highway, the ocean's restless slap and heave, the creak of boat lines straining against the shifting vessels.

He slipped across the grassy lawn to the cars.

With Sugar's pistol he could end this. Take them prisoner, start with Pauly, the most dangerous. Shoot him if he had to. An unavoidable risk.

Or maybe start with Flynn, get him out of harm's way. Back to Leslie's room, slip in, send Flynn for help while he took control of the house room by room. If Flynn would go along. If he hadn't fully converted to their cause. Thorn wasn't sure. This son of his whom he still didn't know.

He was at Sugar's Honda.

Still seeing nothing in the ghostly light, the grass and trees coated with a sugary crust of moonglow. He moved to the passenger door.

Twenty yards away, on the back deck, he heard the dry rustle of footsteps. So he kept walking, going past Sugar's car to the VW.

He went behind the VW, then began a slow meander back to the house.

Until a metal hook caught him around the throat and brought him to a stop. The pry bar's prong was cold and biting.

"You're sneaking around," Pauly said.

The pressure was so hard even a twitch could tear Thorn's Adam's apple loose. A jerk of Pauly's hand and Thorn was gone.

Thorn raised his hands shoulder high. "I couldn't sleep."

"So you went for a walk, checking out the cars. Why? Going to hot-wire one, get the hell out of here?"

"Hell, no. Wouldn't want to miss the party."

"You lie about everything. I haven't heard a straight word come out of that mouth yet. No wonder your boy thinks you're a shiftless asshole. There's nothing to you but treachery."

Thorn could feel a warm ribbon of blood unrolling down his chest. "Okay. Just this once I'll tell you the truth."

"I doubt it. But let's hear."

"Tire iron. In the trunk of the VW. So Sugar can protect himself when he and Wally are alone. That's all."

"One lie after another." Pauly removed the pry bar.

Thorn drew a long breath. "I'm turning around."

Pauly didn't reply.

Thorn kept his arms raised as he turned to face Pauly.

"Get going," Pauly said. "Move it."

Thorn wiped the blood from his throat and cut a glance back at Sugarman's Honda. There'd be no showdown tonight. Maybe he could bring it off tomorrow. Or the day after. There was still time.

Still plenty of time, he thought, as he led the way back to the bedroom.

THIRTY-SEVEN

WHEN MARTA BUSTLED IN TUESDAY morning, Frank was already at his desk.

She came to the open door, stuck her head inside. "Oh, no, what's happened now?"

He reassured her that all was well, then got up and came out to the waiting room while Marta slipped her purse into a drawer and sat down in her chair and flipped on the computer.

"Need an early start. Lots to do. Tonight's the drill."

"The power plant?"

Frank stood in the doorway of his office. "Yep, tonight."

"What happened? It's scheduled for Friday, no?"

"It's time I started calling the shots. With everyone in panic mode, maybe somebody slips up."

"Who?"

"I don't know who. That's the point. Shake the tree, see what falls. The tree's been shaking me too long."

"You can do this? Change the date? You don't need permission from these people, the NRC lady, Sheen?"

"She's been informed."

"So I should call the others, your SWAT group?"

"Tell them we'll meet at the armory at three," Frank said. "I need to run a couple of errands this morning. I'll be out for a while."

"You'll visit Billy Dean? He's at Jackson Memorial, room 403."

"He's first on my list."

"Then?"

"You've got to know everything, don't you?"

"This makes me bad?"

"I'm going to see Ms. McIvey, tell her in person about the drill."

"You want to see her face."

"You got it."

"She won't like it. You taking charge."

"And here I thought I was in charge all the time."

"You were wrong."

Frank had to smile. "You've only met her once, fifteen, twenty minutes."

"She thinks she's the boss of everything. She won't like this change. You tell me later if I'm wrong."

Marta wasn't wrong, but it took him a few hours before he confirmed it.

The National Infrastructure Protection Center was housed in the same downtown office building as the Department of Homeland Security. Sheffield parked in their lot, took the employee elevator to the eighth floor, found the office. A pleasant view of the north fork of the Miami River over the shoulder of the middle-aged black lady at the reception desk. The nameplate on her blouse said she was Portia Jackson-Hibber. The name was familiar.

She was typing at her computer and didn't look up

when Frank walked in and she didn't look up when he
held out his ID. Even clearing his throat got no reaction.

"Excuse me."

That slowed down her typing, but her eyes never left
the screen. "Yes?"

He gave his name and his title, and that slowed her
typing to a crawl.

"Here to see Ms. McIvey."

Finally she ceased. The magic words. "She's in a
staff meeting." Portia was staring at Frank, cocking
her head to the side, a cold appraisal as if sizing him
for a straitjacket.

"This is somewhat urgent."

"Only somewhat?"

Frank felt the blood heating his face. An angry flush.
He was in a hurry to get to the SWAT meeting before
three. It was already after noon. He'd spent too long
with Billy Dean. The guy still gung ho after two surgeries, with another scheduled for later that day. Still some
cleaning out of bullet fragments left to do, then another
operation in a week to repair the last of the damage.

"Let me speak to your superior."

She took her hands off her keyboard and crouched
forward as if she might leap across her narrow desk and
sink her canines in Frank's throat. "I *am* my superior."

"Yeah? And how does that work?"

"The way that works is that as director of the southern district of the NIPC, I hire and fire all personnel. In
this office, I'm the supervisor. Special agent in charge
of Ms. McIvey and the staff she's currently meeting
with."

"Sorry." Clearly he'd stepped into the lady's personal
minefield. "Since you were sitting here—"

"Yes, yes. Since I'm a woman and an African American, you naturally assumed I'm Ms. McIvey's subordinate."

"Since you were sitting at this desk instead of be hind that door marked DIRECTOR, yes, I made an assumption."

"If that's typical FBI acumen, no wonder we've go problems."

"Hey, could we start fresh?"

"No," Portia said. "We have too much history al ready."

"Yeah, well, I need to speak to Nicole about a dril she's part of. The time and date's been changed, an it's urgent I let her know."

"So it's *Nicole* now?"

Frank looked out at the river, searching for its calm ing effect. "I've known Ms. McIvey for some time."

"You have a personal relationship with her?"

Frank took a breath, reached up, and massaged th tightness in his jaw.

"Is that a yes?"

"If by *personal* you mean do I know her outside th office, then yes."

"By *personal,* I mean this." She rolled her cha back a few inches and did two quick pelvic thrusts.

"Jesus, what's going on with you?"

"So I take it that's another yes?"

"What're you talking about?"

"Okay, here's how it is. I don't share this informatic with just anyone, but I know who you are. We've a tended the same conferences several times, but you' obviously never noticed me. That's fine. I'm used to But since you're a man and in a position of authorit someone who might reward Ms. McIvey's pattern of behavior, it's important you know some facts about that pattern."

Frank had put the name and face together. Conferences. Yes, he'd seen Portia give a couple of presentations on sexual harassment. Her professional sideline—enlightening her fellow employees on the subtle ways such conduct occurred in the federal workplace and its insidious effects on morale and the pursuit of justice. She was passionate and smart and told some damn funny stories that always had a serious kicker.

"For the last decade Ms. McIvey has been using her considerable charms to maneuver her way to her current position. This has badly damaged her own reputation and the reputations of several men with whom she's served.

"However, now that she works for me, she will no longer be able to employ these skills. And until I see a radical change in her behavior, I consider myself her personal glass ceiling."

"I see."

"So if by knowing her 'outside the office' means you have succumbed to Ms. McIvey's allure, then you should be on notice that quite possibly you are being manipulated for professional gain."

Frank nodded. "Screwed her way to the top, now you're blocking her."

"I prefer to think of my role as educational. If McIvey to advance any further in the federal system, then she'll have to do it the old-fashioned way."

"Do a half-assed job."

"At least half-assed."

"How about doing me a favor, Portia?"

She cocked an eyebrow at him.

"When Ms. McIvey is out of her staff meeting, have her call me on my cell right away. I need to let her know about the change of plans for the drill."

"I'll be happy to, Agent Sheffield. And I certainly hope I haven't broken your heart. That was not my intention."

"No, I appreciate your directness. And good luck with your project."

He was still in traffic, almost to the office, when Nicole's call came.

"You met Portia."

"I did."

"She can be a handful."

"So I gathered."

"What's wrong, Frank? She say something poisonous about me? I've heard she does that."

"No, nothing." He pulled into a parking lot. This was not a conversation he wanted to have while driving. Might endanger the public.

"Why don't I believe you?"

"Change of plans. We're hitting the plant tonight. Meet at the armory in an hour and a half. We're suiting up at three, going over last-second details. Turkey Point's been notified, Sheen is fine with it, Claude says he's raring to go. Their three-day window starts at sundown today. We'll move in at eleven p.m. Probably be done by dawn." He could hear her breathing. "So get moving. Can't be late for this."

"This cold shoulder, Frank, I'm on your shit list now?"

"You're not on my shit list."

"Then why didn't you consult? Why alert me at the last second?"

"I'll see you at three. We've got a uniform that'll fit you. We'll provide lasers and vests. Weather's supposed to be clear, eighties, light breeze from the south. This won't be Prince Key again. I promise you that."

Just after noon Flynn and Prince returned from a quick run-through, up and back to Turkey Point, to make sure Flynn had the route clear. Flynn was looking relaxed, his face lit up, chapped by the wind and sun. Docking in front of the assembled group, he handled the Whip-ray nicely, slipping into the tight space between Thorn's skiff and the Chris-Craft, coming alongside the pilings without a bump. Cameron tossed the lines to Thorn and stepped ashore.

"Piece of cake," Flynn said to Leslie. "Shouldn't be a problem."

Everyone had gathered at the dock to await their return, Leslie with the cell phone still in her hand. The Chee brothers were perched side by side on the seawall.

"There's been a change," she told Flynn and Cameron, holding up the phone. "Drill's going down tonight. They're going to hit at eleven."

"Why?" Cameron said.

"Somebody got a wild hair. A conflict in schedules. Who can say?"

"Maybe they're suspicious?"

"Don't think it's that. Our guy blames it on some FBI power play."

"And the gator roundup?" Thorn being helpful, one of the team.

"I'll get my gear and you and I will head out now."

Cameron followed Leslie to the house, Wally tagging along. Pauly climbed off the seawall, went over to the

Whipray, pocketed the ignition keys, gave Thorn a long, warning look, then headed up the lawn to join the others.

"Listen, Flynn." Thorn was knotting the bowline to a cleat.

"Save your breath. I'm going ahead with this. What Pauly did to Sugar, that was wrong. He and his brother are seriously fucked up. But the rest of us aren't like that. I believe in this. It's important, worth the risk. Someone has to take a stand or there's not going to be anything left worth saving.

"People your age, you won't be around when the worst of it starts, so it doesn't matter. My generation didn't screw it up, but we've got to fix it if we're going to survive and leave something for our kids. So stop trying to push me around. Decision's made. Just back off."

Thorn looked off to the eastern sky where a single frigate bird was hanging high in the blue distance like the silhouette of some prehistoric dragon. To sailors long at sea there was nothing graceful about that bird's soaring flight. They saw it simply as an ominous sign, a symbol of impending doom. Until this moment Thorn had never entertained such horseshit.

"All right," he said. "I get it. It's completely your call. I don't have a say. But listen to me for one second. Another issue."

Flynn was squatting down beside the rear cleat, retying the stern line. Pauly had halted on the back deck, keeping watch on the two of them. Thorn was pretty sure he was out of earshot. But he kept his voice low.

"There's a pistol in Sugar's car. Might come in handy."

"You've got me confused with somebody else. I don't shoot people."

"I'm not talking about shooting people. You say you want to survive, that's what I'm talking about."

Flynn rolled his eyes up to the heavens and shook his head.

"If you change your mind," Thorn said, "it's in the glove box."

THIRTY-EIGHT

"SURE, MCIVEY. YOU WANT TO drive, help yourself
Just not so fast this time, okay? We're in no hurry. Cur
tain doesn't go up till we walk onstage."

Her mouth stretched into a smile, but her eyes re
mained estranged. Whatever heat there'd been wa
finished, along with Sheffield's usefulness.

Everyone wore black trousers, black shirts with gol
FBI logos front and back, and all of them were fitte
out with laser-sensitive vests. No Kevlar tonight. Minu
Billy Dean, it was the same crew as Sunday night, every
one haggard and hungover from the ordeal, but still fairl
upbeat at the news that no one was going to be docke
for the Prince Key mess.

Out in the armory parking lot in the balmy night a
with the Suburban gassed up, doors flung open, ready t
roll, Sheffield walked from man to man in a last-minut
inspection. One more time everyone presented his hand
gun, opening the clip or cylinder, showing it was empt
working the slide. Worst threat in a drill like this one,
live round snuck into the mix.

Frank took a close look at each of their vests, chec
ing the battery packs, the Velcro fasteners, making sur

their white, reflective armbands were in place. When he got to Nicole, she was slipping her phone in her trousers pocket.

"You were making a call?"

"Texted my dog-sitter. Told her I won't be home tonight."

"You have a dog?"

"A corgi. Why?"

"What's his name?"

"Max. Jesus, you want to polygraph me about my dog?"

Frank turned to the group. "Make sure your phones are off. We're not on the grid tonight. All the way off, not just silent."

When they'd finished checking, he raised a hand for quiet. "Okay, I promise, this is the last time."

To a chorus of groans, he did one more step-by-step repeat of the attack plan. A variation of one of Nicole's scenarios. Very basic: concussion grenades for distractions, slip past the sentries, more grenades, more distraction, move into the control room and take over.

If all went well, no lasers were fired. Rub Sellers's face in how his crew of rent-a-cops were so grossly incompetent, even with advance warning they couldn't stop a group of hostiles coming through the front door. The best possible outcome, besides wholesale changes to security procedures at Turkey Point, would be that Sellers was demoted to latrine duty for the rest of his days.

But something told Frank this simple plan he was selling to his guys was going to be bumpier than he was making out. Yeah, Frank had high confidence in his guys' superiority to the security team at Turkey Point, and he was changing things up, running a hurry-up offense that should have them on their heels, but all afternoon he'd been having the same gut quivers he'd felt out on Prince Key just before Nicole reached for the ice chest. Then a minute ago, catching her with her phone, the quivers ticked up a notch.

As the men were buckling into their seats and Nicole settled behind the wheel, his phone buzzed in his pants pocket. Frank disobeyed his own order. He huddled behind a light pole out of view of the truck. Angie Stevens.

"You find something?"

"I found something. How'd you know?"

"A guess, Angie. What is it? Another software bomb?"

"A virus."

"Can you fix it?"

"It'll take time. A virus spreads and hides. This has gotten into so many nooks and crannies it would be weeks to find it all, and if I missed a scrap of code any where, it would take hold again and mutate."

"This is in the closed loop?"

"Correct. The network that runs internal plant operations."

"So how does it get set off? Someone inside?"

"Could be that, or could be it's triggered by some other signal. Like a surge of data, a flicker in the power source. I haven't figured that out."

"Solution?"

"Quarantine."

"Put a tent over a nuke plant? What is that? Shut down?"

"Just until all the software can be scrubbed."

"Jesus, shut down the whole plant?"

"If you've got a better idea . . ."

"Can't do that, Angie. You keep working, just do your best."

The ride down I-95 at ten-fifteen on a Tuesday night was slow going. Must've been a concert at AmericanAirlines Arena downtown or some damn thing. His four guys were telling jokes in the backseats. A gorilla and a nun are sitting at a bar. When that one's done, Dinkins starts with an old favorite, an Irishman and a Brit and a Scotsman stumble into a pub, Dinkins nailing the accents. The guys laughing from the beginning at the elaborate setup.

Nicole looked over at Frank, alone with him in the front seats. "That talk Portia gave you."

Frank said nothing, watching the traffic breaking up ahead as they left 95 and headed west on the Don Shula Expressway.

Nicole said, "There's another side to the story."

"This probably isn't the time."

The guys were fully engaged with the joke-off in the rear seats. A priest stumbles into a brothel. Voices quieting down as the humor turned smutty.

"Just so you know, Frank. There *is* another version. I'm not the person Portia told you about. She twists everything to fit her political agenda. Every successful woman is a slut, except for her."

"Let's do this later."

She was in the speed lane, clipping along well over the limit. "Fuck it. Believe what you want to believe."

"Everything okay up here?" Dinkins was leaning forward, hands on the back of their seats. His face between them.

"We're cool," Frank said.

Dinkins gave Sheffield a long look, then sat back in his seat.

Frank swiveled around, looked at his guys, everyone watching him. "Okay. So the Dalai Lama goes to see a chiropractor."

Two miles from Turkey Point, Leslie Levine pulled the battered SUV onto the shoulder of the entrance road. The three gators, their snouts duct-taped shut, were flopping around inside the cage, straining the slats, probably agitated by the proximity of the python in the other side of the box.

They were small gators, two years old, the longest only four feet, snout to tip of tail. But Leslie was satisfied. They'd do the trick. Clear out the control room in a hurry and give the whole enterprise the media-friendly weirdness she was after. And the symbolism was on point. The clash of the natural world with the technological nightmare of the power plant.

Though to Thorn, the dopiness of it harked back to those yippie stunts of his youth, revolutionaries showering dollar bills onto the floor of the US Stock Exchange and mocking the mad scramble that ensued. Fine for that trippy time, but in this somber, hair-trigger era, goofing with a nuke plant, gators or not, wasn't going to be anybody's idea of comedy.

It struck him, as they waited in silence, that this felt like a caper concocted in a log cabin way off in the woods, a gang of twenty-year-old ringleaders all stoned and giddy, saying, yeah, yeah, gators, man, and Burmese fucking pythons, yeah, that's fucking perfect. But out on the lonely, dark stretch to the power plant, the smell

of the gators filling the car, as gamy and fetid as stag-
nant water, the mood was not giddy.

Leslie's binoculars were trained on the patch of
lighted roadway a few hundred yards back down the
asphalt, a single streetlamp shining amid miles of utter
darkness. No traffic had passed by since they'd pulled
onto the shoulder. Twenty minutes of waving away
mosquitoes, their whine the only thing that broke the
deadly silence.

Thorn was riding shotgun, Cameron and Pauly in
the backseat. Leslie standing out on the edge of the
road with the binoculars.

"Maybe it was called off." Cameron's voice was tight.

"It's not eleven yet," Leslie said. "Relax. We're fine."

"That ditch is full of water," Thorn said. "They'll
drown, you leave them there."

No one answered.

The highway had narrow shoulders. The deep gully
on one side, a flood canal on the other. A perfect choke
point.

Leslie's cell phone rang, she took it from her pocket,
checked the screen, and answered. Listened for a minute, then said, "Okay, I understand. Loading-ramp door,
it's open? Good." Then clicked off.

Thorn looked at the keys hanging from the ignition.
Scoot over, crank the engine, race down the highway,
he might get a hundred feet before Pauly throttled him.
Or he could hop out here, make a dash. But even if he
managed to outrun them and save himself, Sugarman
and Flynn could be doomed. Sugar, immobilized,
vulnerable to Wally's whims. Flynn left dangling. No
telling how any of that might play out.

Too many variables, all of them risky. He saw no choice but to ride this out a few steps further, alert for his best chance to trip them up.

"It's them," Leslie said. "Get set."

She handed Thorn the binoculars, slipped behind the wheel of the SUV, started the engine, pulled across the road, angling toward the approaching vehicle, then switched on her flashing emergency lights.

"Fucking A," Cameron said. "Let's shut this city down."

In the cargo hold the gators thrashed and grunted in their wooden box as though sensing the rising tension. Thorn set the binoculars at his feet and tightened his seat belt. He watched the headlights bearing down, then turned the other way toward the long stretch of highway, squinting into the darkness where they were headed, where his starry-eyed son was to meet them in an hour's time.

"Don't worry, Thorn." Leslie patted him on the thigh. "Flynn will be safe. I'd never let anything happen to the father of my child."

THIRTY-NINE

"WHAT THE FUCK?"

"Slow down, McIvey."

Dinkins leaned forward, stuck his head between the seats.

"This part of the drill?"

"Looks like an add-on," Frank said. "What do you think, McIvey?"

"What do you want me to do?"

"Is there a choice?" said Sheffield. "We stop, find out what the hell's going on. Could be an accident."

"Doesn't look like any accident," Dinkins said.

"Put your brights on. Roll up close. Everybody stay out."

As Nicole coasted forward, coming to within thirty feet of a beat-up SUV, four people piled out wearing FBI uniforms and white reflective armbands identical to their own. Two of the four had weapons drawn.

"Reverse it, McIvey. Get out of here."

Nicole slipped the shifter into park, drew out the ignition keys, and dropped them at her feet.

"Oh," Sheffield said. "That's how it is."

"Run, Frank? Really?"

"Hey, what do we do, Shef?" Dinkins speaking for the others.

A slender woman with short hair, holding a revolver at her side, stepped into the headlights. A giant muscled-up guy moved beside her, held his hand up to block the brights, another guy hanging a few steps back.

"So how's this supposed to go down, McIvey? You save the day, win a Medal of Honor? Because, boy oh boy, I'd pay good money to see that."

Another man with a ponytail, lean and athletic, loped into the shadows to their right.

"Pauly Chee," Frank said. "Our bomber."

"We being carjacked?" Dinkins said.

"Worse," said Frank.

"Bad night to be unarmed," Dinkins said.

Chee was at his window, tapping on the glass with his Glock, motioning him to crank open the window.

"Or I'll smash it," Pauly yelled.

"These the ones from Prince Key?" Dinkins again.

Sheffield told him, yeah, it was them, the fucking peaceniks.

Looking out his window at Pauly Chee, Frank said to Nicole, "I'm curious. The boathouse, that first night. Was it real? Or just to set this up?"

"It felt real, didn't it, Frank? Isn't that what matters?"

McIvey pressed the electronic lock release on her door panel.

"All this just to get past Portia? That's nuts. You know that, right? How crazy you are."

"Fuck you, Frank."

"We tried that. Didn't work out so well."

Frank's door swung open.

"Which one of you is Sheffield?"

Frank waved a hand.

Chee grabbed his shoulder and dragged him out onto the dark road.

Then Pauly stuck his head back inside the SUV and said, "The rest of you stay put or this shitheel dies."

Leslie kept ordering Pauly to stop. No, no, no. But he ignored her. Taking charge.

Thorn watched as Pauly dragged an agent from the passenger side of the big SUV and shoved him into the glare of the headlights.

And good Christ, it was Sheffield. The feds had sent the first team.

Twice in recent years Thorn had observed Frank in action, seen up close what he was capable of. A smart, savvy guy, grace under devastating pressure. Not the man you wanted on the other side of the ball.

"Cuff him." Pauly left him with Prince and returned to the big SUV.

"Now one by one," he called out. "Step out of the car. Driver next."

Cameron wrestled Frank's wrists behind him and clipped the flex cuffs on. When he was done, Sheffield took a couple of steps toward Leslie and Prince grabbed his arm and yanked him to a halt.

"This is a serious error, Levine," Frank said. "Yeah, yeah, I know who you are and I know what you did. Faked your death so Mom would have a story to tell your little girl, Julie, when she asks about you someday."

Thorn saw her stiffen, the pistol rising, aiming at Frank.

"Am I right?"

"My daughter has no part in this."

"Of course not, but I bet dear old mom has a clue what you're up to, which is what we call conspiracy. It's enough to ship Julie off to foster care. That what you want?"

"My mother knows nothing."

"We'll sort that out later," Frank said. "Meanwhile, best thing you can do right now, put away the guns and we sit down, figure how to handle the next part. So far, I don't see any major crimes committed. Nothing a good lawyer couldn't help you out of."

Pauly had come back to Sheffield's side. "Stop talking. All of you."

"And you, you're Pauly Chee, went AWOL from your SEAL unit three years ago. Ripped off a stockpile of high explosives when you deserted."

Pauly stared into Frank's eyes for a long moment, then raised his pistol and slashed it across Frank's face, drove him to his knees.

Thorn lunged past Leslie and shoved Pauly away. "Back off. No reason for this."

Thorn stood with his arms spread, shielding Sheffield. Chee just smiled. The first one Thorn had seen on Pauly's lips. The tolerant grin of a grown man challenged by a child.

Sheffield's men threw open the rear doors and gathered at the front of the SUV, readying for a charge. Pauly turned to face them, his pistol rising.

"They're unarmed," Frank said. "Don't shoot."

The driver's-side door came open and a woman dressed like the others, stepped out and moved away from the car into the shadows beyond the dazzle of headlights. Only her white reflective armband showed her location.

"Pauly Chee," she called out. "Drop your weapon. You, too, Levine. Hold your arms straight out, let them fall."

"Nicole, stop it now," Frank yelled at her. "Everyone, hold on. Don't listen to Ms. McIvey. She's unarmed. We're all unarmed. Our pistols, they're not loaded. This is a drill. Nobody needs to get hurt."

"Now," Nicole called out. "Weapons on the ground. I'm not saying it again."

"She's bluffing," Sheffield said. "Don't shoot the lady."

With his pistol aimed into the shadows where the armband glowed, Pauly took a step, then another. The emergency flashers continued to count off the seconds in red.

Thorn angled in front of Pauly, put his back to the woman named Nicole, planted his left hand on Pauly's chest.

Pauly looked down at the hand and swatted it away. Thorn stepped past him and into the path of Leslie's gaze. Her eyes were unfocused, mouth open.

"Leslie, wake up. This isn't what you're about. Shooting people, no. This game is done. You tried, it was a noble cause, but it didn't work. We have to stop this right here, right now."

Behind him the woman fired a single shot, and a hot slug against Thorn's left thigh spun him around. As he caught himself and regained his balance, two more shots flared in the darkness. Then two more. The clang of metal as the rounds punctured the SUV's fender. All misses except for the first.

Thorn touched the edge of his thigh. A tear in his trousers, damp and warm, a numb patch spreading like melted wax toward his knee.

Sheffield's agents had taken cover at the far side of their SUV.

Frank was on his feet, yelling at the shooter. "Nicole, goddamn it. Throw the weapon out. Throw it out here now."

"You call that unarmed?" Pauly raised his pistol.

"Goddamn it, Nicole, throw down your gun."

The woman stepped into the halo of light, pistol outstretched, hand steady. A step forward, then another.

"You've been bad." Her voice was cool and vacant as if she were rehearsing a speech alone in a room, simply trying it out. "You've behaved badly for a long time, been dishonest and disreputable. You've brought shame and humiliation on yourselves and your cause. Now it's judgment day."

She was blond and slender, a delicate build, her mouth gritted into a hard smile that was devoid of emotion.

"Leslie," Thorn said quietly. "You can do it. You can stop this."

"No, she can't," Pauly said. "We're too far down the road."

As casually as one might snuff out a candle flame Pauly squeezed off two rounds. The woman bucked as if jackhammered in the belly. Her shriek was short and faded to a moan as she sank to the ground.

Sheffield stared down at his shoes, shaking his head.

Beyond the glow of the headlights and the steady beat of the flashers, the darkness seemed to wobble. An unsteady flicker invaded the light. Thorn fought off the woozy spin, walked across the asphalt to Leslie's side. The left leg was gimpy and uncertain, but it was still supporting him. No reason to explore the wound, see its extent. Not now.

He took hold of Leslie's chin and lifted her face to the light. Her mouth was slack. She wouldn't meet his eyes.

Pauly marched to the spot where the woman had fallen, stood for a moment looking down, then fired once more. He kicked at her body, then stooped and came up with a small automatic. He walked back to the four agents gathered in front of their vehicle, two with their arms raised above their heads, two others standing still, poised to make a move.

"Need more time on the shooting range."

"She wasn't FBI," Sheffield said. "She was a god-damn civilian. She thought you guys were pacifists. Thought she could take you down with a single hand-gun. She wasn't prepared for a shoot-out. She wasn't a hero, a gunslinger, any of that. She was a fucking non-combatant."

Pauly brushed the back of his hand at Frank. Yeah, whatever. "Any of the rest of you assholes unarmed?"

Pauly closed in on the four agents, holding his aim, ordering them to raise their hands, all of them.

"Do it," Frank shouted.

After a moment, the two holdouts complied. Motioning with his pistol, Chee herded them into the blaze of headlights.

"Prince, get over here. Check their weapons."

Cameron passed among the four agents, drew their pistols, inspected the magazines, the cylinders.

"He wasn't lying. They're unloaded. Just these laser thingies."

"Pitch them in the water. Their cell phones, radios. Everything in the canal. And this gentleman's handgun, too." Pauly aimed his weapon at Frank.

One by one, Prince hurled the pistols and phones into the water on the far side of the road.

"Now let's get this back on track," Pauly said. "Thorn, cuff these guys. Make yourself useful."

Sheffield looked at Thorn, their eyes holding. The gash on Sheffield's cheek was deep and ragged. "You're with these people?"

"Seems that way." Thorn grabbed Frank's armpit and hauled him up.

"And Flynn?"

"He's okay," Thorn said. "So far."

Thorn walked over to Leslie. She'd propped her butt against the grill of the SUV, her face smeared by confusion. She had come so far, driven by principles that were clear and defined, making a logical progression of decisions that had led her to this strip of road. It had all made sense. It had all mattered so much. The earth, saving what was left. The war she'd conceived of had cleanly drawn lines of battle, but now that illusion had dissolved and everything was scrambled. They had entered a free-fire zone. No rules. No good or bad.

Thorn stood before her, brought his face into her line of sight, waited till she focused on him. "It's over, Leslie. Look around you. A woman's dead. Pauly's out of control. We can't go on. It violates everything you believe. This is finished. Call it off. You're the only one who can do it."

She shook her head, eyes blank, turning away from him, looking off down the empty roadway.

"We knew there'd be risks," Prince said. "Things could get bumpy."

"You fucking moron." Thorn swung to him, slammed his palms into Cameron's chest, barely budged him. "Is that what you call this, *bumpy*?"

"You two shut the fuck up and cuff these guys," Pauly said. "Or I'll shoot every goddamn one of you, handle the rest myself."

"Do it, Thorn," Leslie said. "There's no U-turn here. We're going in, we're shutting that place down."

Thorn glanced at Sheffield. "I tried."

"Not hard enough," Sheffield said.

Thorn cuffed two of the agents and Prince handled the other two.

"Big mistake, cowboy," one of the agents said. "Big, bad mistake."

"I've made bigger," Thorn said. "You guys relax. You get a chance, roll in the mud, it'll keep the mosquitoes off until somebody comes along and sets you loose. There's not going to be any more killing."

An ankle in each hand, Pauly dragged the woman's body across the road. Frank watched, groaning deep in his chest. Chee rolled the corpse into the ditch.

Prince directed the four agents to lie on the shoulder in the weeds close beside the ditch, then he bound their ankles and left them facedown. One of them kept warning anyone who'd listen that this was a mistake. A big mistake.

After they repositioned the two SUVs back to back, they transferred the wooden cage and Pauly's aluminum cases to the Chevy Suburban. Then Prince parked the battered SUV well off the road, a few yards from where the agents lay. In a medical kit in the back of the Chevy,

Leslie found a roll of gauze. She tore open Thorn's pant leg, flinched at what she saw, then wrapped half the roll of gauze tight around the wound.

With every second the magical numbing agent his body produced was wearing off. She asked him if he was okay, could he make it, or should they leave him here.

Thorn forced a smile. "It's a scratch."

"I'm afraid it's more than that."

"I'm in this. You need somebody sane."

"And that's you?"

Leslie climbed into the shotgun seat of the Suburban. Pauly buckled in behind the wheel. Prince, Sheffield and Thorn crammed into the second row, Frank in the middle. Behind them the gators and python were quiet, alert, probably smelling the blood in the air.

A half mile down the road, Thorn said, "So that was the easy part?"

No one replied.

He rolled his window down and drew a breath of summer air, ripe with the sour mud of the Everglades and the heavy sulfur undertone of its marshy prairie of saw grass and cypress and hummocks of cabbage palm and mahogany, all that thick air mingling with lighter tones—the honeyed bursts of sweet ferns and thousands of night-scented orchids and bromeliads breaking into bloom.

That vast expanse was a few miles distant, but its pollen and its darting night birds and its wild immensity radiated like a beautiful fever beyond its borders, altering the air around them, enlivening their own blood chemistry with its swelling presence in ways no one could fully reckon.

Thorn leaned forward and laid a hand on Leslie's shoulder. "Who's Julie?"

Leslie turned, stared at him. Her face was strained but her eyes radiated an intensity Thorn remembered from long ago—the day she caught her first fish and began to imagine a future brighter than the grim existence she was trapped in—a look of hope. Then she turned her gaze back to the road ahead and the distant glow of the guard gate. "Julie is your granddaughter."

Thorn looked out his open window, at the shadows of trees, the moon half-concealed by ragged clouds, the glimmer of water in the roadside ditch. "That's not possible."

"Flynn made it possible."

"He couldn't."

"Why? Because he's gay?"

Pauly turned and shifted his gaze between Leslie, Thorn, and the road.

"He made a donation," Leslie said. "As a favor to me."

"Why?"

"You'll have to ask him."

"I'm asking you, Leslie. Why?"

"For me, simple. I wanted a child. Time was running out."

Thorn could feel Prince and Sheffield staring at the side of his face. He touched a thumb against the bloody gauze, found the center of the wound, and pressed hard, making the fogginess in his head vanish.

"You wanted a child," Thorn said.

"All right, goddamn it." Leslie turned in her seat. In the green glow of the dashboard lights her eyes seemed to fizz with energy as if hundreds of wild emotions were colliding within them. "I wanted a child who'd grow up strong and decisive, who would never knuckle under o give up on the people and things he loved. Last year when I came to see you that day, you were so distar and out of reach, I decided Flynn was my best chance o having that child."

Thorn squeezed the bridge of his nose and settle back against the seat.

"She's a cute kid," Sheffield said. "Got your eye Thorn. Blue as a January sky."

FORTY

THE GUARDHOUSE RESEMBLED AN AIRPORT control tower at some rural outpost. A square pod maybe twenty by twenty mounted atop a concrete column. A dozen tinted windows gave its occupants a commanding view in every direction.

Along the roof, spotlights illuminated at least an acre of the surrounding grounds and glittered against the heavy chain-link fence topped with razor wire. Their approach along the entrance road was brightly lit by overhead lamps, and Thorn saw surveillance cameras posted conspicuously, starting a half mile away from the steel barrier that blocked the road.

Stationed behind the blockade were four guards, and he guessed at least that many more were manning the watchtower. Two of the four behind the barrier wore the red reflective armbands of the opposing team. They were armed with lightweight machine pistols with folding shoulder stocks.

"Here's your story, Sheffield," Leslie said, swinging round to face him. "The force-on-force drill was canceled. You don't know why. Orders came from DC an hour ago. It's rescheduled for two weeks. You need to enter the plant, speak to Claude Sellers face-to-face, confirm the new arrangement. The NRC rep will be on the speaker and will expect to hear your voice. Cameron, it's your job to make sure Agent Sheffield stays on script."

Leslie handed her revolver to Prince. He smiled and jammed the barrel into Frank's ribs.

"So my buddy Claude," Frank said, "he's your double agent."

Leslie turned back to the road ahead. Silent.

"And you think you can trust Sellers?"

"Where did this come from?" Pauly said, glancing over at her. "This wasn't the plan, taking this fed along."

"Special request," she said. "From Claude."

"Oh, that's sweet," Frank said. "You people, man, you need to ask yourselves why the head of security is letting you inside his facility. You consider that? What his angle is?"

"Keep quiet," Pauly said. "I'm not telling you again."

They were a few hundred feet from the guardhouse, slowing down. The two containment domes and cooling towers loomed a half mile deeper in, and a ten-story building sheathed in elaborate scaffolding and pipe and stairways and an array of exterior ductwork. Transmission lines crisscrossed the grounds in every direction. What looked like fuel-storage silos flanked the guardhouse.

"What I think," Frank said, "the woman you killed back there, Agent Nicole McIvey, she and Claude cooked up this scam. They're a team."

"Team of losers," Pauly said.

"Hear him out," said Thorn.

"They worked together to set you guys up. Nicole

ad her reasons, Claude his. But Nicole was double-
rossing Claude, trying to grab the glory herself for tak-
ng you terrorists down."

"We're not terrorists," Leslie said.

"Yeah, well, whatever you call yourselves. Nicole
as going for the takedown, pulling a fast one on Claude,
nd my bet is, Claude has the same agenda. He's luring
ou into his lair."

Leslie reached out, plucked her cell phone from the
up holder, and punched in a number. When the con-
ection was made, Thorn heard Flynn's voice answer.

"Everything's fine," she told him. "I have eleven
irty on the dot. Remember. Give us an hour to finish
nd exit the plant. If we're not at the rendezvous point
y exactly half past twelve, don't wait a minute longer.
et the hell out of there. You have to promise me."

Thorn heard the voice speak the words she'd asked
r.

"Now get going," she said. "Let's do this."

In the flare of headlights, the guards had come to
tention. The two with red armbands had lasers like the
es Sheffield's men were using mounted on the sight
ils. They were aiming the lasers at the windshield.

laude and Emily Sheen watched the video screen as
e big black Suburban rolled up to the front gate.

"Well, well, well," Claude said.

Sheen asked him what he saw.

"The woman up front in the passenger seat. You
n't recognize her?"

"Should I?"

"Used to work here," Claude said. "Always showing
r pretty face in the newspaper and TV, talking up the

power plant. You must've seen her. Ran the croc reha[l]
program. Before she got eaten."

"That's Leslie Levine?"

"Apparently that croc spit her up, 'cause there she is
at the front gate. Looks alive to me."

Sheffield's voice came over the speaker. Giving th[e]
speech Claude had composed and laid out for Lesli[e]
Drill postponed for two weeks. Needed to speak face-to[-]
face with Claude. Then Claude played his part, trying t[o]
sound reluctant, but saying okay, okay, fine, come to th[e]
conference room, the place where they'd had their plan[-]
ning meeting, and he gave the gate guard the go-ahea[d]
Send them in. Drill canceled. Tell his team to stan[d]
down.

When he was done, Sheen said, "Canceled? No on[e]
told me."

"You don't see what's happening here? This nast[y]
little scam."

"What scam? What're you saying?"

So Claude explained it to the broad, walked h[er]
through it, step by step, watching her confused face tur[n]
worried, then more worried as it sank in. The place wa[s]
under attack. This was real. The croc lady and the F[BI]
guy were in cahoots. These weren't feds. These we[re]
rogue bad guys.

"Then why let them in the gate?"

"You ever hear of a pincer movement?"

"A what?"

You'd think the NRC would hire smarter people [to]
monitor security at a facility as big and complex as [a]
nuke plant. He left her standing there, Sheen alread[y]
digging in her purse for her cell phone, going to call th[e]

to her superiors, see what they wanted her to do, hile Claude headed off to the john.

His last contract gave Claude access to an adminis-ative locker room. He stashed a razor there, deodor-nt, change of clothes, so he could go right from work nd meet the ladies, if there were any ladies to be met. idn't want the stink of radioactivity on him while he as courting.

Down the hall from the conference room, he stood efore the mirror and touched up his Fu Manchu, using s Remington to buzz a few hairs at the tips. Then he n the razor over his slick scalp, nipped some hairs iking up. You never knew what would show up in ash photography. Didn't want to spoil his front-page pearance with a few wild hairs making him look like damn porcupine.

Claude got his bolo squared off, going with the dressy ue-agate tonight, goddamn stone big as a silver dol-r, popping nicely against his canary-yellow shirt. He epped back for the full view, front and side. Claude oking sharp, ready for his close-up.

And ready to unload on this gang of fucking eco-rorists, bring on the heavy weapons, set his men loose, d if a special agent in charge and a bitch from the frastructure police got caught in the crossfire, so much e better.

As he was turning from the mirror, he spotted a ir on his forehead, a photo spoiler if there was one, d he leaned close to his reflection and tried to pluck vith his thumb and first finger, getting his fingernails und it, giving it a little tug before he popped it loose. at's when the lights went out.

Inside the plant, the big, deep hum of the turbine and the nuclear fission and the steam generators and th million volts of current droning through the walls, a those noises that got into your bones and rumbled a shift long until Claude and everybody else at Turke Point was vibrating for hours after they got home—a that stopped.

Claude was in the dark. A goddamn lone straggle hair on his scalp.

He waited half a minute till the diesels kicked i and the emergency lighting fluttered on. Dim but func tional. And the rumble in the walls started up agai right back where it was.

He plucked the sucker, then walked out into th hall, where workers in their hard hats were in low-volum panic mode, hustling here and there, asking each oth what was going on, was this a drill, what about the r actor, and the hubbub grew as Claude walked down th hallway to the security office, where his men, his twel best, had assembled outside the door as he'd told the to do if anything happened tonight the least bit hink such as if the lights went off, or the reactor alarm beepe which had just begun.

Yes, sir, look what we had here, the biggest nu plant in Florida with a Class One Crisis. And wl would be called on to bring it to a successful concl sion? Why, none other than Claude Sellers.

They cruised into the center of the plant without a pro lem. Saw no sign of security, just workers bustli about in golf carts fitted with toolboxes.

Halfway to the reactor building, the overhead ligl went dark, the jangle and roar of the plant ceased.

No one in the car spoke, Pauly driving on.

A half minute later, maybe a third of the lights ightened and the plant's drone and vibration returned. here were shadows now, pockets of darkness around e grounds, near buildings, not the false noontime of efore.

"The diesels," Prince said. "Five minutes, Wally's rus shuts them off."

They drove past the southern cooling tower. Around xty stories high, gigantic, a cement hourglass with a ick middle, a steady stream of bright condensation lling into the black sky.

Off in the distance, thirty miles north across Bis- yne Bay, Thorn could make out the ruby glow of Mi- ai and the beach. A hazy mist of light that hugged the y like cheery smog. They continued to roll deeper into e plant, past the second cooling tower.

"This doesn't strike you as too easy?" said Thorn.

" 'Come into my parlor,' said the spider to the fly." ank looked at Thorn, shook his head. Bad shit ming.

"Do we need this government asshole anymore?" uly said.

"No more killing," Leslie said. "That's not what we're out."

"It is now," Sheffield said. "You're officially in the urder business."

"Sheffield's right," Thorn said. "This smells like a p."

Leslie was silent as they crept toward the office mplex. Two or three hundred yards away, she told uly to stop.

"What?"

"Right here," she said. "They may be right. Time t change things up. Set the first charge. Base of the coo ing tower. No one gets hurt, giant distraction."

"He's going off on his own?" Prince said.

"Cooling tower, maintenance shed. When you've s those two, meet us at the biology lab. From there we tak the airboat to the skiff."

"What about the cage?" Cameron said. "We nee Pauly's muscle."

"We'll take the critters inside one by one. Do Pauly. I'll drive the rest of the way."

Pauly held her eyes for a second, grunted, then g out, went back to the hatch, pulled out the suitcases ar slammed the door, and headed off across an empty plaz

"I don't trust that guy," Thorn said.

"You damn well shouldn't," said Frank.

Leslie settled into the driver's seat and moved th shifter into gear.

As the car began to move, Thorn swung open his do and jumped out. Pitched sideways, his left leg numb, most went down, but caught himself.

"Get back in here, goddamn it, Thorn."

Thorn stood at the open door and watched as a g cart rolled toward them, two security guys giving the a close look.

"Strong and decisive," Thorn said. "Never knuck under."

"But always the knucklehead," Sheffield said.

"Take this." Cameron held out the revolver.

Thorn waved it off. "You guys are going to need

Sheffield bent forward at the waist, straining agai the plastic cuffs. "At least take this." Frank motion with his chin toward his utility belt.

Thorn reached behind Frank and drew the flashlight from its holster. A foot long, heavy enough it could double as a billy club. "Now this I like."

Thorn slammed the door, watched the security guys rolling down the asphalt toward the domed reactor building, a couple of other golf carts with uniformed men converging on the same location.

He saluted Leslie with the flashlight and limped into the dark.

FORTY-ONE

WITH ITS CROWN RIMMED BY hundreds of light the northern cooling tower loomed ahead like som vast pyramid the ancients built to celebrate the invinc bility of their deities. Plumes of steam rose from i stack and were caught and shredded by the ocean breez

Thorn couldn't see Pauly anymore. Lost in the shad ows of adjacent buildings. Thorn hobbled to the base the tower, up onto the concrete walkway circling it. Pov erful fans were roaring inside the structure, and he cou feel the suck of air drawn through the intake openings the base of the tower. Crosshatched steel trusses frame the bottom, raising the tower one story off the grour and allowing for the huge rush of incoming air.

Halfway around its base, he found Pauly on the ba side with one of the suitcases open on the walkway b side him. He was positioning a device the size of tackle box inside the intake gap.

When he sensed Thorn standing close, his ha flicked out, snatched the pistol from the cement wa He swung around, saw it was Thorn and held his ain few uncomfortable seconds, then lowered the pistol a set it aside.

Pauly went back to work, wedging the container into triangular joint between two of the steel columns and he cement retaining wall. "She send you to supervise?"

"I'm here to help."

"Don't need any help."

Though Thorn had no experience with demolition, seemed clear that even a minor blast at that structural oint would splinter the concrete shell of the tower. low bad the damage would be he couldn't guess, but he nagined it would be sufficient to put a lot of engineers nd construction workers on overtime for weeks.

He stood silently in the glow of the overhead spotghts while Pauly finished setting the charge.

When he was finished, Pauly rose, picked up the cond case, and came over to Thorn. "It blows in three inutes. Let's move. This will be ugly."

Pauly headed at a trot in the direction of the southn tower. Thorn tried to keep up, shuffling double-time, shlight in one hand, hauling along his lame leg with e other. From their current position on the eastern edge the property, the bay was only a half mile off. The ading docks were visible, a small cargo ship moored ongside a couple of patrol boats, and to the north across e shimmering expanse of Biscayne Bay, the ruddy lse dawn that hovered over Miami seemed brighter an before, as if the entire city were smoldering.

When he turned back, Pauly was out of sight. Thorn oked up at the sliver of moon, heavy clouds building the east, closing his eyes, trying to recall the layout slie had used to coach them. Thorn believed the intenance shed that was Pauly's next target was off the northeast about two or three hundred feet. Not re than a minute or two away.

As he was heading off, Pauly's device at the base o
the north cooling tower exploded, and the concussio
jolted Thorn sideways into the wall of the building h
was passing, flattened him there for several seconds, fac
pressed to a steel security door. An earthquake rumblin
underfoot, shock waves radiating from the blast, blow
ing out windows, knocking over benches and storag
bins and sending them flying. The gusts, full of debri
threw open the heavy lid of a Dumpster and sent
rolling across a grassy, open courtyard.

Thorn hugged the wall and edged around the co
ner, watching as the sixty-story cement hourglass dis
integrated in a tornado of dust and bits of flamin
rubble. Not like any explosion he'd ever seen. So shatte
ing, and earsplitting, Thorn's vision was dancing an
he struggled to breathe as chips and pebbles of the de
molished structure rained down.

Sirens sounded across the grounds, men's voic
barking orders. Dark figures sprinted across the roac
way and people stepped outside various offices and pr
fab structures, stumbling into the dusty air, dazed, wipi
away blood, the injured with their arms slung over th
shoulders of their comrades.

Thorn struggled on toward the maintenance she
Reeling out of a doorway, a woman with blood strean
ing from her right ear grabbed his arm.

"Oh, my God, you're FBI," she said. "Are these te
rorists?"

"Yes," Thorn said. "Yes, they are."

"Is it over?"

"Not yet. Take cover."

The door of the maintenance shed was locked, b
the windows facing the destroyed cooling tower we

hattered. Thorn shined the flashlight inside and saw
only a row of sit-down mowers and light power tools.

A thickset man in suit and tie carrying a heavy brief-
case came around the corner of the maintenance shed
breathing hard, saw Thorn, and stopped.

"Are they around here?" the man whispered. "Somewhere nearby?"

"No. I need to know where the spent fuel rods are."

"The pool?"

Thorn nodded, coming closer to the man, holding
both palms up. Stay calm, stay calm, don't bolt.

"Oh, fuck. Not the fuel rods."

"Where?" Thorn said quietly. "Which way?"

The man turned and pointed toward the domed building where the nuclear reactors turned water to steam to
spin the turbines.

"South of the containment building." The man started
away, then stopped. "That can't happen. A bomb, something that big in the pool, no, it would be . . ."

"I'll take care of it."

"Is it just you? You're here alone?"

"I can manage."

"Oh, holy Christ." The man dropped his briefcase
and sprinted off toward the distant parking area.

At the entrance door to the one-story building, Thorn
stopped and listened. Inside he made out the grind of
machinery, big gears meshing, and a rhythmic clank
like a tire jack lifting an enormous weight notch by
notch. The door was ajar.

Behind him the networks of roads and cart paths
were filled with people and vehicles, alarms sounding
and distant sirens.

The lights faded, then died out completely.

The mechanical clamor inside the structure ceased Across the grounds a scattering of battery-powered emergency lights were still glowing, and a few vehicl headlamps swept their beams along the sides of build ings, but most of the vast industrial park had fallen int shadows.

Off to the north across the bay, the rosy haze tha floated above Miami had vanished, and the bright feas of stars and galaxies and distant suns that was los every night behind the shield of artificial light had re appeared.

Thorn slipped into the building. A metal ramp ur derfoot, pebbled to prevent slippage. A glow in the ai Blue and green light, the soft turquoise of a bonefis flat covered by a sheet of crystal salt water on a sun mer's afternoon.

Before him on the ramp a man in a white jumpsu and white hard hat and orange rubber boots and glove was sprawled with one arm slung out to his side like drowning man stretching for a lifeline. Thorn knelt ar felt for a pulse. Blood everywhere. No heartbeat. Tw gunshot wounds that he could see.

Thorn rose and inched forward along the ramp. H damaged leg was throbbing and that knee felt spong But it still worked, still kept him upright.

Tubular rails ran along either side of the ramp. Th exposed ducts of an air-conditioning system wrappe around the giant room. Plastic barrels and heavily i sulated wires and cables were strung along the fram work of the machinery.

All the girders and the ramp itself and the ste beams that supported the walls and the roof, as well the lifters and cranes of every size, were painted a bra

ellow, made even more garish by the tint of the blue
low that filled the room. An unnatural light, Thorn
ealized. Not the saltwater flats at all. In fact, their op-
osite.

This was the eerie radiance of enriched uranium-
35 pellets inserted into rods, those rods extracted
esh from the reactor's core, packed tightly into bun-
les, then stored in racks and crammed into the refrig-
ated water where they would stay for decades until
eir radioactivity subsided enough for them to be trans-
rred to dry casks somewhere else on the property. All
all hundreds of tons of uranium still hot from the
actor made the water glow as blue and unearthly as
acier ice.

His long-ago science teacher had explained it all in
at mousetrap lecture, and in the last few days Flynn
d Leslie had briefed him again. For decades they'd
ed the same primitive system. An indoor Olympic
ol, the uranium sunk below forty feet of water to
ffer the radioactivity and slowly, slowly cool the ele-
ents. Now with the main power off and the backup
esels disabled, the neutron absorber and circulating
ter system were both shut down. In only minutes this
ter would boil, turn to steam, and then those solid
aterials would catch fire. Wally had done his job, now
uly was trying to do the unimaginable. Set off one
ant, dirty bomb.

The ramp where Thorn stood seemed to be an ob-
rvation deck. Running directly below him was an
ntical ramp where workers operated the spent-fuel
chinery, adding or subtracting more bundles.

A few feet ahead, lying across his path, were two
re white-suited workers, their uniforms blotted with

red. Chest wounds. Two stories below he saw their au
tomatic weapons lying on the lip of the pool.

Feeling the tremor of footsteps on the ramp belov
him, Thorn leaned over the railing and saw Pauly Che
inching up behind another white-suited security mar
who was armed with an automatic pistol.

Thorn turned away and tried to project his voice ou
into the big room.

"FBI! Stop where you are. Thrown down you
weapons."

While Thorn mounted the railing, both men halted
Pauly looking behind him, the security guy swingin
around, shocked to find Pauly so close.

Thorn tucked his flashlight in his waistband, took
grip on the lower rail, and kicked out over the blue wa
ter, swinging like one of those high-bar gymnas
working up to a full three-sixty, only Thorn was a lor
way past his prime and had only the smallest of wi
dows to sail through. Splashing into that pool was n
an option.

His hands held firm as he kicked out parallel to t
water, then gravity swung him down and he timed h
release, dismounting the rail and flying feetfirst throug
the space between the two ramps, a crazy Tarzan ye
breaking from his lungs.

Aiming for Pauly's head, but mistiming and sid
swiping the guard instead. Thorn knocked the mar
weapon loose, sent him sprawling backward into t
rail, and Thorn thudded down against the steel rar
hard on his rump.

Quick-stepping to the guard, Pauly kicked his m
chine pistol over the side, and it splashed into t
turquoise water. Pauly aimed his pistol at the secur

man's face, but Thorn scooted in front of the guy and struggled to his feet.

"Let him go. He's no threat."

Pauly blinked at Thorn and aimed past him at the man.

Thorn dodged to his left and blocked him again. "This isn't what he meant."

"What?"

"Putting the genie back in the bottle."

"I should never have told you about that."

"He didn't mean to send you off killing people."

"How do you know what he meant?"

"You know he didn't. He meant the opposite."

The security guy had gotten to his feet. A man in his thirties, face shiny with sweat. "Hey, look. I got three kids, a new puppy for godsakes."

Pauly aimed the pistol at him again and told him to shut up and turn around and walk the fuck out of here, then run as far away as he could get.

"Thanks," the man said. "Thanks to both of you."

When he was gone, Thorn held out his hand, palm up. "Give me the gun."

"Yeah, right."

"It's over. We did what we set out to do. Bringing down that cooling tower, man, that's enough for one day. Time for a pitcher of beer."

"Still the funnyman."

"I'm dead serious. We're done."

By now Thorn had seen Pauly's moves often enough to know his mouth went slack before he attacked. So Thorn's hand was already moving to the handle of the flashlight when Pauly drew back his hand and side-armed his pistol toward Thorn's skull. A recap of what he'd done to Sheffield, pistol-whipping him to his knees.

The flashlight blunted the blow and the handgun broke loose from Pauly's grip and sailed into the pool. Thorn pivoted on his good leg, bent low, rammed the butt of the flashlight into Pauly's crotch, and heard the satisfying sound of Pauly's wail as he pitched back against the railing.

But Thorn was wrong. It wasn't a wail.

It was a war whoop, for Pauly bounced off the railing as if it were the elastic ropes of a boxing ring, and he was propelled forward into Thorn's gut, driving his shoulder deep, knocking loose Thorn's breath, then hauling him upright, lifting him overhead, a swiftly executed clean and jerk, then carrying him two steps toward the edge of the ramp. Squirming, Thorn stared down into the irradiated blue, seeing the dark racks at the bottom lurking like a toxic reef.

Helpless in Pauly's grip, Thorn went still and tried to pick a handhold he could swipe at on his flight toward the water. A bundle of wires looping out from a girder looked promising. Thorn focused on that bundle as Pauly made a half turn to his right and tossed Thorn headfirst against the steel ramp.

FORTY-TWO

CLAUDE WAS HAVING CHILLS. HIS pecker twitching inside his boxers. Fucking cooling tower coming down in an avalanche of dust. This half-assed attack had morphed into something else. This would go international. It would be all-time big, up there with the Twin Towers and Pearl Harbor in the annals of disaster lore. It would last for weeks on the front page, take up the full evening news. His pecker might never stop twitching.

This was the end of days, the whole, entire doomsday enchilada, best possible event a security professional such as Claude could dream of. And he was dead center. Claude the vortex. Claude the calm, still eye of the storm.

He waited silently, standing twenty yards from the loading dock that led into the control-room complex. Jim and his six best. In the shadows, next to a Dumpster that was shielded by a slatted wall. Peering through the slats, watching the action. Six more guys waiting aside, his fucking pincer movement about to pince.

They stayed put, even after seeing the north cooling tower coming down, stayed put watching Leslie and

Cameron Prince roll up to the loading ramp, get out, go in through the door Claude had left unlocked, he and his men watching them unload the creatures, start to carry them inside. He waited until both of them were inside the building, Sheffield still in the truck. Bound up, it looked like. Sitting there in the backseat. A gift.

"Hey, Mr. Sellers, shouldn't we be going in?"

"Okay, boys, light 'em up. Go take these mother-fuckers down."

Claude followed his men across the parking lot, taking a detour by the Suburban for a quick hello to his favorite asshole in charge.

Claude Sellers's men, suited up in helmets, flak jackets and carrying AR-15s, rushed into the back door of the control-room complex thirty seconds behind Leslie and Cameron. Sheffield strained at his cuffs, trying to rip them apart though he knew damn well it was impossible. Losing it for a minute.

Then Claude was at the window looking in. A big grin. He opened the door. Giant blue stone at his throat, that stupid string tie. Yellow shirt under his Kevlar.

"Agent Sheffield. How you doing this fine evening?"

"Cut me loose, you jackass."

"As of now, I can't provide that service, but I tell you what I will do."

"This is coming back on you, Sellers, gonna take big bite out of your ass."

"Sure, sure, whatever you say. You just rest easy now, you hear, Special Agent. I got to get inside, lead my men into battle, take care of some badass terrorists. When I'm done, I'll be right back to settle up with you

since it appears you're a coconspirator, possibly even
the gang leader. You sit tight, now, you hear."

Claude took hold of Sheffield's shoulder and yanked
him forward, tugged on his plastic cuffs to see they
were secure, then slammed the door and jogged away,
ducking into the back door. A few seconds after he entered, the door blew open again, and half a dozen civilians poured out. Men and women in street clothes, a
couple in white smocks, wild looks. Several with their
hands clamped over their mouths.

Sheffield called out to them, but no one heard, or if
they did, they didn't glance his way and disappeared
round the side of the adjacent complex.

He sat for a few seconds testing the tightness of the
cuffs. Thorn could've left a little goddamn slack, but he
hadn't. Going along with these fuckers or seeming to.
Frank's guess, the terrorists were holding Thorn's boy
hostage, forcing Thorn to stay in line. But why Thorn?
That, he didn't know.

Sheffield hadn't been keeping up with his yoga and
he'd gained a few pounds around the middle, so doing
the tuck-and-squeeze, slipping his bound wrists under
his butt and down the back of his legs and past his feet,
then bringing them to his front side, well, that wasn't
going to work. Two tries showed him that.

He sat for a minute thinking. From inside the control
complex he heard gunfire, five shots, very deliberate,
then a quick spray of automatic fire. Probably Leslie
and Prince going down. Sheffield was usually a stick-
er for rules. The gang of elves were officially on the
wrong side of this disaster, but the deeper he'd dug into
it the less true that seemed. Given the choice, his first

shot would have been at Sellers before turning his firepower on the others.

Frank stopped. Firepower. Struck by the way words
could pop up, carrying all their associations, like direct
messages from the unconscious, solving shit.

Yeah, of course. Firepower.

Frank brought his bound wrists to his right pants
pocket. Bent sideways, dropping his shoulder down
twisting his spine. Pushing a fingertip deep enough in
the pocket to brush the silver lighter. His old man's
gift, a memento. The lighter that had ignited a thou
sand Lucky Strikes and charcoal barbecues and bottle
rockets on the Fourth.

He emptied his lungs, compressed his right rib cage
and stretched harder toward the pocket, got a finge
around the trigger of his vintage lighter. You saw then
in fifties gangster movies, a femme fatale in an illega
casino lighting up. Press the tiny button, it snaps open
rolling the flint against the steel. On the sides ther
were inlaid green shamrocks. Frank's lucky day. Nev
flint, fresh lighter fluid. His goofy hobby. Keeping th
Sheffield flame alive, by God.

It slipped out of his grasp twice before he hooke
his fingertip around that trigger a third time and inche
it out of the pocket.

More gunfire coming from inside the complex. On
of Claude's men stumbled out the back door, proppe
up by a buddy. Both of them looked to be wounde
One worse than the other. Staggering away into th
darkness.

Frank clicked the trigger, got the flame. Workir
out the logistics behind his back where he couldn't s
a damn thing, having to do this by feel and guesswor

And right away the goddamn flame singed the inside of his wrist. He fumbled it, almost lost it in the crack between the seats. Cursing.

He clicked it again, got another flame, tried to peer over his shoulder, direct his right hand. But the tiny flame burned him again, a deep, scalding shot of hurt, Sheffield smelling his own goddamn flesh, but bearing it, because he could also smell the plastic. It was melting, giving way. If he didn't set his fucking uniform on fire first.

Not more than a minute later the back door of the complex blew open again, and three of Claude's finest squeezed through. Two guys holding up a fellow cop in the middle. Dude was unconscious or dead. Both supporting guys looked torn up. Blood-spattered, faces marked up. The door slammed shut and a second later blew open again and Claude was there. Wild-eyed, a pistol in each hand. Stomping down the back steps, yelling something to his guys.

Sirens now. A chopper circling overhead, maybe two. Frank couldn't tell, so much commotion everywhere.

Sellers marched over to the car and flung open the door. Frank's hands still pinned behind him, feet together. Same position.

"Sounds like your guys are making a hash of it."

"Fuckers got away."

"Slipped through your web. Why am I not surprised?"

"Makes you all the more important, Sheffield, taking down the boss."

"Yeah, Sheffield the terrorist."

"What's that stink?" Claude sniffed at the air inside

the car. "You shit yourself, Sheffield? Big, brave dude like you, you load up your shorts?"

"When you gotta go . . ."

"Some shithead's going to pay for this. And that shithead's going to be you, Sheffield. You're going down."

Claude was breathing hard, a Glock in each hand, a tremble in his arms.

"So it's falling apart, huh, Claude?"

"Where's Nicole?"

"Dead in a ditch out on the entrance road."

"Yeah?"

"These ELF people, they aren't the pussies you thought they were. She underestimated them, just like you're doing."

"Here's what's going to happen, agent fucking in charge of nothing. I'm going to cut you loose. Then I'm going to step back, give you a fighting chance to make an escape, and we'll see how that plays out. See if you stand and fight or make a break. Either way's fine by me."

"You really think you can pin this on me?"

"Got you on tape riding into the plant, using your credentials to claim the drill was canceled, which was not. We got a permanent record of that, Sheffield. You think I didn't cover my ass? You're the one's underestimating."

Claude holstered one of the Glocks and reached back to his utility belt and drew out a tactical knife and popped it open. Big-ass serrated edge.

"Now I'll turn you around to face away from me and I'll cut your hands loose. Then I'll step back and I'll count to three. That's fair. More of a chance than you fucking deserve."

Claude leaned inside the door and stooped forward to slice through the cuffs, his stupid-ass bolo tie dangling down in front of Frank's face.

Frank reached up with his right hand, grabbed hold, and yanked those strings hard and kneed Claude in the face. Broke his nose.

The weapons fell away. Sheffield repeated it, bolo yank, knee smash.

Blood flowing from Claude Sellers's mouth. Blinded by blood, Sellers was clawing at Frank's face, tearing the flesh on one cheek, nails digging into the wound Bauly Chee had given him. Frank did the bolo routine again. Getting a rhythm, putting more force behind it this time. Claude's hands fell away from Frank's face.

Sheffield pushed him back out the door, then held him straight up, a good strong grip on the strings.

"You did Bendell and you did Magnuson. You fried them. Tell me, Claude. It's confession time."

Sellers spit a bloody tooth into Frank's face.

Sheffield hauled him down, bending him forward with the tie, dragging his head back inside the SUV, taking hold of the door handle and lining up Claude's neck, then slamming that heavy-ass Suburban door on Sellers's head.

Claude spit blood and more teeth onto Sheffield's lap.

"You electrocuted Bendell and you tried to fry me, but got an NCIS agent instead, a good man. Tell me you did it and we can close up shop and go home."

More blood and phlegm on Frank's shirt.

Again, Sheffield slammed the door on Claude's head, opened it and slammed it again, opened it one more time and said, "Right here, right now, Claude. This is how you want to go? Turn your brain to mush."

He gurgled something.

"I can't hear you."

More nonsense bubbled from his broken face.

Frank dragged the bolo forward so Claude's eyes were an inch from his.

"One more chance, Sellers. Enunciate this time, use your syllables. You did those two murders, didn't you?"

Claude nodded, swallowing and swallowing, nodding one more time.

Frank pushed him backward out into the parking lot. "Good. Now let's go upstairs and you can tell your boss and the NRC lady what you just told me."

He hauled Claude up the stairway to the back entrance of the control-room complex. Opening the door just as another blast came, this one even greater than the one that took down the cooling tower. An explosion so immense it sent currents of hot wind roaring between the structures and hammered the concrete building, rattled its steel joints, and continued to rumble for half a minute after the blast, shaking loose cement panels from the walls and sending tiles tumbling from the roof, and setting off more screams and more sirens and more turbulence in the air than Frank had ever before witnessed in a long life of turbulence.

HORN OPENED HIS EYES TO the blue iridescent
ow.

Rubbed the lump on his forehead, as large and rough
a peach pit, then felt his nose, which was numb and
t a few degrees off center.

He wiped the blood from his lips, came to his feet.
cked up the flashlight from the ramp a few feet away.
ent to the rail and leaned out to scan the big room. It
s so cluttered with cranes and tanks and control pan-
draped with plastic tarps and a jumble of other ex-
c equipment that Thorn made one pass after another
thout seeing any sign of Pauly. He leaned out to peer
low him, but no one was there either.

As he shuffled down the ramp, heading toward the
tal stairway to take a closer look at the floor below,
caught sight of Pauly, crouched on the ground floor
the far end of the pool, half-shrouded by a yellow
p, some kind of canvas safety barrier stretched
und the sides of the pool.

He seemed to be working inside a manhole, the
tal cover flipped open behind him. The small bunker

was hardly larger than a phone booth, cut into the ce
ment floor, maybe five feet deep.

An access cubicle for plumbing or refrigeration re
pairs or perhaps an entry point for a network of craw
spaces that led into the subterranean realms of th
spent fuel pool. He was bent to his work, hands makin
adjustments.

The physics of what he was attempting was clear. H
was setting the charge as deep below the surface c
the structure as possible to do the greatest damage to th
uranium racks and drain the pool in an instant, alon
with creating the maximum likelihood of spraying thos
irradiated pellets into the upper zones of the atmospher

But after what Thorn had witnessed at the coolin;
tower blast, Pauly's work seemed a pointless precau
tion. The explosive he was using was so devastating, r
matter where he planted it near the spent fuel pool,
would almost certainly pump a mushroom cloud in
the Miami sky, poison the air for years, and guarant
endless days of blood rain.

Maybe it was Pauly's SEAL training and that I
was a compulsive purist who wouldn't settle for an
thing less than perfection. But Thorn no longer ga
two shits about motives. This was down to meat a
bones.

He circled the room the long way around. Picki
his way across the obstacle course of grates and cabl
and metal tubing so he could come at Pauly from b
hind. The water shimmered as if it were alive, as if
were exposed to the wind and the sun and the rand
elements, as if it were filled with fish and crabs, lobs
and white darting shrimp, as if the water were real v
ter, the stuff of life, the stuff that kept Thorn afloat

very way water could accomplish that. But it was not. was none of those things. In this room water was mply a chemical necessity, a slave. A perversion of ater, a liquid hostage in this cellblock, held in isola-on until it was used up, then it was shipped back into e world, a different thing from what it had been.

Ten feet from Pauly, Thorn stopped, surveyed the rroundings, deciding on his final approach. Diagram-ing the path, not the shortest, but the one with the st chance for him to fling himself on the man's back, ming down hard with the flashlight.

He believed he'd have one decent shot. With a solid ull-crusher, things might even up. If he missed that st strike, it was as good as over. Pauly wasn't just ong and quick. He had death-stroke training. A mili-y efficiency. No wasted movement sizing up his emy, no thrust and parry, no feeling out. Zero reac-n time.

Thorn choked up on the flashlight, cocked his arm, k two steps—and the upper door slammed open and nn Moss and Cameron Prince barreled onto the ob-vation ramp. Flynn with a pistol. Cameron empty-ded.

"You in here, Thorn? Hey, it's me, Flynn. You in e?"

Eyes on the intruders, Pauly had begun a slow as-t from his manhole. Flynn and Prince hadn't yet n him, though from the direction they were taking n the observation ramp, his position would be ex-ed in a few seconds. Flynn leading the way, search-the cluttered floor for any sign of them.

Thorn's injured leg made a sprint impossible, so he ed closer to Pauly, keeping his eyes upward to spot

Flynn and Prince. Unless Thorn reversed course, ducke
behind a nearby electrical panel right away, Flyn
would notice Thorn in a few seconds. A word of recog
nition, a shift of eye in Thorn's direction, would ale
Pauly.

Thorn made his move. A clumsy weave through
set of orange highway cones that were marking son
recent construction, then across a stretch of concre
floor, along the lip of the ghostly blue pool, moving
quickly and lightly as his damaged leg allowed.

"Hey, Thorn. Up here. You seen Pauly? Hey, Thorr
Flynn was waving an arm.

The young man had come ashore, violated the pla
An artist, a creative person, a gift for improvisatic
His talent a perfect fit for this moment.

Pauly was halfway out of his bunker, gripping t
orange ladder mounted to the cement wall of the cu
cle. Head and shoulders emerging. Head craning slov
to track Flynn's gaze.

Thorn leapt the final two yards, going airborne, a
raised with the heavy flashlight. Pauly seemed torn. M
ing up a step, down a step as Thorn came at him, sla
ing the heavy club at his head. Missing. Then tumbl
down into the cubicle with Pauly. Ladders on b
sides. Pauly holding to one, Thorn snagging the oth
scrambling to get his balance. An arm's length betwe
them.

"Timer's set for five minutes," Pauly said, a ca
smile in his eyes. "Might want to go find yourse!
foxhole." He looked down at the floor of the cubi
where the aluminum case was open, the device crad
in gray foam.

"Disable it," Thorn said.

"Can't be done. Fuse is set."

Prince and Flynn stood above them on the cement
or.

"Five minutes?" Prince said. "Then we need to get
t of here."

Prince's uniform was shredded in half a dozen
ots, his chest, arms. Blood seeping from each perfo-
ion.

"No," said Thorn. "We can't let this happen."

"Pauly," Flynn said. "You have to shut it down. You
't do this."

"Decision's made. Decision stands."

Thorn chose his spot; coming from below, he back-
ded the flashlight, cracking it hard against Pauly's
n, snapping his head back against the wall. Pauly
ehow managed to keep his grip on the ladder.

Thorn swung again and Pauly was too slow or too
ifferent to block the blow. The heavy end of the flash-
t cracked against his temple, and Pauly dropped his
d on the ladder and fell to the bottom of the pit.

'We've got to get this thing out of here."

'Where to?"

'Anywhere but here."

Thorn climbed down the ladder. Pauly was crum-
d atop the suitcase. No room to maneuver. Thorn
ped him by the armpits and hauled him upright,
ed him against the cement wall.

'horn shut the suitcase, gripped the handle.

As he reached for the ladder, Pauly latched his fore-
across Thorn's throat, an angled lock with his left
levering hard against the back of Thorn's head,
hing his head forward, crushing his windpipe.

Leave us," Pauly said. "Thorn and me, we're going

to stand guard over this gadget. Make sure it goes c
without a hitch."

Thorn thrust backward, slamming Pauly into t
metal ladder, but it didn't break the hold, didn't weak
it. He tried a spin, then a counterspin, tried pulling
Pauly's arm with both hands, tried whipping his elbc
back at Pauly's face. Nothing.

"All right," Flynn said. "Let go, Pauly. Don't ma
me hurt you."

Pauly chuckled. "The man-child speaks."

"There's no time for this. It's your last chance, Paul

"I never thought it was anything else."

From the edge of his vision, Thorn saw Flynn
tend his arm, holding Sugar's pistol, the nine-millime
he kept in his glove box. Sugarman's gun pres:
against the side of Pauly's head.

"Don't make me," Flynn said.

"Go on, kid, you can do it," said Pauly. "Your old n
would."

Thorn rattled against the choke hold one more ti
Shot a hand out, grabbed the pistol, twisted it from I
nn's grasp, and aimed it past his own left ear and fi
into Pauly's face.

The blast, so close and inside the manhole, da
and deafened Thorn.

Pauly's grip fell away. Beside Thorn's face a loc
Pauly's ponytail was plastered to the wall. Pauly's b
lay twisted at Thorn's feet. He rocked back against
wall. The iridescent blue light was spinning around I

"Three or four minutes," Prince said. "Hand it \

Thorn rubbed his eyes clear, then crouched d
and pushed Pauly's body away and took hold of
case and climbed the ladder.

"I'll meet you two back at the skiff. Now go, run."

"You're lame," Prince said. "I'm the fastest. I'm dead
⹀yway." He washed his hand over the bullet holes in his
⹀iform. "My body just hasn't accepted the fact yet."

Flynn was blocking the stairs to the exit.

"Let's move," Thorn said. "I'll take it to the parking
⹀t, a hundred yards, big open area, minimum damage.
⹀n't worry, there's time. I'll heave it, find shelter.
⹀w move."

Flynn stepped aside, looking back into the manhole.
⹀couldn't do it. I couldn't kill him."

"That's good, kid. Keep it that way."

Thorn climbed the stairs to the upper ramp, Prince
⹀d Flynn following. Thorn pushed through the exit door
⹀o the darkness and the whirlwind of sirens, and shouts
⹀d the screams of the injured. The smell of charred flesh
⹀d the thick haze of cement dust from the remains of the
⹀ling tower.

"Listen," Flynn said. "I left the skiff at the loading
⹀cks after all. It's just beyond that building, not far."

Flynn stayed at Thorn's side as he headed toward
⹀ parking lot.

Thorn stopped, planted a hand on Flynn's chest.
⹀elp Cameron back to the skiff. Do it now. I'll be there
⹀ a couple of minutes. Now go, goddamn it. Do what I
⹀ you for once."

Thorn headed off to the parking lot in a clumsy jog.
He crossed a grassy plaza, about fifty yards from
⹀ storage pool. The parking lot was only a half min-
⹀ farther on, Thorn making decent time, when he
⹀s tackled from behind, thrown to the ground. He
⹀ke away as Prince wrenched the case from Thorn's
⹀d.

"Okay, so you had it right, my granddad was a bi
deal to me, a hero. Maybe all that's too late for me. /
least I can do this." Prince got to his feet and set o
running into the dark. Thorn yelled for him to stop, b
he kept going to the north, toward the bay.

Thorn watched Prince crossing the parking lot, th
dull glint of the aluminum case bobbing as he ra
Thorn got to his feet, staggered after him, cupping h
hands to his mouth, yelling for Prince to drop the cas
Get out of there. Drop it now.

But Prince kept sprinting toward the water's edg
due north as though he meant to run beyond the se
wall, clear across the miles of water to the distant isla
where his family once lived. Prince Key. Travel back
those boyhood hours with his family on that faraw
refuge. His strides were long and loping, streaki
through the darkness as if he were bodiless, free of t
dreadful pull of the planet.

Prince was out of time. Making a choice, grabbi
for a legacy greater than what he'd been settling for. I
ran into the darkness until Thorn could no longer s
any sign of him.

Flynn was standing beside Thorn. "Oh, holy Goc

"The skiff," said Thorn. "Let's go."

Flynn and Thorn crossed the plaza and took a wir
ing asphalt road toward the docks.

"Sugarman?" Thorn said. "Is he okay?"

"Fine. He took out Wally. Wally was bragging ab
Pauly blowing up the spent fuel pool. That's whe
took off."

"Leslie?"

"She's waiting in the boat."

"She's all right?"

"Injured," Flynn said. "Prince said there was a oot-out in the control room with the plant security. I ink she'll make it."

A security guard blocked the entrance to the loading ck. He raised his assault weapon and came toward em. He was ordering Thorn and Flynn to halt when e suitcase detonated.

Prince had carried it all the way to the northern sea- ll. The sky brightened and collapsed and sent a sonic om echoing out to sea and back again. The earth shim- ed beneath them. Across the grounds, cars and trucks d fuel tanks exploded. Chunks of pavement flew up- rd as ungainly as prehistoric winged reptiles climb- ; into an ancient sky.

Thorn shoved the guard into the bay and hustled past. Leslie was propped against the front of the console. e'd been shot through the left shoulder. Her face was ite. She was shivering. Thorn wrapped her in foul- ather gear and towels, cast off the lines, and pushed from the loading dock, Flynn at the wheel, maneu- ing past a Coast Guard cutter arriving with assis- ce. He idled out to deeper water before hitting the ottle and putting Leslie's Whipray up on plane.

To the north the city of Miami was totally dark. ple would have a taste of the primitive life. A day or , maybe a week. They'd have to adapt, learn to cope, by on less. Learn a few lessons. It would last for a le.

Flynn pushed on, flat out, no one speaking. A half r later, back in Key Largo, back at Thorn's house, sandra was waiting on the dock. Flynn eased the f up to the pilings, handling it smoothly, an expert .

Cassandra helped Leslie out of the boat. She w
conscious, still shivering, unable to talk.

"She needs a hospital," Thorn said.

"She'll be taken care of."

"A hospital, goddamn it."

A man appeared behind Cassandra. Bearded, lo
dreadlocks, a bearish guy holding a shotgun at port arm
"She'll be taken care of," he said. "We've got docto
friendly to the cause. Trust us, she'll do fine. You gu
did a good thing up there."

"Did we?" Thorn said.

After they'd stretched Leslie out in the back of
Ford van, Flynn came over. Thorn was leaning agai
one of the girders of the cistern. The cistern Camer
Prince had taken such an interest in. Going to build o
like it himself someday.

"I'm leaving," Flynn said.

"What?"

"I'm going with them."

"Where?"

"Wherever they're going."

Thorn opened his mouth but Flynn reached out a
touched a hand to Thorn's lips. "It's what I want to
What I have to do."

Flynn took his hand from Thorn's lips and oper
his arms, and Thorn stepped forward into the embra
For a long moment his son wept on his shoulder. I
son who'd taken such terrible risks for his cause.

Flynn released him and stepped back. Thorn t
him good-bye. Said he loved him. Keeping it simple

Flynn nodded. "And I love you, too, Dad."

He watched Flynn walk away with the bear
man. Cassandra, who had been standing by the v

alked across the gravel to Thorn. As she approached,
e reached to her mouth and pried loose the prosthetic
pliance that had disfigured her face and slipped it
to the pocket of her jacket with the aplomb of an ac-
ss effortlessly shedding one role for another.

Without the misshapen mouth, she was a striking
man. Her cheekbones were sharp, skin glossy and
ar, and her large eyes were dark and electric. Wide
oulders, head held high, an easy poise in her step,
mething vaguely aristocratic about her bearing.

"I want to thank you for your help tonight. You acted
th courage and honor in a very challenging circum-
nce. Don't worry about your son. Flynn's a tough
ung man. We'll watch out for him. Bring him along."

Before Thorn could reply, she turned and walked
ck to the van. He stood watching as she climbed into
nd the van turned around on the gravel drive and
appeared down the entrance lane. He listened to the
gine until the van moved so far away he lost it in
night noises, the dry whisper of palm fronds, the
p and jostle of the restless ocean against the seawall.

FORTY-FOUR

A WEEK AFTER THE ATTACK on Turkey Point, t
case was officially closed, but Sheffield was still
viewing the events of that night. In his room at the Sil
Sands, while he waited for Thorn to arrive, for the d
enth time he watched one of the security videos fr
the night of the assault, playing it back on his TV, t
view from an overhead, wide-angle camera that c
tured the whole control room.

He'd turned the sound down to mute the screa
and gunfire, so all he could hear were the beach sou
beyond his door, the surf crashing against the wh
sands, a comforting noise while he watched Came
Prince, a monstrous masterpiece of muscle, walk bc
legged from the weight of the gator under each arm
the python slung around his shoulders.

Must've been five hundred pounds of squirm
reptiles, but Prince walked with a steady gait, follov
by Leslie Levine, cradling a single gator of four feet,
snout duct-taped. The control room lit by a few en
gency lights.

Frank watched as Cameron and Leslie cut the c
tape, set the creatures loose, and scared the shit ou

gineers and hard-hatted workers who were scram-
ing to get the plant back online before the uranium
ated up to such a white-hot molten state that a great
le would be burned right through the earth's core. As
e hyperventilating news anchor would put it the next
y.

As Leslie and Cameron were fleeing the control
om, a half dozen of Claude's security men entered
d blocked their exit. A quick, sloppy gunfight erupted.
slie wounded, Prince hit several times but seeming
fazed.

Dozens of workers in the big room poured out the
ts, screaming and pushing each other aside, a couple
them wounded in the cross fire.

In the dim light, those half-assed rent-a-cops some-
v failed to see Leslie and Prince slip out a side door,
l they didn't recognize the other members of their
m when they entered. Firing at their own. Rent-a-cop
sus rent-a-cop. A couple injured. A chaotic scene of
dow men shooting at shadow men while the gators
the python roamed up and down the aisles.

Frank ran the video back to the beginning once
in, though there was nothing new to see. No clues,
hing that hadn't already been explained and docu-
ated and substantiated by multiple eyewitnesses. It
all in the reports on his desk at work, typed up
dsomely by Marta.

t had all played out on the local TV and the na-
al news, another Miami-weirdness story, feeding
the clownish narrative that had been established
des back. Miami, that city of eccentrics and wackos,
nation's capital of silliness and gaudy crooks and
esque crimes. Ha-ha. Only in fucking Miami.

But for Frank, watching the video again, the thir
seconds of those two souls staggering under the weight
their reptilian burdens, there was nothing funny, nothi
ironic or goofy. These two were carrying out an hono
able, principled mission. The newswriters had fallen in
the easy clichés and had made the group seem bizar
and cartoonish, and ultimately, in the interests of ente
tainment, they'd undermined the statement the ELF gu
had risked their lives to make. Leslie's miscalculation.

Any publicity was not necessarily good publicity.

Because the media had turned ELF's deeds into
trivial exercise, a fraternity prank gone terribly wror
The reconstruction of the cooling tower was under w
The lights were back on. The chargers were recha
ing, the downtown skyscrapers were twinkling their
deco patterns again, the pulse was pulsing.

Hearing the grumble of Thorn's VW outside in
parking lot, Frank shut off the TV and sat for a n
ment staring at the blank screen.

Thorn stayed seated in the VW, admiring Frank's vi
the blazing white sands through the row of palms.
old motel that Frank was fixing up, staying true to
origins. A side of Sheffield most people never saw.
builder, the preservationist, the beach bum.

The natural kinship between the two of them
strained at the moment because Thorn refused to
cuss Flynn's actions the night of the raid or anyth
that happened afterward. Thorn had described it al
April Moss, Flynn's mother, and if she wanted to r
the information to the authorities, that was her call.
far she'd remained as mute as Thorn on the subject

Despite that lack of cooperation, Frank had covered
r Thorn, testifying that he was an unwilling partici-
nt, basically a hostage. A father trying to protect his
n. Claiming Thorn had wandered into the middle of
is stunt and was an innocent bystander to the events.
iorn was grateful for Sheffield's half-truths, but not
ateful enough to tell Sheffield about Flynn's decision
join the ELF warriors.

Frank came out of the door of his motel room and
aded over to the VW.

Thorn took another look at the postcard in his hand.
panoramic scene of the West Virginia mountains.
th careful penmanship she had written, *F doing fine.*
idn't make it. Thought you should know. Sorry, C.

Cassandra staying in touch. Leslie was gone, Flynn
s some version of okay. Thorn hadn't told Sheffield
iut the card. Surely the FBI had ways of collecting
dence from it. It might reveal clues that would lead
Flynn.

Sheffield was at his open window, bent down, look-
in. "Everything okay?"

Thorn reached over and flipped open the glove box
l slid the postcard inside and shut it. "So where ex-
y is this Motel Blu?"

"Edge of Little Haiti," Frank said.

Thorn got out, walked with Sheffield over to his old
vy.

They drove in strained silence through the midday
fic, up Dixie Highway to I-95, then picked up speed.
'Sugarman doing okay?"

'Few more weeks of therapy, he'll be fine. Barely a
o."

"And you, your leg?"

"A ding," Thorn said. "It's healing."

"What he did, Sugar, disabling Wally Chee like th in the condition he was in, flat on his back, that's pret goddamn amazing. I'd like to hear the whole sto sometime. T heb low-by-blow."

"There's no story. He hit Wally in the head with crowbar."

"How's he come by a crowbar, lying in a bed?"

"I'm not much of a housekeeper. Things get m placed."

"You're a terse son of a bitch. You know that, Thorn

"I do."

Frank parked in the lot of Motel Blu and they sat f a minute looking at the venetian blinds of the sm apartment attached to the back of the place. "Lit River runs behind there. Kind of polluted, but you c picture how it used to be. A pretty place once upo time."

Thorn nodded.

"Neighborhood's getting safer," Frank said. "N tel's got twenty-four-hour security. The girl should fine here. You don't need to worry."

"I only want to see her. See her and go. I'm not ing to try to adopt her."

"She's your granddaughter. It's your right to see Anyway, Geraldine says she wants to meet you, wa to thank you for what you did."

"What did I do?"

"A long time ago you saved Leslie's life, that's h she remembers it."

They sat for a while longer in the parking lot.

Thorn saw one of the slats of the blinds move. "Ju-
. That's a good name."

"It is," said Sheffield. "And she's a cute kid. Got a
tch of Leslie's hair. And those amazing eyes."

"Okay, then. I'm ready. Let's go meet her."

ead on for an excerpt from James W. Hall's next book

THE BIG FINISH

Available December 2014 in hardcover
from Minotaur Books

NE

WAS A BRISK, MOON-DAZZLED November night
en Flynn Moss and several of his closest friends
re gunned down.

For a week, they'd been camping in a forest of ever-
ens on the bank of the Neuse River in eastern North
rolina. Might sound picturesque, but it wasn't. Noth-
 like the majestic Blue Ridge Mountains a day's
ve west, or the gorgeous sweep of dunes and squeaky
ite sands two hours east along the Outer Banks.
ese woods weren't the least bit scenic, and neither
 the flat, barren terrain surrounding them. And good
 l, Pine Haven, the nearby town, if you could even call
 town, was as hellish a shithole as anywhere they'd
 ed an operation in the last year. Even the desolate
 l mining settlement of Marsh Fork, Kentucky, was
 lic in comparison.

 As for Flynn, he was once again nursing an acute
 e of homesickness, the familiar gnawing ache in his

chest, the hard magnetic pull of the seaside city he'
cherished since he'd drawn his first breath. At the mo
ment their campsite in the Carolina forest was just shy o
eight hundred miles from Miami. Eleven hours by ca
a long damn way. But somehow it felt even farther. Lil
suspended animation would be required to travel th
light-years back home to the blue waters and soothir
sunshine and those exquisite breezes flavored with nu
meg and cloves and ripening mangoes.

Around the dwindling campfire the other three we
silent, everyone on edge, waiting for Caitlin to retur
Late in the afternoon she'd received an SOS text fro
one of the two Mexican farmworkers she'd recruited
spies. Their attempt at espionage had apparently go
bad.

With a grim face, Caitlin had set off alone to d
cover just how bad.

Hours later, the group had settled into a fidgety hu:
All the others had finished their dinners, while Bi
Jack was still polishing off his third helping of bak
beans. A brawny guy with black hair and a neck thic
than Flynn's thigh, Billy Jack had played football
Auburn. But after shattering an opponent's jaw in
on-field brawl, Billy Jack was tossed from the team a
would've spent a stretch in jail except his girlfrien
dad bribed the injured man to drop charges.

Caitlin was that girlfriend. A fragile, high-stru
belle, Caitlin had started out as a true believer, a natu
loving free spirit who'd impulsively enlisted in
Earth Liberation Front minutes after hearing one
Cassandra's rousing recruitment speeches near the /
burn campus.

Caitlin dragged Billy Jack along on the righte

dventure. Caitlin full of idealistic rebellion, Billy Jack
mply along for the ride. But in the last few months
eir romance had cooled, and while Billy Jack's thrill
r combat kept him engaged in the group's efforts,
aitlin lost her fervor for the cause. Recently she'd con-
led to Flynn that she'd been sneaking phone calls to
r daddy, and the old guy was begging her to cut loose
d head home. A new BMW was waiting for her, no
estions asked.

In the twelve months Flynn had been a member of
LF, he'd seen recruits come and go, so her departure
uldn't be surprising. But Cassandra would be pissed
cause Caitlin had proved to be remarkably adept at
ing her powers of enchantment to the group's advan-
e. Gaining access to people and opening doors that
uld have stayed shut without her southern charms.

On the log beside Billy Jack, Jellyroll was hunched
er his laptop, his fingers flying. Twenty years old, he
ked thirteen. A black kid from Philly. His mother
ad, father serving life in some supermax joint in Vir-
ia, Jellyroll was the group's computer geek. Back in
y he'd first appeared at a fracking protest rally in Al-
town, Pennsylvania, sidled over to their group, and
establish his hacking credentials he presented Cas-
dra with her entire FBI dossier on the same laptop
was using tonight.

'Half of this is total bullshit," she said when she fin-
ed reading.

'No worries," Jellyroll said. "I'm a wizard with the
ete key."

By midnight, the dinner plates were cleaned and
ved, the fire was down to a red glow, and the moody
nce had grown deeper.

Flynn said, "I'm going to look for her."

"No, you're not," Cassandra said. "We stay together.

"She's in trouble," said Flynn. "She should've bee
back hours ago."

"Wouldn't be surprised," said Billy Jack, "if that gi
has run off. Been months since her last manicure, thos
raggedy nails are driving her batshit."

"Probably her right now." Jellyroll motioned at th
dark tangle of woods, the wobble of a flashlight hea
ing up the trail.

Everyone rose and stood flat-footed, waiting.

Moments later Caitlin came thrashing out of th
woods, halted abruptly, and washed the beam of h
flashlight over their faces.

"It's over, we're finished," she said, panting from h
run. She stooped forward, hands on her knees. "Th
caught Javier, they've got his camera. We need to g
the hell out of here. And I mean right now."

Cassandra squatted by the embers, waved for Cait
to quiet down.

"Whoa, girl. They've got Javier's camera? You
sure?"

"Jesus told me one of the security guys spotted
wristwatch, made Javier take it off, figured out wha
was, and dragged Javier away. Jesus is scared he'll
next."

The tiny spy camera embedded in the wristwa
had remarkable clarity for something so small. The
bought the two watches from an online dealer. U
interface, four gigs of flash memory, audio recorder
battery that could last for two hours of continuous
cording. A hundred and fifty bucks for each.

" 'Took him away'?" Jellyroll was using one fin

o slice and dice the touch pad on his laptop. "Is that a euphemism? Like they killed him?"

Caitlin said she wasn't sure, but it was likely, very likely, because these people were fucking scary, far more dangerous than anyone they'd encountered before. She circled the dying campfire, behind everyone's backs, repeating over and over, We're finished. We need to go. We need to go now.

"Take a breath, Caitlin." Cassandra came to her feet. "Slow breaths, deep. Count them; one, two, three, four."

Technically the group had no leader, but Cassandra was the oldest by a decade and had by far the most experience in the movement, plus she had an intimidating-as-hell glare framed by wild and abundant red hair, so the others deferred to her, even Billy Jack.

"Okay, I've finished the edit," Jellyroll said. "Fifty-six seconds long. It's rough, but there's good shit here. This could kick some serious ass."

Flynn moved behind Jellyroll and the others crowded in to see.

"Did you hear me? We need to go," Caitlin said from across the fire. "If you don't want to, fine. But I'm done. I didn't sign on for violence."

"So go," Billy Jack said. "You see anybody trying to stop you?"

"Javier knows where we're camping," Caitlin said. "If they torture him, he'll confess. They could be on their way here right now."

"Play it," Cassandra said to Jellyroll. "Let's see what we got."

A few days earlier Caitlin, who spoke basic Spanish, had recruited Javier and Jesus and given each a watch and a hundred dollars to wear them on the job. Both were

senior workers, eight years at the Dobbins Farm with free
access throughout the facilities. But Javier was either too
nervous or too hurried to follow the training Caitlin gave
him for various ways to keep the camera steady.

Despite the jumpy, off-angle images, the video was
decent. It started with an establishing shot, the Dobbins Farm sign in green and gold. Then the bouncy drive
up the entrance road. Javier with his arm out the truck's
window, capturing the manure ponds, the giant Rain
Bird sprinklers shooting arcs of hog shit over a pasture.
Not a pretty sight, but nothing criminal.

Then a jump cut took them inside a containment barn.
Noisy hogs full-grown, restless in their tight cages, jostling, snorting, biting each other, scarfing down food,
shitting in their pens. Then another cut. A quick shot of
Burkhart dragging a sick hog by its hind legs out of
pen and into the concrete passageway, then using a han-
sledge to kill the animal. Two hard whacks to its skul
The animal on its side bleating and squirming. Tw
more whacks.

Some of the other hogs were bumping the bars o
their pens in protest. Ten seconds of ugliness, fair!
mild compared to the undercover videos Flynn ha
seen online, hogs being hung by their necks on stee
cables, hogs covered in bleeding sores, their legs givin
way under their unnatural weight, left lying helples
some truly horrendous shit, all of it perfectly legal. E
cluded from state cruelty laws, farm animals were re
ularly subjected to sickening abuse. That was part
the group's mission, to share the revolting realities
industrial food production and put pressure on sta
governments to change those lax cruelty laws. Make
hard for the public to ignore what was going on.

The video moved to a new location. Javier was entering a greenhouse, a Dobbins gold logo over the doorway. He walked slowly down the rows of tall flowering trees, their ghostly trumpet blooms facing downward. After three or four seconds scanning the blooms, the camera turned to the ground, showing the gravel path where Javier was walking, and a quick image of another Mexican worker passing by. The worker was wearing a surgical mask.

"Great shot," Cassandra said. "Rising tension."

Javier entered a door at the far end of the greenhouse, passed by the drying racks that were hung with blooms, and took a seat at a long table where a row of other men were working. All of them in similar surgical masks. Then a few seconds that showed the entire pill room.

The camera was badly tilted, but Flynn could still make out what was taking place. The man sitting beside Javier at the table poured a test tube of fine powder through a paper funnel and filled a small hole drilled into a block of wood. Then the worker inserted a brass tamping rod into the hole, tapped it twice with a rubber-topped mallet, tapped it again, then turned the block of wood over and shook the block until a bright red tablet fell onto the table in front of him. Then the worker scraped the pill into a jar with dozens of other similar tablets and began the process again. A primitive production line.

"Bingo," said Billy Jack. "We got us some major monies."

The video flickered and ended.

Everyone was silent for a moment. Caitlin moaned to herself and stepped away from the others.

"I thought we were here for the hogs," Flynn said.

"We were," Cassandra said. "But this trumps the hogs."

"Sure," Flynn said. "Maybe this could shut Dobbins down, send him to jail, but even if it did, it's a one-off. It doesn't do anything for the big picture. That shot of Burkhart killing the sick pig, that's the stuff we're after, animal cruelty, not some pissant drug operation. That just muddies our message."

"Dobbins is a big deal. Take him down, it's a blow to his corporate bosses, a blow to the industry."

"They'll say Dobbins was an outlier. Throw him under the bus. Their hands stay clean."

"How do we know that?" Cassandra said. "Maybe Pastureland is fully aware of what's happening at one of their farms and they condone this. Maybe they're even getting a cut."

"They make billions on pork. Why risk a sideline in dope?"

Jellyroll raised his hand like a kid in class. Cassandra nodded his way.

"If I'm going to post the video to YouTube, we need to drive over to Goldsboro to hijack a wireless signal."

"Use your damn smartphone," Billy Jack said. "Post itt onight."

"File's too large. Need a wireless connection. That motel we stayed at last week, we could get a room, take showers, upload the video, then blow this taco stand."

Billy Jack was all in for that. Scrub off the putrid hog stink.

"You deleted the video from the watch, right, Jelly? Before Caitlin gave it back to Javier?"

"I did."

"So even if they have the watch, they don't know what we've got."

"Big deal," Caitlin said. "They know we've been spying. They're bound to think the worst. They'll come for us. I know they will. We're finished."

"Once it's on YouTube," Jellyroll said, "we send a link to the authorities. Maybe use Flynn's FBI contact. Someone like that."

"Your buddy Agent Sheffield will handle it, right? If you ask him nice." Cassandra was smiling, giving Flynn some shit.

"He's not my goddamn buddy."

"Okay, your father's buddy." Cassandra and Thorn had crossed paths last year. Sparks flew, but not the romantic kind.

Flynn Moss was the product of a one-night stand between Thorn and April Moss, Flynn's mom, a fact both father and son had discovered by accident a year ago. Flynn had grown up without a father and had no interest in having one now, especially this guy. A hard-core loner, Thorn lived in a primitive Cracker house along the coast in Key Largo and tied custom bonefish flies for a living. The guy came across as mellow, living the laid-back life, but puncture the veneer, piss him off, endanger his friends, and molten lava spewed. The guy could flare so hot it was scary. Flynn had to admit he admired that. The lava part. A year after their first meeting, Flynn still didn't want or need a dad, but damn if he wished he'd inherited more of Thorn's latent ferocity.

Jellyroll said, "I'm going to post on the message

board. Not a mayday or anything, just let our associates know where we are, the broad outline, you know, in case some bad shit happens and we go dark."

"All right, that's it, goddamn it, I'm leaving," Caitlin said. "I'm packing my gear and taking my canoe."

"Happy paddling." Billy Jack shot her a grin. "Watch out for white-eyed rednecks strumming banjos."

Cassandra walked over to Caitlin, took hold of her shoulder, swept back her hair, and leaned in close. Cheek to cheek, Cassandra spoke for half a minute while the others watched. Caitlin's panicked expression slowly dissolved, she nodded, then her head sagged and she looked up at Cassandra.

"Okay, okay," she said. "One more night."

"We're tired, we're spooked," Cassandra said, facing the group. "A lot's been going on. But I don't think we have anything to fear from these yahoos. We've heard their kind of bluster before. Let's just absorb this new get some rest; tomorrow we'll consider our options, figure out the best way to help Javier. He's been loyal. We can't just leave him and Jesus hanging."

"Fuck 'em," Billy Jack said. "They got paid. They knew the risks."

Flynn had first watch. He sat cross-legged with his back against a pine. He'd chosen a spot fifty yards from their campsite on the north bank of the Neuse River.

That Monday before Thanksgiving, the night was crisp and a bright full moon dusted the branches with silvery powder, enough radiance for him to keep watch on the narrow trail that led to their campsite. Only the one way in. These woods were too snarled with thick

ts and vines for anyone to sneak up on the camp from
nother direction.

Cassandra and Caitlin were in their sleeping bags,
tretched out side by side on beds of pine straw, Billy
ack and Jellyroll in the hammocks they'd rigged in-
ide the group's Ford van.

Flynn was armed only with a whistle. If he heard
nyone approaching, he'd blow it twice, a signal for the
roup to abandon their sleeping bags, grab their es-
ape kits, and sprint the half mile along the bank of the
euse to the sandy shoreline where they'd hidden their
noes. Flynn would take a different route to the same
cation. On previous operations they'd drilled for this
ontingency, joking at what seemed like a senseless pre-
ution. But when they reviewed it a while ago, there
as no laughter.

Running from danger was their only option. Weeks
o they'd voted to outlaw weapons, and they'd tossed
e group's single handgun in a river in Marsh Fork, Ken-
cky. Cassandra wasn't happy about parting with her
3, but the group had spoken. Four to one against her.
ving guns led to laziness and lack of ingenuity. If they
uldn't resolve their conflicts peacefully, what good
s their entire mission? Guns were antithetical to all
y espoused.

Above him a breeze stirred the limbs. Flynn lifted
head and listened to them rustle, tried to make
t any human sounds the wind might be concealing.
ound him the strawberry scent of evergreen was
nished and overwhelmed by the harsh reek of hog
nure. The stench of it had given Jellyroll and Caitlin
daches all week. Their eyes reddened and Caitlin's

throat was raw. But their suffering was nothing compared to those in the communities living downwind o
the farm. It's why they'd come. To give voice to the
voiceless, stand against the powerful.

Most of all they were here to mobilize the locals an
bring attention to the outrageous crimes committe
against them. Only they hadn't counted on unearthin
something like this. Their discovery had been uninten
tional, but they saw immediately how volatile their in
formation was.

It was well after midnight. Flynn was in the middle o
a reverie about Thorn's oceanside house in Key Larg
surrounded by dazzling blue waters that teemed wit
manatees, brightly colored reef fish, and rolling tarpor
and the sky above it thick with pelicans and ospreys ar
roseate spoonbills, a gorgeous, Technicolor, heart-soarir
vision.

When the intruders came, the rustle of the drie
leaves jerked him alert and Flynn barely stifled a pa
icky yelp.

After he steadied himself, he leaned out for a glimps

Twenty feet away, out on the dirt track, the poi
man was carrying an automatic weapon and crouchi
low. The man flanking him held a shotgun. The man
the lead wore night-vision goggles, training them fc
ward as he moved toward the campsite.

Silently, Flynn came to his feet, pressing his back
the pine. He raised the whistle to his lips. If he blew
now with the men so near, there'd be no escape
him. If he waited till they passed, the others would
have time to get away.

Shit. He'd set up the watch post too close to can

e saw that now. Stupid mistake. Should have realized
long ago and moved farther up the trail.

Halting, the point man seemed to sense a presence
earby. In the moonlight Flynn saw the snowy bristles
f his flat-top. A guy in his sixties, Burkhart was his
ame, the duly elected sheriff of Winston County and
ead of security at Dobbins hog farm. A cold-eyed guy
ith a military bearing, he'd confronted Cassandra in
wn a few days ago. Reached out a big hand and trickled
s fingers across her cheek. Drawling with mock cour-
sy, a threat masked in avuncular concern. It might be
tter if she and her friends stopped stirring up trouble
d got their sweet asses out of town and didn't return.
is, he told her, will be your one and only warning.
u're a grown lady, so you'll have to decide, but he'd
te to see any harm come to such a sweetheart.

When Cassandra knocked his hand away, the man
ghed, called her a spitfire, and grinned into her eyes
though they'd forged an intimate bond.

Flynn moved behind the tree, squatted down, and
ted a hand across the ground. He risked another peek
und the trunk. Both men had halted. They'd begun
scan the area, panning their weapons in a slow circle.
On the ground a few feet away Flynn found a rock—
nething from his storehouse of Hollywood clichés.
ss it into the nearby brush, misdirect the bad guys,
d while their heads were turned, make a run. Most of
clichés Flynn had absorbed from his thousands
hours of film study were bogus, never worked off
een, but he hoped, by God, this one might.

He stepped back from the pine, keeping the trunk
he attackers' sight line, and he hurled the rock over

their heads back into the woods behind them. It clat
tered into leaves and fallen brush. The man behind Bur
khart swung around, tracking the noise, taking a ste
or two away from Flynn's hiding place, but Burkhar
wasn't fooled. One-handed he adjusted his goggles an
began a slow sweep of his weapon in Flynn's directior

Flynn ducked back behind the tree. His chest s
constricted, he couldn't draw a breath. The man hisse
to his partner, and Flynn heard the dry crackle of the
steps fanning out around him.

Flynn brought the whistle to his lips and blew tw
sharp blasts. He blew twice more as he was sprintir
away, the automatic fire shredding the trees arour
him, strafing the branches, spurting the dirt at his fee
The deafening bursts of gunfire made any more war
ings unnecessary, but Flynn blew the whistle twi
more as he raced through the darkness, leading t
men deeper into the pine forest that smelled so lovely

If his friends had followed their evacuation plan a
fled into the darkness on foot, heading down the ba
to the canoes, everything might have worked out diff
ently. But they panicked, or Cassandra overruled the
and herded them into the van, unwilling to aband
their vehicle and gear. He heard the van's engine cou
and fail to catch, then turn over again. The damn star
motor had been cranky for weeks, but they were sh
on cash and hadn't replaced it. He heard one attac
change direction, rushing toward the campsite, and
heard the engine sputter to life, then the bark of g
fire, howls of rage, and even louder howls of agony.

Flynn veered toward the camp, sprinting low.
didn't know what he could do to help the others, bu
had to try.

All around him the pine forest was thick with scent.
was that rich odor he was thinking of, the sappy
eetness of evergreen, when he felt the hard electric
g on his shoulder, then another in his leg, and a sec-
d later a stinging spray of buckshot, then a creamy
rmth spreading down his back.

After a breathless moment, he felt a surge of unex-
cted joy, a release from the tension of these last few
ys, these last months, an exhilarating letting go, and
the next hundred yards as the mindless bullets ripped
art the air around him, Flynn Moss seemed to float
ove the rough terrain, fearless and strong, his feet
rely grazing the earth as he saw the moonlit water up
ead, the silver current that streamed through this fer-
countryside, flowing and flowing, as all rivers did,
ir waters inevitably returning to the welcoming sea.